LIFE IN THE RAIN

LIFE IN THE RAIN

Justin Radford

VÄINÄMÖINEN STUDIOS

Paperback Edition March 16, 2020
ISBN 978-1-7347929-0-4

Dedicated to all the people who predicted that I would fail in my mission. Faith manages.

01

Chapter One

It was raining.

Not unusual for that time of year, but it was a weather pattern that sparked polarizing opinion. Moans of discontent would rattle throughout the population, as disdain for wet precipitation was common. But there were those that appreciated its calming sensation, a gentle caress on the shoulders of those who walked in the rain.

John loved the rain. When he was a teenager, after a shouting match with his parents, or after an emotional explosion, he'd retreat to the outdoors. As it rained most of the time, his mind associated calming down with the falling drops. He began appreciating, even relying on the rain. This affinity never wavered; even in college, after a disappointing final or an embarrassing date, the rain was his refuge. Nothing else could mask his misery. Nothing else could heal his misery.

Parking in that part of town was a pain to deal with. Apartments were packed tight; open lots and driveways were sparse. He relied on street parking, and that always required a lengthy walk to his destination. John was close to downtown, but the area wasn't dominated by high-rises and massive condo towers. It was denser than a suburb but didn't feel like a busy business district. When somebody walked past him, John ignored them like he ignored most people. Human contact didn't feed him, yet human contact was all John wanted.

He arrived at his friend's apartment, a small brick building with five different two-story dwellings. John knocked on Nick's door. It was under a covered walkway, and already John missed the sensation of the rain. A moment later, the door opened, Nick standing there and nodding. He was slightly shorter than John, with dirty blond hair and wearing an old baggy shirt. "What's up?"

"Hey, man. How's it going?" John said.

"Nothing much, just playing some games," Nick said nonchalantly. He turned around, nonverbally inviting John in. Since John had been there many times before, he wandered around with full access. Here, John wasn't bound by social custom. He didn't feel judged by anyone.

"What is it that you're playing?"

Nick looked over at the television in the living room as John put his coat behind a dining chair. "Some racing game. I know, you're not a big fan of those, but this one is a little fun. You hungry?"

John studied the kitchen behind him and shrugged. "If you have chips or something, I'm down." Since Nick was sitting back down on the couch, John took that opportunity to look through the cupboards to locate the bag of tortilla chips he was searching for. He found a half-empty container of salsa in the refrigerator and poured it into a bowl. Bringing his entrée of bachelor food to the couch, John seated himself next to his friend.

"Damn, graphics are always getting better these days," John said after he observed the game for a while. "Remember that old 2D racing game we played back in high school? And we thought that was the shit."

Nick nodded. "Yeah, and ten years from now we'll think this is pathetic too."

"It's all about the gameplay, really," said John in his sly attempt to soapbox about his opinions on video games. "If you want just the graphics, you're just going to buy the same old shit year after year, bitch about how bad stuff was a year ago, and be a corporate tool."

"Pretty much with you there," said Nick as he was racing. "Speaking of being a corporate tool, how's your job?"

"Hey, fuck you, man!" said John, and they both laughed. After calming down, John continued. "Well, it's about what I can get these days. My degree is doing shit for me."

"How is it still living with your parents?" While they were both twenty-three, they were at significantly different places in their lives.

"It's not terrible," said John with hesitation. "I'm always on the lookout for some good deal or roommate, but I don't want to be broke either. It's sad that chicks look for guys who don't live with their parents but can't afford to do shit. I can take them out and drive them around and have a great time, but fuck, I'm invisible to them. I'm like... To them I've gone nowhere in life. It sucks so bad."

Nick finished his race, placing third out of twenty. "I hear you, man. Sometimes I envy you, not even having to budget stuff. You can just go out and do stuff without worrying about keeping the lights on. Can't believe your parents aren't even charging rent yet."

John chuckled. "Well, if I'm still there at twenty-five, they threatened they would. Believe me, I wish I could just move out. Just want a good quality of life. And working retail at a cheap-ass store ain't gonna help one bit."

Nick offered the controller to John. He held up his hands. "Nah, I want to watch a bit more and get the hang of it first." Nick shrugged and selected the next level. After waiting a beat, John asked, "How's your girlfriend doing?"

"Annoying, as usual."

John got the hint there was more Nick wanted to say. "Okay, so what's going on?"

Nick shrugged. "She adds so much drama to everything. Just being with her is such a chore. It's a full-time job just to get laid."

John laughed. "Yeah, sounds rough, dude."

"I sometimes envy you, not having a girlfriend." Nick's eyes were focused on the current race, but they were also focused on more intellectual food. "It hasn't been that long for you, right?"

After thinking for a moment, John answered. "Well, I went on a few dates with a friend of a coworker back in July. Nothing much came out of that. But yeah, had some fun back in January. But, dude, you shouldn't jump through hoops like that for anyone."

Nick shrugged, but the lack of an answer was an obvious answer. John chuckled at the notion that the two hated their current situations but envied the other's. He distrusted the clichéd theory of the greener grass on the other side of the hill, yet at that moment he bought into it. He wasn't Nick, yet Nick wasn't John. They both were unique, with different friends, coworkers, and histories.

"I've said it once, and I'll say it again," John said. "I just want the one, y'know? The sex I had with Maria wasn't the same as when I was in a serious relationship. You understand what I'm saying? I don't know if it's the sex itself that I want. Hell, maybe it's not the sex at all. It's almost that I think that having meaningful sex is great because it tells you how great the relationship is."

"You really need to get laid," said a deadpanned Nick. They both laughed.

When Nick finished the second race, John jumped in. "I think I'll try a round." Nick handed him the controller, and John went for a spin. He finished ninth of twenty, crashing twice.

While John selected the track for the second race, Nick spoke again. "My lady will never play anything with me. She even hates it when I play."

John sighed. "Seriously, Nick. I hate to be harsh, but why are you even with her? At least my exes would play games with me. What does she get out of dating you if she doesn't do anything with you?"

Nick shrugged. His girlfriend was very attractive, and John's thoughts often lingered when he saw her. Yet it wasn't her specific body that John lusted after. It was any body. Symbols were often desired as an anchor for people's wants, but too often people lacked the reasoning to realize that they were just symbols and not the meat of genuine affection.

The two friends played the game for a while. John's skills improved modestly, but he could still not best his friend. The chips and salsa ran out long before, which prompted Nick to take action. "You want to hit the pub where we took you on your twenty-first? Think it's happy hour now."

"If I say no, call a doctor," said John. They shut down the console, grabbed their coats, and left the dim apartment. Predictably, the rain was still falling, which was a welcome relief from the stale atmosphere in the apartment. John breathed in and welcomed the moisture into his lungs. "How far is it?"

"Several blocks. We can walk," said Nick.

The pair walked side by side on the sidewalk. With the rain pouring down his coat and hair, John became philosophical again. He knew his best friend since freshman year of high school and loved his company. They didn't have to talk much, but they loved doing activities together. There was no one else in his life he'd rather spend time with. Yet there remained an emptiness in his desires.

"Seems that hot women never go to bars," said John. He hadn't realized they had walked in silence for an uncomfortably long time up to that point.

Nick chuckled. "I'm not sure I agree, although I can't take Michelle to one."

"She's not even twenty-one yet?" John asked.

"She's close," said Nick. "All her friends talk about going out all the time, but I never see them where I go."

"They probably go to shitty dance clubs that play shitty

dance music," said John, rather judgmentally.

Nick nodded. "There's an eighteen-plus club that Michelle likes going to. I went once. It was lousy."

"Dude, if she don't play video games with you, don't you fucking go to some lame-ass club with her," said John. "You can't let her hold double standards like that."

Double standards were a sore spot for John. He tried to avoid them, but influences from the patriarchal society mauled his objectivity. He'd take part in a threesome with two other women, yet not with another man. How could he justify that?

Nick and his girlfriend were always fighting. Michelle was happy going to the club with her friends. Nick was happy playing video games and hanging out with his friends at bars and pubs. They had nothing to do with each other. Since no children or obligations were involved, why were they dating? It was better to be alone than to be in a broken relationship, yet their situation was hardly unique.

"What's their food menu like?" asked John. "I don't think I got food last time I was there. Then again, I don't really recall anything at all."

Nick smiled. "Yeah, it's not bad. If you're going happy hour, they have some decent stuff. More than just fries and tots. Their chili dogs are damn good."

John held his stomach. "Oh man, I don't know what chemicals they put in that shit."

"You and your hippiness," joked Nick.

"Shut up. I'm not a hippie!" John said defensively, hinting at his passionate environmentalism. "I bathe and I drive a car that's halfway decent. I just care about what I put in my body."

"Nah, they have some healthier stuff too."

The pair made it to the main road, and right on the corner was The Crawling Pub. There were several neighborhood bars and pubs, but this was Nick's favorite. They avoided a massive puddle on the sidewalk and wandered in.

Fortunately for John's inebriated memory, the interior was exactly as he recalled. Since it was the middle of the afternoon, there were a few tables open, so they sat at one. It was a dark wooden table with matching chairs, with a few scuffs on the furniture. Neighborhood pubs lacked the monetary backing of nationwide chains, but the experience was what mattered.

Even before they sat down, John scouted the room for prospective females. The bartender was a man in his late twenties, and most of the clientele were middle-aged men. In the corner was a woman, probably a few years older than John, with dyed metallic-red hair tied back. She was some distance away, so John couldn't make out any more details.

Since it wasn't busy, the bartender came by quickly to bring them coasters. "Afternoon, gentlemen. Your day good so far?"

Both John and Nick grunted what could be reasonably translated as words of approval. Continuing with his regular spiel, the bartender said, "Awesome. What can I get you guys?"

"I'd like a medium ale if you got one on tap," said Nick. The bartender nodded before turning to face John.

"Have any ciders on tap?" John asked. The bartender responded with a nod. "Great, I'll have one of those, please."

"You got it!" said the bartender as he whisked himself away. While he was working the taps, John's attention went back to the lady in the corner. She was on a laptop, sipping on a beer of some kind.

"Did you see her in the corner?" asked John in a soft voice.

"Who? What?" said Nick as he looked around frantically before seeing the object of John's fantasies in the back corner. "Oh, no. If you had my girlfriend, you'd have to force yourself to stop looking."

"Doesn't sound healthy," said John.

"No, it isn't. It kind of sucks. But she seems alright. Not necessarily my type. Go for it."

John put his hands out sarcastically. "Really? 'Go for it'? That's all you got?"

Nick shrugged. "Well, she's beyond our league."

John appreciated Nick not letting his stunning girlfriend get to his ego. John sighed as he looked over at the mysterious woman. "Yeah, I guess so. But maybe not." He turned to look back at his friend. "I've heard that attractive chicks tend to be single because guys like us assume they're taken or something and don't talk with them. Or if they're flirty with you, they have a ring on their finger. Never fails."

Stealthily, the bartender swung by with their two pints, both filled to the top. The two thanked him in an uneven cadence. The man nodded and went on his way to service the next patron. Both of the friends grabbed their glasses and took a sip to discover the taste. John was getting into ciders and guessed his was a pear cider, a welcome experience for his palette.

"How is it?" asked Nick.

John nodded in approval. Nick took another sip. "Good. I've had this beer before. It's a solid one. Usually get it if there's nothing interesting since most places carry it." He put his glass down to look at John. "Yeah, you may be right. I dunno. We're not an outgoing bunch of guys though."

John looked over at the woman, who was still working on her laptop. "True. And I wouldn't want to bother her. She looks busy." His attention turned back to his cider, and he took a large gulp that placed him ahead of Nick.

"What were you thinking of getting?" Nick asked. He grabbed the small menu from the side of the table and slid it to his friend. "This is the happy hour menu. Check it out."

Even though he was hungry, John's stomach wasn't crying out in pain. His drink satisfied a part of his appetite. Not his hunger appetite, but the appetite of his soul. That mystery woman, over in the corner, could fill up a part of that soul. Would a relationship replace the need for alcohol consumption?

Such thoughts assumed John knew anything about that woman. She was pretty, had red hair, owned a laptop, and liked dark ales. She was an enigma, and John was projecting his desires into her. Assuming she was single, she could be something that didn't agree with his sensibilities. She could have been careless about the environment. She could show no care toward stimulating conversation. Worst of all, she could show no care toward ambition, her pride existing in the vapid accomplishments of her potential offspring. An empty desert of wasted potential.

Or she could be the woman John always wanted.

"Have you guys decided on food?" asked the bartender, who again snuck up onto the table and almost startled John.

"Oh Jesus, yes, sorry," said John with a nervous laugh. "Yeah, I'll have the personal pizza, please. No pepperoni, just the cheese."

"Got it," said the bartender while writing the order on his notepad. Without looking up, he continued. "And for you?"

"The chili corn dog for me," said Nick, followed by more scribbling on the pad.

After he was done, the bartender looked up. "Right, we'll get those out to you in a few minutes." He then left to relay the order to the kitchen. Nick finished sending a text message on his phone when he looked up at John.

"What you thinking about?" Nick asked, more as a polite gesture than with any genuine curiosity.

"Ah, nothing really. Chicks, I guess. Thinking about what I'd say to her if I had the balls to talk with her."

Nick smiled. "Well, if you want to talk to her, go for it. I got no suggestions though. Worst-case scenario, she says no, and even a worse worst-case scenario, she says yes and she's still a better girlfriend than Michelle."

John cackled at that comment, and Nick followed suit with a smaller bout of laughter. When the chuckles subsided, John collected his thoughts again. "Funny, I was just telling you about how I never see hot women where I go."

"Well, you're the one who thinks she's hot. I can't tell from here." Nick took a quick peek over at the mysterious woman. "Someone with that hair, drinking dark beer. You never know, she could be a lesbian."

"Or bisexual," suggested John.

Nick shrugged. "Have you ever met a bisexual outside of porn?" He waited for John to not respond. "Exactly."

"I'm not talking bisexual as in 'oooh I'm gonna have a threesome with one of her hot friends.' Not that I would say no."

Nick interrupted. "Good man."

"But yeah, I'm not going to live my life expecting porn to happen to me. I was just saying, just because she likes other women doesn't mean she can like a guy." Once in a while, John would step outside his body and wonder if he came across as desperate. This was one such moment.

"I think some of Michelle's friends are single," said Nick, "but they annoy the crap out of me. Wouldn't wish that on you."

"Thanks, I appreciate it." John mused that his social anxiety in this situation resulted from him being afraid his fantasies wouldn't come true. That could have been his issue. Why not see what the mystery woman could add to his life? More importantly, why did he spend the past ten minutes exerting the extra effort in developing potential personalities for the red-haired woman when he could have gone over and talked with her?

That had to wait, for the food arrived quicker than both John and Nick anticipated. The bartender brought them a second round as they began their early dinner. John's pizza was actually quite tasty; it wasn't the typical frozen fare most bars handed out, and even though it lacked toppings, it had plenty of flavor. He got into his food so much he didn't realize that the woman had stood up from her table and started heading out the door.

"Now's your chance," said Nick. His voice wasn't urgent; it sounded almost bored. He could predict what John wouldn't do next.

"It would be awkward now," said John, confirming Nick's predictions. "Yeah, probably not worth it. Plenty of other women out there."

After taking a big bite from his chili dog, Nick offered his opinion: "I don't know what it is. But there's a lot more attractive ladies out there now. Back in high school, it was like finding Waldo. Now, everybody has got it going on."

John nodded. "I think you're right. That or our standards are way lower than they used to be."

With the distraction gone, John spent the rest of the time focusing on hanging out with his best friend. His mind no longer focused on his inner turmoil, just on enjoying good food, beer, and company. After three drinks each, the pair paid for their meals and started walking back into the neighborhood.

"So yeah, you're more than welcome to hang out, but my girlfriend is coming over," said Nick. It was starting to get dark, and although the rain eased up, John still felt its trickling sensation. "If I knew we'd get naked, I'd kick you out, but I'm not holding out hope. You can stay, although it may be boring with her."

John shook his head. "Well, that was a lot of fun. Thanks for having me over. I'll head back now."

Nick smiled. "Cool, see you later."

The two went their separate ways. John's car happened to be on that block. He had his car for about a year; it was a five-year-old gray sedan, but it was comfortable, had no issues, and never broke down. Its previous owner maintained it quite well. The sound system was decent, and unlike his last vehicle, John didn't have to worry about shifting since it was an automatic. He got into his car, shut and locked the door, and set his hands on the steering wheel. Taking a deep breath, he sighed. It wasn't a sigh of relief.

"Why the fuck didn't I talk with her?" he asked himself out loud. That conversation with himself happened too often. He had a wonderful time with his best friend, but he was more depressed now than before. John wanted to avoid needing someone else to satisfy his existence. John was complete. Life wasn't terrible; he enjoyed working his retail job, and he had a nice circle of friends, even if most of them were disposable. Everything was satisfactory.

Except the red-haired woman wasn't in his life. But she was just a symbol, and John had to remember to want what the symbol meant, not the symbol itself.

02

CHAPTER TWO

Despite having an easy job, John sometimes burned out for no reason. There weren't any unreasonable customers or overly long hours. Yet something clicked in John's subconsciousness, urging him to get out of there as soon as he could.

Instead of driving home, John decided to go into town and hit up one of his favorite pubs. It was too late to invite one of his work buddies, and Nick was probably entertaining his girlfriend, so John set out to visit the venue on his own. Sometimes going to a pub solo was satisfying. Drinking and eating alone without having to prepare something often cleared his mind, especially when rain wasn't available to meditate in. Occasionally, John would catch a conversation with another patron or bartender to stretch and enrich his mind.

John drove up to Uncle John's Public House, which had some of the best food and drink in town for a good price. It wasn't raining at the time, but there were puddles John had to avoid in the parking lot. Being a little after the new year, it was still dark at that hour, and the local lighting wasn't the most forgiving. He managed to make his way into the establishment with little drama.

It was a Thursday, but the place had a decent crowd. There was a homey feel to the pub. It had a lot of wooden fixtures and furniture, but it was brighter than most bars. Wanting a drink right away, he went right up to the bar and began pulling out some cash.

"Hey there. What'll it be?" asked the bartender, who finished serving a couple.

"Hmm," said John. "Thinking of going with something a bit heavier than cider. I'll go with the pale ale."

"You betcha," said the bartender as he turned around and tapped a pint. John had the money ready by the time the bartender returned to him with the drink. "That'll be four dollars."

John handed him a five-dollar bill. "Keep the change," he said, grabbing the glass and heading toward an empty table. He had barely taken a few steps when a woman backed up from the bar and almost bumped into John. He held his drink up into the air to avoid contact with her as much as possible.

"Woah!" he yelled, startled by the stranger.

She turned around to face him. She had very dark hair that went a few inches past her shoulders, with longer messy bangs in the front. Pale complexion with subtle, if any, makeup. She was wearing a black leather jacket and a long gray skirt. Her eyes widened when she realized what happened.

"Oh my God!" she exclaimed. "I'm so sorry! Please tell me you didn't spill anything."

John played the situation cool. "No, no, I'm fine actually. Are you okay?"

Her widened eyes turned into a smile. "Oh yeah. I was just going outside to call a friend. So noisy in here."

"Yeah, it's a bit chatty in here." John observed the room in a little more detail, noting the empty tables and volume levels. "You here by yourself then?"

She pouted. "Right now, yeah. My friends bailed on me. Just got off work and needed to unwind, but I hate being out on my own."

John shrugged. "I just got off work too. But I don't mind being alone. I love eating out and drinking and watching people. What makes you not like it?"

It was her turn to shrug, except she kept her shoulders up a lot longer than John did. "One of those stupid non existent judgmental things, I guess. Oooh, what are you drinking?"

He looked at his own glass. "Oh, it's the pale ale here. My best friend really likes it. Say!" He looked out to the nearest empty table. "Since we're both off work and by ourselves, wanna grab a table so we can complain to someone who might care a little?"

She giggled. "Yes, sure. Let me grab my drink." She turned back to the bar, where an unaccompanied glass was sitting. Grabbing it, she went back over to John, who then directed the pair over to the empty table. He held out a chair, and she sat. He took the spot across from her.

"So where do you work?" asked John, before taking a sip from his brew.

"I'm a nanny for a two-year-old, and I freaking hate it," she said with lots of disdain in her voice. "It pays the bills, and I guess I'm good with kids. But I feel like a slave sometimes, especially when my employer is a snotty couple."

"Sounds rough," said John before taking another sip.

She shrugged. "The kid's fine though. Best part is when she sleeps, I can relax and read and dream. What do you do?"

"Big-box retail," said John with his own sigh. "Pay sucks, but it honestly ain't bad. If you don't have many expenses, I think that's the way to go, if you can handle the corporate soullessness of it."

"I want to open up a small shop," she said. "I don't know what. Coffee shop, craft shop, art gallery, something. Something small that isn't stressful. I don't care if I don't make any money on it. I don't care if I live in the damn place. But it would be so fun."

John smiled. "That would be. That's a great dream to have."

She finished the sip from her transparent drink, set it down, and looked directly at John's eyes. Her eyes were dark brown, almost black, but they were mesmerizing. "My name is Isabel."

"Isabel? That's a very lovely name," said John. "Do you have any Spanish heritage?"

"Thank you!" she said, grinning. "And not really. I mean, sure, a little bit. I think my great-great-grandmother immigrated here from Spain."

John put his hands out in a welcoming gesture. "Well,

Isabel, my name is John. Unfortunately, my name is not as cool as yours."

Isabel blushed. "Oh, thank you! And I like John. Some of the best people ever are named John."

"Oh, like the pope?"

"Wasn't really thinking that, but I'm sure there are some great popes named John." She took another sip from her drink. "I don't know what the hell this is, but it's alright. Some guy at the bar bought it for me."

"I've always wondered what it's like to have people buy you drinks," said John. "I guess I can always visit a gay bar or something."

Isabel laughed. "It's not as great as you think. It's one of those stupid social norms that women have to put up with. Even if it was acceptable for me to buy drinks for random guys at a bar, I sure as hell won't do it. I work too hard for my money."

Already, John found Isabel endearing. It wasn't her physical appearance that drew him in, yet she was plenty attractive. Her comment about social norms was what mesmerized him.

"You'd think with the onset of the feminist movement that many of those norms would have gone away," John observed. "I know so many guys who treat the bar scene like an auction house. Women bring themselves to bars willingly to be auctioned off to the sleaziest dude in the room. That's the reality, and it sucks that people aren't more disturbed about that."

Isabel leaned in. "I know! It's so nice to meet a guy who realizes that. Your girlfriend is one lucky woman, I bet."

John wondered if Isabel was slyly asking if he was available or not. It was early in the conversation, but it was too premature to make such assumptions. He ignored them for the time being.

"I never knew someone imaginary could feel so lucky, but you learn something every day." John took another sip.

It didn't take long for Isabel to register the joke. "Oh! I'm sorry. I just assume that guys like you are always coupled."

"Or there's always being gay."

Isabel thought for a second. "Well, I didn't think you were, but my radar does suck. I've dated a gay man before, in college. Neither of us knew. It was a little confusing."

"You'd think they'd have it figured out by then." He was hypnotized by his new found friend. He enjoyed being in her company, despite knowing so little about her.

The conversation reverted to basic information about the two by the time a bartender came by their table. They ordered a second round of drinks with some dinner. Isabel was the same age as John, a college graduate with a degree in anthropology. After their drinks arrived, John delved further into her personal life.

"Whereabouts are you living right now?" he asked.

"I have two roommates. They're both nineteen, in college. They had a third room in their place that they needed to rent. It was cheap, so I took it. One of their parents owns it for their rental home. They keep begging me to buy them booze. But if I'm not going to buy booze for a hunky guy at the bar, I sure as hell am not gonna get cheap liquor for some babies."

John laughed. Isabel took another sip. "How about

you?" she asked.

It was a question John always tried to avoid, but there was no way around it. He didn't think Isabel was shallow about that particular social norm, but he wasn't sure. Just in case, he took a rather large sip of his cider before answering. "Well, you know, college graduate, haven't found a good job, working part-time. Parents sure are understanding, let me tell you."

"Oh I bet," said Isabel, but her smile hid something else. John feared she was disappointed in him for that. Before he could fret more, she continued. "I'm sure if I was in your shoes, I'd do the same."

"What do you mean?" asked John, perplexed.

"Well," Isabel started but had trouble continuing. It was obviously a difficult subject for her to discuss. "Let's just say my family and I aren't on speaking terms. Haven't been for a while."

That relieved John of his initial fears. Her timid reaction wasn't a reflection of him, but rather an unfortunate series of events in her past. "I'm so sorry. Is everything okay with you?"

She shrugged. "Oh yeah, I'm fine. I've been doing pretty well without them, and they obviously don't need me. The way I look at it, you don't choose your family. Why should you be forced to accept who they are? People always tell me that you can pick your friends but you have to always make peace with whoever your family is because you always have them. And you know what I say to them? Fuck that."

John giggled before putting his hand on his face, realizing that could be interpreted as not taking a serious matter seriously. "I'm sorry. No, I completely understand where you're coming from."

"No, it's fine," she said. "It was a silly way for me to put it. But seriously, if your family doesn't accept you for who you are, or has opinions or perspectives that are just downright rotten, just because they are family, I have to tolerate them? My genetic code is not linked to my social code. Blood or no blood, if someone is a dick, they're a dick, and I won't give them the time of day."

"Well, you are right," John said. "My family is pretty good and loving, so I've never had that conflict myself. But your principle is perfectly sound. Never thought of it like that before, but I may have to adopt your... methodology."

Isabel smiled. "Thank you. But still, be glad that your parents are cool. You probably want to get out of there, huh?"

John nodded earnestly. "Oh yeah."

There was a pause as Isabel quietly looked into John's eyes. She might not have been saying anything, but she was thinking. He couldn't figure out where her thoughts were going.

"I'm glad I ran into you here," she said calmly.

It was John's turn to smile. "I'm glad I ran into you too." He leaned back. "What prompted that?"

At that time the cook from the back brought out their two plates and set them down. Isabel ordered a Cajun cheeseburger, while John received a grilled bacon and cheese sandwich. Both of them looked up and said "thank you" in near unison. The cook smiled and retreated back to her work.

"I don't know," she said. "I was sad that my friends

weren't here. You were just someone to talk to. But now, I don't know." She laughed nervously. "Whatever, I'm eating this."

"It looks damn delicious!" said John, and the two ate their meals in silence.

Isabel finished half her burger before putting ketchup on her plate for the fries. "Well, this may come across rather callous." She ate a few fries, this time watched by an overly attentive John. "You're pretty cool. I don't come across pretty cool people very often. Almost always they have a douchebag side to them. And it's fucking stupid that I think that way about someone. I'm prejudging you, and that's not right."

John shrugged, finishing a few bites from one of his sandwiches. "It's fine. I understand where you come from. Most guys are terrible. They're the type that always makes their ladies suck while they don't offer anything in return."

Predicting a massive laugh attack, Isabel put her hand over her mouth while working hard to keep her food in. She swallowed what she was chewing before saying, "Oh man, that's so wrong. So funny though. But man, is that true!"

"No kidding, most of my female friends say that." John only had a few female friends, and they were all coworkers. He figured it was safe to stretch the truth. "That problem is an indicator about guys like me and how we view and treat women like you. It's dumb."

Again, Isabel looked at John silently for a few seconds. "Do you like being a man?"

John set down the sandwich and looked at it for a few seconds while he collected his thoughts. "You mean, if I could change my gender, would I?"

"No, not like that," she continued. "I mean, are you proud of being a man?"

"I'm not proud of what men do," he said. "In general. I do my best, but I'm not perfect. But I am ashamed of what guys my age are doing. I went to college. I've been to parties. I've seen shit go down that I am not proud of seeing. I look in the mirror sometimes and think that I'm capable of the same shit. It's not a cool feeling to have."

Isabel nodded, and John wasn't sure what she thought of that response. Instead, after finishing most of the second half of her cheeseburger, she looked at her phone to check the time. "I didn't expect to be out this long today. Probably head out soon."

"Yeah, I didn't intend to stay out this late either," said John, "but I'm definitely glad I had a reason to."

She smiled. "Let me get you in my phone." She played with her phone for a minute after John gave her his number, and then she put it away. What seemed like a coincidence at the time, John's phone buzzed in his coat pocket. He took it out and saw he had a message from an unknown number: *This is Isabel. Call me when you want to go out again* :).

"Thank you, I will," said John. Isabel giggled as she finished her fries. As if on cue, the bartender came by with the bill and, per social norms, handed it to John. He thanked the bartender.

As the bartender walked away, Isabel grabbed the check from John and pulled out her debit card. Before he could say a word of protest, she said, "I know I just said that I wouldn't buy a guy a beer if it was socially acceptable. But you know what? Fuck it. I like you, and I want to thank you. And I want to turn what is socially acceptable around because fuck all these other people."

John laughed. The bartender returned and grabbed the card for processing in the back, which prompted the two to slowly get their coats on. "Well, what's your work schedule like?"

"I work when the parents work, so it's pretty normal hours. Feels long though." The bartender returned her card and receipt. She signed it and added a tip. "Goddamn that kid."

"I thought you said you liked the little guy?" asked John with confused curiosity.

"Little girl, but whatever," said Isabel. "I may be okay with kids, but I'm not really comfortable with them. They just remind me that, biologically, I can be forced to grow one of them. And that's just a crappy feeling. Yeah, birth control and abortions and stuff, but it's the principle. I don't want a kid. I never want a kid. I just want to rule the world."

John stood up with Isabel, disoriented from her declaration. "What? Really? I have never heard a woman say that. It's usually douchebag dudes who are afraid of having a kid."

Isabel walked next to John. "Well, the stereotype that women don't want to fuck like men do is false too. Same with kids. Not every girl out there wants a kid."

"Well, yes, I can imagine that," said John. "It's just, with women, they're brainwashed into wanting children from a young age."

"Exactly," she said as she got to the door. "I avoid these

stupid social expectations if I find they're stupid. But men can enjoy fucking and not have to be forced to grow what will turn out to be an annoying runt who poops and cries." They were now outside, and it started to rain.

"Where are you parked?" asked John.

"Oh right here," said Isabel, gesturing to a car parked right in front of the building. She turned to face John, her eyes a couple of inches lower than his. Before he could contemplate the next move, she leaned forward on her toes and kissed him on his lips, then backed away. Lacking the usual first-kiss nerves, he leaned down and responded to her show of affection with a kiss of his own. She smiled. "It's your turn next time. Give me a call this weekend."

She turned around and got into her car. John had a big grin on his face. He waved to her and walked over to his car, avoiding the large, nasty puddles he remembered seeing on the way in. He had a new friend, and he was excited to see where their friendship would go.

03

CHAPTER THREE

Over the course of the next three weeks, John went on three more dates with Isabel. After their initial meeting at Uncle John's, the pair met up for lunch the following weekend at a fantastic sandwich shop. From there, they went to the local art museum to view an exhibit on traditional Japanese artwork, where the two learned about the depth of the other's knowledge. A traditional dinner followed by a hilarious comedy was next, and the fourth date was on the table.

"I'm picking this one out," she said over the phone.

"Okay," said John. "What do you have in mind?"

"You like stir-fry?"

"Sure. Know a good Asian restaurant?"

"Well, yes, but I want to make you some dinner on Friday," she said. "Got a good TV show that I want to show you. Think you'd really like it."

Isabel was taking the next step. She was inviting him over to her house. No doubt her roommates would tease her about bringing a man over. He still had to temper his expectations. John remembered Nick going on about five dates with a woman. He was invited to her house, and when he made a move, he was rejected. Such obvious setups weren't always what they seemed.

"Sounds like fun!" he said. "Should I bring anything?"

"Just you," she said in a gushy, romantic way. "I have some beer we can drink. One I know you'll like, Mr. I-Hate-Beer-That's-Darker-Than-Piss!"

"Hey now!" he said, raising his voice.

He heard laughter on the other end. "You don't work the next day?"

A forward question. "No."

"Well, I don't want to keep you too late. Just meet me here at six on Friday. Talk to you later!"

John was working every day between Wednesday and Friday, and his shifts couldn't pass quickly enough. It was a joy every time the two met, and John hoped this time would be no different. After he got off work at four on Friday, he went home to get out of his work clothes and changed into a button-up green-gray sweater and dark blue jeans. Once he was looking his best without suiting up, he was off to the address she had messaged him.

He pulled up and parked on the street in front of the house. It was an unassuming dwelling. The neighborhood itself was older, but that particular house was a much newer construction, probably built in the past ten years. Isabel's car was the only one parked in the driveway, and the porch light was on. Being mid-winter, it was still dark. It was dry but chilly, so John wore a heavier peacoat he bought while shopping with Isabel.

John locked his car and walked down the driveway to the front porch. He was never sure if it was appropriate to knock or ring the doorbell. Knocking seemed more aggressive, so he opted for the more tranquil option. The bell rang deep inside the house, which prompted a nervous sigh from John. He saw his breath shoot out in a puff of steam.

Moments later, the door opened. Isabel was wearing a dark-green ribbed long-sleeved shirt with some jeans. Her hair was tied back, and she wore a silver-colored necklace. She smiled. He smiled.

"Hey there!" she said softly but with great exuberance.

"Hey," said John. "Nice place."

She put her head outside so she could get a view of the exterior. "No." They both laughed.

"Well you live here," said John.

"Awwww," said Isabel. "It has no character, no soul. But why don't you come in?"

"Maybe I will," he said as he walked into her house. It had a generic suburban feel despite being several miles from the suburbs. It also had the feel of a sorority house, no doubt due to the influence of Isabel's housemates. There was hardly any artwork on the walls, and there was a lot of pink and purple everywhere.

"Love the pink blankets," he said.

Isabel laughed. "Yeah, Christina and Kat are girly girls. In the annoying way. The kitchen's back here."

She led him past the living room adjacent to the entryway and made it to the kitchen in the rear of the house. She had a wok going on the stove, cooking an excellent concoction that smelled delightful. John nodded in approval. "Girly girls in an annoying way?"

"Yeah. Well, I'm a girly girl too, but in a different way." She stirred the vegetables in the wok a bit. "They're all show. They wear cute pink tank tops and plaster smokey eye shadow on their face and talk about such intellectual topics like something dumb their friend said. My girly girlness is better."

"Quite the ego there," he said with a sly smile.

"Well, you know what I mean," she said. "They sometimes make me ashamed to be a woman. At least you and I have that in common."

"No kidding." John leaned against the wall. "Where are they?"

"At some dumb dance club," she said, grabbing some plates from the cupboard. "Someplace you'd never see me at. They're probably not coming home tonight either."

"My friend's girlfriend probably goes to the same place," he said. "Need help?"

"If you can get the silverware from that drawer, that would be cool," she said, setting the table while pointing at a drawer. John grabbed forks and knives from the drawer and set them beside the plates while Isabel lit the candle in the middle of the table.

"Awww, how romantic," said John with jest.

"Hey!" she said, smiling. "Sometimes I like cliché. Besides, we can turn the lights off and save electricity. You know, the environment and all."

"Yeah, yeah, appealing to my heart."

She turned off the stove and grabbed the two plates from the table. John turned off the light switch, got the soy and peanut sauce from the counter, and brought them to the table. By the time he sat down, Isabel had come by with two plates of beautiful stir-fry and set them on the table. Without missing a beat, she retreated to the refrigerator, grabbed two bottles of a medium ale, and opened them on a refrigerator-mounted bottle opener. She then sat down across from him, providing him with his bottle.

John looked up at Isabel's smile, the soft light of the candle casting soft shadows on her face. He responded with his own smile.

"Thank you," he said softly.

"You're welcome!" she said, even softer. "Why don't you start? It's really good."

He grabbed the peanut sauce and added some to his plate. Grabbing the fork, he began to eat. It was wonderful; John didn't believe he ever had a meal so tasty. It could have been because he was distracted by the woman across from him. It could have been because that woman cooked with great skill.

The meal was silent. They enjoyed the food, stared into each other's eyes, and occasionally giggled. Nothing needed to be said. John could read her eyes better than he could hear any word she said. The beauty of that moment superseded all of John's previous romantic moments. He had known her for less than a month; it was too hasty to call it love. It was beyond infatuation though. The more time he spent with her and the more he delved into her secrets, the more John realized the cause of his attraction.

She wasn't the same as John. They had different interests. She didn't fancy video games; he didn't fancy crafty hobbies. But they both respected their respective interests. They both offered something the other could learn from. She was a rare person whom John could truly lose himself in. Rather than struggling to escape, he'd rather absorb her web of knowledge and passion. She was greater than him, and John didn't mind that realization.

Both of them finished at the same time and they sat in silence. They looked straight into each other's eyes, gauging what the other was thinking. John smiled first, followed by Isabel.

"That was very good," he said, maintaining the soft volume.

"Thank you," she said, waiting a few seconds before continuing. "There was that show I wanted to show you."

"Yeah?" John said.

Isabel stood up and walked around the table to John's side. His eyes followed her. Right as he began to stand up, she pulled the chair back while he was seated, creating a gap between him and the table. She put herself in that gap and sat on John's lap, facing him, her legs straddling him underneath the armrest. Running her hands through his hair, she gently kissed him. John closed his eyes and moved his hands to her hips.

When she pulled back, she said, "I'm not sure if I want to show it to you right now." She lowered her head again and kissed John's lips, this time more passionately. After each date, elongated kissing was the climax. This was different: the setting was different; the vibe was different; even the kissing was different. It was less intense, more refined. It was the beginning of something else.

Soon their hands explored each other's bodies, their mouths moving to their cheeks and neck. John's heart rate was accelerating. Without a second thought, he pulled Isabel's shirt above her head, and she lifted her arms to accommodate him, exposing a dark-green bra. The two continued to further explore each other in the candlelight. She pressed her forehead against his, looking down as she swiftly undid his shirt buttons, exposing his own front.

When John moved his hands back to unsnap her bra, Isabel whispered, "They may come back tonight. Let's go into my room."

John complied. She stood up and grabbed his hand, pulling him away from the chair, forgetting her top. The rest of the house was dark, but Isabel didn't bother with any of the lights and led the way upstairs. Hers was the first room on the left. She turned on the warm night-light as John closed the door behind them. The room was small, but it was a lot different from the rest of the house. Pictures and art covered the walls, handmade blankets of earthy colors lay on the bed, and there were several plants on her desk. There was almost no floor space left.

Isabel sat down on the bed and pulled John toward her. They resumed their kissing as John removed his shirt and Isabel removed her bra. Their chests pressed together as they ran their hands along their naked torsos, discovering each other's sensations. John gently pushed Isabel back on the bed and worked along the sensitive spots on her breasts while slowly undoing her jeans. He made his way awkwardly onto the floor, trying to pull the pants and underwear off her legs. When those reached the floor, he continued his kissing in a new location entirely.

It had been over a year since he went this far with a woman, but he wasn't completely out of practice. Isabel's soft breathing turned to audible moans. Her hands alternated between feeling herself and feeling his hair. The intensity increased, the pace of her breaths increased, and the volume of her moans intensified. His tongue eventually wore out; he was sure she didn't finish. But when he stood up to look at Isabel, she was lying comfortably, her eyes closed, her breath quick but calm, a slight smile on her face.

Her eyes opened to look at him. Without saying a word, she sat up and reached for his belt loop. She did have trouble with it, so John helped her out enough to where she could drop his jeans to the floor. He lifted his feet to get out of the pants while her hand rubbed him back and forth. As he was getting more aroused, Isabel gestured to her dresser. "Look in the top-right drawer, underneath my socks."

Obediently, John walked over to said dresser, and looking under the socks, he found a condom package. He pulled it out and brought it over to Isabel. Her hand found its way back to him, getting him as excited as possible. She broke the package and put the latex barrier on him. Once it was in place, she lay back down on the bed. John got on top of her and made his way into her. The pace was slow at first, as Isabel adjusted to having someone new inside of her. Her hands wrapped around his back and helped him guide the pace. She stared into John's eyes, like at the dinner table.

"Oh, John, kiss me," she said. This wasn't the appropriate time to be a rebel, so John obeyed. That kiss was the longest and most passionate one they ever had. No woman in his past had ever wanted him to kiss her after he went down on her, so this was a brand-new experience for him. Once the moment was over, John adjusted himself to an elevated position again, and Isabel guided him to a quicker pace. As he sped up, their kissing became more lustful, more primal. Their breaths quickened, and both of them began moaning. It had been a while for John, and even with a condom, he was nearing his end.

Isabel knew the moment was imminent. "Look at me," she whispered as if she was out of breath. John stopped kissing her, and when he finished, he did his best not to lose eye contact. His attention was all on her, all on her thoughts, all on her emotions, all on her pleasure. John let out a grunt and collapsed onto Isabel's body. They wrapped their arms around each other for a few moments before John disposed of his latex device. Isabel curled up on the bed, still above the covers, waiting for his return. He lay down next to her and welcomed her into his arms.

Even though neither fell asleep, they lay there in silence for a long time, feeling each other's hearts. Isabel pulled back and ran her hand across John's face.

"Hey," she said, grinning.

"How are you doing?" said John.

"I can't put it into words." She took several deep breaths before continuing. "I've never been with someone in that way before."

John's eyes widened. "Wait, are you serious? This was your first?"

Isabel giggled. "No, no, no." She kissed him on his nose. "I've had other men inside my body. But I've never had men inside my heart."

He contemplated her comment for some time. "What makes you think that?"

Her smile continued. "I asked you to look at me when you finished. That's the one moment where people can't lie. You didn't close your eyes. I didn't become an anonymous fuck toy to you. You didn't forget about me. You saw me."

Now John smiled. "I've never let someone have my heart like that before either."

Isabel waited a beat before responding. "Well, it's also been a long time for me, so it did feel pretty amazing."

They both giggled. John broke the soft laughter. "Does that mean we're boyfriend-girlfriend now?"

She nodded. "Yes."

"So what about that show you wanted to show me?" asked John, followed by a poorly executed wink.

"We'll get to that in a bit," she said before kissing John on the nose again.

04

CHAPTER FOUR

"This place isn't too bad," Isabel said as she stood in the living room and looked up the stairway inside the duplex. It was a skinny apartment with a small living room and kitchen on the first floor and a bedroom and bathroom on the top floor.

"I'm not used to small," said John, looking around at the downstairs living space they were standing in.

She looked at him. "I thought you were fine with small? It's a better carbon footprint."

John shrugged. "I know. Going from my parents' place to something like this is an adjustment."

The landlady looked up from her clipboard. "So what do you two think?"

John and Isabel had been together for nine months. It was a blossoming relationship that improved every day.

They had done so much throughout the year, spending a week camping in a remote location and visiting the beach many times. He was learning so much about his significant other, not just her quirks but also her perspectives and a bit of her past. She was still shy at disclosing information about her family, but John didn't pry too hard at such subjects.

Two months earlier, John got a new job that had more hours and higher pay. It was deeper in town. That prompted him to start looking for a place to live, but rather than John having to find a random roommate, Isabel offered herself. She was never too pleased with her housemates but didn't want to move into a cheap place in the suburbs. The two figured they'd move into a small apartment or duplex.

"I love it," she said. "We can grow a garden in the backyard. Put all sorts of artwork all over the place. What do you think, John?"

John nodded. "Yeah, I like this. What if we fight? We can't run from each other."

Isabel glared at him. "Always the practical one, aren't you?"

"Well, not like we don't get along, but if we have an argument, we'll have to stay with each other. Or hide on each floor."

Isabel looked at the landlady. "Can we talk in private?"

She smiled. "Sure! I'll be upstairs."

After she went up the stairway, Isabel walked over to John. "What's wrong?" She wasn't angry or accusatory, but genuinely concerned.

"I've never done this before," he said. He reached out to hug his girlfriend, and she accepted. "I'm twenty-four and finally moving out of home, with a brilliant, beautiful woman with dreams that I only wish I had."

She smiled.

"I don't want to hurt you," he continued. "I know with my inexperience that I'm gonna do some dumbskull thing and we're gonna fight and hate each other, and I don't want to hurt you."

Isabel looked up at him and moved one hand through his hair. She stood silently for a few moments.

"What are you thinking, Bel?" he said, using his personalized nickname for her.

"I think I love you," she said. They first confessed their love two weeks after their consummation, but they didn't say those words frequently. Its scarcity made the word more impactful. "And I also know that life can go in any direction. We may fall out of love, we may get angry, we may cheat. We've talked about this before. Let's just live in the moment. And the moment is wonderful."

"I know it is," said John. His breath held back, and Isabel picked up on it.

"What is it?"

John released her from the hug and turned away, making an effort not to look at her. "This isn't the time to say it."

Isabel's face spelled concern. "What do you mean? We've talked about moving in for weeks. Do you want to wait?"

He continued to look away. "No, I don't. I love you too, Bel. I love that you live in the moment. But I look at possibilities in the future. What if we get to the point where we marry and then hate each other? I see so many couples, both our generation and my parents' generation, where that shit happens. All the time."

She backed away a few steps. "Are you actually considering marrying at some point?"

By that point John was freaking out, putting his hands on his face and walking away. "Forget I said anything. Let's go. I don't want to hurt you."

"No, no, no," she said, taking a few quick paces toward him before reaching out and grabbing his arm. "I want you to answer the question. And like always, be honest. Don't be afraid to say something that may be hurtful."

John turned around to face his lover. The dam blocking his tear ducts weakened. "I'm not sure. I want us to love each other on our own terms. If marriage is something you want and we get to that point, I guess I'll be fine with it."

Isabel's face remained statuesque. "That open mind is why I love you." She went over and kissed the distraught John on the lips, then pulled away. "Did you seriously think I ever want to get married?"

A shocked John shrugged. "Well, ummm, I don't..."

Before he could finish mumbling, Isabel interrupted. "It's okay! Marriage sucks. It's so misogynistic and bullshit. Kids suck. Society's expectations for relationships suck. I thought you knew all of this about me."

John managed a small smile. "I do, Bel. I do! I just wanted to be sure. It's been ingrained in me that everybody wants that."

"Let me tell you, we are not Nick and Michelle. Who knows why the hell they are getting married? I know you have a lot of concern for your friend, and I'm glad you do.

But that's them, not us. Have I ever told you about my dream house?"

"No," said John, now in a more coherent state.

She turned to look outside the window. "I want a nice stone cottage somewhere. In the country, in the city with a lot of green space around. I don't care. Small. One room, maybe two. With a bathroom, of course. Maybe even smaller than this. I want to grow moss on it and have a big garden all around. Maybe a creek or pond in the yard. Woodstove to keep warm. Have some electricity, but we wouldn't have to use much."

"Sounds beautiful," said John, who walked over to Isabel. He put his arms around her front and rested his chin on her shoulder. Her hands clasped his. "Kind of awesome, actually. Still civilized but be part of nature."

"I've dreamt about the place since I was ten," she continued. "I can't afford it now. Maybe I can never afford it. I always imagined living there by myself, making crafts and growing trees until I grew old. Never really cared about boys much. But life comes across new experiences. So even if that doesn't happen, I want this to be my cottage. I want it to be our cottage." She lifted his hand and kissed it gently.

John squeezed her body tighter. "I'll help you make it happen."

There was a pause, as if Isabel lost herself inside her mind. "What was that?"

"We'll move in here and make it the best place it can be. We'll see if we still are the same dreamy couple in four or five years' time. We'll save up our money. We'll find that house, and we'll make it happen."

She turned around and smiled. "On one condition."

"Yes?" said John, confused by the ultimatum.

"You have to find your own identity," she said. "I've found myself in love with a brilliant man, but don't make my dreams your dreams. I want John to be John. I don't want John to be Isabel's boyfriend. I don't want to date myself."

"That could be interesting," quipped John.

Isabel pinched him, causing him to yelp. "You know what I mean."

"I do," said John. "I've always wanted to live in a home that was eco-friendly, but I never made it romantic-sounding or thought too hard on what that would be. Your cottage is everything I ever wanted. We'll make it happen together. And I'll continue to play video games, just how you like it."

She giggled for a bit before pausing to gaze at John. "Are you okay now?"

John nodded. "Yeah, I am. Thank you. Kinda relieved too. Now I just have to ignore my mom talking about wanting to be a grandmother."

Isabel walked around the empty room. Even though most of it was carpet, her footsteps still had a slight echo. "Anything you see wrong with this place?"

John shrugged. "The only thing missing is your magic."

She grinned. "Good, let's go let her know." She took several steps toward the stairway and raised her voice. "Samantha! We're ready!"

When he listened for a response, John made out a muffled phone conversation that was soon concluded. After the talking ended, the landlady walked down the steps with her clipboard and faced the couple. "Well, what do you think?"

"We want it," said John.

"Alright, let's get the paperwork signed!" The three of them walked over to the kitchen counter and huddled around it. They signed documents and asked final questions outlining the details. When that was all done, the landlady smiled and said, "Great! We'll complete the background check. Then I'll get you your keys on Wednesday next week. Then you can move in whenever you'd like!"

When the two parties said their goodbyes, everyone left the empty duplex. John and Isabel walked to John's car in the driveway. John was fearful of what was coming. He had never moved before, and not only was he moving for the first time, but he was moving in with his girlfriend. Both steps were huge, but they were steps he had been preparing for. Even though there were still aspects of Isabel's past that remained a mystery, he was more confident with her than ever. Even her anti-marriage confirmation, while unusual, was oddly reassuring.

"Where to?" asked John after getting in his car.

"Frozen yogurts," said Isabel. Her face was serious, even though it was the middle of autumn.

"Alright, let's go!" He turned the ignition, backed out of the driveway, then drove down the street. "We'll have to share the driveway with the neighbors."

Isabel nodded. "Can't wait to meet them. She said they were good. Gay couple, mostly keeping to themselves."

"Yeah, there's that," he continued. "But mostly thinking about our car situation. We got two cars. One of them will have to be on the street. Which isn't terrible, but now that we live together in the city, and we're both relatively close to work, do we really need two cars?"

She shrugged. "I like the independence. Don't feel too bad. It's not like we drive gas hogs." She looked at him. "We'll see how it goes. We might keep both of them but try relying on one for a week or two."

They continued the rest of the drive in silence. John had fallen in love with this woman faster than any other woman he had loved. He wondered if he even knew what love was before. But he had to take it one day at a time. Tomorrow he might want children; tomorrow she might want children. Tomorrow he might even leave her. The reality was that tomorrow he and Isabel would still be an item and that next week they'd be living together. Able to spend fragile moments with one another, able to create memories.

The frozen yogurt shop was about a ten-minute drive away, and fortunately, there was a small parking lot John squeezed his car into. Both hopped out of the car, noting that the wind had picked up and the clouds were starting to come in. The shop was small, with seating for six people. A bar with self-served toppings lined the wall, and in front of the cashier, a weight machine calculated the price. Both of them grabbed small bowls, filled them with their choice of toppings, and met up with the cashier.

"That all for today?" he asked with a hint of droll boredom. He looked to be in high school, or maybe he was early college-aged.

"Yeah." John pulled out his debit card and predicted a glare from Isabel. Smiling, he turned to her. "This is my treat."

She didn't say anything. She grabbed her bowl and sat

down at one of the empty chairs.

As soon as John concluded the transaction, he joined her and delved into his dessert. Like during the car trip, the two were silent, although the silence was more pronounced and awkward. John was usually good at gauging Isabel's silent thoughts, but this felt new. This sort of silence was one John had met in most of his past relationships. Until now, Isabel hadn't acted like that. Until now, she hadn't shown signs of normalcy.

When she was almost done, she stared at her bowl for half a minute, concentrating on the food. Her eyes betrayed her intense thoughts. John thought to inquire but instead continued eating. Right as his spoon went to his mouth, she said, "My mom got me frozen yogurt last time I saw her."

John froze. In the nine months he knew her, that was the first time she referred to a specific family member. He finished what was in his spoon, then set it down. His eyes fixed on her with thoughtful concern and curiosity. Isabel looked right at him, gave a nervous laugh, and then went down to her bowl.

"When I moved away to go to school, Mom took me out afterward to get frozen yogurt. After that, it kind of became a tradition of mine to get it every time I move."

Her hand rested on the table, and John took it in his. He only smiled, as he didn't want to ruin that cherished moment. He saw her eyes were close to welling up. She looked at him. "This is the first time I've had frozen yogurt with someone I've loved in six years. And I couldn't ask for a better person to buy me some."

John continued to smile. "It's okay. Thank you for

telling me that." He looked down at her empty bowl. "You want to wait a while, or are you good to go?"

She was starting to snap out of her mood. "Yeah, I'm good. Let's go home." He must have looked confused, because she clarified, "My home."

They left the frozen yogurt shop and went back into his car. Traffic was getting worse, so the drive to her place took longer than anticipated. It gave John more time to reflect on what happened. While he was still curious about what exactly caused the falling out with her family, he saw a crucial moment with her. He never saw her close to tears before; there was still pain about that part of her life. It made him feel closer to her. It might be another nine months before she mentioned anything else, but it'd be worth the wait.

When they arrived at her house, one of her housemates was home but remained in her room. John tried his best to socialize with them per the rules of etiquette but found it hard to relate to them. They were nice enough individuals, not quite the immature teenagers Isabel portrayed them as, but they lacked good conversation skills. Isabel reheated some pasta she had the night before, and there was enough to feed the two of them for their dinner. With the living room vacant, Isabel broke her house rule by setting their dinner on the coffee table so they could watch a movie while eating.

"This linguine ain't that bad," said John between spats of his mouth being full of food. "I like the mushroom and tomato sauce combo. Good work, Bel!"

"Thank you," she said in response. "It's reheated, but it works."

"I like microwaved foods," he said. "When we finally move in and start cooking, I'm totally down with leftovers and seconds and stuff. Keep things cheap. Don't want to let things go to waste!" With that final sentence, he stared deeply at Isabel.

She blushed. "Okay, okay, yes, throwing out food is bad. I'm working on it. We both have a lot of work to do if we're going to save this planet."

He leaned over and put his arm over her shoulder. "We do have the rest of our lives to make a difference."

Her head leaned on his shoulder. "I'm looking forward to it."

After their movie concluded, they cleaned up their dinner. John wasn't sure what to do. It was still early enough to go back home if he wanted to. She sheepishly walked from the kitchen to the front room, where John still was, and shyly looked away. "Do you work tomorrow?"

John shook his head. "No, we were overstaffed, so I volunteered to take the day off."

She nodded. "Did you want to stay here tonight?" Her face turned and her eyes focused more. "I'm on my period right now, but we can practice actually sleeping-sleeping together."

John smiled. "I would love to stay with you tonight. Are little kisses okay?"

"Of course," she said, her face starting to beam.

O5

Chapter Five

With the sky veiled by overcast, it was hard to tell if it was dawn yet. The clouds were brightening, but the need for lights prevailed. John wrapped his coat around him tighter with one hand while keeping his flashlight in the other. It was winter, and he was struggling with the cold.

"It isn't much farther," said Isabel. She didn't have a cap on, and her hair flowed openly behind her. She looked back at their friend Misty, who was bundled up and carrying photography equipment. "How are you doing, dear?"

Misty nodded. "Fine, but it's damn cold."

John noticed she was struggling with her equipment. "You need some help?"

She flashed a quick smile. "Thanks." The two stopped, and she passed a backpack of equipment over to John, who slung it over his shoulder and continued walking. They were a half-hour from where they parked in the road, hiking along an unknown trail and going into the woods a few miles out of town. Misty let out a puff of steam. "Have you been here before?"

"I went once when I first moved into town," Isabel said. "It's not really advertised."

"I'm definitely getting excited," John said. Isabel looked back at him and smiled.

Despite the conditions, the rest of the walk went smoothly. Visibility was improving, and they noticed they were near the top of a hill. A small path branched off to the right, around a large rock formation, and followed a rather steep cliff. The three managed their balance and made their way around the rocky formation to a section not visible from the main trail. Tall grass and a soft mist further hid where they were going.

When the trail went away from the cliff and toward this mist, the air got warmer. It wasn't the arrival of the day, but it was the source of the mysterious mist. The shivering lessened, and John started to relax. After another minute, the trio arrived at their destination. Inside a small cropping in the rock formation were several pools of hot springs.

"Wow," said John. "This is pretty cool."

"Just like I remembered it." Isabel set down her pack and turned around. "Not quite light enough yet, but check out the view."

Through the dim lighting, past where the cliff dropped off, they could see the tops of trees stemming from the lower elevation. Proper illumination meant they could see quite a distance, at least all the way to the road where they had parked their car.

Misty set her gear down and pulled out her camera. "The lighting I'll need will probably be here in twenty minutes. And if you guys don't mind, I'm gonna warm my hands by this water, because it's fucking cold."

Isabel laughed. "Good idea."

The three of them finished putting their belongings on the ground around the largest pool. Misty got down on her knees and put her hands by the water, testing the temperature to make sure it wasn't scalding. Isabel went a step further and took off her hiking boots and socks. She sat down right by the edge and slowly lowered her bare feet into the water. John followed his partner's example.

It took some time for him to adjust to the temperature. He took a deep breath, taking in the mist and feeling the humid air soak into his lungs. It was very relaxing. With his eyes shut, he slowly dipped his feet into the pool.

John looked at Isabel and saw a tepid smile on her face. He couldn't help but grin. Even after five months of living together, seeing her face brought him joy as if it was the first time he had ever seen her. She eventually noticed the attention, and she returned a soft smile. Their eyes were locked for longer than either realized, and they had to be interrupted by Misty.

"Alright, you lovebirds. I'm gonna start setting up my shit. I'll be over there if you wanted to get ready."

The couple let their feet soak another minute in the hot springs before they stood up and got to their bags. They carried their packs over to the opposite side of the pool, next to the large rock formation, and unpacked their necessary supplies. Keeping the change of clothes inside, they took out large beach towels and laid them out. John had a wool blanket that he held around his arms as Isabel walked right up next to him. They leaned into each other, and their noses touched.

"How are you doing?" asked John.

With an equally monotonous tone, Isabel responded, "Good."

"I brought this that we can strip down in."

"Sounds good." The two broke their somber facial expressions with a smile.

After unwrapping the blanket, he swung it around Isabel and put himself into its sheath. They giggled as he awkwardly adjusted the blanket so it would stay up and cover them. It wasn't too heavy but definitely warm. John nodded at Isabel, and she began taking her clothes off. He kept her shielded from the elements as she shed her layers. Some pieces were difficult, as shown by some awkward smiles.

When she was done, she took over the responsibility of holding up the blanket and left John to his own devices. He took off his upper wear before awkwardly taking off his pants and underwear. It was chilly even with the blanket and the warm springs nearby. He took off his cap, revealing what was undoubtedly messy hair, and threw that down on the ground nearby.

Gaining his composure, he maneuvered the top of the blanket around his arms as he put them around Isabel, bringing her body right up next to his. It was always a beautiful feeling, the touch of her warm shape against his skin.

"It's a bit nipply," quipped John, and they both laughed.

Isabel followed with a vocalized *brrrrr* sound. She rested her head on his shoulder. "Can you wrap the blanket closer?"

John sighed. "I'll try." He did his best to squeeze her body within his arms while wrapping the blanket as tightly as possible around them. While it helped a little, it didn't help that the blanket didn't reach the ground, and a cold draft came up from below. "I feel my balls shriveling."

Isabel laughed, followed by another violent shiver. "My lips have sewn shut by now, probably."

Over in the distance, Misty yelled, "Are you guys decent?"

Calling back, Isabel yelled, "Our naughty bits have frozen off. We're fine to look at."

Even with a bit of distance between the two parties, John could hear an audible sigh. Both he and Isabel chuckled. He looked toward the sky, and the clouds were now closer to a light-gray color, the light bright enough to make out more of the surrounding woods. Carrying a reflective umbrella, Misty approached them from that direction. She found a place near where the couple was standing and set the umbrella down, facing both the pool and the overcast sky.

"Almost ready?" asked John, his shivering not improving.

Misty raised her camera to check the light meters. "Everything looks good. Do you want any pictures of you going into the water?"

The two looked at each other, their eyes repeating a verbal conversation they had the other day. Isabel's eyes went back over to Misty. "We want to put these up on the wall. Not sure how guests will dig us being all nude and everything."

"I think my friends will dig you being nude," quipped John. He whimpered after feeling a stealthy pinch.

"Awesome." Misty lowered her camera. "I'll turn around and you guys can go in."

After she turned away from the couple, John dropped the blanket to the ground. The already-chilly air became even colder, but he was braced for the difference. Isabel wasn't prepared for the swift change and yelped. She continued to hold onto John for a few seconds before breaking away. She wrapped her arms around her torso, shivering like she was at the epicenter of an earthquake. Keeping her thighs together, she hobbled toward the pool and slowly lowered herself to the ground. John was soon behind but delayed himself enough so he could examine her figure as she immersed herself in the pool. The view never got old.

As he was sitting himself down next to Isabel, she began sliding in, wincing from the difference in temperature. John discovered the same issue, as the water seemed hotter than it was earlier when he first dipped his feet in. The warmth passed through the rest of their bodies.

"Feeling better?" asked John, noticing that she wasn't shivering as much.

She shrugged. "A little bit. And you?"

"Just waiting to get used to the water." After another minute, John took the brave first step and slid himself into the pool. It was grassy at the edge, so he had to be careful with the blades, and once his rear was off the side, he was holding himself up with his arms. His arms slowly lowered his body in. When his feet hit the mysterious bottom, the water was up to his abdomen. Thinking about the ground,

John became concerned about the mysteries he couldn't see due to the mist. Were there needles or glass lying in wait? It was a risk both he and Isabel had agreed to take.

John looked back at Isabel and offered his hands. Isabel put her hands around his shoulders and used him as leverage.

"It's warm!" she said with a mischievous smile before straightening her legs and landing on the surface. Due to the shallowness of the edge, her breasts were still exposed to the open air, which became an issue when they heard a shutter snap. Their heads darted toward the origin of the sound, revealing Misty taking shots with her camera.

"Sorry," she said, eyes still in the viewfinder. "Just getting a few preliminary shots. You have very artistically pleasing boobs."

Isabel blushed, looking away. "Oh, thank you." She gained her composure and returned her gaze to Misty. "Topless is okay. I'd rather have my boobs for the world to see than my hoo-ha." Both John and Misty laughed at the word choice.

Misty lowered her camera. "Well, if you don't mind, why don't you guys start your posing there? You two look great. Well, Isabel does anyway."

"Hah, hah, hah." John tried to make his laugh as fake as possible.

The two stepped several paces from each other, and the photoshoot began. John and Isabel had been talking about doing a couple's shoot for some time since there'd be no engagement or wedding photographs. They also wanted to do something that appealed to their sensibilities: the idealized country cottage in a misty forest for Isabel, with the warm-water comforts for John. These seldom-known hot springs were the perfect location for such artistry.

They started at the shallower edge of the pool, approaching each other and embracing with unknown certainty. The shutters of the camera punctuated the background noise of the forest. John and Isabel began feeling each other's bodies as if they had never seen another human being before, their hands caressing every inch of their skin above water in a nonsexual, exploratory way. After several shots, John led Isabel into the depths of the middle of the pool.

Mischievously, John splashed Isabel with the warm water. She gasped and splashed back. They played around for a bit before John broke the silence by suggesting, "You know, if you go under and slowly stand up, you'll look like Venus."

Isabel shyly considered his suggestion as she played with her hair like it was a prized possession that couldn't be tainted. She bent her knees, lowering herself into the pool, the tips of her hair floating on the surface as the rest of her head slowly submerged. The heat might have been too much because she didn't stay under for very long. Regardless, Misty captured her slow, seductive rise out of the water. Her long hair ran partly down her face, connected to her skin, and streamed down her chin to her breasts. When her bearings returned, her eyes connected with John's and remained fixed on him.

He could only shake his head as he said, "God, you're beautiful."

Isabel smiled.

Despite his belief that Isabel was a powerhouse of intelligence and reason, she also was an unadulterated ray of the pale sun. She was a forest nymph, a water sprite, a Goddess of nature. She was Isabel.

Within that serenity, Isabel slowly approached John, the resistance of the water slowing her down. It appeared seductive, but he knew it was a walk of joy.

John took several steps forward to meet her, locking her into a loose embrace with scant space between them. He fanned back her dark, wet hair to expose more of her face and skin to him and the clicks of the camera. In turn, she ran her hand through the hair behind his head. Both exchanged smiles before the tension grew too great and they leaned into each other for a deep, warm kiss. The shutter sounds intensified in frequency.

"That's really nice, guys," Misty said, her eyes still in the viewfinder.

Turning his head toward her, John said, "Now don't be getting off over there." Isabel giggled.

Misty smiled. "Nah, man. That'll make a really good picture. You have no idea how good everything looks." She lowered her camera so there were no visual obstructions between the two parties. "Want to keep going? Got room for a few more shots."

Now it was John's turn to smile, yet his smile hid something more devious. "Yeah, sure. You good, Bel?" He waited for Isabel's silent nod, then looked back at Misty. "You ready?" He waited for Misty's nod, and before she could raise her camera back up, John dipped to the left, quickly shifting his arm deep into the hot water, and caught the back of Isabel's knees. With a quick pivot to the right, he caught the side of her knees in his upstroke, sweeping his partner off her feet and into his arms.

Isabel let out a soft shriek as John leveled her out, and there she was, cradled in his arms, partially obscured by water. Once she got her bearings, she put her arms around the back of John's neck. The buoyancy made carrying her much easier. Her lips soon formed a smile.

"Hey now!" she said, her minor protest unbelievable.

"I think I got a few shots of getting her in your arms. Her expression was hilarious." Misty had been kneeling on both of her legs and went into a standing position. "I'm getting nipple here. Isabel, if you wanted to strategically place your hair, get some safe-for-family shots of you two."

Giggling, Isabel took a free hand and moved her wet hair strands around her breasts to hide the naughty bits that society deemed unacceptable for public viewing. Even though the rest of her body was bare and visible, she was now ready for prime-time viewing. The shutters and clicks of the camera continued as the two lovers continued to look at each other. Isabel reached her hand up and felt John's face, a touch that brought warm sensations to his heart and soul.

Eventually, he eased her back into the water. Once she found her footing, she grabbed onto his arms and positioned him so he was facing toward the open air. She turned to face the same direction, her back against his chest. He wrapped his arms around her, and they stared off into the soft sky, the perfect position for Misty to get a few more shots.

"Perfect," she said, lowering her camera to reveal her face. "Got plenty to look at."

John rested his chin on Isabel's shoulder. "How long

before we can get prints?"

Misty shrugged. "A few days. Don't want to rush that process." She stood up and began disassembling the gear she had set up. "What are you guys going to do? Gonna stay here or what?"

"It's pretty warm," said Isabel. John held her closer to him, and they both smiled.

"Well, I'm gonna head on out then, leave you two love-birds alone here." It didn't take her long to break down the equipment and put everything away in cases.

"Can you find the way back?" asked Isabel.

"Yeah, no sweat. The trail's right over there and it just goes back right to where we parked." She slung a bag over her shoulder while carrying other ones in her hands. "See you lovebirds later. I'll call you when I have shit ready for you."

Misty walked back the way she came, around the rocky cliff face, and was soon out of sight. John released his arms gently as Isabel turned around to face him. Their gazes spoke not of joy, of laughter and smiles, but of intensity, of studying. It was a look they gave one another during moments when verbal speech was incapable of betraying anybody's thoughts.

Minutes into this muted conversation, John broke the peace. "Did you have fun?"

Isabel betrayed a tiny smile. "Yeah. Yeah, it was wonderful." She ran her hand down his cheek, observing his reactions. She closed her eyes, retreating to her other senses. John's breathing was masked by the quiet hissing of steam coming out of the pool, the chirps of the birds, and the gentle wind.

Opening her eyes, she betrayed her thoughts. "I love you."

"I love you."

Their lips locked soon after.

06

Chapter Six

"How the hell can you do something like that and not expect me to freak out?"

All relationships had minor squabbles. But after being inseparable for nearly two years, a fight of greater proportions was due.

Isabel looked back at John coldly.

"I like to think about myself as being open-minded," continued John, "but Jesus, Bel, what the fuck? Did you do this with other boyfriends?"

Isabel continued to stare in silence.

. "Isabel!" yelled John. Outside of sex, he rarely used her full name. "Did you do this with other boyfriends?"

"Why should it matter?" she said, breaking her silence.

"What do you mean? I want to know if you fucked them over too!"

"I didn't fuck anybody over."

Sighing, he turned around and took several steps to the wall of their duplex. Hands on his hips, he spent several seconds collecting his thoughts. "I just want to know what I can expect."

"We both agreed that our past relationships don't matter," said Isabel. "Why are you bringing that up?"

John held his breath, unable to contemplate how to word his next sentence. "What I meant by that was details. Little bullshit that doesn't affect anything. But hanging out with a guy, doing nothing to stop his advances, and then letting him kiss you? Kind of a big fucking deal."

"And you think it's my damn fault?" said Isabel with more fire in her breath.

He hesitated. "No, that's not—"

Then Isabel came down on him with an intensity he had never seen from her before. "Fuck you, John. That's exactly what you're doing. Placing that blame on me. I didn't do anything."

"I know that, but—"

"But you are still shaming me." Isabel continued her icy stare, taking several paces toward John until she was right in his face. "My friend may have had ulterior motives, but at least he wasn't a misogynistic asshole."

John raised his voice to match. "Then what the hell am I supposed to do? Please, tell me. Tell me how I should act. How any boyfriend should act."

"Boyfriend." Isabel said the word as if it was the most disgusting idea she knew of.

"What the hell do you mean by that?"

"You're acting like any boyfriend would act, that's for

damn sure," she answered. "Being a self-centered asshole. Did it occur to you that I didn't want to be kissed by him?"

"You should have known he was into you."

"Answer the question!" she demanded.

"It doesn't matter, Isabel. All men have ulterior motives. I know they all want to fuck you."

"So you talked to me when we met because you wanted me to be your little whore."

"I… no. Jesus—" But John was cut off.

"Whatever, John. Go fuck yourself." Isabel turned around and went upstairs.

She had never used that language against him, not with that potency. She also never had anybody else kiss her, at least to John's knowledge. He sighed and sat down on their loveseat.

"That son of a bitch," John muttered.

The two of them started taking a gardening class on the weekends to help with their dream of the country cottage. They made a few friends, including a man named Theo. Even though the three of them hung out at first, soon Theo only invited Isabel, without John's knowledge. Isabel thought he was a good friend, and they had a good time with each other.

Isabel came home the night before, crying but unable to talk about what happened. She finally admitted to the kiss and to their exclusive hangouts.

John wanted to blame Isabel for everything. She was the responsible one. She was the one who had a boyfriend. She wasn't naïve either; it was obvious what Theo was up to. John wasn't keen on placing blame on him. If John was interested in somebody who was taken, and his interest kept hanging out with him alone, that indicated a sign.

It was all misogynistic thinking on John's part though. Isabel wasn't the one who initiated. Theo's actions betrayed her. She did nothing. But John couldn't wrap his mind around that. His outburst drove Isabel from sadness, to coldness, then to open hostility. She never defended what she did or didn't do. She was only defending herself from his verbal assaults.

Isabel had said the word "boyfriend" as if it was a four-letter word. The disgust in her voice couldn't leave John's thoughts. Perhaps she had those feelings for months, and they only manifested themselves during that argument.

This was no ordinary fright or unease. John's fear could cost him the most important person in his world. He was petrified, and he couldn't act out. Sitting wasn't doing him any favors, so he stood up, scanning the room for anything to take his mind off things.

Walking over to the wall, he saw numerous framed pictures. Some were monochrome, others in color. The setting of all the photographs was a film of mist over a pool of water. In all those pictures, the subject was a man and a woman, looking like they were having the time of their lives. A premier stage actor couldn't replicate the way the couple looked at each other.

Their photoshoot from the forest turned out beautifully. Misty had done a fantastic job, capturing a feeling and time and preserving it for history. John couldn't replicate that feeling in his heart. Instead, he was sad and lonely and started crying. He put his face in his hands and banged it against the wall. It was painful, but not enough to overcome his thoughts of failure.

He was in love with Isabel. He knew that with certainty. Yet he hurt her. There was no way he could forgive himself for that betrayal. The tears streaming down his face couldn't eject the guilt from his soul fast enough. In his emotional state, he wished to be in one place: in Isabel's arms, his head in her lap, her hands caressing his hair.

His mind went back to that dirty four-letter word: "boyfriend."

He thought she loved him. He knew she loved him. There had to have been motivation behind her inflection. She did tell him the truth. She did feel shame for what happened.

Why? John thought. *She did nothing wrong.*

At that moment, it was made clear to John; she'd do everything not to hurt him. Placing a false feeling of guilt on herself made that point clear. John repaid her self-sacrifice with anger and shame. It was an act of instinct, but it wasn't an act of logic. John failed himself.

The pain had to be healed. The thought of walking up the stairs was even more painful. Would she be sleeping? Would she be crying? Or worse, would she show no emotion? A blank void would be worse than seeing her tearfully pack her bags. Everything made him feel sick. Normally he'd double-down and things would mend themselves, but not this time; this time he messed up.

Boyfriend.

Sick of hearing that in his head, John got the courage to walk up the stairs and confront his inner demon. It was oddly quiet, save for the moans of the stairs as he walked up them. Making it to the top, he found his way into the bedroom. The door was open, the room well-lit with outside light. Isabel was on the bed, lying down and facing away from the door. John watched for a while. He tiptoed to the side of the bed closest to him and sat on it. He looked at Isabel's back, his mouth silent.

Nothing changed for several minutes. Eventually, Isabel rolled over and faced John. There were no tears, but her face was flushed and moisture had collected around her eyes. In her hands, she was playing with a necklace John had given her. Their eyes locked.

"You hurt me." Her voice was calm but quivering. She was doing an okay job of burying the implied emotion.

John's eyes flitted away. "I know." He waited a beat before continuing. "I hurt you, and I can't take it back." Another tear streamed down his face.

Isabel's face showed some confusion after another moment of silence. "Is that it?"

His gaze returned to her. "How can I ask for your forgiveness?"

Isabel's face showed even more confusion.

"We inflicted so much pain on each other. To think that we, as human beings, are capable of that. I thought I was better than that. And look what I said. I projected myself onto Theo. Theo is not me."

"Theo at least kissed first."

Isabel's face slowly changed as she realized what she said. He tried to keep it together, but he couldn't stay in the room anymore. He stood up. Isabel leaped from her position, her arm reaching out to John.

"John! Please, don't go."

He looked down at Isabel, who was on her hands and knees facing him. Now it was her turn to not look him in the face.

Holding back the tears, she said, "Why are we like this? Why are we horrible?"

He sat back down on the bed, this time his legs over the side so he was facing away from Isabel. "We're human."

"No, we're not," said Isabel, tears slowly taking control. "We shouldn't be. I thought we could be better than that. A moment ago, I thought you were a monster. And now I'm a monster too."

John turned around, seeing Isabel's face buried in the comforter. "You're not a monster, Bel." Soon tears streamed down his face. "But what you said hurt."

"I know," cried Isabel. Lifting her face up a bit so her voice wasn't so muffled, she said, "I just wanted to be friends with Theo. I knew he liked me a little, but I thought we could be friends. Why did he have to ruin everything?"

"Do you think he ruined everything?" John was partly asking himself that question.

Isabel didn't answer, but she sat up, trying to recover from the onslaught of tears. John pivoted to face her. At first, they had trouble looking at each other, but eventually, their eyes connected. She hesitated for a moment before saying, "I don't think so. But he did ruin a fantasy."

"That we'd be perfect?"

She nodded. John contemplated her words before chiming in with his own perspective. "I don't know if both of us are perfect, but I do know that you are perfect enough to not deserve what I said downstairs."

For the first time, she smiled briefly. Chuckling, she looked down and shyly said, "That's sweet of you."

John slid his hand across the comforter, fingers stretched out. "Nothing was your fault. You should never put up with what I did again."

Isabel's hand slid to barely touch John's. "You shouldn't change because I'm a bitch."

Their hands were lightly caressing each other's. "Well, what I did was worse. You deserve more than a jealous douchebag."

Eventually, they were holding each other's hands. The two looked at each other, their quiet gazes holding their attention.

"I'm sorry, Bel."

"I'm sorry, John."

The two leaned over and embraced, hugging each other tightly, not wanting to let each other go. Their relationship and their egos took a bruising that day. Yet they were healing together, mending their pain and moving forward. They continued to cry, not from anger or pain, but from relief. It was a difficult moment for any relationship, but they made it through. Still locked in their embrace, they leaned over and lay down, continuing their peaceful gesture until they both fell asleep.

Several hours passed before they woke up. Isabel's eyes opened first, for John woke up to her hand running through his hair.

"Hey," she whispered.

"Mmmm," he said in response. His eyes opened slightly. "Hey you."

"Are you hungry? I want to make us some food."

"Mmmm," he said again, releasing Isabel from his prison. Before she could get up on her feet, inspiration struck John. "Hey, wait."

"Yeah?"

John sat up, rubbing his eyes in a feeble attempt to eliminate his grogginess. "Let's go on a date."

A surprised smile broke onto her face. "A date?"

"Yeah, sure, we haven't gone out in a while. I mean just the two of us. We've done the garden class, but I just want to take you out."

"Okay," said Isabel contentedly. "What did you have in mind?"

"I dunno," said John. "Let's just go on a walk and see what happens!"

Still overcome with the aftereffects of the nap, the two took their time getting ready. The couple made a deal that when they would go out, they wouldn't get ready in the same room, to emulate the days when they were dating before moving in together. Isabel grabbed her clothes and got ready in the bathroom; John remained in the bedroom. He put on a tighter-fitting long-sleeved shirt with no collar, a few buttons undone at the top. Dark jeans and Isabel's favorite peacoat completed his look. Moments later, Isabel left the bathroom, wearing a purple sweater, tights, and a skirt that went down to her mid-shins.

"Wouldn't you get a bit cold?" asked John.

"Think I'll be fine."

The two went downstairs and left the duplex. It was around 6:30, so the sun was low but not too dark. While they held hands, there was still a sense of awkwardness between the two, and they didn't talk a lot. It was still an enjoyable walk, and after cruising down several blocks, they went into their neighborhood bar and grill. They had been there a few times before; there was nothing too special about it, but they had good hamburgers and it was within walking distance.

"What happened to us not eating beef?" asked Isabel between bites, referencing their awareness of the environmental effects of cattle farming.

"We had a rough day. We need a short break," said John. Isabel nodded.

They kept their drinks down to one each. Satisfied, they left the premises and continued walking around the neighborhood. It was starting to get darker, but the setting sun didn't dampen their mission of re-exploring places they had already visited.

Eventually, they found the local park they frequented. There were still several people out, some jogging, others playing frisbee with their pets. The couple found a bench close to a baseball diamond and parked themselves on it, studying the myriad of activities around them.

Night crept forward, and the last few people were dispersing from the park. It was getting late in autumn, so it got cool at night. This prompted John and Isabel to continue their walk before they started freezing. They were in the middle of a wooded area when John broke the silence. "How are you?"

Isabel stopped walking and, after a moment of contemplation, answered with, "I'm okay. It was a rough day."

"I know." John continued studying his surroundings, managing to make out most of the nearby trees despite the worsening light conditions.

"How are you?" asked Isabel.

"I'm better now." He looked over at Isabel. "I want to be good for you. If there's anything you want me to change, please tell me."

Isabel did an inaudible chuckle at the ridiculous state-ment. She turned to face him. "John, it's okay. You're…" She paused for a moment. "You're a good man." Her face betrayed her wandering thoughts.

"What is it?"

She gave a half-smile. "You know, I was thinking. Say we weren't together, but we were friends. I still think you'd be way cooler than Theo."

After a beat, "You think so?"

Isabel nodded. "Yeah. He's cool, but he's not John cool."

They both giggled. John quipped, "You were thinking about a threesome, weren't you?" He was half-joking but was curious about Isabel's thoughts.

She wasted no time in answering. "I am a young woman who is comfortable with sex-positivity. Would you hon-estly believe me if I never envisioned being plowed by two dudes at the same time?"

John laughed. "No, I guess not. Hell, maybe someday we can find a cool cat who's half as cool as me. Not Theo though."

Isabel smiled and nodded confidently. "Not Theo. Maybe when they invent cloning I can have two of you."

"Well, if we're doing that, why not make like ten of us and have a massive orgy?"

She laughed. "As long as the clones clean up. I'm not dealing with that shit."

They got to another bench and sat down. There weren't any park lights nearby, so while it was hard for the couple to see others, it was also hard to see them. They stared at each other, for different reasons than before. It didn't last long before John grabbed Isabel and gave her a long, deep kiss. She offered no resistance and grabbed onto John's shoulders to return the embrace. The deep kiss was followed by other kisses in quick succession, which soon spread to their necks and ears. At this point in their relationship, they thrived on nonverbal communication. Both of them moaned in delight.

Isabel rolled over so she was straddling John, and her tights mysteriously fell onto the ground. They did their best to keep as quiet as possible, but they were having too much fun out in the open. Isabel started getting tired, but the timing was impeccable, for John buried his face in her bosom to cover his loud moan as he finished. She kept up for a little longer before she collapsed forward into John's shoulders.

"I love you," she said.

John had the biggest smile on his face. "I love you too."

Looking around to make sure no one was watching, Isabel stood up, which let John zip his jeans back up. She went into her purse and found some tissue to clean up the mess. Finding her tights on the ground, she put them in her purse. With the scene of the crime erased, the couple walked home, holding hands with smiles drawn on their faces.

Their pace was quick but not rushed. They weren't in a hurry; it wasn't chilly, and their spirits were rejuvenated. Thanks to their poorly timed nap, they didn't feel sleepy. When they got back, it was 9:30. After turning on the lights in the apartment, they put on a movie. Wanting something relaxing, they chose a comedy and cuddled with each other. It was enjoyable; they laughed at the jokes, and the story made sense in its context.

After the movie ended, John felt emboldened, playing with Isabel's hair. "Hey, Bel?"

"Hmmm?" she said, her eyes focused on the darkened television.

"I feel like I owe you one for the park."

She turned to face him. "What do you mean?"

"I mean," he said, before nibbling on her nose, "I think you can use a bit of lovin' too."

Isabel barely said, "Oh yeah?" before John was at her neck—a paralyzing attack to her. She stared up as her body surrendered to him. His head slid down her body, stopping past her belly button. John spent as long as required to fulfill his promise, and Isabel offered no objection.

07

Chapter Seven

"Come on in!" said John, backing out of the door.

Nick stepped into John's duplex. He stood in the entryway, studying the walls and furniture arrangements. It was hard to beat a plethora of wall art, small sculptures, and homemade crafts filling many shelves and tables. Thanks to Isabel, it was a place to be proud of.

"Damn, I really wish Michelle was this cool," Nick said with resigned conviction.

John picked up on the impression as he shut the door behind his friend. "So how's married life? What is it now, nine months?"

"Ten months, I think. However long ago June was." He sighed as he walked into the living room and sat on the couch. There were a few nights when Nick slept there, to escape the troubles he often faced with his wife. Unbeknownst to him, that couch was also host to a few nights when John and Isabel were creating a fair bit of trouble themselves.

"Any plans for your one year?"

Nick shrugged. "I don't know. She wants a kid. She got off birth control but I'm stocking up on condoms. It's just a mess."

John walked over to the couch and sat on the other side, holding a bag of chips. "Gotta watch it that she doesn't poke your stash with a pin or something."

"Yeah, that would suck." Nick reached over and grabbed some chips out of the bag. "Now how long have you and Isabel been together? I mean, you're practically married."

While John didn't like the term, it was a fair way for others who trapped themselves in anachronistic social norms to understand the relationship they had. "Over three years now."

"Is it still great?" asked Nick, a hint of malignant envy in his tone.

John smiled. "Yeah. Yeah, it's still kickass."

John heard dull footsteps creeping above the ceiling. Nick looked up. "Sounds like she's still here?"

"Yeah," said John with a bit of food in his mouth. "Their plans got delayed a bit."

Every other Saturday, John and Isabel would have a friends day, where they split up for the day and did activities with their friends separately. They would switch who would get the house and who would go out. Sometimes it wouldn't work out due to schedules, but overall, it functioned well. It had been two months since John hung out with Nick, so today was especially noteworthy. Isabel was meeting up with her friend Annie, although John wasn't sure what they'd be doing.

"Alright, well, got anything going on?" Nick looked forward at the television.

John stood up and walked toward the TV. "Yeah, got this movie that's supposed to be freaking hilarious."

Nick put his arm on the top of the couch. "Can't wait. It's been a while since I've seen a good movie."

Returning to the couch after putting in the movie, John chuckled. "Let me guess. She picks?"

"Yeah." Nick grabbed a chip. "She loves those dance movies. You know, like those underdog sports movies but with dance teams."

"Fun," said John, grabbing his own chip and dipping it in the salsa.

Their movie began. They silenced their conversation so they could sink themselves into the narrative. A door opened upstairs, followed by footsteps down the stairs. The two looked over to see Isabel dressed up to go out: leather jacket, green shirt, black pants. She flashed a smile.

"Hey, Nick," she said.

"Hey, Isabel. How's it going?"

"Oh, just about to head out." She watched the TV for a few seconds. "Oh Jesus, this movie?"

The two men laughed. John said, "Hey, it's gonna be great!"

She giggled. "Yeah, you're probably right. I'll end up watching it later, I'm sure." She leaned over the couch and kissed John. "I love you. I'll be back late afternoon, probably. Have a good time!"

John and Nick waved with poorly rehearsed synchronicity as their attention drifted back to the movie. John heard the front door shut, and Isabel was gone. Unlike Nick, John was never relieved when his partner left and never felt he had to act a certain way while she was around. John was John, and he appreciated how easy it was to fit into any social situation, whether it was with Isabel or Nick or in any group setting.

An hour and a half went by, and John and Nick laughed more times than what would be otherwise healthy for a comedy of questionable intelligence. Life didn't need to be constantly highbrow. This was especially true when he was hanging out with Nick, but sometimes even he and Isabel needed some dumb entertainment.

"Oh man," said Nick, looking at the empty chip bag and salsa bowl. "And Isabel would like that?"

John shrugged. "Sure, why not? I mean, it wouldn't be her favorite movie, but she would laugh, I'm sure." He looked over at the clock. "So what's going on, then? Picked up a new game if you wanted to try it for a bit."

Looking at his watch, Nick sighed. "Yeah, the missus probably wants me back now."

John put the movie back in its case. "You don't want to go back, do you?"

Nick inhaled through his teeth without saying anything.

"You know, have you ever thought why Michelle is so needy of your attention?" John thought about turning on the video game console but decided against it. "Seriously. Have you tried talking to her?"

Sighing, Nick said, "I try, but she gets fussy. I really

want to know what it is with her."

It took a lot of willpower for John to hold in what he really wanted to say. There was no love between Nick and Michelle. Michelle was insecure and constantly needed attention. Meanwhile, Nick would say he'd never have the companionship of another woman. He enjoyed the intimacy he had with Michelle when it was available.

John's phone buzzed with a message. He casually looked at the phone and saw a message he didn't expect. "Huh."

Nick glanced over. "What is it?"

"Oh, it's Annie. Isabel's friend. Bel isn't there, and she's wondering where she is."

"Huh," said Nick. "That's weird. Has she tried messaging Isabel?"

"Yeah," said John, who typed up a quick response indicating that Isabel had left two hours earlier. John and Isabel weren't in constant contact, but it was odd that she wouldn't follow through with plans. "Probably nothing though."

Nick looked at his watch again and offered his not-so-rare sigh. "Well, think it's time for me to get back to the woman."

"Can't think of anything more important than video games except for getting laid." They both giggled.

"Well," said Nick, "here's hoping. I could use that. I know you horndogs are probably going to do some weird *Kama Sutra* shit tonight."

The two got up and headed to the door. "Well, make sure you're wrapping it up."

"Oh I will," Nick said. "You might want to check up on Isabel, see if she's okay."

"Yeah, I'll do that." John opened the door. "Well, that was fun. Anyway, good luck."

Smiling, Nick said, "Yeah. You have a good one, John."

"You too!" The door shut behind Nick, leaving John alone in the duplex. He looked back into the rest of the apartment and felt something different from what he was used to. There was a dustiness in the air, a thickness that was both visible and tangible. Dust particles occupied the sunbeams as they snuck into the home, and while they were drifting about, there was also stillness. John couldn't hear any noises from the outside, as if his entire world had entered a stasis.

This minor distraction proved temporary when John remembered Isabel and sent her a message on his phone: *Are you at Annie's yet? She was looking for you.* Not wanting to clean up the party yet, he sat down on his couch and closed his eyes. While John craved the company of Isabel and his friends, there was the rare moment when he desired the calm state of solitude.

His idle sitting soon became a two-hour nap. John sighed as he checked the time to confirm, then stood up to begin the cleaning process. Fortunately, the two didn't leave a big mess, as there were minimal salsa and chip crumbs on the table and floor. Soon, all evidence of Nick's presence was erased. John continued his constructive behavior and cleaned the rest of the room.

Twenty minutes later, as John was starting in the kitchen, his phone rang. Wiping off his hands, he went into the living room to see who it was. John didn't recognize the number.

He answered. "Hello?"

"Hello, this is Dr. Harner at Kaiser Medical. Is this John Poland?"

This wasn't the call he was expecting. John didn't know a Dr. Harner, and he didn't think Isabel had a physician by that name. Stuttering, he responded, "Uh, yes. Yes, this is John."

"Hello, John," continued Dr. Harner in a professional tone but with the taste of concern doctors spoke with. "I'm calling about Isabel Breton. Several hours ago, she was in a major car crash and was rushed here by the EMTs."

John froze. His breathing stopped. His heart rate heightened. His anxiety showed no restraint in filling up every fiber of his body with poison. "John, are you still there?"

"Yes," he said, gaining back some of his autonomy. "Yes, sorry, I'm here. Is she okay?"

"John, I'm calling you because we have spent the past two hours trying to locate someone who we can consider the next of kin. We can't find any record of parents or family, but after going through her phone, I assume you're the boyfriend."

John wasn't sure how to answer. "Well, Doctor, I consider myself her partner. We're not legally married but we've lived together for three years. Is she alive?"

"Yes she is, John." But his tone offered no reassurance. "Would you mind coming to the hospital as quickly as possible?"

"Yes, yes, I'll be there right away." John hung up the phone without waiting for a proper goodbye. Flying to the coat rack, sailing to the shoe shelf, John defied the laws of physics to ensure he was out of there quickly. He wasn't even sure if he locked the door, but their physical possessions were unimportant compared to the needs of his beloved.

Thankfully, their talks of downsizing to a single car never materialized. He ran to his aging car, got it going, and spun out of his driveway. The irony of potential reckless driving wasn't lost on John, as he drove carefully.

How long was she there? She never even made it to Annie's. Isabel was probably rescued from her crushed car while Nick and John were laughing hysterically at a movie. He sped past the speed limit, but not enough to warrant attention from police officers. Yet the drive seemed drawn out. The seconds on the clock had no hands to reach him; John was on his own.

He made it to the hospital, parking by the emergency entrance. He easily found a spot. Almost as fast as he flew into the car, John soared out the door, shutting it and jogging into the multi-door entry.

He saw several occupied wheelchairs sitting around, with people of all ages and creed. He didn't see Isabel waiting for him in any of them. John looked around anxiously as he walked toward the desk, trying to find anything to signify where Isabel or Dr. Harner were. Sensing John's distress, the man at the front desk called out to him. John approached him, and their brief conversation provided the answers he was looking for.

"Thank you," said John. Not even waiting for a response, he rushed off to the wing Isabel was in. Fortune again greeted John as he didn't have to travel very far, just down a few hallways. He found the door, but it was locked like the man at the front desk had said. John pressed the buzzer.

"Yes?" a female voice said on the speaker.

"Yes, I'm John. I'm here for Isabel. Isabel Breton." A few seconds of silence was followed by the door opening, and on the other side stood a short nurse with a half-smile on her face.

"Come this way!" she said, and John obliged. He was in a large room that was a care station for nurses, with computers and several medical professionals milling about. She pointed to an open area in the side of the room. "Please wait here. I'll get Dr. Harner."

There were several chairs that seemed inviting at first, but John was too strung up to even think about accepting the tacit invitation. Fidgeting his hands in his pocket, he looked down at the floor, thinking about how gaudy a lot of hospital décor was. At least Isabel had better taste for much lower budgets.

The feeling of stasis returned. It was an open room, but John felt claustrophobic. He wanted to hide in plain sight, not paying any attention to anybody else in that room. He wanted none of them to pay attention to him. The nurse was sweet enough, but he couldn't stand being around her. Looking up, he saw what were probably two dozen adjacent rooms, all likely occupied by patients. One of those patients was undoubtedly his lover.

"Mr. Poland?" said a familiar voice. The shock of attention jolted John upright, and he spun around, seeing a man with a wide face and a full black beard. He held out his hand. "Hello, John. I'm Dr. Harner."

John nervously smiled as his right hand left his pocket to meet the doctor's. "Hi. Hi, Doctor. Yes, I'm here. So what's going on?"

Dr. Harner's voice remained calm and reassuring while maintaining an edge of somberness, as it did on the phone. "I'm afraid to say the accident caused very severe injuries. Multiple broken bones, internal bleeding, spinal injuries."

"Oh God," said John, feeling his eyes well with tears, his soul feeling the onset of what he believed was utter dread. "Is… Is she going to make it?"

Dr. Harner's broad shoulders heaved up and down with his sigh. "Well, that's the tricky part. The easy answer is yes, but I'm going to be honest with you. There was a lot of trauma. We've done all we can for her, but she's in a coma and can't breathe without being on life support."

John cocked his head to the side, the full brunt of the news not quite reaching him. "Well, what do you mean by that? So she's going to recover?"

"Well, the hope is that she comes through on her own, of course. But a case like this, well, most people never wake up. We can sustain her for a while, but…"

At that point, Dr. Harner stopped because he knew John had to process the reality of the situation. No, Isabel wasn't dead. She survived the car crash. But she wasn't going to go home. His emotional side felt she'd wake up in a few weeks, but his rational half knew she'd be comatose for the rest of her natural life. While she wasn't dead, Isabel was gone.

The reservoir of tears released. There was no cry of anguish from his mouth, no words uttered from his throat. Just a waterfall covering his cheeks. His gaze no longer met the doctor's eyes but floated at something. Or nothing. They drifted to the side, unable to focus due to the blindness of tears.

"John," said Dr. Harner, his voice still maintaining its comforting tone. "I am so sorry. I would leave you alone, but I do have some important questions to ask you."

John didn't know why, but Dr. Harner's voice penetrated his bubble. "Yes?"

"We talked about this briefly on the phone. Unmarried persons' next of kin is usually their parents or adult children. Now Isabel was—sorry, *is*—young, so we tried to find out who her parents are. There was nothing on her. We checked quick with government offices. They're still looking but they haven't found anything yet. I'm hoping you can help me. I'm sure her family wants to know as much as you do."

With a small delay, John shook his head, finally returning his attention to the doctor. "No. I... No, I don't. She never talked about her family. She briefly mentioned her mother once, but that's it. I never bothered to ask. That was her business."

Dr. Harner looked down and nodded. "I see. Typically, in cases like these, depending on their belief affiliation, some families would take their loved ones off life support and end their suffering. I'm not partial either way, but it would be good to know."

"What about me?" asked John, rationality returning to his grief-stricken state. "We weren't ever planning on getting married. We would just be partners." That statement brought a second waterfall down his face.

"I understand," said the doctor, forever reassuring. "We'll have to see about a common-law marriage and if you two had one, but I don't have an answer right now. Normally we don't have these talks with boyfriends or girlfriends, but I understand your relationship so I'm making an exception."

John realized he missed an important question, perhaps the most important question: "Can I see her?"

There was hesitation on Dr. Harner's face, a fight between his compassionate side and his limited knowledge of the legal issues. He nodded. "Yes. John, I don't want you to make a decision today. It may not even be up to you if we can find her parents. But do think about what we talked about. I'm sure your input would help one way or another. You were the most important person in her life. I'm sure that will count."

The inverse was true as well; Isabel was the most important person in his life. Isabel *was* his life. Isabel's witty banter, her smile, her kind eyes, and her ponderings meant everything to him. Everything John wanted in his life manifested itself in her. That encounter at Uncle John's Public House was a fluke; he wasn't sure he believed in "soulmates," but he randomly found someone on a rainy winter evening who saw the world through his lens. More accurately, he saw the world through her lens; she was the better, smarter person.

Dr. Harner led John toward the door, their pace slow and introspective. They got to the door right down the hall, Room 12. The doctor faced John, looked him up and down, and said, "If you need anything, just ask the nurses. Again, I'm so sorry." With that, Dr. Harner walked back the way they came, leaving John at the edge of the doorway. Before he stepped forward, nerves struck him, and a sinking feeling dragged his stomach into the floor. His legs weakened. John didn't understand why he was nervous; maybe he was afraid he'd see something different, that it wasn't Isabel. Maybe he thought Isabel would be scarred up so bad she wouldn't be recognizable.

With a deep breath, John walked in. It was a small room, smaller than the ones they showed on hospital dramas on TV. There wasn't much in there, but there was a bed, surrounded by all sorts of medical contraptions, and a person in that bed. The foot of the bed was facing him, so he had to walk farther to make out more details. Whoever was in that bed, their arms were exposed, IV tubes coming out of the veins. And covering their face was a large breathing apparatus hooked up to one of the machines in the room. The machine was forcing air in and out of the comatose patient.

Silently, so as not to disturb their sleep, John crept to the side of the bed. A third smaller waterfall poured down his cheek when he realized his nightmare went beyond the imaginary. "Oh God." The dam broke.

Isabel lay on the hospital bed, the life support machine providing the only motion. From what was visible, she seemed alright: some bruising on her arms, a big ugly bruise that had swelled up on the left side of her forehead, some cuts on her lips. Even so, it was Isabel, and she was still beautiful.

John fell to his knees, his cries of anguish not relenting. "Oh, Bel!" he cried and reached out to touch her body. There was a warmth to her that was usual. What wasn't usual was her response. What she should have done was roll onto her side, open her eyes at John, and offer a small smile. She couldn't say anything with the respirator on her, but at that point, John wouldn't care if she lost the ability to speak. He wanted them to stare at each other and offer nothing but devotion and care. Or if all else failed, he at least wanted them to have a chance to say goodbye.

While John was enveloped in this fantasy, the reality was a still, unresponsive body. No reaction to his touch or his cries. There was a breath, but there was no life. John buried his face into her arm as he grabbed her hand in his. He didn't stop crying for a long time, staining her arm with his tears. All the while, the machine worked effortlessly, providing her crippled body with the air its lungs still craved.

When his body emptied its well of tears, when his mind escaped the imagination of them looking at each other, John glanced up at her covered face. With his other hand, he reached up to her hair and felt it, searching for some familiarity in that hour of despair. John wondered if Isabel could hear him, if she knew he was there but just couldn't respond. His limited knowledge of human biology indicated there was a possibility such a thing could be true, so it wouldn't hurt to try.

"Hey," he whispered, caressing her loose hair. "It's John. I'm sure you know that though." Another tear ran from his eye; he didn't understand where they were coming from. "I had a wonderful day today. Nick and I had a great time. You'll love that movie. I know you will. Maybe I can bring it in some time and show you when you're feeling a bit better."

John sniffed and quietly cried out before continuing. "Bel. I love you. I love you so much. I'm going to get that country cottage for us. I'm going to live that life that we wanted to live. But I would trade all that for a shitty apartment to have you back." He leaned forward to rest the side of his head on her torso, trying not to disturb the life support machine. It was faint, but he heard the heart he fell in love with.

"I hope that they can help you. They say they can keep you like this for a long time. Medicine is getting so damn good these days." John sniffed. "I don't know what's going to happen. The doctor is trying to find your family. I know you don't care about them, and I know you don't want them in your life. I'm going to fight for you."

John paused to wipe the mess from his face. "But let's not talk about that right now. I love you so much. I will love you always and forever. I want to be with you forever." He squeezed her harder. "I hope you know that. I hope you know that no one will ever have what we have. When you wake up from your nap"—John paused, knowing what he said was likely a lie "—I will wait for you. I will be here for you. Bel. Goddammit, my beautiful Bel. My north star. My eternal partner. I love you." His weakening voice collapsed into tears, his spirit broken.

08

CHAPTER EIGHT

Driving home from work in the agonizing July heat five days a week was horrible. Coming through the door, his shirt unbuttoned halfway down his chest, sweat permeating his clothes, John threw his messenger bag on the floor and sighed. Another day of his existence checked off. Thousands more were expected to come.

With his wearied body, John stumbled into the duplex, unbuttoning the rest of his shirt and practically ripping it off. He looked around, making sure everything was still in place. The arrangement of the art and the furniture, the life of the apartment, was unchanged from when Isabel left for the last time.

John threw himself onto the couch, setting his shirt down on the empty seat next to him. He unbuckled his belt to loosen the strain on his waist and let out a big sigh.

Shutting his eyes, he leaned his head back on the cushion. Like most evenings, his time would be spent doing little. He was content with that since there was little to be content with.

The hospital could locate none of Isabel's immediate family. They couldn't even come up with their names. Her past was as much of an enigma to them as it was to John. As such, her power of attorney was going through the legal system. While there was a push to make her a ward of the state, Dr. Harner was kind enough to help John get spousal rights, a lengthy process that was finalizing. It would also help cover her hospital costs.

Isabel herself was the same. John's visits went from every day to four days a week. Every visit he told her about his day, even if John barely did anything anymore. Even though there were friends, those friends had no place in his void. Her physical wounds had healed, aside from small scars, but otherwise, she looked like she always did. The hospital even moved her to a long-term room.

After several minutes of silent contemplation, John opened his eyes and got up to go to the bathroom. He walked up the stairs, heaving his anchored body into the appropriate chambers. Looking up into the mirror, he saw he had more than a five o'clock shadow going on. Was it a five-day shadow? John couldn't remember when he last shaved, and as long as his work mentioned nothing, he didn't care.

"Bel would hate this," he muttered, and he was probably right. Yet he was sure if she woke up and he rushed to see her, she wouldn't mind a bit of fuzz.

The phone ringing downstairs took John by surprise.

After the initial round of offers of condolences, his social life began resembling the universal microwave background. He ran down the stairs, finding his phone on the coffee table. "Hello?"

"Hey, it's Nick."

John hadn't heard from Nick in a while. "Oh. Hey, man. How's it going?"

"Not bad, mainly calling to see how you're doing!"

"Yeah," said John, which might not have been the most sensible answer to that question. "Yeah, it's the same."

"Well, I got some good news."

John feared what was coming regarding Michelle's desire for a child. "Yeah?"

Nick laughed. "Well, Michelle is hanging out with her mom all day tomorrow. Want to grab a bite for lunch?"

It wasn't the first time Nick had offered to meet up since the accident. John had declined the other two times, but wallowing in never-ending misery wasn't working out. "Oh. Yeah, let's do it."

"Awesome," Nick said. "Been to Hopscotch? It's a newer brewpub that opened a bit ago."

John had wanted to go there, but his self-inflicted isolation hindered his efforts. "Sounds great, man. What time you thinking?"

"Let's do one."

John nodded. "Sounds good. See you then."

The rest of the night was uneventful, save for some unfocused video games and random channel-surfing. John was waiting for the night to end and for Saturday to bear fruit. He wasn't sure why it was worth waiting, but the uncertainty of the next day was worth more than the emptiness of the current day. It was a terrible existence, but it was a conscious existence.

That next morning, John put on a T-shirt and some cargo shorts to help beat July's punishing heat. Grabbing his keys and sunglasses, John left in his car and found the new pub. It had been opened for a month, so the initial crowds had dissipated. It was also early enough that it wasn't too busy.

The bar was on the first floor. There were many high stools and tables littered across the floor, with the physical bar along a long wall. While he was scouting for a table, Nick came up behind him.

"Hey, man. Looking good," said Nick with a sly grin on his face.

"Hah," said John in a droll voice. "You too."

Nick pointed at one of the many empty tables. "Let's get that one."

The pair soon found themselves seated at the table, checking out the freshly printed menu featuring in-house beers.

"Thank God they have something for me," said John.

"It's summer," said Nick. "Of course they have all your water beers."

"Funny." Since it was slow, they were quickly approached by a waitress.

"Hello, boys," she said. She seemed a little younger, probably still in college, but she definitely showed enthusiasm that was usually lacking in veterans of the service industry. "How're you two doing today?"

"Oh, not too bad," said Nick.

"Yeah," said John.

"Boys want anything to start off with?"

"I liked that medium ale that I had last time. Think I'll go with that again." Nick set his drink menu down and looked over at John.

"And you, sir?" asked the waitress.

"I'll go with your pilsner that you got." John continued to stare into the void, not making eye contact with the waitress.

"Great! I'll go get your drinks, and I'll bring over a food menu too." The waitress bounced off to fulfill their order.

There was a half-minute of silence between the two friends. Nick sighed, eventually shrugging. "I think for the first time in several years, I envy myself more than you."

John managed to make eye contact with his friend. "Really?"

Nick shrugged. "Yeah, I hate to say it, but I really envied your life for a long time. Fuck it, I'm not going to lie: you and Isabel were a much better couple than Michelle and I ever were, and you weren't even married."

The waitress arrived with their drinks, two coasters, and some food menus. After setting everything down on their table, she left while the two of them went over the new menu. John sighed. "Well, I'm not sure how that's supposed to make me feel."

"Well, never mind," Nick said as he was reading the food menu. "You seem to be doing okay otherwise. I mean, financially speaking."

John set his menu down. "I got a decent raise at the beginning of the year. Plus, Bel and I had been saving up since we moved in together, so we've been living under our means pretty well. And…" He paused to take a large drink from his glass. "I just have not been eating as much."

"Yeah, you look a little skinnier, now that you mention it." Nick took a swig of his beverage, then proceeded to stare at it. "Ah, still good. How's yours?"

Shrugging, John said, "It's okay. It's cool that it's local, but I'm not a huge fan."

Nick nodded. "I know. This is your first time living alone, huh?"

"Yeah," John said. He took another large drink from his glass. "Went from parents to living with Bel to… well… not living with Bel."

"You boys figure out what you'd like to eat?" They weren't sure if she was oblivious to the seriousness of their conversation or if she was trying to be upbeat.

"Think I'll go with the mushroom swiss burger," said John. "No sides please."

"Okay," said the waitress as she jotted down some notes. "How about you, sir?"

"I'll go with the chicken enchiladas," Nick said, "and some hot sauce to go with it, if you don't mind."

"Not at all!" The waitress grabbed the menus off the table and smiled at the pair. "We'll get that going for you right away!"

With the distraction gone, the two returned to the topic at hand. Nick asked, "How about your parents? I know you told me they liked her."

"Yeah, they were sad for me." He took another sip. "But I don't think they saw her as a wife. I mean, I'm not into that whole marriage thing, but dammit, Nick, that's about the closest thing she was to me. I think they saw her as, like, I dunno, a college fling or something." Tears started to form, but he kept them in check.

Nick offered a half-smile. "Yeah, your view isn't too common. What can you do?"

It was a profound question. John had no answer. He couldn't do anything. Isabel's body was kept alive by a machine, making her existence that of a rudimentary robot.

John continued to be silent, outpacing Nick's drinking by almost a factor of three. John seldom drank on his own, reinforcing his commitment not to fall into the shroud of addiction. Yet there were moments he wanted to splurge.

After tapping the table with his fingers in sequence, Nick continued the conversation. "Have you thought of what you're going to do?"

"Hmmm?" There was a delay between the question and John's nonanswer.

"Well, you did say the other day you were going to have legal rights or whatever over her soon. Is that still happening? What are you going to do?"

John shrugged. "I don't know."

Nick let out a soft laugh. "And now I'm remembering those debates we had back in school. You were for assisted suicide. I was against it."

"I know." John took another sip of his beer, finishing it. Despite the possibilities spelled out to him, if he kept Isabel around long enough, a cure to her condition might eventually develop. Selfish beyond a doubt, for sure. She could be tied to that machine for decades. At her side, John promised, in his darkest moment, that he'd be with her forever and always. Sustaining her existence fulfilled that promise, but was she also suffering?

Nick looked at his friend between sips of his brew. As soon as John's second beer arrived, he began drinking.

"I thought you didn't like it," said Nick.

John shrugged. "It's not bad enough to bother trying something else." He took another sip.

Nick swallowed. "I think you could use help."

Setting his glass down, John stared at it before finally making eye contact with Nick. "I'm not an alcoholic, man. It's just hard right now."

"I know it is, which is why I'm not talking about drinking." Nick tapped the table, trying to think of what to say next. "I told you this before. I lost two grandparents before I was eighteen. It was difficult. So I can't even imagine what it's like to lose a friend, a parent, or—"

"You have no idea," said John.

"Yeah, John, I don't. I want to help you, but I can't. I don't know what's going on in that brain of yours. But you can't go on like this, man. You're fucking miserable. This is the worst I've seen anybody. I'm busy as hell with Michelle, but even when I'm free you do nothing. Your beard, I don't even know what the hell, man." Nick sighed. "You can't continue like this."

John's tear reservoir built up. He was the person Isabel didn't want him to be. Four years earlier, he was a loveless idealist. Now, he was a loving nihilist.

"It hurts."

"I know, man."

John looked over at the waitress carrying their food. "But Bel. I... just... don't..."

"Here you guys go!" she said as she set down their dishes on the table. "You ready for another one?"

"Yes please," said Nick, unrolling his napkin to grab a fork. The waitress strolled off without a word. Before Nick took a bite, he looked back at John. "What was that about Isabel?"

"I can't just abandon her. I know she's not coming back, not anytime soon, but I feel if I get over myself and move on, then my love for her was not real."

Nick took several bites of his meal. He shrugged before he finished chewing. "I don't know." After some reflection, he amended his statement. "Let me tell you this. I can't believe I'm going to say this, but fuck, man. You know what? If Isabel died today and you moved on tomorrow and forgot about her, in fifty fucking years you would still love her more than I ever loved Michelle."

John's welling tears subsided. He gave Nick a quizzical look, unsure if he was being genuine or just trying to cheer John up. Nick hadn't finished his first drink when the second arrived, yet he smiled and nodded at the waitress.

"Wow," was all John could say.

Nick took a few more bites and shrugged. "Well, what can you do?"

With the attention off his plight for the moment, John started eating. His mushroom swiss burger was one of the best he had ever had. Even though his drinking slowed, he still washed down his food with his pilsner.

After a minute of eating their meals in silence, Nick wiped his lips with a napkin. "Well, Michelle and I haven't fucked in like two months. I'm just not into it with her. She's not really into it with me."

"But she wants a kid?"

Nick laughed. "I know, right? I don't think she knows

where babies come from." He took a sip from his brew. "Like, it sucks. I feel depressed because it took me not getting any to realize that I'm not in love with my freaking wife. It's, like, sex made me happy, you know?"

John made a muffled snicker. "Yeah, tell me about it."

"And I was going to have a talk with her about this, how maybe we both could be happy if we had an open marriage or whatever. Like, fuck other people."

John nodded. "Well, assuming she's not asexual, that means she may be cheating on you." It was an itching suspicion John had had for some time.

It was Nick's turn to nod. "Yeah, maybe. Maybe that's why I want to sleep with other people. She's doing it, and I'm jealous. But hold on!" He put his hand out as if to stop the conversation, even though he was in command of it. "We're getting sidetracked here. There's a point to this!"

"Okay?" John wasn't sure where his best friend was going with the disjointed sermon, but he took it as an opportunity to take another bite of his burger.

"So me getting laid helps me ignore my problems. So I was thinking, maybe you getting laid can help with your problems."

John wasn't expecting that sentence. It caught him off guard, enough that he put down his hamburger and pondered what Nick said. "Wait, are you saying that you want me to cheat on Bel?"

Nick tilted his head and smiled. "Oh jeez, man. You really do love her."

John returned with a half-smile. "Yeah."

"Look," said Nick, "I'm no expert, so don't take anything I say seriously. You are lonely. I remembered how much of a hopeless romantic you were. And I liked most of your girlfriends, but none of them really made you as happy as you were with Isabel. You guys didn't break up, but she… she more or less died. I don't know how else to say that. And that fucking sucks. It would be a lot easier for you if she did actually die, as sick as that is to say."

John nodded as he took a drink.

"I can't say if she wants you to move on. Maybe she doesn't. I dunno. I think you have it in you that if she's breathing she is still your girlfriend. And I'm not saying you need to start dating anyway. I think that's a terrible idea. I just think you need to find a girl, get wasted, and fuck her brains out. Or fuck her sober. Doesn't matter. It won't be the same, but you'll be a lot happier. Happier than you are now. It's gonna help me, and I think it'll help you too."

If John was in any other mood, he'd consider those words insulting: insulting to Isabel's memory, insulting to John's sensibilities, and insulting to women in general. While he used to think more like that, his time and discussions with Isabel had evolved his viewpoint. It was possible that Nick's relationship with Michelle soured his own opinion on women, but John was in no place to offer judgment.

"Maybe," said John.

Nick finished chewing his mouthful of food. "Well, think about it. We're both shy, but there are dating sites online. You can find somebody on there. Hopefully they're as desperate as we are."

John chuckled. "Yeah. But what about Bel?"

Smiling, Nick said, "Leave her as is for now. You're

not ready to make important decisions or anything. But please, for your sake, have fun."

They finished their meals. With the weighted discussion out of the way, they focused their talks on movies and video games. After a third round for each of them, they decided to take off. It was already mid-afternoon. The outside temperature was almost as hot as a fission reactor.

"That was fun," said John as they arrived at the door. "Thanks for calling me."

"No problem," Nick responded. "How are you?"

John shrugged. "Better, I guess. It's gonna take a while. A long while."

"Yeah. Well hey, remember what I said. I'll let you know if it works out for me, but seriously, I think it can help."

"I'll think about it."

The inside of John's apartment remained cool on the ground floor, so he stayed down there for the time being. He was originally planning on visiting Isabel, but going out with Nick drained him for the day. There was always the next day and the day after that. One day, Isabel might finally give up and refuse her machine the honors of providing her with life. One day, he might make that decision for her.

That day wasn't soon. John looked over at their photo collage on the wall. Her long, wet, dark hair clinging to her nude body. The smile on her face. The spark in her eyes. John saw the spark in his own eyes too, on what was still one of the greatest days of his life. A tear ran down his cheek as he wondered if it was one of the best days of her life. She had said before how much she loved that day.

John needed to hear it from her again.

His hand reached out to touch her face on the photo.

"I love you," he whispered.

The photo did not whisper back.

Surrendering that moment to the past, John went on with the rest of the day. He put on a fun, quirky flick about a high schooler who got pregnant. Throughout most of the film, John's thoughts weren't on himself or Isabel, but on Nick and Michelle. Considering Nick's personal admission, John didn't understand why Nick would continue to delude himself into continuing the marriage. He was always afraid of being single, but if Nick had the opportunity to explore other women, then he'd learn that his fear was unfounded.

"I'll never forget you, Bel," cried John, thinking about his own loneliness. "You'll always be in my thoughts."

When the movie ended, he put his face in his hands, agonizing over his situation. As tempting as it was, he didn't have the will to kill himself. Yet he couldn't remain where he was, falling into the endless chasm. He could breathe. He had life. He had friends. Did he have hope?

John was now out of options. If he was to continue to survive, to exist, he had to change something. Standing up, he went upstairs. It was now late enough in the evening that the apartment had cooled. His computer was on the dresser in the bedroom, so he retrieved it and lay down on the bed. He opened the computer and signed onto his first online dating service.

09

CHAPTER NINE

John's stomach became an anchor. Only calm breathing
cured it. Nerves were something he never understood.
After a deep, long breath, he opened the door and got out
of his car.

There was justification for his nervous behavior. He
was meeting someone he had never met before. She was
also not the first person he met in those particular circumstances.

About four weeks after signing up for online dating,
John met Shantelle at a bar downtown. She was a few
years older and a single mother. The thought of becoming
an adoptive father to a child was not appealing, but the
relationship John was seeking wasn't for the long term.

John met her under false pretenses. In his profile, he
didn't state what he was genuinely looking for, nor did

he mention the reason he was on there in the first place. When he met Shantelle, she was already inebriated and confident in her sexuality. They had a few drinks before she invited him back to her place. John didn't feel comfortable, so he ended up driving home.

A week later, he met Staci. Staci was sweet, but she was also much younger. She was cute, freckled, and had curly brown hair. John was the older gentleman, the mature man with his own place. While they left their meeting amicably, there was no follow-up, no chance at a physical connection.

Next was Tess, who was closer to John's age. During their date, she often spoke about hooking up with her coworkers and how that well had run dry. She was looking to satiate her appetite elsewhere. It was promising, as her lifestyle lined up well with what John was looking for.

John drove her back to her place, and she invited him in. He quickly found himself making out with her on the couch, but guilt overcame him. Guilt for being physical with a woman other than Isabel, and guilt for lying to Tess. They continued to where their clothes fell to the floor. John's unhappiness translated to his physical arousal; Tess tried many tricks with her mouth and tongue to get John ready, but the combined efforts left him limp. Nauseous and embarrassed, he put his clothes back on and left her house, never hearing from her again. He wondered what she thought of him and if she'd complain to her friends about how lousy he was. The experience left him throwing up in his bathroom.

John returned to the dating site and gave his profile an honest overhaul. He wrote that he recently lost his partner and was still healing but ready to explore new avenues. It was unrealistic that a woman with any self-worth would be interested in someone in John's state, but the lie wasn't working. Something had to change.

Three weeks later, John started talking with a woman named Bethany. She was twenty-two years old and had recently graduated with a degree in psychology. They arranged a date at the coffee house that John had just parked at. Early autumn was rolling in, so there was a nice cool breeze, yet the sun still dominated the blue sky and the leaves still clung to their branches. It was too warm for his peacoat, but he wore a nice brown sweatshirt with some dark denim for the occasion.

Stepping inside, he scanned the coffee shop for someone matching Bethany's description. Not finding her, he walked up to the counter to order; fortunately, there was no wait. A young barista came up to the counter and smiled. "Hey, welcome to People's Coffee. What can I getcha?"

John chuckled. "I'll take a peppermint hot cocoa. A medium please." He didn't need caffeine to stress his nerves.

With the barista working on his request, John took another look around. It was a smaller shop with seating for two dozen people. Befitting of its name, there were posters depicting themes of communism. John remembered one of Isabel's dreams of opening up a similar coffee shop. Small and intimate yet uniquely quirky. He wouldn't put it past her to make her coffee shop communist-themed. There was a certain appeal to that ideology.

"Here you go!" said the smiling barista. John smiled, placing a small tip in the jar, and found himself a corner table. His thoughts were on Isabel, even if it wasn't a good time for that. He still visited her three times a week, telling her about his day, his job, or his normalizing social life. John still hadn't told her about his dating aspirations. He never wanted to lie to her, as they were always open with one another. Yet deep in her comatose mind, maybe she'd still be hurt.

"John?" a voice said. Startled, John looked up, freeing his thoughts from the anchor weighing him down. The voice wasn't Isabel's. It was scratchy-sounding but also light and calm, reinforced with curiosity. Standing next to him was a young woman with curly dirty blonde hair, a freckled face, and blue eyes. She was wearing a tan sweater with a dark brown scarf around her neck, accompanied by black slacks.

Her appearance matched her pictures, which was promising. "Uh, yeah!" He stood up, his nerves returning. "Bethany?"

She gave a slight smile. "Yes! How are you?" She reached out her hand to offer a handshake. He took her up on that offer.

"I'm okay. How about yourself?" After a quick beat, he added, "Uh, why don't you sit down?"

"Okay!" Bethany said, followed by a nervous smile. John wasn't one to accurately gauge people's emotions, but he figured Bethany was as nervous as he was, which made him feel better. As the two were sitting, she continued. "You looked so deep in thought I almost didn't want to bother you."

John shrugged. "I like thinking, I guess."

Bethany smiled. "Thinking about whether I would look like a troll in real life?"

Both of them giggled. "No. Just about life."

"Life is good." Bethany had her own drink and she took a sip. "What did you get?"

John looked at his hot cup, which was still sitting on the table. "I got their peppermint cocoa. Looked pretty good."

"Mmmm, I can definitely smell that. Sounds tasty."

Silence settled on the table as the two looked at each other. John had trouble focusing on her eyes; he wanted to run away from her gaze. It was oddly frightening to him, even if it reflected thoughts of curiosity and understanding. John took a sip from his own drink and forced a sentence out. "So how was your week?"

She smiled. "Not too bad. Still looking for work. This economy is starting to suck. Four years I spent to get here, and I'm living back home with my parents."

"You went to school out of state?"

"Yeah," said Bethany. "Got lucky with scholarships and grants. We grew up poor, so I guess getting even this far is fortunate."

John nodded. "That's good to hear. Yeah, I hope my job is going to be okay."

Bethany furrowed her brow as if she was pretending to read John's mind. "You live on your own, then? No roommates?"

"No roommates. Not anymore. Yeah, so no... no roommates."

Beth ignored his uncomfortable statement. "Yeah, I spent all four years in the dorms. A lot of my friends rented houses. Just seemed like a waste to me."

With the wave of awkwardness swept aside, John breathed in deep and continued the conversation. "So you weren't a big partier then?"

"Oh you kidding me?" she said, smiling. "The dorms had all the best parties. Oh man, the things that we did."

Isabel had kept quiet during her college years, concentrating on studying and socializing with small groups. Like John, she wasn't a fan of huge parties. Bethany seemed like an extrovert, although that wasn't a knock on her. John had matured in the past several years and judged women less for their differences.

"What are you trying to do, like, job-wise?" It seemed like a vapid question, but he was trying his hardest to keep the focus on her.

"I'd love to be a school counselor. I prefer elementary, but I think middle school has the biggest impact. Young teens can really be a rough bunch, let me tell you."

"No kidding," said John. "We didn't even have social media, and it was still awful."

"Yeah, I just feel my life experience can really shape a young woman's future. If we don't treat our children well, what makes you think they'll take care of the world when they're in charge?"

"Definitely a valid statement," said John as he sipped his drink. She might have been a social butterfly, but she also had passion.

"But enough about me," she said, smiling. "Tell me about you. You have a job, your own place. I've never lived by myself. How is it?"

John tried to phrase his response as positively as possible. "Well, it's quiet. The couch is always yours. And you never have to worry about being judged."

She set her hands on the table as if she was opening

up to this stranger. "I'm guessing you used to live with someone."

"You could say that." John didn't want their conversation to go down that road. He took another sip of his hot drink.

Bethany looked away. "You know, I studied how to deal with loss and sadness and depression for years. I never felt I knew it all." She looked back at John, her eyes projecting more concern. "Would you mind telling me what happened to her?"

His heart sank. John should have known that an educated psychologist would delve into the uncomfortable parts of his life. "Well, like, so…" John stopped.

Silence again paused their meeting. John's eyes sunk to the table, but Bethany's remained calmly fixed on him. "I'm sorry. Is it still too hard for you?"

At that point, John realized he was on a date and that he had to bind the pieces of his heart together if he was going to maintain Bethany's interest. He wanted to surrender to her question, despite the difficulty.

"No, it's fine." He returned his gaze back to her eyes. "So I kind of simplified the story I told you online."

Bethany gave an understanding smile. "I figured."

"So she was in a car accident, and right now she's plugged in over at Kaiser. They say she's probably not gonna wake up. So I mean, in a way"—John sighed—"maybe I did tell the literal truth. She is dead."

There was a pause. "I'm sorry," said Bethany.

John shrugged. "It happened back in April. I just… I just need to go out there. Meet people. Meet people who understand. Meet people like you. I shouldn't hide the pain, but I don't want to live in the past either."

"I think that's healthy," said Bethany as she smiled, "and I do understand. I'm going to also be honest with you. I've gone on a few dates the past couple of weeks. There just wasn't a spark. But there's something about you, and I don't know what it is."

Trying to make light of the situation, John said, "Maybe you just found out that confident guys aren't your thing."

Bethany laughed. "Yeah, maybe. I like men with emotion. I mean, you have a lot of red flags, but you have emotion, and I like that."

"Well," said John, looking around at the communist-themed décor in the shop, "if you're gonna have red flags, this is the place for it!"

Bethany laughed even harder. "Yeah. Trying to rally your comrades, huh?"

It was John's turn to smile. "Well, I did rally you here."

Bethany blushed and took a sip of her coffee. "Yeah."

John leaned forward. "So, Bethany, is this a date for you, or are you using me to practice your skills?"

She shrugged. "I dunno. Both?" She nervously laughed. "I do like you. I mean, I don't know you well. But I have to say, you are pretty hot."

John's heart fluttered. She was more forward than Isabel. "Oh, well, thanks."

Bethany giggled. "Well, how are you feeling? About today? About me?"

John had spent months coming to this point. Honesty worked so far but could tip things over the edge. But beating around the issue could delay healing or outright cancel it altogether.

"I'm not sure. I've gone on a few dates too, but it was so uncomfortable. But there's something reassuring about you. Like I trust you. Like I want to be with you."

She nodded slowly. "You want to hang out and maybe, I dunno, cuddle?"

John smiled. "Cuddling is good, yeah."

Bethany mirrored his smile. "Okay. I don't feel comfortable going over to your place yet, but my parents are out of town for the weekend so you are welcome to come by. I don't want you to have expectations though."

"No expectations," parroted John.

"Okay. You can follow me but I'll give you the address just in case." She found a scrap of paper in her purse and wrote out the address for John. They stood up and left the shop together, then split off outside to go to their respective cars. Bethany drove an SUV, which brought some ire to John, but he didn't want to let something like that impede his healing process. His idealism now had limits.

Bethany pulled out of the parking lot, John following her. She was a cautious driver, so there weren't any sudden movements to throw John off. She lived a few miles east, out toward the suburbs but not quite out of the city proper. It was a thin slice of town generally occupied by families in a lower-income bracket.

Fortunately, the area was a decent neighborhood. The houses were older and smaller but they were well-maintained, and a certain liveliness exuded from the homes and their small yards. Bethany pulled into her parents' driveway, and John parked on the street so as not to block her in. Her parents' house was small but cozy, single-story white walls with flowers dotting the front yard.

John was walking over as Bethany was unlocking the front door. "Come on in!" She got the door opened and disappeared inside. John followed and shut the door behind him.

"Were you a single child?" asked John.

Bethany giggled at his funny word choice. She put her purse on the dining room table in the next room. "Yeah. I don't think I could have survived with a sibling. You?"

"Same," said John. The house didn't have a proper entryway; the front door went right into the living room, which had a couch and an older television on the entertainment center. The dining room was to the left, and farther back appeared to be the kitchen. A lot of the light fixtures and furniture had an older quality to them, yet they weren't quite vintage. "I've always liked old small houses."

"Easy for you to say," said Bethany as she approached John. "I grew up here. It's old and I want something new. I really want to get a nice big house one day. Don't think I'll have one unless I find a sugar daddy." They both giggled.

Bethany motioned John over to the couch. He followed her advice and sat down on it. She played with the lights until she found a mood, then sat down next to John.

"So," said John.

"So," said Bethany. "Are you comfortable?"

"Yeah," replied John. He wasn't kidding either; unlike his previous date, he was relaxed and at ease with Bethany.

"Good. Come here." She opened up her arms, and John fell into the invitation. His head fell onto her shoulder, and his arms weaved their way under her armpits and wrapped themselves around her back. John closed his eyes, relaxed further, and offered a subtle moan.

"You haven't hugged someone in a long time, have you?" Her scratchy voice was easy to understand at the softer volume.

"Not really," said John, who made no effort to quiet his voice. "I mean, I got hugs from parents and friends after the accident, but the last time I felt a connection was with Isabel."

"Isabel." Bethany repeated the name of John's lost love. "Isabel. That is a nice name. I'm sure she was very special."

"She was." A single tear came out of his left eye. "I called her Bel though. That was my name for her."

"That's sweet." Bethany put one of her hands behind his head, cradling it against her shoulder. She turned her neck and gave him a peck on the side of his head, something that caught John off guard. She took a finger and made a token effort to wipe his tears off. "What did you two like to do?"

John giggled. "Everything. Well, no anal though."

Bethany laughed. "Smart girl." She wiped more tears off his face. "But that's not what I meant."

"Oh. Well, we liked walking, cooking, debating, gardening. Kissing." His voice became weak.

Bethany leaned forward and kissed him on the forehead. "How was that?" she asked.

"It was good." John was hesitant.

"Do you want to sleep with me?" she asked. "I know you're probably confused. I'm confused too. Don't worry. I just… want you, in your super-attractive emotionally depressed state. Do you want me?"

John's brain began overloading. There was a shackle that swallowed his body on the day of the accident, a straight-jacket not even Houdini could escape from. His emotional availability was stunted, his virility extinguished. While there were background songs of grief playing in his mind still, his masculine prowess stirred in ways it hadn't in months. Something about Bethany clicked with his primal urges, and it was occupying his focus.

"I... yes. Yes, Bethany, I do."

Bethany leaned forward, and their lips connected. The nerves stewing in John's stomach were flushing away, and his heart fluttered. He felt lively and welcomed the dormant emotion.

Several seconds went by before she backed off. John didn't react. She asked, "What is it?"

John lunged forward, capturing Bethany in his grasp, and he returned the kiss, dominating the encounter. There was a muffled yelp from Bethany, but no struggle or denials. Her arms wrapped around his body, and they pressed against each other. John's hunger finally passed the threshold of his pain. When he pulled back, both he and Bethany were gasping for air, panting from the sudden spurt of energy. She had a surprised smile on her face. "Wow. Hi!"

John laughed. His hands ran down the sides of her body, eventually reaching the top of her thighs. Instinctively, they opened slightly. John shyly said, "I've never hooked up with anybody before."

Bethany grabbed his wrist and slowly led his left hand. "Well, I don't want you to go too far and be uncomfortable."

"I know," he said, still catching his breath. He dove headfirst into her lap, kissing her slacks. Bethany's breathing intensified as she ran her fingers in his hair. Sliding down the side of his head, she wedged her hand underneath John and unzipped her slacks. John sat up slightly. Her slacks weren't skin-tight like a lot of denim was, so she slipped them and her underwear to the floor without performing tricky acrobatics.

After a minute of John's oral passions, Bethany pulled his head off of her. "Wait," she said. John was confused but obliged. She didn't seem anxious or scared but took a moment to settle down. "This is my parents' couch. Let's go to my bed."

She grabbed her slacks off the ground, and wearing only her sweatshirt, she walked toward the back of the house. John wiped his face and followed her. They ended up in a narrow hallway that branched off from the kitchen and turned into her room. It was a lot smaller than John's room, with a small bed against the far wall.

Without a word, she took off her sweatshirt and a tank top underneath. John followed the invitation and stripped down, watching her as she took her bra off with her back facing him.

"Lie down on the bed." Remaining silent, John complied with her request. When he was lying on his back, Bethany crawled on top of him, supported by her hands and knees. She kissed him all over, from his neck to his chest. When he closed his eyes, his sense of touch heightened. He responded to her marks of affection with short breaths of air. Unlike his encounter with Tess, it didn't take much to get him ready.

Bethany stopped. Concerned, John opened his eyes and looked down to see what was delaying her. She had reached over to her nightstand and grabbed a condom and put it on John. Without another word, she adjusted her hips and lowered herself onto him. Their eye contact remained locked as her gyrations started, first a slight movement but eventually becoming more powerful. Both their breaths intensified. John tried to lean up to kiss Bethany, but she put her weight down on his shoulder, keeping him flat on the bed. Instead, she leaned forward and kissed his forehead, cheek, and neck.

Bethany kept asking John if everything was okay. He was relaxed and comfortable. They were having fun, even occasionally giggling. Eventually, John couldn't hold it in anymore and released himself, shutting his eyes and letting out a long, deep moan.

It wasn't the greatest orgasm he ever had, but it was better than none at all. She kissed him on the forehead and continued to run her fingers through his hair. But John's moment of elation melted away, and his moment of clarity began.

He had sex with someone other than Isabel. He abandoned Isabel to purgatory at the hospital, to sleep around with other women without her knowledge. It didn't matter that she no longer resembled the woman he fell in love with. It didn't matter she would never know John slept with someone else. She was alive, and John betrayed her. He burst into tears.

Bethany frowned. "Oh, John, it's okay." She lowered her whole body onto his and hugged him tightly. He appreciated the affection, hugging back. It wasn't her fault. It was nobody's fault. Everything confused John at that point.

"I'm sorry, Bethany," said John between sobs. "I really like you. I don't know…"

"Shhhh," whispered Bethany. "Everything will be fine."

For the first time in a long time, John felt safe. His tears might have been from sadness, but they were a mark of the healing process. Finally, he found comfort in someone else, a connection to another human being. And despite his tears and cries of sorrow, that was very comforting.

10

CHAPTER TEN

"That's so sweet that you do that!" Michelle said to John. She turned in her chair to face Nick. "I miss that you don't do anything like that anymore!"

"Yeah, honey, I'll make it up to you," said Nick with a thin air of resentment that John picked up on.

Bethany touched John's arm. "Yeah, this boy knows how to make a girl happy."

Fortunately, John's outburst in Bethany's bedroom didn't end things prematurely. They met up again at another coffee house the following weekend. Bethany felt that John wasn't ready for a relationship, long-term or otherwise, but he disagreed. He was at his happiest since the accident, and he wanted to continue seeing her. She was busy finding work but found time to spend with him. They dialed themselves back, keeping festivities to platonic dates and hangouts.

His self-esteem and passion for life trickled back in, but he never lost sight of what mattered to him the most. The visits to Isabel decreased to twice a week, due to his more active social life. Isabel's unresponsive body was still unaware of the new developments. A thought sprouted in his mind: maybe Isabel would be happy for John and would want him to meet new people.

As the year wound to a close, Bethany warmed up to John. They got physical again, starting with high-school-style make-out sessions. Soon, they brought back intercourse. To his shock, she got him a wool blanket for Christmas. It embarrassed him because he had no gift to give her, so he promised Bethany a gift every week for the next month. He delivered on that promise.

After Christmas, they spent more time with each other, leading to a double date with Nick and Michelle at a nice restaurant downtown. Nick was more comfortable with the setting, since he often took his wife out for fine dining, but John was reserved about the choice. He loathed upscale establishments.

"So you guys exclusive yet?" asked Michelle with a sly smile.

"Oh no, we're just good friends," said Bethany.

John laughed. "Yeah. Things still aren't normal for me yet, but that's slowly turning around." He turned toward his date and smiled. She responded in kind.

"There's just too much man meat to pass up!" joked Bethany.

"A new guy every day, right?" joked Nick.

Michelle slapped his shoulder. "Seriously, babe? That's

not a nice thing to say!"

"I don't have a problem with it," said John. It was likely Bethany had been exploring her options since that first date, as she continually insisted they weren't monogamous yet. "Hell, if she keeps coming back to me, that just tells me I ain't too bad."

All except Michelle laughed. Bethany continued. "Yeah, not enough hours in the day. Sometimes I have two or three guys at once. The line is out the door!"

John giggled as he took a sip of his beer. Nick and Bethany both had wine glasses in front of them. Michelle usually drank wine or a cocktail, but she was having water that night. John suspected he knew why. He thought Nick was in a sour mood because of a fight the two had, but maybe there were bigger things on his mind.

"Well, if you guys will excuse me," said Michelle, standing up out of her chair. "I'm going to powder my nose. Bethany, I'm sure you'll want to freshen up too!" Nick's cough did not sound authentic.

"Oh yes!" Bethany said, turning to the side and giving John a quick peck on his cheek. "Be right back!" Bethany left to follow her new friend into the restroom to gossip.

"Oh Jesus God," said Nick.

"How're you doing?" asked a concerned John.

Nick sighed. "Well, you know. The usual."

John decided to subtly ask the question burning in his mind. "So I notice she's drinking water. Is she changing her lifestyle, or is it what I'm thinking?"

"Yeah, it's what you're thinking," said Nick with the tone of ultimate defeat. "We just found out a couple of weeks ago."

John could hardly imagine Nick being a father. They were still young, and their relationship wasn't the healthiest. John nodded. "Yeah, well, how do you feel?"

Shrugging, Nick said, "I don't know. I should have seen it coming. The rare times we do get it on, she's freaky. I can't say no. Even knowing she wasn't on anything anymore. It's just really rare that happened. With her."

"How about with other people?" asked John, knowing Nick wasn't being altogether faithful with his spouse. "Is that going to continue?"

"Damn, I don't know. I feel bad about it, man, but it feels so damn good."

"Yeah, I get that." John's mind went out of focus as he thought of his dual relationship with Bethany and Isabel, or whatever relationship he still had with Isabel.

"Well, I know you can get pregnant from one time, but what are the odds that she got her oven cookin' when we've been fucking once or twice a month?"

John nodded. "Yeah, those are far odds. DNA test, maybe."

"Yeah, maybe." Nick took a sip from his glass, his lips puckering. "Anyway, job still okay?"

"There were some layoffs, but my department was mostly unscathed. Bethany is still looking for something though."

"Yeah, she graduated at a shitty time, with the economy crashing like it did," Nick said. "Not looking forward to a depression."

John laughed. "Don't think there's gonna be a depression. But how 'bout you? You've been scared for a while."

"There's another round of layoffs happening soon, and the company is stripped enough as it is." Nick took that opportunity to have another sip of wine. "I have a feeling I'm next. With a baby on the way, it's gonna suck hard. But going back to you, I like Bethany. She's a cool chick. Not bad looking. Kinda surprised you managed to score her."

"Hey now!" John's fake offense was a terrible ruse, and the two friends laughed.

"So I know you guys are 'just friends,'" Nick said while giving air quotes, "but she's good for you. That's all I'm saying. She's smart, hot, funny. I know you like to compare her to Isabel, and that's fair, dude. But look at it this way, after Isabel, Bethany is by far the best woman you've been with, and I've known all your girlfriends. She's good for you."

"Thanks, I appreciate that." On cue, the two women returned from the restroom. John pulled the seat out for Bethany. Michelle sat down without acknowledgment.

"So," said John, "got any good gossip?"

The two women laughed. Michelle slapped the table. "Oh, John. You."

"Is powdering a nose actually a thing anymore?" asked Nick.

"Well, if you're a cokehead, sure," said a blunt Bethany. "Wasn't my thing though."

John looked over with wide eyes. "You've done coke?"

"Yeah, once or twice," said Bethany calmly. "It was kind of cool, but that shit can fuck you up, so that's all I did."

"It's great at keeping your weight down," Michelle said with pep. Michelle was thin for all five years John had known her. He always gave her the benefit of the doubt, but her enthusiasm for cocaine gave him pause. John didn't care either way, but he wondered how it affected her relationship with Nick or how it would affect his unborn child.

"Yay cocaine!" declared John, and the table laughed.

"I miss hanging out with you, John," said Michelle. He didn't know if she was sincere, but it had been some time since they were together. Aside from right after the accident, it had been over a year. It was a similar double-date back then, but John had another companion.

"Yeah, I haven't even seen Nick that much either." John was subtly digging at Michelle for how she controlled her husband. She was oblivious to the accusation.

"Well, we'll make an effort to hang out more," said Nick, looking at John.

"You guys are so awesome," said Bethany. "I'm really glad we got together. John does have some good friends."

"Oh, thank you!" said Michelle.

The evening settled down. Drinks were finished, the bill was paid, and they left. Nick and Michelle were parked near the door, but John and Bethany had to brave the cold wind as they walked down the street toward John's car. Despite wearing a thick coat, Bethany shivered.

They snuggled up against each other as they walked the two blocks to the car in absolute silence. It was after eleven but there was still bustling activity downtown, with many cars darting around the dark streets and people of various sobriety levels making random noises.

As they got to his car, John broke the silence. "Did you want to come over tonight?"

Bethany didn't say anything for a moment. She shivered silently. "Really? Are you... are you sure?"

John nodded. "Yeah. I think I'm good."

He opened the door for Bethany, and the two got in. After igniting the engine, he wasted no time in turning up the heat to stave off the wars of winter.

"So what did you two talk about?" asked John.

"More like what did she talk about," said Bethany, disappointment filling her voice.

"Oh?" John got his seat belt on and turned onto the street, making sure there was no oncoming traffic.

"I think she just wanted someone to talk to about her life," she said, adjusting her seat belt strap to be comfortable. "Apparently she's pregnant."

"Yeah, Nick told me tonight as well."

"Very chatty. Talked about what she wanted to do with the baby. Names, what toys to get, how to decorate their room."

"Sounds dreadful," said John, his eyes focused on the road. He had told her how Isabel and he decided to never have children, so she knew of John's stance.

"Well, babies are cute and I didn't mind that part." Bethany was more accepting of children than Isabel was. It was a typical mindset and conflicted with John's perspective on the issue, something that would cause friction down the line. "But she just kept bitching about Nick. How he's so awful, how he forgets things, how he's inattentive and often ignores her."

"Doesn't surprise me," murmured John.

"Really? 'Cause I liked Nick actually. I can see how you two got along for so long."

"Well yeah, that's what I mean. They've been having problems for a while. We'll see what this baby will do to them."

"I hope they get it figured out, for the baby's sake anyway."

Casual conversation echoed in the car for the rest of the drive. Fortunately, he remembered to leave the porch light on so they could see the door when he pulled in.

"Wow, you live closer in than I thought," said Bethany as she undid her seat belt.

"It's a nice little place." The two got out of the car as a large wind gust came in and made them more uncomfortable. They haphazardly attempted to jog. He fumbled for the keys before he got the front door unlocked. He let Bethany inside first before closing the door behind him.

After grabbing her coat, he turned on all the lights downstairs so she could see. As John was hanging their coats up, he asked, "Want a drink or something? I have some cider in the fridge."

"Yes please," said Bethany as she walked past the entryway. John ventured into the kitchen, leaving his date to her own devices. He grabbed two bottles of hard cider from the refrigerator and spent a minute finding his bottle opener. As soon as he got the bottle caps off, he heard a voice from the other room. "Is this her?"

With his hands full, John followed the voice. He found her facing the wall. In front of her were the framed portraits of John and Isabel, nude while wading in the hot springs. Slowly and silently, he walked over to stand right behind Bethany. In his haste to get her to come over to his home, he blanked that reminders of Isabel were all over the place. Nine months later, the duplex still remained unchanged. All her art, crafts, pictures, and furniture arrangements were all untouched by John and untouched by time.

"Yes," said John solemnly, looking at the blissful happiness in the photos. "Yes, that's her."

"She's beautiful," said Bethany. There was no jealousy in her voice, nor condemnation. Just admiration. "I can see now."

John sighed. "Look, Bethany, I didn't intend for you to see this."

"No, no!" She turned around to face John. "No. Not at all. I actually wanted to see what she looked like." She laughed as she turned back to the wall. "Stupid as it sounds, I wanted to meet her. Strange, isn't it? If I was able to meet her, I wouldn't be in your life to begin with."

"It's an interesting paradox, for sure."

She took a step toward the portrait, whispering, "So happy." Then, louder, her scratchy voice more pronounced, "You are so happy here. I've never seen you happy before."

John looked down and shuffled his feet. "Sorry."

"To be honest, I don't think I've ever been as happy as she looks here." Bethany sighed. "It's amazing to think about. It's all relative. Our pain, our sadness. My life has been good. My parents struggled, but they did okay. School was good, if useless. But I have never been truly, honestly happy. And she had that. And I wonder why that is."

Unfair comparisons aside, Bethany was an observant individual who understood a lot. She was a great companion to John, whether in a platonic capacity or otherwise. His heart betrayed him every day, and Isabel's greatness lingered on a pedestal in his mind. He had to make do with what life gave him.

Bethany gave out a soft laugh. "And you're really hot in these pictures too."

John smiled. "You're beautiful as well." It was the first time he had said those words to her.

She turned around, her arms folded on themselves. "Really?"

"Uh, yeah."

Her smile turned into a wide grin. "You're so good with words."

Ignoring the sarcasm, he offered the bottle to her. "Would you like to sit?"

She grabbed the bottle from his hand. "Yes. Thank you."

John was the first to turn around, navigating himself to the couch that was home to his drawn-out purgatory. There used to be beautiful moments here, but John didn't wish to dwell on those memories. A new change was coming, and he had to work to make sure he could catch up. He looked back at Bethany, who was still looking at the portraits with a subdued wonder on her face. Catching all the emotion she could from the art, she turned away and followed John to the couch.

"How are you doing this fine evening?" he asked.

"I'm warmer." They both giggled. "How are you?"

"I'm doing better than I have in a while."

Bethany took several sips from her cider with a hint of surprise in her eyes. She took a hard look at the bottle. "I need to turn you on to wine."

"Oh?" John said. "You don't like it?"

"Oh, no, it's great," she said, "but wine is a world you need to be exposed to. Step out of your comfort zone. And it makes you a distinguished gentleman."

"So I need a monocle now?"

Bethany laughed. It wasn't the time to express his opinions on social norms and forced conformity, but it was a conversation he'd like to have with her. Despite her flaws, there was enough good in Bethany to make her worth keeping. Yet John was curious if the only attractive element she had, aside from her physical appearance, was that she was there for him when no other woman was. Was there really anything else he saw in her?

"Before I forget," she said. "Sorry, this seems random. But if Nick wants someone to talk to, someone who's neutral, let him know he can talk to me."

"I'm sure he'll appreciate that." He sipped on his bottle. "And I can give you glowing reviews."

Bethany smiled. She set her bottle on the coffee table, putting her hands in her lap. "What do you feel like doing?"

John took another quick sip before setting his bottle down. "Well, I am feeling better than I thought I would. So that's good." He stretched his arms out and laid them along the back of the couch.

Smiling, she scooted closer. His arm slipped off and connected with her shoulders. They wasted little time before they kissed, their hands caressing each other's shoulders and backs. Even though John wanted to continue on the couch, Bethany whispered into his ear, "I bet your bed is really comfy."

Not picky about location, John led them upstairs and into the dark bedroom. After finding the lamp on the nightstand, they removed their clothing. Bethany shivered.

"I'll get the heat going," said John.

"Yay!" said Bethany with muffled celebration. John adjusted the thermostat and felt the warmth almost instantly. He returned to Bethany, her attractive silhouette standing patiently against the backdrop of the bed lamp.

"Damn, you are beautiful," said John, and the two resumed kissing. When the pressure became excessive, they fell sideways onto the bed, bouncing slightly. She rolled him onto his back, his heart eager with excitement. After making sure he was ready to continue, she guided herself onto him, and once in position, leaned forward to give him a long, deep kiss on the lips.

This was their first time without a condom. She mentioned before she was on birth control but insisted on condoms as long as they were casual. What was purely physical before was now something else: romantic. Everything was different now. Even Bethany was reacting differently, her moans stronger and more authentic. She played with herself like she had never done with John, and her reactions spoke for themselves.

When John finished, he cried out before falling back to silence. Bethany sat straight up, panting heavily as she looked down at his body. She rubbed her hands all over his sweaty chest and giggled. They had come a long way, and John's dysfunctional tics were extinguished. She finally found the boyfriend she had been seeking, a man with feelings and intelligence and a deep understanding of her needs. He finally found a girlfriend, one who could explore his passion with him and who understood his emotional needs. Isabel briefly entered his thoughts; John recognized her for what she meant to him and how important she was to his life, but he didn't let her misfortune take control of his life that evening. He was with Bethany, and that was enough.

11

CHAPTER ELEVEN

John wondered if the familiarity of the room indicated obsessive compulsion. He was sure some of the staff felt that way about him.

"I wish more people were like you," the woman behind the counter said.

John looked up from working on the form he was given. "What do you mean by that?"

"Well, you're kind and gentle and understanding," she said. "I see family members come in all the time who are so demanding. They want better treatment for their loved ones. Outrageous demands. This and that. They get so rude sometimes."

"I can imagine that gets annoying after a while."

"Well, you get used to it." The woman sighed. "You keep to yourself. But every time I've talked with you, you're such a peach."

John teased out a smile. "Thanks. You guys here are great as well. You do a good job taking care of things. I just wish I didn't have to come though."

The woman frowned. "I know. Not many people keep coming week after week. It takes a saint to stay faithful."

John didn't answer. He didn't want to disclose the reason he was there. Looking down, he finished filling out the waiver and signed the date: April 12. He passed the clipboard back to the woman.

"Thank you," said John as he stepped back from the counter and walked down the white corridor.

April 12. He had been dreading this day for months now. He'd flip through his calendar, whether at work or at home, and freeze when he caught sight of that date. His stomach turned and agonized as he approached the room he had visited over a hundred times. This day was different from all the other days.

After walking through the door, John let out a long exhale. Even though he was more used to the circumstances, it never got easier. He walked over, trying not to make any sound, so as not to disturb Isabel as she lay lifeless in her bed.

April 12, the one-year anniversary of the accident.

The staff at the hospital kept excellent care of her, even if she wasn't able to appreciate their efforts. She was always clean, they changed her clothes and bedding, and they moved her enough to stop bedsores from forming. Her breathing apparatus never ceased its work. Like clockwork, the oxygen entered her lungs, prolonging the life of her unresponsive brain. In and out, nonstop for the past twelve difficult months.

"Hey, Bel," said John in his usual upbeat tone. Even if he had a rough day at work or something unfortunate happened at home, saying that greeting was almost always the highlight of his day. He grabbed her lukewarm hand and held it, rubbing his fingers over it with a delicacy he couldn't conjure anywhere else.

"How are you?" he asked. Even without proof, he knew somewhere deep in her mind, in her soul, she had an answer. Even if she couldn't vocalize or even show him in any fashion, she still had an answer. John, as always, pretended she told him what that answer was, and he smiled.

"I had a good weekend. After work on Friday, my coworkers and I went out and had a few drinks, played some darts. I wasn't last, believe it or not. I got a higher score than Sam. You remember Sam. We hung out with him and his wife a few times. They're doing well."

He reached out and ran his hand through her hair, adjusting her bangs so they weren't in her face. "Can't say the same thing about Nick. Michelle is about four months along now. I didn't think their relationship could get worse, but it did. Since he got laid off, things have been bad for him at home. She's still working, but now she's placing a lot of pressure and stress on him. He's not handling it very well. I wish I could help, but my work took a hit too last fall and we can't take anyone else on."

John looked up, shaking his head. "You knew this was going to happen. You talked about how the big banks would fail us. We didn't trust them with nothin'. All they do is hurt the poor, and they did. It feels empty, Bel. It feels empty. It sounds cynical, but I wanted to celebrate being right. But I can't celebrate. Not without you. There's no one else worth celebrating this horrible thing with." He lifted up her hand and kissed it.

"The lettuce I planted last month, it's starting to take. I felt like shit last year. I didn't keep up on our garden. I really wanted to, but I was hurt so much that I couldn't get much out of it. Maybe you'll forgive me someday for it. But gardening really reminds me of you, especially when the sun shines. I know I was all about the rain, but there's something about the warmth of the sun in the early spring breathing life to our plants. It's like I have a helper, just like you were a helper. We helped each other. So don't feel too guilty. I know you're there."

He sniffled. He wasn't the broken mess he was, but he still would receive random injections of unimaginable grief. Tears were bound to happen, but he kept his composure for the time being. "I took up yoga. I think I told you that last week. I forget sometimes. Hope you don't mind me telling you things more than once. You never did before. But it's been fun. Not really into the spirituality of it, not sure I ever will be either. I wonder if that's a good idea though. I kinda wish I had your opinion of it. I think you would have gone with me. You'd enjoy it, for sure."

All those words, all those lucid fragments, were John's attempts at delaying the inevitable. He couldn't stomach his purpose yet. Swallowing, feeling his heart beating faster, he went on. "Your opinion. Your opinion I valued so, so much. So much. I guess it mattered so much that it became fact. Or something. But a lot has happened, and hearing your thoughts on everything is a comfort. No, it's one of the many comforts I miss. You were always so, so, so much smarter than me."

A tear slid down his cheek. His wall finally broke. It was his body's way of saying what he meant, and there was no holding back anymore. He sighed, gripping her hand more firmly. "Bel, my love, it's been a year since you fell asleep." A second tear. "It hasn't gotten any easier. It's worse today, in fact." Third tear. "I can vividly remember that day. Nick coming over. You coming down those stairs. That phone call." Fourth. "I know you're not supposed to think about or worry about the bad things, only the good. But that's the last time we saw each other. The last time that you saw me."

All bets were off as John let out a sustained cry. "And I know it's selfish how I wish you woke up. I know you want to wake up more than me. It's your body, for God's sake. You had such a life to live. But here I am, and I have to make do with my life. Bel, I couldn't take not having you anymore. I... I met somebody."

John's knees collapsed and he sunk to the floor. Not caring how painful the impact was on the hard surface, he leaned forward and muffled his cries in her body. He did not stop; he could not stop. It was his most painful admission, his most hidden secret, revealing itself. A cocktail of emotions wrecked his inner compass as he was bombarded with guilt, sorrow, love, betrayal, and helplessness. There might have been more, but John wasn't in the place to isolate every one of those swiftly orbiting emotions. He just hurt.

Isabel remained lifeless, save for the occasional rising of her abdomen. It was unfair to John that he couldn't know her reaction. His assumptions jumped all over the place, from sadness to anger to approval. There was no way to know, and he'd likely go to his grave never knowing. And none of that was Isabel's fault; rarely was anything her fault. This was all on him, all his actions destroying him inch by inch.

Minutes of sobbing went by, and when his cries finally subsided, he turned his head so his cheek rested on her body. He could feel her clothes soaking wet, no doubt a result of his emotional outburst. There was a small feeling of guilt as he realized the nurses would have to go through the hassle of getting her into a new gown. The thought subsided as John's own selfishness kicked in, reflecting his own pain.

"I didn't want to find someone else," whispered John, his ear glued to her body, listening to her artificial breathing. "I spent months completely fucking miserable. I couldn't go on. I hated everything. My life. My job. My existence. I told you about this. I've been telling you about this for the past year. But I couldn't kill myself. Imagine if I did that and you woke up." More tears stained her hospital gown. "There was nothing for the pain. I tried to find it. I knew it was somewhere out there in the world. And I did find it. It… helped, but it's not totally healing. I don't think it ever will completely heal. I met someone, Bel. She's a little younger than us. She's cool. I think she could have been our friend in a different lifetime."

John lifted his head up and stared off into the abyss of the room. "Oh, what the hell am I saying? You probably hate her. I don't blame you. You probably hate me too. I don't blame you. I wonder how I'd feel if you were me right now. But you're not me, you are you, and no matter how

I'd feel in this situation, it doesn't matter."

He looked back at Isabel. "It sucks because I still always think of you. When her and I are... together in that way, my mind wanders to you sometimes. A lot of times, actually. It's not fair to her. I'm sure she would be happier if I was focused totally on her. But I can't. And I wonder why that is. I've told you many times before: you are the love of my life. It's so kitschy for me to say that. So fucking dumb. But if your body chooses not to come back, and I have to live, am I going to be that grouchy hermit that you and I both vowed not to become? Someone who is dry of love and passion for years and years against their will, an asshole to everyone around him? An asshole to existence? I'm only human, Bel. I wish I was better than human, but I'm not.

"Listen to me. It's fucking pathetic, isn't it? I'm trying to justify this to you. I know better. There's no justifying this. I can only hope that you are okay with my choice. I'll never know, but I hope so, because it's the only way that I can live with myself."

John slowly got up, hand still firmly gripping Isabel's. "I love you, Bel. I hope you won't forget that because I never will." He wiped his face with his free hand. "It burned me to keep this from you for so long. No secrets, ever. Remember we had that vow between us? Well, I broke that promise. Maybe that's the worst crime of all. But now you know. Now I atoned for committing that sin. I have nothing to hide anymore. Her name is Bethany. Not my favorite name, not as pretty as yours, but honestly I don't think anything really compares with your name. Like I said, she's good to me. She's kind. Understands me for the most part, I think. I feel more alive with her than I ever had in the past year. But I wish I didn't need her to be happy."

John bowed his head, his thoughts following through on his previous statement. "Maybe, just maybe, that I wish I didn't need anybody to be happy. That I don't need you to be happy. Wouldn't life be easier that way? People just wandering around aimlessly, content with their internal desires. What a world, right? Experts keep saying that you should be whole with or without companionship. And I know what you'd say to that." John giggled softly. "You'd say, 'Fuck them. Humans are social creatures. We want to be with others.' And I know you'd be right. A generation of self-obsessed wanderlusting people who are too cool for each other. Fuck, now I'm just ranting."

John closed his eyes, breathing in and out while processing his one-sided discussion. Calmer, he opened his eyes to reconnect with his silent love. "But yeah, people need other people to be happy. And we can't change that. But I do wish I could change who that other person is."

After a gulp, he rubbed his hands around her face and hands and smiled. "But, Isabel, my Bel, I will always love you. Beth may end up becoming my life partner, and we may fall into a deep love, spending the rest of our lives with each other, and it may be great. But she will never have all my heart. And you, you don't have to do anything. You just lying there is enough to make me love you. Who else has it that easy?" Some tears streamed again, but they rained more gently this time.

He patted her hand. "Goodbye, Bel. I'll see you later." Wiping the tears on his sleeve, John stood up. Before he walked out, he leaned over to kiss Isabel on her forehead. With one last smile for that visit, he turned around and left the room.

12

Chapter Twelve

Moving was categorically a hard job, no matter how in-shape one was. Some people moved from home to home frequently, and their experience helped the move go swiftly. Others moved once or twice, a reality affecting John as he set down a box to wipe sweat from his forehead.

"At least this is the last trip," he said between heavy breaths.

"No kidding," said Bethany, who was stretching out her back after moving a small corner table. "You have a lot of stuff, that's for sure."

John had lived in his little duplex for four years. It was the first time on his own, so he had a fondness for the place. Yet it was also his home with Isabel. While there were many beautiful memories there, her absence placed a specter on the apartment. John could still not separate

Isabel from that place.

"Do you need help with that, hon?" asked Bethany.

John shook his head. "Nah, I got it. Thanks though." With a heave, he lifted the box back up and walked it to the short stack of boxes in the living room. John, his arms now free, paced around the room to walk off the fatigue.

Once they became a monogamous couple, John considered getting a new apartment for both emotional and economic reasons. He didn't mind downgrading to a smaller place to save money. Bethany continued to live with her parents but found a part-time job at the same retail store John used to work at. She wasn't happy working at a job she was over-qualified for but managed to accept its reality.

"There's one last thing, I think," said John, his panting easing up.

"Yeah, the dining room table." Bethany walked over to the front door. "Let's get it now and be done with it."

There were nine months between John meeting Isabel and them moving in together. Those nine months seemed like a long time, and nothing felt rushed. John had known Bethany for about a year, yet it wasn't long enough.

However, the alignment of events made the move a smart choice for both of them. John burdened himself by maintaining his duplex how Isabel had left it. He didn't have the heart to do otherwise. He was about to move out when Bethany, wearied by her living situation, decided to rent a room in a shared house closer to her work. It'd force Bethany to enter into a one-year lease, locking her there no matter what happened in the interim.

John had an innate feeling they'd want to move in together eventually, but then they'd have to wait the year. He chose the pragmatic option, pushing their relationship to the next step. A riskier step.

Bethany's SUV proved a convenience, much to John's chagrin. John provided most of the furnishings and supplies from his old apartment, but he opted for a new bed and couch. John crawled inside and grabbed his dining table, while Bethany pulled it from the outside. Once the table was clear of the SUV, John swiveled around so he'd walk backward up the stairs to their new place.

The new apartment was a fourplex not too far from John's old location. Since he was providing the larger chunk of the financial backing, he wanted more of a say over the location, as Bethany wanted to be closer to the suburbs. He made a promise to Isabel, and even though she wouldn't be able to litigate a breach of that agreement, he opted to keep it. City or country, but no in-between.

It was a single floor but had higher square footage than John's old place for roughly the same cost. The economic downturn affected many people, and landlords were willing to ease prices to hold off vacancies. John and Bethany were now experts at carrying large objects up their stairs, and they managed without any significant difficulty. Once inside, they navigated around some box stacks and set the dining table in the dining section. After a quick sigh, John ran to the door and closed it.

"Well, we're done."

Bethany smiled. "Well, that took longer than I expected."

"No kidding." John walked over to Bethany as she leaned against the table. "Last time I moved, we had a lot less stuff with us. We ended up buying almost all our furniture. It was easier, but a hell of a lot more expensive."

"I bet," said Bethany as she touched his arm and leaned in to kiss him. When her eyes opened, she smiled. "How are you doing?"

"Tired." The two laughed. "But fine. You?"

"Okay," she said. "It is a big step. Just hoping we don't kill each other in two months."

John smiled. "I'm glad we share that same concern." He wrapped his arms around his girlfriend and embraced her. They moaned as their hug softened and became more loving.

"But there's so many boxes," said Bethany, pulling both of them out of the moment.

John chuckled. "Yeah, it sucks. We may be eating pizza for a while."

"We're so lazy!" She pulled away from John's body, looked at him in the eye, and smiled.

"It's a shame we don't have a couch yet," said John.

"Or a bed," she said in response.

"Well, you know," said John, mischievousness in his voice, "we do have a new mattress though, and it is in the other room." His hands were getting less casual with her.

She toyed with his hair for a moment before they ran off to the bedroom and made sure the mattress was comfortable for more than sleeping.

While the mattress was fitted with sheets, those sheets were now all over the place. John and Bethany were in a tight, sweaty embrace, breathing heavily again. This time, they didn't mind the physical exertion. They played with each other's hair, giggling stupidly as neither of them could come up with anything to say.

"Well, John, just think," she said, her voice scratchier than usual. "It'll be more fun once we have a frame."

"It's always fun with you," he said, smiling.

Blushing, she reached in to give him a long, loving kiss. She rolled her head to stare at the ceiling. "You're too sweet sometimes. And you know what, when the couch comes, I'll even help you test the legs on that."

That statement shocked John. Bethany's tastes were more vanilla, yet as their relationship matured, she became more amicable to different desires and passions. Isabel was adventurous right away, but at least Bethany had the flexibility to adapt.

"I won't complain too hard about that," said John.

Bethany smiled. "It's amazing to think how far you've grown."

The mood of the room changed. John's calm smile transformed into a concerned frown. Her words were condescending and insulting. Who was she to judge him on those merits?

"What do you mean?" said John sternly.

Bethany picked up on his change in attitude. "I mean, well, you know."

John propped himself up on his elbow. "I don't know what you mean, no."

Sighing, Bethany rolled onto her back. "Great," she muttered under her breath. John left the sarcasm alone. She sighed and continued. "It's nothing. I didn't mean anything by it."

Despite not believing her, John nodded. "Alright then, cool. I'll start on some boxes." He stood up, tried to collect his discarded clothing, and left the bedroom. Fortunately, the box stacks were organized, so he had little difficulty finding what he was looking for.

Starting with the kitchenware, John began taking out all the utensils, cups, knives, pots, and pans and placed them on the counter. They had not yet consulted about how those objects would be stored, but for the time being, he'd organize items similar to how things were in his old kitchen.

A few minutes later, John heard footsteps come out from the bedroom and enter the main room. He heard her stop and what sounded like her opening up some boxes. It was good she was helping out; sometimes labor could simmer arguments.

Isabel and John rarely had arguments, beyond the philosophical and rational. Hypocrisy was explored, double standards exposed, traditions broken down and eliminated. Every debate made John less of a misanthrope. Bethany's views on relationships were more standard. Those conflicts were still uncommon and were of no immediate cause for concern, but the underlying fear of their normalization was legitimate.

Bethany went around the corner about ten minutes later to look at John. He looked back while continuing to unbox the last of the kitchenware.

"Look, John," she said, "I do love you, but you have to know that I only feel that way about you based on how you are now. A year ago you were a freaking wreck."

"And that's supposed to help?"

"No, no, no," she said, her trademark scratchiness coming through more. "I thought I saw something in you that just needed to grow, and I was right."

John crossed his arms. "Glad I could help."

"John, hon, you are a wonderful person, and you've grown so much."

"Okay, hold it right there." Beth stopped, and John sighed as he looked toward the stovetop. "You keep saying that I have grown up, matured since we first met. That I am a better person now than I ever was. You did not know me two years ago. I am the same fucking person I am now as I was then. All this maturing and growing up you're talking about happened years ago."

"John," said Bethany, but John continued.

"You, Beth. You have no idea what I went through. You never even saw the worst of it. I didn't just lose a girlfriend. I lost a partner. I didn't grow up since then. It's just the pain went away. I have always been me."

Bethany had a defeated look on her face as she also looked away. "I... You know. You are right. I may not know what you went through, but dammit, I can be empathetic. It's what I went to school for. And I feel you don't give me enough credit for getting you out of your slump!"

John stared intently at her. "A slump?"

"I healed you!" Bethany said, emphasizing each word. "But I don't want a medal for that. I just want you to realize that I was there for you and that I do try to understand the best I can."

Despite her reassurance, John had an inkling of doubt about whether she'd hold that against him in the future. She was correct, however; she did accelerate his recovery from despair.

"I know you were there. I wanted you there. You did save me, maybe saved my life. And I do love you too, Beth.

But please don't think that you made me something I wasn't before. I am what I was before."

Bethany nodded. "Yeah, I get what you're saying. I'm sorry." She walked over to John, intending to hug him. John accepted the embrace, and they held each other. After a minute of silence, she asked, "When are you going to see her again?"

John sighed. "Well, the move threw off my schedule, but probably after work tomorrow."

Over a year and a half since the tragic accident, John still visited his comatose partner. She was still his partner, and he was still her legal guardian. Because of the move, he hadn't visited her in over a week.

Bethany played with his hair. "I'm just glad that you're still doing that. I know you know, but I'm not jealous." Her inflection was difficult to read.

"Well," said John with a smile, "I keep my promises. And just know that you can trust my promises too."

She smiled. "Yeah, maybe that's why I like it."

Both of them knew if Isabel woke up and had some level of self-awareness, John would run out the door and immediately pledge himself to her. Despite its unlikeliness, it was an unspoken wedge in their relationship. John could sense a slim amount of apprehension in Bethany every time they were on that subject.

Resting her head on his chest, she asked, "Are you still going to put up her things?"

"Yeah," said John. He donated all her clothing to a homeless shelter but kept her personal possessions and crafts in several boxes marked with green ink, her favorite color. Those boxes were worth more to him than anything else he had, and he would take them to the end. His plan was to set up a bookshelf to display her crafts and several photo albums of her. As a compromise to Bethany, none of their couple pictures would be displayed, including the ones at the hot springs. They would still be kept in the boxes underneath everything else.

She nodded. "Good." If the response wasn't genuine, she did a great job at masking the deception. With nothing to worry about, John kissed Bethany on the forehead and returned to unboxing. He was about finished with the kitchen, so she went to the other room to continue what she was working on. Peace was secured, and that satisfied John. Appeasement, a mindset John had repugnant feelings toward for most of his life, was now acceptable.

With the kitchen prepared, he went into the main room with Bethany, trying to figure out what to tackle next. Even though it wasn't important at the moment, John walked to the side of the room with the stack of boxes with the green marks. The bookcase for the shrine was already set up. He adjusted its position to make sure it was out of the way but still visible. With its position secured, John unboxed Isabel's life. She would still live through her art and crafts.

After John worked on the display for some time, Bethany walked over to his side of the room and gave him a big hug from behind. "Hi, babe!" she said, peeking around his shoulder.

"Hey, Beth," said John, who was never sold on the concept of pet names.

"It's looking good." The scratchiness of her voice was more pronounced than usual, which usually indicated honesty. "She was very talented."

John smiled. "Way more than I ever could be."

"You ever wondered what it would be like if our roles were switched?" she asked, continuing to look at Isabel's works and pictures. "If we were married for a few years, I die or go into a coma, and you found her?"

The question made John tilt his head.

"You're actually thinking about this, aren't you?" asked Bethany.

"Yeah, it really piqued my interest," said John. "Never thought about it before."

"Well, one thing I can tell you is that it'd suck for me." They both giggled. John could see Isabel cracking the same joke if she was in Bethany's place. Knowing that his former lover could pass off the dreadful situation with light-hearted gallows humor put a smile on his face. It was comforting, in an odd way.

"You think we'd be married?"

Bethany shrugged. "I mean, yeah, it would be a different relationship. I think without her influence, you'd probably be more open to the idea. But that's just me."

John wasn't sure if that was accurate, but Bethany might have had a point in regard to Isabel's influence. Maybe there were many minor things Isabel influenced John on without him knowing. He always considered himself his own person, but who was he to argue with someone who had education on that subject?

Maybe he was more misogynistic than he thought. Maybe he hadn't grown as much during his relationship with Isabel. Maybe he was still the lonely, bitter, cynical twenty-three-year-old. Maybe he wasn't good enough for her, or for Bethany.

"Yeah, maybe," said John. "But at least you'd know I'd visit you often and would have a shrine erected in your honor."

Bethany laughed. "That's so beautiful. I cannot deny your passion, that's for sure." She then bit into John's shoulder.

"Oww!" yelped John, completely surprised at her course of action. "I'm the one that does the eating around here, not you!"

"Oh, you think so?" she said. "Well, let's order some pizza or something and get through a few of these boxes. Then maybe you can demonstrate that a bit later."

The two exchanged a quick kiss, then returned to their work, with Bethany calling the local pizza delivery shop.

Finishing the display, John opened up the final green-marked box. He didn't take any of the contents out, but he wanted to look at them. The pictures at the hot springs always brought a smile to his face, yet he could never replicate that moment. It was a disgrace that such a work of art was sentenced to such isolation, that John would be the only one to ever appreciate the pictures' beauty.

John had one last quick look at everything else before closing the box. He took it to the closet in their bedroom. It would always be there for him, his own special memory. No one would ever take that away from him. Not even his girlfriend.

13

Chapter Thirteen

John rarely left work in a good mood. Not that work was ever a terrible experience, but most days were average or forgettable. There was some worry in the aftermath of the recent recession, but the news of the day swept away that worry. He couldn't wait to tell Bethany about what happened.

It was her day off, so he wasted little time driving home. Traffic wasn't bad, his venerable car still running well. Despite his excitement, he kept his speed down; he rarely sped or drove recklessly since the accident. He couldn't put his girlfriend through the same ordeal he went through.

He made it to their fourplex quickly. His excitement continued as he ran up their stairs. Almost throwing his keys out of his pocket, he unlocked the door and raced into the house. "Beth! Beth!"

"Yeah?" said a voice from the back. John darted in, initially forgetting about the open door. Going back to shut it gave Bethany enough time to meet John in the hallway. She was still in her pajamas.

He planted a long, deep kiss on Bethany's lips, causing her to give out a muffled cry. When they were done, her face was startled.

"Oh my God, Beth. My boss talked to me today. They're finally giving me a promotion."

Her startled look turned into a face of pure joy as she smiled. "Oh, that's so wonderful!" She hugged him hard. "I'm so proud of you."

"I know. About five damn years with this company. Recession didn't help things, but the company is finally starting to turn around."

The couple ended their embrace, Bethany's face still beaming. "Fuck yeah. You got the management position?"

"Supervisor, but yeah, ain't too shabby. Help out at least while you're looking."

"I know," said Bethany, her face strewn with guilt. "I'm sorry I'm not contributing as much as I should."

"Don't worry about it," said John, still smiling. "It's fine, sweets. I know you're still looking hard for something better too!" He took further note of her pajamas.

"Well it's getting close to the end of the school year so I'm keeping an eye out for districts hiring." She started playing with the buttons on John's shirt. "You know what this means, right?"

"All night of raunchy sex, with you begging me to do unspeakable things to you?"

Bethany laughed. "Well, not to say that can't happen

as well."

"So what do you mean?"

Bethany's gaze fell down toward John's shirt rather than up at his eyes. "Well, with this good news and how long we've been together, we can start looking at things a bit more long term."

"Oh yeah?" John wasn't expecting a serious conversation. "That can mean a million things, honeybun."

"Let's relax a bit first. Want anything to drink?"

"No, I'm good." John took off his light jacket while Bethany went into the kitchen to grab herself some orange juice. John smiled at seeing his girlfriend pouring her cup. He took off his shoes, walked into the main room, sat down on their couch, and sighed. "Okay, Beth, don't keep me on edge."

"Well, I know we're not, like, married or anything like that, so your money is yours and mine is mine. So I feel kind of silly talking about this." She appeared in the room with her glass and sat next to him.

"It's fine. Your words do matter to me."

Bethany smiled. "Thank you. I dunno. I just get so depressed. Been out of college almost two years now, and I'm working a retail job making pennies while my manly man is making the big bucks. It's so old school, and I thought my life would be better by now. And just to think, if it weren't for you, I'd still be at my freaking parents'."

John put a hand on her leg. "Listen, I've told you this many times before. It was the same thing I told Bel. Money is not that big a deal to me like it is for most people. If I'm the breadwinner, whatever. If you are, I don't care. I am in love with you, and that's worth it more than financial fairness or whatever."

Bethany smiled again, this time more sheepishly. "Thank you, John. But that's kind of what I'm talking about." She sighed and closed her eyes. "I am in love with you too. You are slightly strange, but you have a wonderful heart and are kind and… just wonderful. It's crazy to think that we've been together for over a year. But this version of our relationship, I want it to change, to get better."

"Okay," said John, drawing out the last syllable. "I'm still not following."

"Well, let me put it this way," she said. "In five years. We're still together. What's going on? Are we living here? What's happening? Maybe I have a better job. Maybe I don't. Whatever."

John nodded. They had never had a discussion about their long-term future. Isabel had the goal of the country cottage, of independent living, of never marrying or succumbing to the playbook. He assumed the same in this new relationship without realizing that dating a different person would have a different future.

"Well, having a house would be great. But that would have to wait for you to have a better job."

"Of course, hon. Having a house would be great. I knew you always wanted a house, and of course I want one too, so that just went without saying. But… but I'm talking about other things." She paused and put her hands in her lap. "John, do you love me?"

He smiled. "Yes."

"With all your heart?"

"Yes."

"Do you though?"

John was taken aback by that statement. He took his hand off her thigh and positioned himself defensively, creating some distance between the two. Before he got too far, Bethany grabbed his hand and turned to face him.

"I know you love me, John. I love you too. You are my heart's commitment. Am I it for you?"

Stammering, John couldn't answer that question. He finally understood where the conversation was going. The timing wasn't optimal, thanks to the two-year anniversary of the accident recently passing. This was the conversation—the poison—John knew would rise up and present itself like an old wound.

"I've told you that I do believe in marriage personally," continued Bethany, "but I've always been fond of your beliefs too. And they can coexist. Marriage is what you make of it, not what others tell you. I've always agreed with you that most marriages are business agreements, are shams, are forced by religion on us. To me, marriage is the ultimate form of love. Really, we both want the same thing. They're just under different names."

"Are... are you proposing to me?" he asked.

She laughed. "No, silly. I don't want the marriage talk now. Fuck that. Neither of us are ready. I just want to let you know that relationships are compromises. Sometime in the future, we both get what we want, but I just want a little more formality to it."

John grit his teeth. "But the ceremony?"

Now it was Bethany's turn to rub John's thigh. "Oh, John. If we get married someday, we can do whatever the hell we want with the ceremony. Throw together a drum circle. It'll be unique and fun. But that's still not what I'm getting at here." She took a deep breath and continued. "If we're going to commit fully to each other at some point in time, I'm going to fully commit to you, and you will have to fully commit to me."

She turned her gaze to the bookshelf on the side of the room. She stood up to approach it, then picked up a photo album on the top shelf. She opened it. "I know you love her deeply. I know that she will always be important in your life. And I've always told you, truthfully, that I am so glad you have that. And I've told you that a part of me wishes that what happened never did, even if that means I would have never met you."

John looked over at the album in Bethany's hands. He took a deep breath, not wanting to start a confrontation. "So what do you want me to do, Beth? I can't just forget her."

"I'm not asking you to do that. I can't ask you to do that. I don't control you. That's not what love is. Those pictures of her. She's absolutely gorgeous. I always could tell, despite never meeting her, that she was witty and brilliant and funny and just awesome. And I know when you look at those pictures of her, you have those thoughts too."

A surprise tear ran down John's cheek, his eyes fixed on Isabel's shrine. Neither of them acknowledged it.

"You want to know what I think?" she asked. "Your love is of the woman in these pictures. And that's fine. I'm not sure if your love of her is directed toward... well, actual her."

John continued his silence.

"I don't know how the laws of relationships work in

every case. I know that when your significant other dies, your monogamous obligation to that person is freed up and that it's okay for you to see other people. I mean, yeah, it's painful and sucks, but society at large is okay with that. Isabel is, well, still alive. You guys never broke up. What do the relationship laws say about that? Do you treat coma patients like they died?"

"I don't know," said John, now trying to hold back more tears.

She walked back to the couch, holding onto the photo album. Sitting, she reached out and grabbed his hand. "I don't know either. And that's fine that we don't know. But we are both monogamous people. If this is going to become more long term between us, I think you have a conflict of interest going on. And I hate to be frank, but I can start to see myself getting jealous and hurt."

"So what do you want me to do, huh?" said John, his voice becoming angry and defensive. He turned to face Bethany. "Break up with her?"

Bethany smiled with concern on her face. "No, John. No. I can't ask you to do that. I know you don't have it in you. I wouldn't have it in me either. This sucks for you. I'm just here for you."

John nodded as he looked down. "I know."

"You've confided in me that you're conflicted about her future. You've told me that you want your own plug pulled and that I want my plug pulled too. But the two of you never had that talk."

A few more tears escaped his eyes. "We're in our twenties. There was no need for that yet."

"I know." Bethany took that opportunity to wipe a few

tears from his face. "I really feel for her too. There's the hope that in ten, twenty years, doctors will figure out how to fix her. But her body may give out completely before then, and even if she lives long enough, it won't be Isabel. That"—she pointed at the pictures in the opened album—"is Isabel. That is the woman you loved."

He didn't want to admit it, but he started to agree with Bethany. Yes, he still visited the hospital once a week to talk with her, but those visits were slowly turning from conversations with a person to conversations with a tombstone.

"I… don't… know," said John, his words broken up by sobs. Bethany leaned over to give him a hug, but John didn't return the embrace. He continued to sit, torn by his internal struggle.

"What about if she is in great pain?" she asked, whispering into his ear. "Her body is calm, but her brain is suffering."

"I don't want her to be," he said, sniffling.

The couple was silent for a few minutes, to give John time to calm down. Surprisingly, Bethany developed a tear or two herself, and they soaked into John's shirt. Noticing, John pushed her away to look at her face. "Are you okay?"

"Yes!" she exclaimed, laughing under the tears. "Oh, John, I love you. Here you are, having a bad time, and you still care about me."

"I try," he said. "I love you too. I'm sorry I'm so indecisive."

"Well, my love, I don't want you to make any decisions now. I want you to think about this. It's only fair to you and to her. But if I'm going to be callous enough to offer a suggestion, she has been like this for two years. A long time with no improvement."

"Maybe," said John.

Bethany looked toward the front of the room. "Sorry I threw this on you today. You came home to celebrate, and we can still do that. I just… The whole love and marriage thing, I've been thinking about that since Nick and Michelle's divorce. How awful that relationship was, how awful that kid's future is going to be. No way in hell do I want that for us. But at the same time, it got me thinking more about us and how things can maybe work out for us if we do a few things. It's just… We both want one on one with each other, but it's not fair that I give you my commitment when, well, when I don't have yours."

"I know," John said with defeat in his voice.

She nodded. "But we both are honest about this and have put on the table what we want. I think that's great. Not many couples can do this. Believe me, after all the couples I worked with during senior year, what we have ain't common."

John always compared Bethany to Isabel. What he had with Isabel was unique, but it would never happen again. Hopelessly maintaining that for so long was wearing him down, a long struggle that made him jaded about love. He didn't want that attitude to transfer to what was otherwise a great relationship. It wasn't fair to Bethany. It was as if clinging onto Isabel was poisoning his life.

He never imagined fantasy being poisonous and conformity being the antidote. John living his fantasy of half-dating a glorified cadaver would force him to throw away a terrific thing. Bethany was delightful, and a dispassionate analysis would tell him she was right. Yet sacrificing some of his values in the process would be a lot for him to consider.

"How are you doing?" she asked softly.

John nodded. "I'm okay. Thank you for talking to me."

"Thank you for being you," she said, smiling. "I wouldn't have it any other way."

"Really?" he asked.

She kissed him on his lips with careful precision. "Of course!" Leaning back, she smiled. "I'm so glad you got that raise."

John laughed. "Switched back to that so easily, huh?"

Shrugging, she said coyly, "I mean, today should have been about that. So let's make the rest of the day a celebration. What would you like to do, babe?"

"And I'm assuming I'm paying?" he said with a sly grin on his face.

"I'm not broke, you know!" She poked him on the nose. "What would you like to do? I mean, we both haven't eaten yet. Let's go out! Where do you want to go?"

"Well, there's that new cider bar that even you loved. They got great drinks and food!"

"Perfect, I love that place!" she said. "Let me get some proper attire so I don't embarrass you."

As she left to go into the bedroom, John remained seated on the couch, having a moment of sedentary relaxation. It was the middle of the week, so he'd likely have to deal with work the next day with little sleep.

Bethany was quick to get back into the room, having undergone a swift transformation. Her hair was down in its curly glory, and she was wearing a maroon sundress tied around the waist. It was the first warm day of the year, so she took advantage of it.

"Ta-da!" she said, eliciting brief laughter from both of them.

"Damn, Beth," he said, "you always look so good."

She walked over to the couch. "So do you."

John stood up and adjusted his button-up shirt. "We're just so attractive we can't help it."

Bethany laughed. "Well, yeah."

They held each other in their arms, although this embrace wasn't one of comfort, but more of affection. Their heads bowed, leaning on each other's foreheads, as their hands caressed each other's arms and shoulders. Soon, this turned into a kiss, which made Bethany moan slightly.

"You know, if we bow to our instincts, we'll never leave this apartment tonight," she said, her scratchiness more pronounced.

"By that logic," replied John, "we may never leave this apartment again."

"Death by unrestricted sexual pleasure."

"Sounds good," said John. "With that being said, I am kind of excited for cider."

Bethany giggled. "Yeah, that does sound good. Then maybe you for dessert?"

John shrugged. "Desserts are small. I'll have you for a second course. Maybe a third."

"Ooooh, I like that line," she said. "I'll drive."

The couple got their keys and wallets and headed out the door. John had some tough decisions to make, but tonight was about him, and there was no one he wanted to celebrate it with more than Bethany. His career was gaining importance in his life, and he knew Bethany would find one soon. She was young and had plenty of time to blossom.

14

CHAPTER FOURTEEN

"And just one last signature here," said the nurse, holding back the other papers on the clipboard to expose the bottom page.

John felt his hand trembling as he etched his name. There were many fail-safes in the process, and he had to remind himself his signature was just another step.

"How are you feeling? Doing okay?" asked the nurse, grabbing the clipboard once John was done signing.

"Nope," said John, a feeling of sickness growing in his stomach. "Part of me felt like I should have done this two years ago."

"Well, if I was to give you my opinion on this, whether you did it two years ago or now, either way, it's the right decision." He took the clipboard and pinned it in his armpit. "I'll go get Dr. Holsteen for you."

The nurse turned around and disappeared around the corner. John stood by himself at the desk. He wanted to do this alone. As comforting as it would be for Bethany to be there, it was his burden. Bethany had never met Isabel, and it would remain that way. John wanted to be alone with her one last time, a time that would be all he'd ever have for the rest of his life. He couldn't squander the moment; he kept his focus on all the details, to memorize every sight and sound. If he messed anything up, there was no turning back, no repeating the moment. It was now John's responsibility to keep her alive, but in a different, more noble way.

Dr. Holsteen had been a doctor in that department since Isabel got transferred there for her long-term stay. John didn't talk to the staff much at first but grew to respect them. He trusted nobody else to do what needed to be done. Dr. Holsteen switched departments a few months earlier but agreed to do this for him.

Several minutes went by, and Dr. Holsteen came through the door behind John. He turned to look. She was short, her hair slightly grayed from the passage of time. Neither of them smiled, but the rest of their faces communicated an understanding of the situation. "How are you doing?"

John's eyes focused on the tiled floor. "Not well."

"Come this way," she said, and he followed her as they took a stroll down the hallway, toward the room he had visited hundreds of times in the past couple of years.

"I've been mentally preparing for months," said John, noting their slow, strolling pace down the hall. "I thought I would be more ready."

"Doesn't matter how long it was. No one is ever ready.

I've seen it a thousand times, but the pain on the faces I see never gets easier. And for as long as you've been here to visit her, I know this one means a lot."

"Thank you for doing this," he said softly. There was a scratchiness to his voice that reminded him of Bethany.

"It's just you today? Never did find her family?"

John shook his head. "I did a little bit of searching, but it's not my thing. I don't think she'd want them here anyway."

"No friends either?"

"I'm still in contact with a few of our friends. I'll make sure they come to the service." John sighed. "But I want to be alone with her one last time."

"Understandable," Dr. Holsteen said. They had stopped in front of a familiar door. She looked at John for a brief moment before asking, "If you want to be alone for a moment, I'll wait right out here until you're ready."

"Thank you," whispered John. He closed his eyes, let out a burdened sigh, and reached his hand to the handle. Dr. Holsteen turned her back to the wall to lean against it and had a sigh of her own. She was probably annoyed at having to wait herself. He didn't care much for her annoyance. This was his moment. This was Isabel's moment.

Opening the door to a familiar sight, John stepped into the room. The atmospheric noises were different; lots of distant chatter and subdued cacophony filled the hallway, but in this chamber, the respirator unit dominated. Air being pushed in, air being pushed out. Constant clockwork for over two years.

"Hello, Bel," said John. He didn't pay heed to the fact that it was the last time he'd say that to her living body.

The lights were off, but the blinds were open, and it was a sunny autumn day.

The sound of his footsteps punctuated the dull hum of the machine. Isabel physically remained the same, permanently in a state of tepid calm. John had fantasized she would perpetually look like that for as long as she was in a coma; he'd be eighty years old, his body decaying, his friends dying, yet Isabel would remain a young woman in her mid-twenties. He knew that wouldn't be the case. Isabel would age as he would. Her body would naturally deteriorate as it silently marched through the field of time. She'd gray alongside him, her wrinkles matching his. She'd suffer from aging without enjoying the wonderful life age afforded the conscious.

Some point along the way, Isabel would make the decision to give up. In a way, she already had. Minutes after her accident, her body made that choice. It was through good hearts and competent technology that an extension was allowed.

"How are you?" asked John, kneeling beside the bed. Her hand was already above the blanket, lying out in front of him. It was as if she knew he was coming and had readied her hand to be held. Not refusing the invitation, he grabbed her lukewarm hand, embracing her body heat that was soon to go away. "It's been... a hard couple of weeks. I'm sorry I haven't visited you in a while. If I saw your face, I don't know if I could have gone through with what I'm doing. What we're doing."

Crying, he wiped his cheek with his other hand. "I love you, Bel. I've told you that a thousand times. You've told that to me a thousand times, enough to know that you still mean it. I've been wishing that you would wake up. But I've also been so afraid. What if you did? Two years gone, and my life is different. It's getting more different every day. Your life is frozen. Your life will always be that moment, that afternoon in April. As much as I want to continue sharing that moment with you, I look back and see that it's fading away. Slowly. So slowly. I didn't realize it at first, and it hurt when I started thinking about it. I don't think it will ever not hurt.

"But I'm not even sure anymore, Bel. I'm not sure if I want to go back to that time with you. We weren't where we wanted to be. There was so much more life and growth in us. It's not right that you got stuck. Maybe that's why I'm sad. Our times are no longer aligned. It's harder and harder to share moments with my younger self, because that's all I've been doing." He shed more tears.

"Beth... Beth is aligned with me though. The alignment isn't as good. It needs adjustments every once in a while. But our lives are linked. There's no two-year gap between us. Oh, Bel, that gap is just going to grow harder and harder. I do love Beth, and there is a future for us. It's not the future you and I had planned, but it is a future. And it hurts me that you were robbed of that."

He sniffled. His eyes watered to the point he could barely make out his lost love. "You know that saying 'time heals'? I think it's bullshit. Pain never dies. The pain of losing you will never die. But pain will stretch. It's always there to hurt us, to hurt me, but it'll get stretched out. I hope my memories of you won't stretch in the same way."

John wiped his eyes to focus his vision. "Anyway. I love you, and I know you've been in so much pain. It was fucking selfish of me to keep you in this state. It was wrong, and it's time I make it right. I don't want you to suffer anymore." His vision blurred yet again. "I love you, Bel. I love you. I love you, I love you, I love you."

His words blended into crying. He was no longer capable of vocalizing his most inner feelings. He knew this was the last moment, and words utterly failed him.

After several minutes of solid crying, John regained control and took another look at Isabel. He managed a smile. "I'm going to get the doctor in here. She's going to make you better." He ran his fingers along her hairline. After a beat, he leaned forward to kiss her forehead, still with the slight prayer she'd respond with a stir or a muffled moan. When that prayer exhausted itself, John stood up, letting go of her hand, and walked to the door.

He opened it, and Dr. Holsteen was dutifully waiting for him. She gave him a look, probably noting the reddened eyes and blushed face. John nodded. "We're ready."

Dr. Holsteen had a half-smile on her face, one not necessarily of acknowledgment, but of sadness. She walked into the room. John shut the door behind her and walked back to where he once was. He remained standing. Dr. Holsteen moved to the other side of the bed and fiddled with the vitals monitor. She was shutting off the alarms and speakers so it didn't disturb the fragile peace.

Once it looked like everything was ready, Dr. Holsteen took one look at John and asked, "As Isabel's legal guardian, do I have permission to take her off of her life support?"

After all the signatures and meetings, the lectures and legal work, this was the final fail-safe. This was the hardest decision John had ever made in his life. He doubted anything would come close; even if it was Bethany, he at least had her permission in advance. Once he went past that line, there was no return, and John would have to dedicate himself to the rest of his life. His hesitation choked his breathing. His mouth went dry. He had committed to this decision weeks earlier and had no plans of backing out. But once again, emotion strangled logic into submission.

All those thoughts happened within a moment. Then, with a soft stutter, John said, "Y-Yes."

Dr. Holsteen looked down at Isabel's lifeless body, which only moved when the machine filled her lungs with air. She grabbed the mask and began undoing the straps. "Alright, Isabel, I'm going to take your breathing mask off, if that's alright with you. It should make you more comfortable." Dr. Holsteen was a professional and conducted the operation with little emotion. Perhaps it was a defense mechanism against her true inner turmoil, or maybe she had been desensitized after all her years.

The mask came off, and Dr. Holsteen set it aside on the table. For the first time since she walked down those stairs to leave for her friend's house, John saw Isabel unobstructed, her entire face free to the world. Her lips were badly chapped from the years of the mask, but it was the same Isabel John ran into at the pub, nearly knocking over their drinks. It was the same Isabel that invited him to her home to cook them dinner. It was the same Isabel that made love to him. It was the same Isabel that kissed him. It was the same Isabel that made him think. It was the same Isabel that gave him the world.

"Oh, Bel!" cried out John. The familiar sight of her stomach rising and falling ceased. There was no reaction, no gasps for air, no autonomous movement. Isabel remained passive in her bed. John's watery eyes kept looking for a response that never came. Her eyes opening, her mouth moving. Maybe it was the machine that kept her comatose. Maybe all she needed was to free her body from the machine. But with all those last hopes fading into the past, John had but one wish. Even if she was passing beyond the realm of the living, an inevitability that was impossible to stop, he only wanted a proper goodbye. Isabel acknowledging it was her time to sleep forever. A word, or a look, or a touch. Something to let him know so he could truly accept her passing.

Nothing.

He glanced over at the vitals monitor. There was a disturbing lack of sound coming from it, but the visuals were still apparent. Dr. Holsteen was studying it. Everything from heart rate to blood pressure was falling. Isabel's body was finally slowing down, ending its perpetual suffering.

John looked back at Isabel. Of all the senses, the body's ability to hear and interpret sound was the last to go as the body transitioned to eternal darkness. If Isabel could truly hear John for the past two years, then this moment would be no different. But this moment was in haste.

"Goodbye, Bel."

He knew that Isabel, with how much she loved him, would want to end her life hearing his voice.

"I love you so much. I will always be here for you. I will never forget you. I don't care if I spend decades with someone else. I will never forget you. You have my soul. You are my life. You are... my... Isabel."

Without checking back on the vitals, without caring

what Isabel's condition was, without seeking the approval from Dr. Holsteen, John leaned over and for the last time kissed her on the lips. Her lips were parched, but John did not care. She didn't reciprocate, but John did not care. He hadn't kissed her like this since before the accident, and it was going to be his final living memory of his partner. He hoped, however unlikely, this was her final living memory of him.

After what seemed like an eternity, John released the kiss. He whispered, "I love you." He then stood straight up. There were no audible cries, only occasional tears. John's eyes fixed themselves on the monitor, seeing the dangerously low readings. He gripped Isabel's hand. Her heart was stopping, but he still felt warmth. There was still blood pressure, but it was minimizing. John tried to control his breathing as a massive panic attack loomed closer. Calling on his yoga training, he slowed his breathing but retained a tight grip around her hand.

A long minute went by. John's eyes going back and forth between Isabel and the monitor. Dr. Holsteen's flitted between the monitor and John. Utter silence. When that minute went by, Dr. Holsteen took one last look at the life signs and nodded. She punctuated the stillness with her voice. "I think it's time." She looked down at her watch. "I'm calling it now: 5:38."

Isabel was dead.

John remained frozen, holding her hand. He gave no reaction. He only focused on her unchanging face. Dr. Holsteen waited for his move, but not finding it, she continued. "I'll get the guys to take her out of here. We'll let you know after the arrangements are met."

Without a nod, John lowered Isabel's hand onto her body, making sure to set it down gently. With no acknowledgment, he left the room. It wasn't just his body that was leaving; he could feel his emotions chasing after him. He didn't want them to catch up, to stab him in the heart and leave his body broken. Through his brisk pace, he couldn't feel his legs. It was as if he was floating through the hallway.

John left the building. It was still light outside, and the sun was unwelcoming. It was not raining. At no other point in his life did John want the rain to fall more than in that moment. That prolonged moment offered no mercy to his situation. There was no time to calculate, to plan. His only option was to continue flying away from the finality of his decisions.

Without a drizzle to hide his pain, he rushed to his car. He had forgotten where he parked, as his mind wasn't focusing. Eventually he found it, extricating himself from that horrific place. He would never visit that hospital again.

His drive was random, lacking any sense of priority. He didn't exceed any speed limits, but he made some poor choices in regard to turning. He heard a lot of car horns, but he ignored every one. None of those irate drivers knew what had happened. To them, they were expressing outrage at an awful driver who needed to go back to driver's ed and learn the gravity of their ineptitudes. To John, those drivers were not in his life.

There were many things missing in his life at that moment. But there were also many good things in his life. He needed time to rediscover them.

A whole day passed, the sun rose and set, and John remained in a haze; his memories weren't locking in. He stumbled through his apartment door, not sure how late it was. His answer came when he found himself in the doorway of his bedroom, seeing Bethany in bed, looking at him as he walked in. She had a book in her lap. John could imagine what was going through her mind and how disheveled he appeared to her. He was sure he wasn't a pleasant sight.

"Hey," said Bethany.

John leaned against the doorframe. "Hey."

Bethany breathed in heavily. "How are you?"

He looked down at himself. "Can't you tell?"

"Did you do it?" she asked.

John folded his lips into his mouth in a poor attempt to mask emotion. "Yes."

Silence fell over the room. "Honey. I'm so sorry."

He nodded, his eyes still focusing everywhere but on her. "Thank you."

"You were gone longer than I was expecting."

"Well," said John, "I told you I needed some time alone afterward. It just… took a while."

She tilted her head. "John, you're exhausted. You need to sleep."

"Maybe," he said in response, wondering if it was snark-iness or delirium dictating his speech.

"You don't have any burdens anymore," she said. "I know you may not think that to be a good thing. But she's free now. I know that's what you wanted."

"I'm never sure what I want." John hobbled to the bed. "Except for one thing."

"What is that?" she asked.

John sat down on the bed, right next to Bethany. He looked up and down the outline of her body underneath the covers. Eventually, he made eye contact with his girlfriend. She was the only one in his life now.

"John? Is everything alright?"

"I love you, Beth."

She flashed a smile after hearing his weary words. She had heard them many times before, but this time there was something different behind them. Despite his exhaustion, there was a certainty in his voice. "I... I love you too, hon."

"I am tired as fuck right now, and I had the second-worst day of my life yesterday. I really feel like shit. But I'm sorry about the emotional rollercoaster I put you through."

"Shhh!" hissed Bethany before placing her hand on John's back. "Never apologize to me about that. It de-legitimizes your feelings for her, and I know you don't want that."

"But now I have to look forward," said John. "You are now the only person I love who draws a breath. You are more important to me than anyone else, and I don't want to lose that."

She smiled again.

"So this isn't probably how you thought this would happen when you were a kid, but..." And John stopped, closing his eyes. He took a deep breath and sighed. Another decision of great importance weighed on him. He opened his eyes and looked straight at Bethany. "Beth, do you want to get married?"

Her smile was accented by a small bit of exposed teeth. A tear came down her eye before she responded. "John, you don't have to do this now."

"I know," said John, "but we've been ready for this for a long time. You and I both know that. I would have asked months ago, but I knew you didn't want to while there was someone else. I think I'm finally ready to spend the rest of my life with you. Hopefully."

Bethany laughed at his addendum. When she calmed down, she got out from under the sheets, crawled to John, and hugged him. "That's so you. I love it."

John returned the embrace with a tight squeeze of his own.

She continued. "Yeah, this isn't the romantic on-the-knee-in-Paris proposal, but that's not you. I love the real you. And this is perfect." She waited a beat. "Yes."

15

Chapter Fifteen

John was glad to get out of the early-summer sun. It wasn't sweltering, but the late-afternoon temperature was still uncomfortable. All the decisions going into the wedding were a matter of many compromises. That John agreed to have a wedding at all put a lot of decisions in his favor, but Bethany still insisted on scheduling it during the sunny season.

"So much cooler in here," he said, scanning the reception hall. It was already filling up with his guests.

"You and your rain and clouds, man," said Sam, sipping on a wine glass.

John looked at his coworker. "Think you've known me too long, Sam. It's time to kill you."

Sam elbowed John in the ribs, cracking a smile. "You know it. Gotta find where my wife ended up. You should find where your wife is too!"

Your wife. It was the first time John had heard that phrase. Not "your girlfriend," "your partner," "your fiancé," "your future wife." But just "your wife." It hadn't even been half an hour yet. Both John and Bethany were secularists, so the officiant was nonreligious. There were many things that differed from a traditional ceremony. John didn't feel comfortable with the way brides were given off by their fathers to their future husbands like they were property, an anachronism that should have died centuries earlier. Not only did Bethany's father walk her down the aisle, but John's mom walked him down the aisle right afterward.

"Congratulations!" said Amanda, who walked up to him. She was an old friend of Isabel's. "Damn if that wasn't the best wedding ceremony ever. I loved how the two of you walked down the aisle."

John smiled. "Thanks, Amanda. And thank you for coming. It's been a while."

"Yeah, I don't think we've seen you since the cremation," she said.

"Yeah, it's definitely better circumstances this time around."

Amanda had a long look in her eye. "Well, this is the happiest I've seen you in years. This Beth chick seems pretty cool. We need to hang out with the two of you guys. I don't know why we haven't done it yet."

John shrugged. He knew the reason. Amanda and her husband Jacob were joint friends with Isabel and John. Once Isabel was out of the social equation, it would have been weird to continue having couples' nights. So much time had passed, and it was time to move forward.

It was also awkward to be talking about John's deceased partner at his wedding with his second partner. But Isabel was Amanda's friend first. It made sense for her to come up in conversation, even at that particular time.

"Well, honeymoon's pretty short. When we get back, let's do the first Friday."

"Sounds good, John." She looked around the room. "I'll find your wife. You should find a drink."

His wife. John wasn't sure if he was comfortable with the implication of ownership. It was one of the many reasons Isabel abhorred the concept, a reason she passed on to John. Yet Bethany wanted the title, and her presence in his life was worth many compromises. The music came on, and John found himself over at the open bar on the other side of the hall. It was a smaller wedding, about thirty guests, so the room didn't need to be extravagant. They were hesitant to have an open bar due to the expense, but John's parents covered the cost, chiefly because they wanted one in case they didn't get along with Bethany's side of the family.

"Congratulations, man," said the bartender. He had a nice buttoned-up shirt, but his sleeves were rolled up, revealing numerous tattoos on his arms. Not something John expected to see at a wedding.

"Thanks, appreciate it. Oh shit, I don't have my wallet on me, otherwise I'd tip you."

"Hey, it's cool, man. I do these weddings where these early twenty-something bachelorette chicks who weigh a hundred pounds get totally trashed, and they don't tip shit. Your crowd is a lot better, so don't feel bad."

"You're a good man, my friend," said John. "Well, it

looks like you got my favorite cider, so I'll have that."

The bartender smiled as he opened the appropriate bottle. "Funny coincidence, considering you guys picked the drink list." He handed over the bottle. "Cheers."

As soon as John took a sip, a body pressed against him from the back, arms reaching around to trap his torso. "What are you doing?" asked a scratchy voice.

John smiled as he turned around. "I am enjoying what we paid for, my sweets."

"Oh yeah?" asked Bethany. Despite the special occasion, she didn't do much to her hair. She had grown it out since the proposal, so it was the longest John had ever seen it. The blonde curls covered her exposed shoulders, and she looked fantastic. She wore a simple strapless yellow dress, opting to avoid the usual bland white. "You know, people drink wine at weddings."

John himself wore a brown suit with a pastel yellow shirt. Also unorthodox for a wedding, but the look complemented his wife well. "Well, I guess you didn't marry a person!"

She laughed. "Never thought I'd be a trailblazer in cross-species relationships!" She looked over at the bartender. "Hey, looks like you have some Pinot ready!"

He looked down at the display of filled glasses in front of him. "I wouldn't get the gigs if I weren't good at them."

Bethany grabbed a wine glass and raised it to him. "Well, I wish you good fortune in your life." She turned around to give John a quick kiss while Amanda walked over to them.

"Well, why am I not surprised?"

Bethany blushed a bit as she turned to face Amanda.

"Sorry, but this nonhuman I picked up at a coffee house is just too damn hot."

While the two began a conversation, John saw a familiar face in the corner of the room, seated alone at one of the tables. He was sipping on a beer and had a lonely look on his face. Not wanting anybody to feel left out at his party, John walked over and pulled up a seat next to him.

"Hey," said Nick. While he had groomed and dressed up for the occasion, there was an underlying aura about him that told astute observers that many things weren't right in his life.

"Hey," said John in response. They both took a swig of their respective bottles. "Thanks so much for being best man. I know it's rough for you."

"Dude, you were the best man at my wedding. Of course I was going to do it for you." Nick stared away at the wall. "Damn. Been about four years since I got married. Man, how time flew. You remember that?"

John nodded. "Yeah, it was a bit bizarre. Michelle's family was a tad bit weird."

"Not just her family," said Nick, taking another drink from his beer. "She was crazy too. I remember Isabel taking me aside and saying that she'd buy me an unlimited supply of condoms to keep that family from reproducing more."

John laughed hysterically, enough to catch the attention of nearby guests. "Oh man. I did not know that. Neither of you ever told me that story."

Nick shrugged. "At the time, whatever. I think it's much funnier now." He paused, collecting his thoughts. "Sorry to bring her up today."

"No, it's fine," said John as he waved his hand. "Some of our old friends are here too. Haven't seen them since I sprinkled her ashes at the hot springs."

"That was a rough day," noted Nick, who also witnessed the sorrowful event. He looked behind John and toward Bethany and Amanda. "But it looks like they're liking her okay. She's a good woman. In the time I was with Michelle, you were two for two with your ladies."

"Have you talked to her recently?"

Nick blew a heavy sigh through his narrowed mouth. "Not really. I visit our kid once per week. I don't talk to her much when I visit. Things are pretty awkward."

"Well, you know. Before Isabel, remember how I was a third wheel to the two of you? Well, you're always welcome to come over and hang out with us. Bethany loves you."

Nick gave a half-smile. "Thanks. It's rough right now. Couch-surfing, doing odd jobs here and there. But I think I can have fun every once in a while."

The reception proceeded without unplanned hijinks. Some of the older family members were dancing, but otherwise, socializing was the favored sport among the younger crowd. So as to not be embarrassing, toasts were kept to a minimum. Nick and Bethany's best woman, Chloe, gave flattering speeches about the newlyweds. While Chloe was quite inebriated, Nick was strangely sober. The time since the divorce had led to many drunken nights. Fortunately, he kept his count down that night.

"I love you, Beth!" screamed Chloe into her mic.

"I love you, Chloe!" Bethany yelled back.

"I love you too, Beth!" screamed out a faceless male voice from the crowd. Everybody laughed.

With the speeches over, the music came back on, and it was time for the reception photographs. It was early evening, but the daylight was still strong, so Misty, being the official photographer, shuttled everybody so the light from the glass wall would illuminate them. She had also taken the official wedding pictures earlier. John never told Bethany that Misty was the one who shot the pictures at the hot springs. It might not have been appropriate for her to know the connection. Ironically, these new pictures were going to end up being John's replacements for the hot springs shoot. New pictures that would hopefully never see the depths of a cardboard box.

The small crowd began trickling out, so it was time to end things. Chloe and John's parents would handle the aftermath, freeing the couple to go on their way. Everybody who was still there took one last toast, and the couple ran to their car. They opted not to go for the rice farewell. The two waved as they made it to Bethany's car. John was about to get inside the driver's side when Bethany pushed him aside.

"Hey, buddy, I'm driving!"

"Oh yeah?" he said, not offering much resistance.

"I don't need no man!" she said. The two laughed as they got into their respective sides of the car, and they drove out of the parking lot.

"Well!" said John as he looked at the world speeding past him out the window. "I guess I'm married."

"You know, if you're getting cold feet now, we're not going that fast. I'm sure you'll only break a few bones rolling out."

"It's a technique I've been mastering for some time."

He looked over at Bethany. They both smiled.

"You know," she said, "I'm really freaking hungry right now."

John was puzzled. "Oh?"

"Yeah, like, I need food food." She spent a moment making a right-hand turn onto another road. "We just had some snacks and stuff. And drinks. Everyone else is probably gonna go out and get dinner. Why not us?"

"In our wedding clothes?" asked John.

Bethany shrugged. "Sure, I mean, why not? This is what we did for prom. Show up in our ridiculous dresses to eat at Applebee's. And besides, it's not like I'm wearing a traditional wedding dress anyway. Most people would just think I'm a bridesmaid or something."

John gave Bethany a hint of side-eye. "I didn't know you went to prom."

She laughed. "Yeah, once. Had my date pay for everything, since we were so poor."

"Yeah, I never went to prom. Thought it was dumb."

"Well, let's at least get an appetizer at a pub. I know that would make you happy."

They made a quick stop at a nearby brewpub. Ordering some chicken strips and a round of lagers, the couple made quick work of their basic meal. Some curious bystanders recognized their odd clothing, but no one said anything. Since Bethany was driving, John paid the bill, and they were back on the road.

Their travels led them out of the city and into the surrounding countryside. They had booked their wedding night at a nice country inn in a small town about an hour away. Bethany drove slightly faster than John would have, but the excitement of the day made it easy for him to ignore. By the time they arrived, the sun had set behind the mountains, casting a red hue along the western sky.

The hotel itself was right along a creek. It was small, about ten rooms. The lobby was still open, so the couple dashed in to check in. It was a quick and painless process.

"You kids look a little old for prom," said the attendee behind the counter. She wasn't much older than John.

"Yeah, they permit dads to go with their daughters," said a quick-witted John. Bethany started cackling hysterically.

Blushing, the attendee handed the keys and papers to the couple. "Here you go. Checkout is at 11:30. Um, have a good stay!"

There was a five-year age gap between the two. Topping things off, John had joined the Thirty Club earlier that year. Although it was an obvious joke, it was rooted in reality. His parents already had him by that age. The newlyweds hadn't spoken about children yet, but John knew the pressures society placed on married couples. Was that another step he had to surrender to at some point?

They found their room and unlocked the door. John turned on the lights as Bethany brought in their two suitcases. It wasn't a super-fancy or large room, but still a far cry from the cheap highway motels John frequented when he was a child. There was a welcoming queen-sized bed surrounded by wooden fixtures and ornamentation. Pictures of wildlife and nature occupied the walls. There was a small kitchenette on the side of the room, in addition to the bathroom on the far side. Drawn curtains covered the window that looked over the creek, darkened by the night.

Bethany ran off to the bathroom, having contained herself all day while drinking wine and the beer they had at the pub. John didn't have to go, so he walked over to the bed. He sat down on it and bounced. It was softer than their bed at home, a nice change from the usual. Kicking off his shoes, he was about to lie back when Bethany emerged from the bathroom. She had a mischievous look on her face.

"Hey, babe," she said, softly and seductively.

"Hey, sweets." John had a feeling where the evening was going.

With a sway in her steps, Bethany walked over to where John was sitting. Her movement drew John's attention to her hips. "So now that we're married, I suppose I have to start performing my wifely duties, huh?"

John looked up at her face. "Start? You've been holding back on me?"

Smiling, she kneeled on the ground, laying her arms on his thighs and looking into his eyes. "Well, I've been holding back all day. God, you looked so hot today."

"You're so fucking gorgeous in that dress," he said, feeling his heart flutter. They had made love hundreds of times in the two and a half years they had been a couple. He wasn't sure why he was nervous. "It's a shame our guests don't know how fucking beautiful you look out of it."

Bethany leaned forward and kissed John with deep, calm intensity. They began exploring each other as their heart rates increased. She backed off of John before he was able to control the situation. She lowered herself, locking her eyes on John while she undid his pants. Her eye contact didn't stop as she lowered her mouth onto him.

John leaned back and propped himself on his elbows, worshipping Bethany with colorful language. She'd occasionally stop and giggle. Right before the point of no return, she stopped. Displaying faux fury, John picked her up and threw her onto the bed. They wrestled before they found themselves in the opposite position; this time Bethany was lying on her back, her eyes having difficulty focusing on anything while John worked his own style of magic. The two of them were experts at this point in their relationship, knowing what to do at the exact pace and rhythm.

John was still distracted by his nervousness; it wasn't overt, but there were small flutters. However, his confusion wasn't enough to distract himself from his duties as a newly christened husband.

When Bethany had been satisfied, the two continued their wrestling. This time, though, the wrestling was more of an excuse to put each other into different positions and for John to spend time inside his wife. Eventually, John found himself on top of her in the traditional position. Bethany's eyes were focused on John, but John continued to be distracted and had trouble meeting her gaze.

The cause of his unease became apparent as soon as he climaxed. Letting out a loud yell, Bethany gasped as she witnessed her husband's orgasm. When he finished, his mind was clear. He was now married. He consummated his marriage with his wife. He never planned for this to happen. There wasn't supposed to be a wife. He wasn't supposed to be married. That was what he had discussed with Isabel, through hours of thought-provoking conversation. Even though his thoughts of love and affection were toward Bethany at that hour, he betrayed his old partner. He betrayed the love they had. A love never invalidated or second-guessed in the years since her accident.

What would Isabel think of John letting go of his convictions? Her hypothetical disappointment entered John's mind and poisoned his soul. John had convinced himself marriage was a new stage, a new experience, distinct from untitled courtship. His nerves were a reflection of that newfound belief.

Was Isabel correct? Did he buy into the sham? Did he make a mistake? John loved Bethany and didn't wish to hurt her. Marrying her was the right choice; it was the only choice.

He did, however, hurt Isabel. He broke into sudden tears.

"Oh, John," whispered Bethany, cradling the back of his head in her hand. He rested the side of his face on her upper chest and continued to cry. Tears flowed and formed waterfalls, building paths along the curves of her skin.

"Oh, John. It's okay," she continued. Her words were enough to tell John she knew why he was crying. She wasn't a perfect psychologist, but she knew her husband. He'd recover in a short time, and their emotions could move forward. All that was needed was time.

16

CHAPTER SIXTEEN

Following another sleepless night, John completed yet another day at his job. Corporate America dictated he continue his labors unabated, so he dutifully fulfilled his obligations to the machinery of society. He had been at his current position for over two years; even though he recognized that upward mobility was usually glacial in its pace, he'd still get impatient.

After shutting down his work computer, he left his office and walked into the parking lot. His car had started giving him troubles, and he wasn't sure if he should continue putting bandages on the endless issues or get a new vehicle. It was a decision he could afford either way. Buying a new car conflicted with his belief in sustainability, but his decision would ultimately come down to the needs of his life.

His conversation with Bethany about long-term goals led them to getting married and to solidifying their future together. That future was an unchanging monolith on the horizon. He had still not achieved his goals of owning a home and moving forward with his life. John thought that future was soon, yet they were still at the same fourplex they had been renting for several years.

The car started okay. Sighing again, John steered the vehicle out of the parking lot and onto the road. It was overcast, the glow of the sun spreading evenly across the cloud cover. It had been raining for the past several days, but the precipitation had eased up. Some of the roads were still stained with moisture, yet it wasn't enough to make the roads slick.

Bethany had been at her retail job long enough to get some seniority perks of her own. She was getting more hours and had some pay raises based on added responsibilities. She still made nowhere near the wage she'd make as a counselor, but there was at least some progress on her financial front. She had toyed with the idea of going back to school to get a master's degree, since that was what many of her friends had been doing. However, it would put the house on hold for at least another three years. Now that she was married to John, she'd also no longer qualify for many of the low-income grants she received as an undergrad. Student loans were a nightmare the two wanted to avoid at all costs.

Despite the potential financial issues, John was still in love with Bethany. They recovered from their disastrous wedding night, although he took a little while to find his sexuality again. Things had been going well much as they had before; the familiarity that plagued many couples hadn't affected their physical relationship. John had also crossed a new threshold in his life; he had now been with Bethany longer than he had been with Isabel. Isabel's shrine was still in the side of their main room; he refused to let his marriage interfere with that.

Their social life had also taken a turn for the better after their wedding. John reconnected with Amanda and her husband and they did regular game nights together. Sometimes Nick came over, though he was working a graveyard shift at a janitorial job that sapped the life out of him. He had his own place again, but it was a shell of the bachelor pad the two played video games in back when they were in their early twenties. John wondered if Nick was happier when he was married to Michelle. Nick had a fear that if he wasn't with Michelle, he'd be alone. As far as John knew, Nick wasn't seeing anybody at that time. Nick's prophecy was self-fulfilled.

John parked his car at home and noticed that Bethany's car was absent. She wasn't scheduled to work that evening, and she didn't mention any plans about going out. He got out of his car and went up the stairs into his apartment. It was recently cleaned, so it looked nicer than usual. He scanned around for any written notes or indications of Bethany's whereabouts, but he couldn't spot any. He noticed his stomach gurgling, so he cooked himself a small meal.

After getting some vegetables boiling in a pot on the stove, his phone beeped. He got a new phone for his birthday, and it was more advanced than anything else he had ever owned. Still getting used to the upgraded interface, he pulled up a message from Bethany saying she'd be home soon. Not knowing what she meant by "soon," he continued with his meal. John was still in the dark about the situation, so if she came home hungry, she was capable of producing her own nourishment.

He buttered up some French bread and put some leftover pork in the microwave. Everything was timed perfectly, for the vegetables were done at the same time. With his quick meal ready, he brought it to their table and started devouring. They were out of alcohol, so he drank some lemonade instead. In the middle of enjoying his meal, he heard footsteps going up the stairs. They were quick.

The door opened and closed rapidly. Bethany ran around the corner and found John. She ran over to him with a huge smile on her face and hugged him. John stared blankly.

"John! I got the job!" she exclaimed with glee.

"What! Really?" John knew she had been going through the application process for a job but had no clue she was on course to get the position.

"Yes! Middle school counselor! Oh my God, John!" She squeezed him harder.

"It's what you always wanted!" he said. He returned the embrace.

Bethany let go and sat down on the chair in front of him. She set her purse and keys on the table, still wearing her jacket. Smiling, she said, "I wanted to surprise you. Had my second interview last week and we finalized the contract today. I start the next school year. End of August!"

"That's so wonderful!" Now John was smiling. This changed their situation. She'd now make almost as much as John and get large swaths of time off when the children were on their breaks. Changes to their lifestyle could begin. "That's only a few months away!"

"I know. I'm not even nervous or anything." She looked at his half-eaten dinner and ignored it. "I'll probably keep my job for a couple months, probably through the end of July. Then that will give me a month off to get my head in the game and prep."

"That sounds wonderful, honeybun," he said. He reached his hand out across the table, and she responded by grasping it.

"You know, we could take a trip," she continued with great excitement. "You have some vacation time to spend."

While the prospect of a trip seemed seductive, especially considering how short their honeymoon was, John was mindful of other plans. He had to consider saving up for a down payment for a home, as well as the possibility of replacing his car while it was somewhat manageable. "You know, you haven't started yet. We still have to be careful."

"I know!" said Bethany, staying positive. "Then we can take a short trip!"

They both giggled. "You know, I don't think I'll mind."

Bethany stood up to take off her jacket, which she hung on the chair behind her. "But yeah, it'd be nice to start saving for a house right away. The market is still recovering so now's the time to do it. Get out of this apartment and have a real home."

John's mind immediately went to the stone country cottage, the fantasy placed in his mind years earlier. He wanted to get the small house as an honor to Isabel, but given his limited funds and time, he wasn't sure if that decision was economical. If they were to get a house, John would have to consider Bethany's wishes. John's life was in a much different place than it was five years earlier. Back then, he wasn't attached to his job, and he and Isabel had the flexibility to chuck their careers and make their way wherever they lived. With Bethany, her job was her dream, and her attachment to it was paramount to her happiness. John was also more attached to his job now, enjoying his elevated position while putting more effort and soul into his work. Sometimes he wondered if he was further surrendering to society by filling the role of corporate stooge, but he shook those thoughts from his mind. He did what he had to do to meet his new standards.

"Well," said John, "hopefully things are still stable for a while. We can save up for a year or two, get a really nice down payment on a house here, and score. In more ways than one."

Bethany's giggles were muted, much to John's surprise. "Well, yeah. But do you really want to keep living here that long?"

John shrugged. "I mean, it's not terrible. Now knowing that we're making the big bucks and have an actual time frame to work with, it makes it more bearable."

"Yes. But, John, we could buy a nice house much sooner. Out in the burbs. It'll be a bit of a drive to our jobs, but we'd save money and have it sooner."

This debate came up every once in a while during the course of their relationship. John still maintained his attachment to living in the inner city, with its culture and lifestyle. If the country cottage was an unrealistic prospect, then a house in a nice urban neighborhood was an excellent second option. Bethany always fancied the suburbs, dreams of Americana with the white picket fence and the yard for the dogs to run around in. Her point was valid, but John still felt the suburbs lacked the character that he enjoyed. He also remembered that Isabel despised suburbia. Yet those were Isabel's thoughts, not John's.

"I mean, I guess, yeah," he said, looking down with a hint of defeat in his voice. "I've been wanting a home for a while. But it's so much cooler in town."

"I know," said Bethany. "There's more to do here if you go out, sure. But I think that there's more to do in our home if you go out a few miles. We can get a bigger house. More room for us, and room when we decide to grow our family."

The children conversation was one John tried to avoid or deflect. They didn't bring it up often. He knew Bethany wanted children at some point in the future, and she had expressed that point early in their relationship. She was patient on that front though. She agreed with John during their discussions on the topic that they should meet their ambitions first before they surrendered their lives to start the next generation. Her new job was her ambition. Perhaps she was emboldened by that. Bethany was ready to propel her life forward into an unknown but exciting chapter.

"That could be cool," John said with hesitation.

Bethany smiled. "We can be responsible with this, you know. I know you have concern about the future. I mean, Christ, you've opened up so much to me. I got rid of my SUV because of you, and I loved that car. Maybe if we get a house we can plant a few trees to help offset things."

"I'm not sure that's enough, but it's something."

"You have concerns beyond your world, and that's wonderful. Attractive, even. But, John, I almost feel that you've lived your whole life thinking that you're helpless. You can't help save the world, so you have to hurt your own well-being to compensate because it's easier. But it's not easier. There are things we can do. You can help save the world."

John smiled. "Well, when you put it that way."

"See?" she said. "You're better than you thought you were. I knew it. I wouldn't have married you if you weren't."

John grinned. "Well, I figured since we celebrated my promotion, we should celebrate your new job. Wanna go somewhere?"

With an apprehensive grin on her face, Bethany stood up to walk next to John, his meal still not finished. She bent over to whisper in his ear. "Finish eating your food, brush your teeth, then come into the bedroom and eat me." She licked his ear and stood up.

John nodded intently and ate the remainder of his meal shockingly quick. Bethany laughed and slowly walked toward their bedroom in the back of the apartment.

17

CHAPTER SEVENTEEN

Most people bought houses in the summer. Late autumn wasn't an optimal time to purchase, but fewer people looking meant less competition and lower prices, something John and Bethany wanted to take advantage of. Both of them were from the area, so the rain didn't deter them much.

"It's always nice to get one final look at the place before signing the paperwork," said John.

"Considering we're committing to this for thirty years, I agree," said Bethany.

The couple had been pre-approved for a mortgage through John's credit union. Because of the current state of the housing market, they had a wide variety of places to check out for their home. Although this was their first home, they also wanted to make sure it lasted a long while. While

John wasn't eager to move into the suburbs, they did find a thirty-year-old home that looked like an older house. On the front side, it had brick going up three feet from the ground, and the rest was gray painted siding.

Inside, the first floor had a small entryway; on the left was the living room, and on the right was the dining room. Farther back into the house was the kitchen, the master bedroom, and a large bathroom. Off to the side was the garage. The top floor had the family room and three bedrooms. The backyard was small but modest, and the front yard was open and inviting.

"Garden's definitely going in the back," said John. Their fourplex had no room for gardening, so he hadn't grown anything in several years.

"Sounds exciting," said Bethany, looking out the back window with him while standing in the master bedroom. "What are you thinking? Tomatoes, corn, squash?"

"That, but also some berries too. Think of all the blueberry and raspberry bushes we can fit!"

"Mmmm, you're making me hungry." She looked back into the empty room. It didn't feel like home yet, but their two visions gave them optimism for its future.

"Also want to plant a bunch of trees too."

Bethany tilted her head to look at John. "Are you sure we're going to have the room?"

"Doing our best for the environment is very important." John sighed and turned toward his spouse, leaning against the wall. "Look, if we're going to live way out here and drive longer distances for our work commutes, I want to offset that. And if we're going to be here a while, it would be pretty badass seeing those trees grow."

Bethany nodded. "Well, seeing them grow like that would be cool."

John smiled and shook his head. "Here I am, dictating all the things I want. What do you want?"

"Well, I'll leave outside up to you. As far as in here"—she looked back at the empty room—"we have what we have, but we'll get more stuff over time. Think I've got a better eye for art and that sort of thing."

John smiled as he ran his fingers through her hair. "Well, that's good. I trust you on that. Decorating was not my strong suit."

Bethany stepped closer to John and sighed. With the realtor outside waiting on their visit, they didn't want to waste his time. Still, they conveyed their emotions without the need for physical contact. "I have to be honest, I'm not so sure about where to put Isabel's shelf."

John nodded slowly but deliberately. "Yeah, I had a feeling you're not really keen on having it in the living room anymore."

Offering a half-smile, Bethany shrugged. "It's just awkward to be married to a wonderful man yet having to stare at, well, his previous partner's stuff."

"Probably wouldn't want it in our bedroom either," joked John.

Bethany shook her head with a straight face. "Don't want you fucking me with a paper bag on my head while you're admiring her."

John laughed. Bethany's black comedy was a treat when it revealed itself. It had been a long time since the accident. It was fair to be comedic about such events, as long as John kept remembering his true feelings. "Well, we can put it in one of the spare rooms. I made a promise to her that I won't forget her."

Now smiling, Bethany responded, "I know. I've told you before, it's good to know that if I go, you'll have no troubles remembering me."

"But if I kicked it," said John with sarcastic concern, "would you even remember me?"

"Mmmm, maybe," said Bethany. "You'll be hard when rigor mortis sets in. I'll have them make a mold of your cock for me. But that's about it."

"Such a romantic," he said. They both giggled. John used his hand to bring her closer to him for a quick kiss. When he let her go, he continued. "Well, I'm ready to sign the papers if you are."

"I'm game," Bethany said.

The two left the house and let the realtor know their decision. Pleased with the outcome, all parties agreed to meet at the agency's office after work the following afternoon to finish the paperwork. The home inspection had already passed the week before, and they signed the mortgage papers. It was a long, arduous process with a lot of legalities.

When they finished the following day, the couple walked out to the sidewalk. The rain was lighter than the day before. Their eyes connected, their faces blank, but their minds were full of relief and happiness. They embraced one another, much to the confusion of others walking around them.

"We own our own home!" said Bethany cheerfully.

It might not have been the country cottage, and it might not have been in a hip urban neighborhood, but she was right. It was a major milestone in John's life, and it was cause for celebration. "This is freaking awesome."

"And I'm hungry," she noted, changing topics on a whim.

John broke off the embrace to take out his phone to check the time. "Anywhere you want to go?"

"No, this time I think I'm letting you pick!"

John squinted his left eye as he looked back at Bethany. "This isn't going to be one of those things where I suggest a hundred places and you say no to each one."

Bethany smiled, offering a barely audible laugh. "Oh Jesus, you know me better than that. Maybe not something new, but anywhere we've been before I'm good with."

Luckily, there was a familiar Thai restaurant close by, so they walked over; the rain wasn't too harsh. The place was busy, but the greeter found them a small table right away. It was next to the front window so they could watch everybody walking back and forth. John enjoyed seeing who was bothered by the rain and who was not.

"What would you like to drink?" asked their waiter when he came up to their table.

"I'd like tea, please," said Bethany.

"Make that two," John followed up. The waiter nodded and hurried away. John looked back at Bethany and said, "It's Friday. Surprised we aren't getting drink drinks."

Bethany's eyes shifted back and forth. "I'm not really feeling it right now. Maybe later. Besides, you don't even like their beer here!"

"Well, I guess that's true," admitted John. He had tried some of their imported beers from Southeast Asia, but they were too sour. He shrugged. "Anyway, I guess we're going shopping this weekend for some new furniture."

"Let's hold off until we get all our stuff moved in," said Bethany. "We'll see what we need and go from there."

John nodded right as the waiter came back with their teas. John went over the menu one last time while Bethany ordered a pumpkin soup dish. He ordered a lemongrass chicken dish. With everything settled, the waiter grabbed the menus and took his notepad to the back.

"Well," said John, "we still have a month and a half on our lease. I guess we're not really in a hurry."

"Well, we're getting the keys on Tuesday, but I'd like to at least get everything moved as quickly as possible." She took a sip of her drink.

"Yeah, but at the same time, since we're paying for another month's rent, the apartment does have the advantage of being closer to work. It would be cool to be able to use that for as long as we have it."

"Mmmm," mumbled Bethany.

John took a quick sip. "Well, what I'm thinking is that we move over the stuff we really don't need. The TV, my video game systems, the storage boxes, the tables. They can go right away. The bedroom and kitchen can wait a bit. Spreads it out so we're not super stressed."

Bethany nodded with a distracted look. "Yeah, that does make sense. Make it easier for us. I dunno. I was hoping to sleep there as soon as possible."

"It would be nice. We can flip them, keep the nonessentials at the apartment." He took a sip. "I dunno. I guess my thought was that if we're going to do it over multiple weeks, no matter what order we do it in, we're not going to be fully moved in until we're done. So while we're in the process, we can save some gas money. Just makes sense. We can do it the other way though."

"No, no, that's fine. We can do that." Bethany seemed disappointed in the decision, but John didn't dwell on that. Their food arrived, and the two ate their meals in relative silence interjected with occasional banter and quips. John became more concerned about Bethany's distractions, but he chose to ignore them. They finished their meals, John covered the check, and they drove themselves back to their apartment.

The drive back was even more silent than their meal. John would glance over at Bethany, finding her in a contemplative state, staring out the window, but not looking at anything in particular.

When they got back, it was approaching dark, but fortunately, the floodlights on the fourplex lit their way from the car to the stairs. The rain had eased even more, the sprinkle now little more than a drizzle. John found his key on the way up and unlocked the door. Even though they now had a de jure home they could claim as theirs, this apartment was still very much a home to them.

Once they were inside and their coats and shoes were shed, they made their way to the couch. The stress of the home-buying process was behind them, and despite the mental fatigue of the process, their relief was profound. Both of them sighed as they sat. Before she had time to position herself, John took her in his arms and held her with a gentle embrace.

"Hey, honeybun," said John.

"Hey," said Bethany, her voice less enthusiastic.

"I love you."

Bethany looked at him and smiled. They were silent for a moment as they stared into each other's eyes, their souls. Eventually, Bethany relented, breaking eye contact and sighing. "I'm sorry, John. I thought I would be happier. Maybe the house is just distracting me. I dunno."

Her words further confused John. The mysterious behavior wasn't a result of the house. John ran his fingers through her curly hair. "Well, what is it?"

There was a long pause as Bethany collected her thoughts. "So I went to a follow-up appointment this morning."

John had to think about what appointment she had recently that would qualify for a follow-up. "You mean your gynecologist?"

"Yeah." She fidgeted.

"You didn't tell me that you were going to go in again," said John, a little more concerned.

Bethany shrugged. "I got the morning off. It was no big deal. We were checking up on something, and I was going to wait to tell you. I just... didn't think I'd feel so scared?"

"Are you okay?"

She relaxed some and looked at John. Her face had a half-smile on it, but John could tell it wasn't genuine. "John. I'm pregnant."

Two words that inflicted fear and unknowingness into even the most prepared couples. John's eyes bulged, his breath becoming inconsistent. He nodded in silence.

This had been a hypothetical since before their engagement. Bethany had talked to John about the prospect of kids and how she wouldn't want children until they had a house and solid jobs. John loved Bethany, but he also had doubts about how long their love would hold. Being able to share that love with another human being, especially one of his progeny, was a scary prospect. He eventually relented. Bethany had told him she was coming off birth control, but he didn't realize she'd become pregnant so quickly.

"We weren't sure when I went in last week," she said, "and the house was not a sure thing yet. Trust me, if we didn't have a house signed and then I found out, I would have aborted it. But with the papers signed today, I think… I think… I think this is the time." Her eyes were full of fear.

"Okay." John was also full of fear.

"Oh, John, I'm scared too. Part of me thinks I'm too young, that I'm not ready. But I've met all my goals. All my dreams. If I can't have a kid now, when will I ever be ready?"

John appreciated Bethany's nonchalance with motherhood. That wasn't the focus of her life. If she said she was ready to start a family, John knew she was genuine. He was happy she was where she was in her life. Bethany had accomplished what Isabel never had a chance to. She even accomplished more than what John dreamed of for himself, even if he wasn't sure what his own ambition was. He couldn't stand in the way of her triumph.

Still not getting a reaction out of him, Bethany finally had a legitimate smile. "John, I love you so much. I wish I knew what you were thinking."

John thought he'd always be childfree. The reality was that he didn't really give much thought to the question of children, at least not until Isabel entered his life. Even if he told himself he was doing it to limit his carbon footprint, the real reason would be the loss of his independence. The more he thought about that independence, the more he realized that independence was an empty trophy that had stopped offering benefits a long time ago. The freedom to hang out with Nick was meaningless, as he no longer lived in the area and had the responsibility of his own kid. His other friends were starting families of their own. He couldn't even claim that society won, that society defeated him. He wouldn't even say that he defeated himself. His life just changed.

"I don't know what to say, Beth. This is going to change everything."

"I know," she said. "What are we going to do? Do you think I should have an abortion?"

John took a deep breath, feeling his heart pump heavily. "No. You're right. We're as ready as we'll ever be. No point in getting rid of it if we'll just try again in six months."

Bethany rested her head on his chest. "This isn't how I thought this would happen. I thought we'd be so happy."

"Let's get the move done, everything settled first. We don't have to worry about this now. Once everything settles down, I think everything will turn out right. It always has."

Bethany smiled.

18

CHAPTER EIGHTEEN

Since it had been raining for the past several weeks, the ground was damp and muddy. John made sure to wear his hiking boots and suitable clothing for the occasion. Luckily for him, the sun was shining, and the clouds were sparse. It could have been much worse.

It was a hike John had done many times before. He never took Bethany on this particular trail, however. Since it was unmarked, hardly anybody from the area knew of its existence. With a growing population, who knew how long it would be before the area became a tourist destination? A treasure soiled by scores of people who didn't appreciate the history behind the area. It was special to John, and he wanted to be alone on this day, holding the memories inside his heart.

The first time he hiked that trail, the weather was clear,

if cold. Since then, it always rained. Usually, John appreciated the soft grace of its touch, but not while hiking in the forest. He always hiked the trail at the same time every year, so the weather was always the same. Yet his memories of those other visits were vague; only that first visit meant something.

Looking ahead, he could see some steam rising above the treetops. To the average observer, it looked like the sun was evaporating the water in the mud. But not to John. He hiked ahead, slogging through the mud as he made his way up a slight incline. Despite the sun showing its rare face, it was still cool under the coniferous trees.

Once he hiked to the top of the hill, he took a right turn away from the trail and around a rock outcropping. It was a narrow path, but still manageable. On the other side of the outcropping was the source of the steam: several pools of hot springs radiating warmth to the surrounding area. John wasn't equipped to go into the pools, nor did he have the desire. Yet he sat down next to the largest pool. It was good to relax after a hike, even if his stop wasn't for a break. It was his destination.

After taking in a deep breath, John closed his eyes. The average person, standing where John was, would look around and see nobody. To that dispassionate observer, John was the only person in that forest. John felt differently. He knew differently. He could observe what others couldn't. There was a hidden history there, and John took advantage of that knowledge.

"Hello, Bel."

Somewhere, in the deep sediment of the pool were particles of ashes that were deposited there some time ago.

The ashes didn't originate from a fireplace or a campfire. They were all that physically remained of a person, a person John had devoted himself to. Those hot springs were Isabel's final resting place.

John's words, when spoken in the hospital room, were uncertain, pained, weak. Yet his words in the forest were calm, reassuring, and happy. Isabel was freed from the physical world. John was more comfortable talking to her echo within the mysteries of the forest than talking to her broken body on the bed in that sterile hospital.

"It's a beautiful day, isn't it? This hike kinda sucks when it's raining. I know it's not possible, but I sometimes wish that you controlled the weather here. Then I know the rain is just you smiling every time I visit. It's obviously not true, but it's fun to think about. I only visit you twice a year now, so I have to make it worth it."

That day was special, but not in a good way. It was the fifth anniversary of Isabel's car accident, the day he truly lost her. It remained the most dreadful day. Despite the years since that painful time, the anniversary still haunted him. He secretly noted the day in his calendar every year, anticipating its coming with dread.

John giggled to himself. "I was thinking not that long ago. About why I'm such a hardass about the environment. Why I was such a hardass to you. To Beth. It's because of the rain. It's always about the rain. When I'd go on walks in the rain as a teenager, I would walk to the local park, and just, I dunno, feel more at peace there. The rain, the trees, it was the total package for my serenity. I guess that's why I cared so much, because I wanted to protect that everywhere I went. Don't know why it took me this long to realize it. Kind of a dumb reason why I'm a hippie environmentalist. At least it's a secret I'll keep with you."

The second day of the year John visited her was the anniversary of her final death, her silent mercy. Its third anniversary was coming up that fall. John's memories of the cremation were vague. Five of their mutual friends, including Nick, made that same hike a week after her formal passing. John carried the container of her ashes. Isabel never had a chance to tell him where she wanted to rest, but he took it upon himself to make that decision on her behalf. She would rest where they had their best memory. He could think of no better place.

"You have no idea what's happened since I last talked with you. I'm going to be a father. Can you fucking believe that? Beth's pregnant with our kid. We're expecting to have it in a few months. I still can't believe it's happening. Hell, I don't think Beth believes it's happening either. Beth... Beth is a good person. She has doubts but also has hopes. She's really not that much different from you and I. I thought for the longest time that she was different in every way, but really, she's not. Different personality, maybe."

He looked to his right, over the cliffside. The view was magnificent: it went over the treetops for miles. He remembered seeing that scene for the first time in the early-morning glow. Now with the benefit of the unobstructed sun, it was a sight to behold. It was a sight he wished would never change. After studying that beautiful landscape for a few minutes, he went back to his conversation.

"I still wonder sometimes about us, where we'd be at. We would have had our eighth anniversary a couple months ago. Goddamn. Maybe we would have had our cottage. Maybe we wouldn't. But what would we have done with all that time? Would we just have made love to fill up all of our free time? Turn it into something mechanical, a checkbox to fulfill ourselves? I know that's what we wanted to avoid. But we weren't together long enough to know for sure. Bethany and I have been though. And as hard as it was for me to admit, there needed to be a change."

John rubbed his eyes and took a deep breath. While the air itself was clear, the warmth from the hot springs made it hard to breathe. "Holy shit. I just realized something. I've always compared Beth to you. On, like, everything. I always had you on a pedestal. I know, that's totally unhealthy behavior and I know you would scold me for it. I don't think Bethany knows how big that pedestal really is. How big it was. I'd like to think I did a damn good job at that, despite your protests. But here we are, five years later. I built a nice pedestal for Beth now. And your pedestal... Well, yours is crumbling now.

"She doesn't know I'm here either. As much as she says she cares and understands, I have trouble believing her. What I felt five years ago, it's a pain I can't forget. And it's not something I could have dreamed of. I doubt anybody could. I told you before you died that time doesn't heal—it only stretches. After all this time, I think I have a pretty good idea now. I still think I'm right about that."

He ran his hand through the damp grass, feeling the blades between his fingers. Feeling her hair between his fingers. "I miss you, Bel. Even now that I'm married and soon to be a dad, I still miss you. Having you in my life would make my world better. Even if you were just a friend.

You made a lot of people's lives better. Our old friends that I'm still in touch with, they all still love you. I think it's the only reason they put up with me, to be honest. But I also wonder how long they will remember you. How long will I remember you?"

That thought brought the first tear of the day, but no more followed. "Why did I even think that? You were so important in my life. I would not have gotten where I am today without you. Your passion, your drive, your love. I put it upon myself to carry on your existence with me, and I damn well will keep that promise. If I take care of myself properly, then I'll have many long years to uphold that promise. I think I'll carry you in me that whole time."

John lay back in the grass, shutting his eyes to block out the bright sky. He could feel the moisture from the grass on his neck, but it wasn't wet enough to dampen his clothes. There were no more words he wanted to say. Each visit was less verbose than the one before. John wasn't sure if he was becoming detached to his lost partner. Before the accident, one of his fears was Isabel losing genuine interest in him or even him losing interest in Isabel. They hoped there would always be something to talk about, always conversations to be had. Never a dull moment in the decades they would live with each other. John had been pulling the sled of conversation alone. Perhaps he was becoming tired. There were only so many new topics to talk about.

After getting those thoughts out, John continued lying down calmly. It was a good day to lie in the forest. The chirps of the occasional bird. The still sway of trees rustling their limbs. The cool dampness on his neck. He must have stayed in that position for a long while, for when he opened his eyes, the sun had moved and more shadows covered the ground. Wanting to get back home before nightfall, John sat up and turned toward the warm pool.

"If it ends up being a daughter," said John, "you have no idea how much I want to name her after you. I don't think Beth would allow it. I don't think she wants to be reminded of my ex every time she calls our daughter. But maybe she will. Maybe a middle name would work. I don't know. But I do want to instill in our children your values. You and I may not have wanted kids, but I'm going to raise them in a way that will make you so proud."

Smiling, John reached his hand out to dip his fingers into the pool. It wasn't scalding, but he still winced. After some relaxing, he further submerged his fingers into the pool and squeezed his hand. Isabel no longer had a hand to hold, but the metaphor still worked in his heart.

"Goodbye, Bel. I'll see you in a bit."

He released his hand. After standing up with a final smile, John turned around and walked back the way he came. Another visit to the tomb of his heart. How many more visits would John appreciate before his own inevitable end? One thing was for certain; John wished Isabel's resting place would remain frozen in time, unchanging throughout the seasons, unmolested from human intervention. Every visit would have the same sights, the same sounds, the same feeling. Could John keep feeling the same?

19

CHAPTER NINETEEN

"Did you want to cut the cord?" asked the doctor.

John wasn't sure what to do. He was being asked to do something he never thought he'd ever do. Admittedly, his memory of his birth was a little hazy.

"Um," said John in a drawn-out manner, wondering who he was at that moment. "Yeah, sure."

He analyzed the surgical scissors he was given. They were sharper than any scissors he was used to. With an easy snip, he cut the umbilical cord to his newborn daughter.

His newborn daughter. The doctor held her, a shriveled extraterrestrial covered in gross fluids. It was difficult for him to focus on the present, but deep inside, he knew it was even more difficult for Bethany, who had just finished nine long months of unimaginable stress. Five years earlier, the moment was inconceivable. Yet Bethany wanted it, and because of that, John wanted it too.

Childbirth wasn't as clean as in media depictions; John was now an eyewitness to the messy reality. His child was wrapped up in a blanket to dry off. Then she was passed to Bethany, who was still reeling from the postnatal shock.

"Hi there!" she said in her scratchy yet weakened voice. "Hi there!"

The baby was calm by that point, having partially adjusted to her new world. John wasn't sure if Bethany expected an actual response, but he wasn't one to judge in that moment.

Bethany looked up. "Look at her, John!"

John slowly sat down in the chair by her side. This time, the room was more calm, more joyful. He leaned over and set his head on her shoulder while taking his hand and placing it on their daughter. "I see her," he said calmly. Were the endorphins supposed to kick in soon? John was worried about his apathy. "She looks like an alien."

Even though she was weak, Bethany gave a laugh. "Oh, John, I just knew you'd say that." She laughed again. "You are right though."

One of the nurses intervened at that moment. "Would you like me to bring the grandparents in?"

Bethany nodded. "Yeah, bring Mom and Dad in." She smiled again, focusing on her baby. She wanted her parents there at the hospital, but not during the birth itself. That was just for John and the staff.

While the nurse left, Bethany turned her head to focus on John. "You still okay with the name?"

John nodded. "Emma Sophia is a good name." Sophia

was Bethany's great-grandmother's name. She had immigrated from Greece. Bethany never knew her but had heard stories of her growing up, and Bethany admired her strong character. John kept silent on what he really wanted. He did like the name, but the name was a compromise to John; it was a hill he chose not to die on. John figured it would be best to give Bethany more choice over the name for the first child. If there were other children, John would have more confidence in voicing his opinion.

At that moment in time, other children were the last thing on his mind. A couple of years earlier, any children at all were the last thing on his mind. In a few more years, John could well be a collector of human cubs, uncaring about his environmental impact as his family grew. He tried to cast away those thoughts, but his reaction to Emma's birth placed him in an introspective mood, and he was trapped there.

"Oh my gosh!" exclaimed Lisa, Bethany's mother, as she walked into the room. After a life of hardship raising Bethany, having a granddaughter was a triumph for her. She always had an underlying disdain for how her adult life turned out, having become pregnant with Bethany at a young age. Yet that disdain vanished for the first time that John had ever noticed. She walked over to the bed with a big smile on her face.

"Hi, Mom," Bethany whispered. Behind Lisa was Bethany's father, Jim, who smiled at his granddaughter without saying a word.

"Oh my gosh, she's so gorgeous!" said Lisa calmly so as not to disturb her granddaughter. She had experience with babies, experience both John and Bethany lacked.

"Hi, Dad," Bethany said with a slight smile.

"How are you doing, Bethany?" he asked in response.

Bethany nodded. "Been through hell, but otherwise alright." She sighed and looked down at Emma, her breathing visible through her thick blankets. Breathing that required no machine or apparatus. "Do you want to hold her?"

"I'm first!" her father said as he reached over toward Emma. John helped the baby off Bethany and into his father-in-law's arms, and he cradled her with fatherly compassion. John had known Bethany's parents for a while now, knowing them better than any of his exes' parents. It was a forced relationship, but John kept it cordial for Bethany's sake. That was what he liked about Isabel; there was no family to deal with. It took some time to get used to in-laws, but it wasn't bad.

"So you decided on a name, right?" asked Lisa.

"Yeah, Emma Sophia," confirmed John.

Lisa smiled nostalgically. "I'm glad you named her after Grandma Sophia. She was my favorite grandparent, but don't tell the others."

Bethany squinted and gave a skeptical smile. "But they're all dead, Mom."

Lisa waved her hand. "Ah, I still miss them though."

John still had half his grandparents. Both of his mother's parents were still alive, but they were divorced long before he was born. His grandmother's second husband was still alive, but his grandfather was a widower. But would his grandfather still be a widower if his first spouse was still alive?

John didn't care much for those thoughts. His mind,

although partly displaced, was in the moment. He was now a father. He could hardly believe it. Could he ever believe it? The evidence was right in front of him, but she was still foreign to him like she didn't belong.

Bethany's father had been singing to Emma for a little while. An oddity, for he was usually quiet. Bethany's mother got antsy waiting for her turn, having become bored talking with her daughter. Isabel had told John about that situation: the grandparents see the grandchild as a free prize to them, a prize for completing the rigors of parenthood themselves. The prize was more important than their own children. John hoped he was projecting his fears, psyching himself out needlessly.

While Emma was passed from one grandparent to the other, Bethany moved her hand over toward John. John grasped it, and the two looked at each other. They smiled.

"How are you?" asked Bethany with hints of a sweet smile.

John was taken aback. "I'm, uh… I'm fine. But why are you worried about me? You just shot a giant head out of you!"

Bethany smiled, a tired look in her eyes. "Yeah, I did. But we're in this together, you know. It's not just me."

"Well, you're too kind."

Bethany looked over at her parents, ogling the warm fussy bundle they were holding. She lowered her voice even more so they couldn't hear her. "I just know how you felt about all of this, and I know that I did kind of drag you kicking and screaming."

John's stature deflated. "I love you, Beth. I knew how important this was to you. I was willing to make this work."

Bethany continued staring, but John knew her eyes were no longer focused on her parents or child. It was a more distant, vacant stare. "I know. I was ready. We were ready. But I all of a sudden feel bad for everything."

John tilted his head. "Don't tell me this is that postpartum depression we were warned about."

"Probably." Bethany laughed. "Oh well. We got this."

Lisa eventually passed Emma to John, who held her while remaining seated in his chair. John wasn't sure what to do, and his body language gave his weakness away. At least he was holding his daughter correctly, but John wasn't sure if he should sing or talk or remain silent. Before he had a chance to test a course of action, Emma started crying.

"She probably needs to be fed," Lisa said. John nodded, trusting her expertise in those matters. He wished his parents were there. They were the ones he trusted in matters of parenting advice. John set Emma down on Bethany as she prepared herself for breastfeeding.

"Yes, so sexy," Bethany said, her sarcasm thick. Lisa started shooing Jim out of the room, and John felt it was a good time to get some fresh air himself. As he stood up, Bethany gave John a worried look. "Hon, you can stay, you know."

"I know," he said with a quick smile. "I'm just gonna call Mom and Dad. I'll be right outside."

Standing up, he could feel an ache in his back he hadn't noticed before. That pain was unfamiliar to him, and he couldn't immediately diagnose it. He hadn't been sitting for long. Perhaps the stress of the situation had caused his muscles to tighten. Perhaps the birth of his first child was a subtle signal to his body that he could begin the aging process. Even though he was in his early thirties, he largely felt the same since high school. For years he remained a youthful man and had stayed active with hiking and yoga. John wasn't sure if he could maintain that level of commitment to wellness with a newborn daughter in his arms.

It was the first time he left the room in over two hours. His commitment to Bethany's labor was solid, but now that same commitment could be more relaxed. He stood in the corridor, looking both ways to find his father-in-law, but to no avail. Jim was probably looking for some food or even a restroom. With no one else in the hallway, John took that opportunity to pull out his phone and call his parents.

"Hey, Mom," said John, his voice filled with weariness.

"John!" he could hear her yell. "Well, what's happening?"

He paused for a moment to collect how he'd convey the news. "Well, you're a grandmother now."

On the other side of the line, he could hear an audible gasp. It wasn't one of shock, but of joy. "Oh my God, John, that's so wonderful! What did you name her? Did everything go well? How's Beth?"

John chuckled at the rapid-fire questioning from his mother. Taking a more measured approach, he responded to each question sequentially. "Her name is Emma. We both picked that one out. It felt modern, but not like it will age badly."

"Didn't you have a crush on an Emma when you were in grade school?" asked his mother.

John had forgotten about that. There was a girl in grade

school who he did have a crush on. He hadn't thought about her in years. She was a nice girl, but John couldn't remember what happened to her. There was no memory of her in middle or high school, so perhaps she had moved and John was unaware. Regardless, his youthful infatuation with a girl named Emma might have been a latent memory in his mind. Even if he couldn't actively recall the association, he may have been subliminally attracted to the name.

"Yeah, I did," said John. "I dunno. The name sounded good to us. Anyway, birth went very well, no complications. She was in labor for five hours, so it wasn't too intense."

"You know, I was in labor with you for twenty hours. Tell Beth she's lucky."

"I'm sure she'll appreciate it, Mom. But anyway, birth went fine. Everything is smooth. Beth is doing okay. She's feeding Emma right now. She's probably very tired, but she's strong. She's very strong."

"She sure is," said his mother. "How are you doing?"

John nodded without realizing his mother couldn't see him. "I'm fine. Not really sleepy tired, just drained. I just... I still can't believe it."

"You stay there with her. Remember that!"

"Yes, Mom, I'm not going anywhere. Anyway"—he turned back toward the door to Bethany's room—"I should probably be back in there. She's probably needing my help soon. But I'll call when you can come by. It may be a couple hours, but I'll wait until Beth's ready."

"Okay, John! Love you!"

When the call ended, John focused back on reality. He walked back toward the closed door to Bethany's room but stopped. It wasn't the first time he had walked into a hospital room where his love was resting inside. This time, the circumstances were very different. The other time was filled with dread and sorrow he couldn't comprehend, even all these years later. This time, while still unnerving and uncertain, it was far more beautiful. He had a daughter, his wife was healthy, and everything was going as planned.

20

Chapter Twenty

Christmas lights burning out were always an annoyance. John sighed as he found the culprit and promptly replaced it. All the blue lights reactivated, their calming hue returning to the Christmas tree in his living room. Filled with many colorful lights, it featured few ornaments, mostly little trinkets and a commemorative Baby's First Christmas for Emma. It was enough for their house; both John and Bethany didn't want to make things too gaudy with holiday debauchery.

The rest of the room was dark, which accentuated the colorful glow of the tree. John smiled. He had loathed Christmas for years thanks to his time working retail a decade earlier. There was some small reconciliation during his time with Isabel, but it was only recently, now that he owned his own house, that he could truly enjoy the aesthetic again.

Being dark outside and quiet inside was itself an unusual combination. Most nights, John wasn't home alone. Emma was always there with him, and often Bethany was as well. That evening, Bethany was visiting her parents and brought along their grandchild, leaving John alone with his thoughts—a rarity at his age.

John looked at the outdated Baby's First Christmas ornament again. Emma was now nearly a year and a half old, and her physical and mental changes during that time were outstanding. He was used to the passage of time among adults; children's perspectives were radically different.

Outside of raising a toddler, their lives had been progressing routinely. Bethany was happy with her counselor job and continued to be enamored with working in a field she was always passionate about. Meanwhile, John kept working in his current position, receiving pleasant annual raises but no new promotions. That situation was satisfactory. He had been working at his company for ten years, the management appreciating his dedication. He had wished he was as passionate at his job as Bethany was at hers, but that was a reality that would never change.

In that dark room, John found the couch and sat down, sighing with satisfaction. They had reservations about raising a child, but Emma was very healthy and calm. While it was difficult, he had the impression child-rearing would be worse than it was. Perhaps they were lucky with Emma's disposition; perhaps the warnings were overblown. Life was going well for not just him but for everyone in his circle. At first, he couldn't imagine a better life. Soon, though, he concocted an alternate scenario in his mind.

"I wonder what you'd think of this," said John out loud, his eyes closed. Most of John's thoughts were usually on Emma. Without his family there, those stray thoughts returned.

John opened his eyes. He smirked and shook his head. He had no reason to think that when his eyes reopened, Isabel would be there to answer his question. For a fraction of a second, he wished that was possible. He'd never know her opinion on his family.

"It's not a stone cottage, but it is home," he muttered, a defense mechanism against any hypothetical judgment on her part. John sighed and shut his eyes again. That conversation brought about a question with two potential answers. Was Bethany and Emma a distraction from his past life, or was being alone a distraction from his current life? Five years earlier, the answer was simple, but as time wore on and stretched his pain, he wasn't sure anymore.

His phone rang. The volume was low, but the sudden noise forced his eyes open. Picking up the phone, he looked at the caller ID. To his surprise, it wasn't Bethany calling to let him know she was on her way home. It was Nick. He hadn't spoken to him in over six months, something John didn't even realize until that moment.

"Hello?" said John.

"Hey… hey," said a pained voice on the other end. The voice was tired, lacking any spark, and seemed to lack any semblance of hope. "It's Nick."

"Hey, man," John said, smiling. "How's it been? It's been a while."

"Yeah, I know," said Nick. John could hear a long sigh on the other end. "It's been okay. Actually, John, not gonna lie, life hasn't been peachy."

John nodded. "Yeah, I get that. Do you want to talk about it?"

"Can I come over?" Nick asked, a hint of desperation in his tone. "I'm in town now, so I can swing on right over."

John wasn't even aware Nick had moved far away. Aside from phone conversations, they hadn't seen each other in over two years. He was in no mood to entertain the demons of his past, so John was happy to oblige his best friend's request.

"Sure, Nick. Beth has Emma, and they're not due back for another hour or so. Faster you get here, the more time we got."

"I'm about fifteen minutes away. I'll be right there."

When the line disconnected, John got up from the couch and turned on the porch light as well as the lights in the kitchen and living room.

Even though he was three minutes late, Nick showed up at the front door and knocked. He had an unkempt beard, as though it had grown unmolested for months. His eyes were the saddest John had ever seen them, punctuated by the hint of a permanent frown on his face. His clothes were in good condition though. The two embraced each other, but the moment was brief because of the cold.

"Fucking December, man," said Nick.

"Yeah, you just never get used to it. Come on in. Want a beer?"

As they walked through the door, there was a beat in Nick's response whereas there never had been before. "Yeah, I guess I'll have one. Sure."

"Well, sit down over there then." John pointed to the

couch he had been sitting on as he went to the kitchen and pulled out some lager cans from his refrigerator. After opening both of them, he returned to the living room, passed a can over to Nick, and sat himself down on a nearby chair.

Nick looked at the thinly decorated Christmas tree. "Damn, dude, really rocking the décor these days."

John laughed. "Not really. Just a tree. Beth and I wanted to celebrate at least a little bit, but we're not going the route of our parents."

Nick nodded with more life in his demeanor. "No kidding. Don't look too bad." He proceeded to look over the rest of the room. "Don't look too bad at all."

"I didn't even know you left town. I don't think I've talked to you since May or whenever."

Taking a sip from his beer, some liquid spilled onto his beard, so he wiped it away with his sleeve. "Yeah. Michelle wanted to get back with me."

John's eyes bulged. His lips parted to complete the reaction. "What? No fucking way. What's the story there?"

Now it was Nick's turn to laugh. "Dude, I don't know. Like, I think I told you she moved to the other side of the state a couple of years ago. Wanted to live closer to her mom or something. Took our kid, of course."

"How old is Alex? Five now?"

"Yeah, he turned five a couple months ago. He's gonna be starting kindergarten next year. Can you believe that?" Nick took another sip from his brew. "Got to grow up and I barely got to know him." He looked down at the coffee table in front of him.

"That sucks. But no, seriously, what's the story with

Michelle? I mean, she did leave you originally."

"Yeah, that's the thing," Nick continued, his expression changing from defeat to resentment. "I actually was kind of doing okay. Job had solidified a bit, better hours, no more shitty graveyard. Had a place. So when Michelle moved, she hooked up with this guy and got pregnant again!"

"Oh sweet Jesus," said John. "That girl needs sterilization."

"Yeah, since she's freaking insane!" He set his beer down on the coffee table, ignoring the coasters. While John would normally mind, he was too worried about Nick to care. "Anyway, boyfriend moves in with her and her mom. Crazy, of course. I knew nothing about this, by the way. I visited my son last year, but only her mother was around. Michelle was off with her boyfriend and I didn't see her. Anyway, that whole family is crazy. So they break up in March. Boyfriend moves to bumfuck nowhere, Michelle is left with two tiny ones and her crazy mother, and she's not working at all. Mom is on social security. So she calls me up."

John finished taking a swig from his drink. "I kinda see where this is going. Continue."

"Pretty much what you'd expect. She calls me up, not telling me any of this. But she says she regrets breaking up with me. She says she truly loves me, wants to come back to me. But she's taking care of her mom, so I have to go to her. Now I've been pretty single for a long time now, and I gotta admit, Michelle is still pretty hot. So I let my penis decide for me. Quit my job, move to her. Town's a shithole, but thankfully I got a job right away. Got an apartment. Michelle moves in with me with our kid and this dumb fuck's kid."

"How did you feel about the other kid?"

Nick shrugged. "Well, it's a packaged deal. So I dealt with it. Basically got to experience the years that I missed out on with Alex. Alex and I bonded again. It was good. And let me tell you, John, the sex was amazing."

John nodded pensively. "The sex with Michelle, that is."

Nick giggled. "Yeah, yeah, probably should have clarified. Yeah, she's still a beast in the sheets. That never changed. Remember before we divorced how we'd have sex like once a month, maybe? I dunno what, but it was like the early days of dating. She was a wild rabbit." Nick's grin grew bigger and more devious. "It was awesome."

"So now she's pregnant with a third kid."

"Oh God no," said Nick. He had to chase those words with a chug from his can. "No, remember I got snipped after she left me, once I got my job? And hey, if she did get pregnant, then I know that she didn't really actually change."

"So you're in a town of less than ten thousand people, nothing fun to do, really, and you're working some crappy country job and you're just blowing loads into your ex-wife every day." John leaned back into his chair. "You know, it's not great, I wouldn't want it, but I have to admit, it's not a bad gig."

"It was a giant shitshow, and I rode it longer than I should have," said Nick.

"That's what she said," John quipped.

Nick shook his head and silently laughed. After he

composed himself, he continued. "Anyway, so yeah. Her other ex came back into town. This was two months ago. They get back into contact, presumably for their kid's sake. The guy finds out who I am. I run into him at a bar while I'm hanging with some coworkers. For some reason, he hates me for stealing his girl or whatever, just verbally berates me. Whatever. He gets kicked out but jumps me when I leave."

"Shit, man, you okay?"

"No, I'm fine. It was a light scuffle. We were both drunk, so we were too stupid to hurt each other. But it gets worse. Couple of days later, her mom is watching the two kids. I get home from work, and this douche is sitting on the couch getting a blowie from Michelle."

"Ahhhhh," said John.

"Yeah, so the apartment's mine, Michelle's not paying anything, so I kick both of them out. I pack up her shit, and she picks it up later that evening. Moves back in with her mom. I don't know where douchecanoe ends up, but I don't see him again, thankfully. I wanted to talk to Alex about what happened because I don't trust his mom to say anything truthful. But Michelle won't let me see him. I try to be a gentleman so I don't force my way in or anything. I just let it be. Figured I take her back to court if I had to. Then, as I'm leaving, she tells me, and I don't know if this is true or not, that she invited that guy back into town because she wanted to hook up with him and I wasn't meeting her womanly needs or some bullshit."

"Is that woman on drugs?" asked John.

Nick shrugged and finished his beer. John was only halfway through his can, but Nick finished his story. "I knew she did coke a bit when we were dating, but she stopped years ago. But I did check her stuff when I was packing it, just to be sure. She really needs help, and that town is not a good environment for her, let alone for the children. And I do feel guilty for abandoning my son."

"You didn't abandon your son," said John. "It's not your fault, man."

"I know." Nick's voice changed to something John had never heard before. It no longer felt like their regular banter to him. Now, Nick's voice sounded pained, lost, defeated. He was on the verge of tears and was trying everything to seal them away.

"I just…" Nick started again, catching his words before they left his mouth. "I just wanted to see Alex. Those five months with him were so amazing. He's so smart. He's my freaking kid, man. I came back into his life at the right time. He's got a personality. I can talk with him."

John nodded. Emma was at the age where she was a barely functioning automaton, so he couldn't share that same experience with his friend. But John could look into the future and see where Nick was coming from. He wouldn't want to be ripped from Emma.

Nick composed himself, his eyes misty but not leaking. "I started drinking pretty heavily. It got bad. Showed up to work drunk a few times. They let me go. I had some money saved up so I could finish up the lease, but I started drowning in the bottle. Didn't apply anywhere, just sat at home, playing stupid childish video games and getting drunk on not even good beer. The beer in that town sucks!"

John laughed but quickly calmed himself while waiting for Nick to finish his woes.

"A week ago, I realized that my whole life was shit, and I wasted it because I wanted to get laid. Michelle was so easy when we first got together. I stayed with her despite her being shit because I hoped I would get some. Years with her, and I saw you with Isabel and then Bethany and both of them were the greatest women I've ever met. I'm so stupid to spend eleven years or however long it was being a stupid guy. I'm not a man. I'm a cock with legs on it. I'm fucking worthless."

Silence permeated the room. John had always known Michelle wasn't an ideal partner for his friend. He always tried communicating that to Nick. John wasn't Bethany, though, and couldn't hope to offer the guidance Nick was subtly begging for. John wondered if he should have made his opinions plainer. He couldn't blame Nick for his decisions.

"Well, you did come back," said John, not sure if his words were appropriate.

"Yeah," said Nick, his tone quieter. "I couldn't stand being within a hundred miles of her. I still had the rest of the month but said fuck it and just left. Haven't drank in a week. Nobody's hiring right now, and I've been hotel hopping. My savings are almost gone. My parents are on a cruise for the next two months. My sister is out of the country for another year. I have no one right now. Nowhere to go for Christmas."

Thus, the reason for Nick's visit was made clear. It would be easy to dismiss Nick's sudden appearance as selfish. Nick had messed up, quitting a stable job and moving hundreds of miles to a town with no support mechanism for a relationship that was dubious at best. Optimism had saved John many times before, but not all stories had happy endings.

John continued to be silent as he pondered the unasked question. Nick continued. "I don't know how Bethany would feel if… if I could stay with you. I don't know how long it will take. I know it's not a good time. It's Christmas, and you're a newer family. I get it. You want to stay with each other."

"You can stay." John's statement was firm. He didn't hesitate.

Nick leaned back. "What? Really? I-I-I didn't think you'd say yes."

"Why?" asked John. "Remember when Bel had her accident, and you dragged me out to a bar and we had a drink when I probably shouldn't have had a drink?"

Nick looked down at his empty can and grinned. "Yeah. The tides have turned, haven't they?"

"You're me. I know what you're going through."

"But what about Beth?" asked Nick.

"You know, fuck what she has to say about it." John always worked with Bethany when they made decisions, but he made an exception for his oldest friend. "You need family right now, and I will be your family. Stay as long as you like. I don't care. You'll do fine. I know you will."

For the first time, Nick's face lit up with a genuine closed-mouth smile. "Thanks, John. Thank you so much. I'll never forget this."

"Merry Christmas, Nick."

"Merry Christmas, John."

21

Chapter Twenty-One

"God, I've barely said anything since I got here," said John. "There just hasn't really been anything new in my life. Am I really that depressing?" He stiffened his back. "And the damn funny thing is, is that most of the time, I'm fine with that. I only get guilty when I hang out with you. I'm not sure what the hell that means. It really makes me wonder who I am. I thought I knew that before I turned thirty, but hell, I'm starting to think it may be until I'm forty before I find out, if I find out at all."

John sighed, closing his eyes slowly. "Did either of us really know who we were? I ended up changing. Granted, it was required of me. I wonder if you would have changed too."

Opening his eyes again, he looked over at whom he was talking to. After a second sigh, he reached out his hand, but instead of touching somebody's shoulder, he dipped his hand into the hot pool. It was a familiar yet infrequent sensation. The day was slightly cloudy, yet it wasn't too cool. There wasn't a lot of moisture on the ground, so John could sit without getting his pants wet.

"Bel, I really struggle sometimes. I keep my promises. Your memory is mine forever. But the stretching has made everything so mangled. It's really hard to imagine what my life would be like without Emma. She's two now. Takes after her mother for sure." He swallowed. "Could I have convinced you to have a kid?"

John looked away as if a door had opened and Medusa was standing in its arch. "No, what am I thinking? That wasn't you. But it wasn't me either. That... That was then. Then is always going to be the past." Eventually, he willed himself to make eye contact with the pool. "Even in death, you're a stronger person than I am. You would have said no to Beth. I could not."

He wiggled his hand in the water and smiled. "Goodbye, Bel. I'll see you in a bit." With his usual farewell, he stood up, brushed some foliage off, and walked back the way he came.

That visit to Isabel's resting place was yet another milestone; it was the five-year mark of him terminating her life. Half a decade later, it was still the hardest decision he had ever made. John doubted that would ever change. Bethany had the end-of-life talk with him. Any decision he made on her behalf was made with her agency. The decision made for Isabel was nothing more than a guess.

He still made the trek to the hot springs twice a year, on the two anniversaries associated with Isabel's fall. Yet each visit was shorter, less verbose. He was unable to keep her alive as much as he thought he could, hoping he'd have hour-long conversations with her remains all the way into old age. But it was hard to muster the will. He didn't want to admit that the whole ritual was a chore, but there was an obligation on his part to keep her memory alive.

John made his way to the shallow downward slope leading to where his car was parked. The leaves of the deciduous trees had begun to change, and even though a few had fallen, they were still mostly attached. During a visit two years earlier, he saw another group of people far off in the distance. It was the only time he saw other people in the sacred area. He wasn't sure if they saw him, but he wagered they were just hiking around and not interested in the hot springs. Realistically, other people had to have bathed in its warmth; after all, somebody else originally told Isabel about it. It seemed morbid that people would bathe where a person's ashes had settled, but at the same time, it seemed oddly okay. The warm pools weren't Isabel's or John's. They were the memory of a wonderful time the two had. Isabel would be more than happy to share that happiness with others.

"Five years. Half a decade." He still remembered bits of the actual cremation ceremony, but when he was in the mood to think dark thoughts, he rarely thought about that day. Instead, his memory drifted to the hospital room, with that machine off her mouth, her diaphragm no longer rising and settling.

John shed a tear and sniffled. Emotional outbursts were becoming rarer as more time passed. A couple of the more recent visits had no tears. His mind continued going back to that final kiss on her chapped lips. Another tear dripped down his cheek. Those emotions were more natural, what John was hoping he'd feel—the self-inflicted pain he craved.

"I miss you," whispered John.

Every visit was still a secret from Bethany. It was possible that she was aware, as she might have remembered the date of Isabel's death because it was the day before John's ragged marriage proposal. Yet every time he returned home, his love for Bethany was renewed. He praised the universe for bringing her into his life. Bethany saved him in his blackest hour in ways Isabel never did.

He completed the rest of the hike in thoughtful silence. He found his newly purchased car along the side of the road. His old car had finally broken down with a massive engine failure. He had driven it for twelve years, and replacing it was prohibitively expensive. He donated it to an automotive department at a local high school and purchased his first new vehicle. It got better gas mileage than his old one, yet John's complacency made him forget about the carbon costs of building a new vehicle in the first place.

After he pulled back onto the highway, it took about thirty minutes to drive to Emma's babysitter's house. She was the niece of one of Bethany's friends and was inexpensive. John and Bethany trusted her. Emma was playing with some Duplos when John arrived at the house, but she was quite eager to leave when she saw her father. John picked her up and got her into her car seat in the back. Once she was secured, John took off.

During the short trip, Emma fell asleep. Being careful so as not to disturb her, John got her out of the car seat with a delicate touch and carried her into their house. With his daughter still sound asleep, he put her into the crib and watched her for a moment. Her hair was sandy-colored, a trait she got from Bethany, although it wasn't curly, which John assumed was of his doing. She had vivid blue eyes as well. Emma was also very talkative with Bethany. John didn't mind his exclusion too much, although he did have small worries about how that could affect their relationship as she got older.

He left her bedroom to visit the other spare room. Nick had spent nearly a month there the previous Christmas. Bringing Nick into his regular life also eased leftover anxiety from his youth. Even though Isabel was gone, Nick was a constant in his life. Bethany ended up being thrilled to host him for the holiday, and he was great with Emma.

Fortunately, Nick managed to get a decent job right after the New Year, but he remained with John for a couple of weeks until his first paycheck. Rent in the city was more expensive than when Nick last lived there, but he got a room at a house nearby.

John didn't spend as much time with Isabel's shrine as he used to, but he made sure to at least dust it every few weeks. Her pictures and crafts remained timeless, showing no age. There were several pictures John wanted to see but weren't displayed. As he dug through the closet, he realized it had been over a year since he pulled them out of their box.

John found the first box with green ink markings on it. He dragged it into the room and opened it. Thankfully, its presence inside a closed closet meant it hadn't collected dust, but it was still seldom visited. One of the hot springs pictures was at the top. Despite all the wonderful moments he shared with Bethany, he doubted that he would ever again feel the happiness he felt during the hot springs photoshoot.

Before John could pull the framed picture out of the box and fully appreciate it, he heard the door open. Instinctively, he stood up and walked into the front room downstairs. Bethany, wearing a light coat and a lengthy skirt, had closed the front door behind her.

"I'm home!" she said as if John wasn't in the room, even though he was several steps from her.

"Hey, baby mama pumpkin," said John teasingly as he embraced her and kissed her softly on her lips.

"Baby mama pumpkin?" Bethany said with faux disgust after he pulled away from her.

John shrugged. "It sounded better in my head."

She giggled, then took off her jacket. "I think that goes with a lot of things you say." She went down the hall and put her coat on the coat rack. "Emma sleeping?"

"Yeah, she passed out on the way home." John shuffled behind her, trying to gauge where she was going next.

"So how was your day off?" She came back into the living room and sat down on the couch to take her shoes off.

"It was good to just relax," said John, joining Bethany on the couch.

Bethany nodded. She leaned her head onto John's shoulder, and he pivoted to embrace her.

"You do know what tomorrow is?" asked John.

"Yeah, I'll never forget your proposal." She kissed John on his ear. "I love it, you know. I have friends who proposed on mountain tops and at the Grand Canyon. But I wouldn't change it for anything."

John grinned. "Well, good. Can you believe that was five years ago?"

"I know!" Bethany lowered her head into his lap. "Our five-year anniversary is next summer. What's the material supposed to be? Something weird like copper or wool or something?"

"They're all pretty weird," John noted, "and I have no idea either."

She continued to lie down in silence, and John joined her in the peaceful ritual. No words were spoken, yet no words needed to be spoken. Earlier that day, John felt awkward about not being able to speak with Isabel, who wasn't there, yet he was content with not speaking to someone right next to him. John stroked her hair. She was tired, but her eyes remained open as her thoughts were free to wander.

"I know what you're thinking," Bethany said, breaking the momentary silence.

"Oh yeah?" asked John, genuinely curious.

"Our baby is asleep in her crib. We're alone. We haven't really seen each other much in a couple of days."

"Interesting analysis." John now understood the implication yet decided to be playful. "Not sure what your conclusion is."

Bethany quickly sat up straight, her hair tousled from John's touch. She leaned toward John instead and locked in on a kiss that was more passionate than the last one. John smiled.

Bethany nodded. "There is something you should know

before we fuck each other's brains out."

"I'm surprised we still have secrets."

"I'm pregnant."

Unlike the first time, this announcement was less dramatic. She had already dealt with one pregnancy. This time, they had discussed dropping birth control because the hormones were messing with Bethany. The two weren't actively trying to have a second child, but they were ready.

"Okay," John said, equally deadpanned. He started processing this new development. Things wouldn't settle down at home until Emma started school in a few years. Now, not only did they have to raise another baby, but they would have even more years of daycare and commitment.

Bethany had a laugh that she tried to cover up. "Well, how do you feel? Is it too soon for number two? I think we're ready."

"Yeah, probably." John smiled too, now seeing that Bethany was reacting nonchalantly. "Well, it's gonna be weird. We're both only children. I know you liked that, and I didn't mind that. Do you want the same for Emma?"

Bethany shrugged. "Emma will be almost three when number two is born. I think that's a pretty good spread. Honestly, I think it'll be easier if they can distract each other. More time for us."

"I love how you're so calculating of this whole thing." John leaned forward to kiss her. "Most parents probably think we're monsters."

"I'm fine with that," she said, and they both laughed. After staring at each other in silence, she continued. "I'm ready if you're ready."

"I don't know what the hell we're getting ourselves

into."

Bethany smiled. "Me neither."

"This is our last one, you know."

She nodded. "Yeah, I can't be stretching my body again after this. I want to be a milf, you know."

John delivered a half-grin. "Well, you're my milf."

"I like where this is going!" Before she could say anything else, John forced her back.

Their play was interrupted by a faint cry from upstairs. "Mommy? Daddy?" John stopped, and both of them sighed.

"Well, I guess this will have to wait another week," said Bethany, her disappointment turning into cynicism. John frowned and sat upright. The two of them stood up and walked upstairs.

John had completely forgotten about the open box in the extra room, which would likely turn into the second child's room. That meant the special box would have to move to another location, possibly the garage or someplace that wasn't so easily accessible. And Isabel's shrine would be moved as well. The third bedroom was a den with their computer and bookshelves, and Bethany spent a lot of time in there. Whether the shrine's next move was into a box wasn't on John's mind for the rest of the day.

22

Chapter Twenty-Two

Having double- and triple-checked Emma's backpack to make sure it had everything she needed, John walked over and gave it to her. "Here you go, sweet teeth."

"Thank you, Daddy!" she said. She turned around so John could put the straps on her.

"I think you're now ready for kindergarten!" John was especially proud at that moment. Here was his daughter, who started out as an alien look-alike in a hospital room but was now ready to go to her first day of school. She was wearing a black dress with a white ribbon around her waist; everybody who saw her said she looked adorable.

Emma ran down the stairs and into the living room, where John's parents were sitting. They made sure to not miss their granddaughter's first day of school. That was fair, as they weren't there when she was born. Bethany's parents hadn't retired yet and were unable to get the day off.

He followed her down the stairs at a slower, more careful pace. Both of his parents were on the couch and had been playing with Olivia, their second granddaughter. Olivia saw her older sister run into the room, and she squealed and hobbled over with her limited motor skills.

John hadn't intended on having two daughters, thinking he was going to have one of each. But instead they had Olivia Isabella. Her first name was entirely Bethany's decision, but John claimed full authority on her middle name. Isabella was a slight alteration and a safe compromise. It was important to John, in case of death, that Isabel's memory carried on for a little longer, even if it was only part of a name.

"Emma, play!" demanded an excited Olivia. She fed off the general excitement in the room without being aware of the reasons for the excitement.

"I can't! I got school!" said Emma in her best attempt to sound as mature as possible.

"I *have* school, you mean," said Brian, John's father. He was a nice man but liked to correct children's grammar whenever he could. If he could get away with correcting adults' grammar, he'd do that as well.

"I have school, Olivia!" repeated Emma with the correct wording, albeit sassier than before.

"Oh!" said Olivia, trying to process the meaning of the statement.

"You'll be in school in a few years too!" said John.

Olivia nodded while staring at John. She was definitely quieter than Emma when she was that age, but Olivia had a curiosity that surprised even both sets of her grandparents. John hoped this curiosity would continue as she grew older and that she would study the world for what it was and what it wasn't.

"Bus is coming in five minutes!" said Bethany from the other room. Their school district released software that allowed parents to track how far away busses were via GPS. Bethany had it installed on her phone, but she still lacked complete faith in its accuracy. "Better get out there!"

"You ready, Emma?" John said. She smiled and nodded enthusiastically. His daughter had no fear. Another trait bestowed to her exclusively by her mother.

"Okay. Mom, Dad, we're gonna wait outside. Bethany, you coming?"

"Yeah!" she yelled, still in the other room. She had finished cleaning up their family breakfast and ran into the front room. Brian and Carol, John's mother, sat up and prepared their phones so they could film the festivities. They had filmed John's first day of school on an old VHS camcorder. They had dug up the tape and shown it to the family earlier that week. It was partially for the nostalgia but primarily so Emma could better prepare and understand that it was a safe and normal undertaking for any child.

"Daddy!" John looked down and saw Olivia, who was unsure of what was going on and holding onto his legs. He smiled, bent down, and picked her up.

"Gotcha!" he said playfully. Olivia giggled. John made a final glance around. His parents were going out the door, and Bethany was behind them. Presumably, Emma was ahead of everybody else. John followed the caravan out the door to their front yard. The pickup zone was two houses down, and there was already one of the neighborhood kids waiting, a fourth-grader. It wasn't his first day, as school started a week and a half earlier for the older children.

Emma, at the head of their family pack, ran down the sidewalk and toward the spot. John hollered at her about running too far away from them, but Bethany grabbed his shoulder.

"John, she's fine."

He nodded while gripping his younger daughter harder. "I know. This is so new."

"It is," said Bethany, who quickly squeezed his rear end with no one else noticing, "but trust me, it's all good. I know these things. Besides, I'll be driving to the school once she leaves anyway, so I'll be there to settle her in."

"I guess so." They had walked up to the bus stop but maintained distance from Emma. She was already chatting up the fourth-grader. It was obvious from his expression that he didn't care to talk to someone so much younger, but seeing several adults around, he reluctantly entertained her. Emma really had no fear, talking to another kid twice her age, especially one she was unfamiliar with.

"It's amazing that you two are letting her ride the bus," said John's mother, fiddling with her phone to get its camera ready. "Seems like every one of your generation drives their kids to and from school every day."

"We're too cheap to pay for the gas," quipped Bethany. John smiled. His mother tended to be judgmental about the younger generation and would often blow stereotypes out of proportion.

"Mom, people don't do that as often as you think," he said, adding weight to the conversation. "Emma's smart. Look, she's already making friends with the big kids."

"She's quite the butterfly," Carol said.

"Make a good politician," said Brian, although John couldn't figure out if he was being serious.

"What's politician?" asked Olivia with sketchy pronunciation.

"Someone who makes very important decisions," said John, trying to find a balance between immature baby talk and adult discussion.

"Oh," said Olivia. John wasn't sure if she even understood that simplified explanation, but he was glad Olivia never asked *why* repeatedly like many young children did. Perhaps she wasn't old enough yet to know how to deliver torture.

Almost on schedule, the bus drove down the street and stopped in front of them. Another child, accompanied by one of her parents, had joined their crew by that point. The red lights of the bus flashed on, and the door opened. The bus driver waved at the four adults, and they all waved back.

"Bye, Mommy! Bye, Daddy!" Emma waved back at them.

John's stomach seemed to jump up into his midsection, something he thought was anatomically impossible. "Bye, sweet teeth!" he said at the same time as Bethany's goodbye.

"Bye, Grandma and Grandad!" Before John's parents could even respond, she turned around and ran on the bus first. They could see the bus driver talking with her and directing her into one of the front seats. There appeared to be another young student up there with her. That relieved John's anxiety slightly. After the third child found a seat, the door shut, the lights flickered off, and the bus drove away. Emma was waving through the window the whole time, and her family was responding in kind.

"And she's off," said Brian.

"Where did Emma go?" asked Olivia, despite being told many times before.

"She's going to school! She'll be back later today!"

"Okay!" she said.

"Alright, time to haul ass and get to the school." Bethany kissed Olivia on the cheek and then John on the lips. "I'll get Emma settled in. Should be back in an hour or so." After her farewells to Olivia and her in-laws, she rushed off to her car, which was back at their house.

"Well, that's that," said John, still reeling from the event.

"She's going to be fine," said the other child's parent, whom John recognized but had never properly met.

"Yeah. I know she'll be." He turned toward his own parents. "You got all that?"

"Yeah, we both did," said his father, putting away his phone. "We'll be showing her that one at her graduation party."

"Man, I'm not even thinking that far ahead. That's a long ways away."

"You say that now, John, but twelve years will go by before you know it. Trust me, the same happened with you."

The more John thought about it, the more his dad's words matched his perspective on reality. On the surface, twelve years seemed like a very long time. But John thought back twelve years. He was living with Isabel in their duplex. That brought his father's point home more than anything. The memory of Isabel being fully alive, while a more distant memory than John would have liked it to be, was still easily remembered. Considering how fast the past twelve years had transpired, he could imagine how quickly the next twelve years would go, especially now that he was older.

"I'll be fifty when she graduates," said John solemnly.

His mother laughed. "We've been past that point a while, John. I think you'll live."

While he wasn't yet decrepit, he wasn't as spry at thirty-seven as he used to be. Regardless, his clean diet had kept him and Bethany slim, and their short outdoor hikes with the children had yielded some benefits, but they had to keep those journeys short to avoid whining children. They had discussed taking on rock climbing, but life had unusual ways of preventing them from starting.

"Do you still want us to take Olivia for a few hours?" asked his father.

"Yeah. Beth and I took the day off so we could get some rest. If you still don't mind."

"Oh no, we don't mind at all!" said his mother, who walked over to John, her eyes on Olivia.

"Hey, Olive, do you want to go to Grandma and Grandad's?" asked John.

She raised her hands high above her head. "Yay!"

The three adults laughed, and John handed over his youngest daughter to his mother. She wasn't yet potty trained, so John had to run back into his house to grab her bag. He met them back outside, with Olivia already in the back of his parents' car, secured in her car seat. After hugging both of them and thanking them again, he took his leave, watching them pull forward and down the road. Watching Olivia go with his own parents was a lot different from watching Emma leave on the bus.

After his parents cleared the corner and were out of sight, he checked the time on his phone. Bethany would return in forty-five minutes. That gave John some time to do some tidying up for her before she got back. He went inside, concentrating on the kitchen. Bethany had already cleaned up most of it, so the details didn't take long. Olivia had made a jumbled mess in the living room, so he tackled that next. In the master bedroom, he made their bed and got all their clothes off the floor.

When Bethany came back home, he greeted her with a powerful kiss. She couldn't escape, being trapped by John's arms. Yet she didn't struggle.

"Hey, John!" she said sweetly.

"Hey, sweets," he said. "How is Emma?"

"She's great! We found her table. She introduced herself to her neighbors. I met some of the other parents. Lots going on but things seemed to be under control. Mrs. Garcia has some help so everything will be fine!"

"She'll be back around two-ish?"

Bethany nodded. "Yeah. Something like that."

John pulled her closer to him again for a second kiss. She moaned this time, and he could feel her knees weakening as she felt heavier in his arms. "What are you thinking, babe?"

"I made the bed," he said, whispering in her ear. "I really want to make the bed a second time today. I was wondering if you could help."

"Okay," she said, following her husband into the master bedroom. They barely got through the door before they tore each other's clothes off, clawing at each other's bodies. John, with the best effort he could muster, threw Bethany toward the bed. She barely had time to crawl onto it when John grabbed her hair and held her face down into the comforter. There were no considerations for foreplay; they had been craving this for weeks. Bethany gasped every single time John made a thrust. He was relentless. She tried to bury her head in the bed to muffle her screams, but John objected, pulling on her hair to force her head back, forcing her cries to be heard.

Once John was spent, he collapsed forward on top of Bethany's back. His powerful grip on her hair turned into a gentle hand, finding a way to wrap around her sweaty body. John lay there, hearing the chorus of their heavy breathing.

"I love you, John," Bethany said, barely making out words between her breaths.

"I love you, Beth," John responded in kind.

"I missed you," she continued. She reached back with her hand to feel his body.

John didn't respond at first. He wasn't as spirited as he used to be, and the fatigue was wearing down on him hard. Words were even difficult to plan in his mind, let alone speak out loud.

"Tired?" asked Bethany with a sweet innocence John knew was false.

"Yeah," he said, managing to muster some words. After a few more heavy breaths, he continued. "I'm out of practice."

"It's okay, hon," she said reassuringly.

"Maybe we should hit up rock climbing. I'll get back in shape and then we can fuck like we're in our twenties again."

Bethany closed her eyes and smiled. "Mmmm, I definitely won't mind that. We just have to worry about the kids though. Olivia won't be in school for another few years."

"We'll just have to get our parents to watch them more," he said with a mischievous tone. "I love our kids, but I really, really miss just fucking your brains out."

She moaned. "I'm glad you miss that. I'm so glad that kids didn't make us go stale."

John nodded. It was one of his fears going into parenthood. He knew so many coworkers and friends whose sex lives had vanished. Even though they had to carefully schedule alone time, they were lucky that their passion had never gone away.

23

Chapter Twenty-Three

When John was younger, he avoided flying. He was more concerned over the pollution than he was in saving time. Now that he understood the frailty of time, he had a change of heart.

"I remember Beth and me making this drive when we were dating," he said to the man sitting beside him. "She had never gone since she was so poor growing up. I had gone twice as a kid, so figured it was worth it."

Normally, when someone was trapped on an airplane, the incessant rattle of a neighbor was an unwelcome nightmare. This time was different. The man looked away from the window. "Yeah, took several days, didn't it?"

"Yeah, we hauled ass down the highway." John sighed, recalling the memory. "Damn, Nick, could you imagine taking both of our families down to Disneyland in cars?"

"Don't make me think about that bullshit," said Nick, and the two silently laughed.

Ever since Nick stayed with John that one Christmas, his life rebounded. After he got his own apartment, he received several promotions within the first year at his new job. He started dating again and was much happier with the experience. Eventually, he formed a partnership with a woman named Ashley, a shy but lovely woman who John quickly warmed up to.

During that time, Nick learned that child protection services had gotten involved with Michelle's home life. Seeing an opportunity, he sued for sole custody of Alex, their child. It was an easy fight, and Nick finally won custody. Ashley welcomed the newcomer to their budding family and talked with Nick about having a child of their own. Nick proposed, and the two married, with John fulfilling the role of best man for the second time. A year later, the newlyweds welcomed Chloe into their lives.

John turned around in his seat, looking toward the back of the plane. A few aisles back, he could see Bethany with their two children. They were now old enough to appreciate the visit to that fabled park. Emma was already in the fourth grade and was participating in her school's student council. Olivia was a few years behind her, finishing up the first grade. Unlike her older sister, she was more reserved but explored her creativity. She was already a competent artist, winning several contests and awards for her drawings.

He studied the three of them having a conversation about something he couldn't hear. The strain of turning his back got to him, so he pivoted to face the front, accidentally brushing the unknown passenger sitting to his left.

"Sorry about that," said John. The man nodded and continued reading his book.

"They doing okay back there?" asked Nick, gesturing behind him without making the extra effort to turn around.

"Oh yeah, they're great. How about your peeps?"

"Nobody is dead yet," he said, deadpanned. His family was sitting on the other side of the fuselage a couple rows in front of them. Alex was already a teenager; Chloe was only a few months younger than Olivia.

"Man, I wonder what it's like to be the only boy in the pack," noted John, thinking about Nick's oldest child.

"Well, probably would be better if he had a more stable life growing up. He still has behavior issues, but they've been getting better the past year or two. They say it's better to have a teenage son than a daughter, anyway."

"Ah, fuck me," said John. They both laughed.

"Anyway, I think it's good that Alex got to see Chloe being born and all. Don't know the science behind it, but having that older-brother gut instinct from the start made him get his act together."

John nodded. "You think the age gap would be a problem. Beth and I didn't want to deal with that."

Nick tilted his head. "You'd think so, but I think it's good in his case. He would feel more responsible because he's the older brother. Fixed some of his issues faster, I think."

"Yeah, probably." John studied the cabin. It was April, so school was still in session for most families; John and Nick decided to take their children out for a week. It was a gamble that would hopefully afford them shorter wait times for the more popular rides. Mostly adults of all ages and backgrounds occupied the plane.

"So, John, had a weird thought." Nick waited for John's acknowledgment. "Do you think Alex and Emma would date when they're older?"

"Jesus, dude!" John said louder than he wanted. Several heads turned to react to John's outburst, including Nick's family. Their attention didn't hold as they lost interest.

Nick laughed and shrugged. "I mean, didn't you tell me that Emma had a crush on him?"

John's eyes bulged out as he recalled that memory. "I mean, yeah. But that was a couple years ago. She was, like, seven at the time. He's just the only older boy she knows well."

Nick nodded. "Yeah, but it makes you think. In a couple of years, they'll both be old enough to date. Do you think it could happen?"

"Well, what's that rule again?" asked John, trying to recall the formula in his mind. "Something like half your age plus seven?"

"Hmmm, that sounds right." Nick furrowed his brow. "So if Alex is, I think, three, four years older, that means he would be twenty-two. She'd be eighteen."

"Freshman and senior in college," John said, analyzing the math. "It's a smaller gap than between Bethany and myself."

"Or me and Ashley."

John nodded. While Nick was talking in jest, it made John think about his daughter's dating. In two years, Emma would be in middle school, and she'd start having interests beyond friendship. She'd want to explore those emotions.

Upon first learning of Emma's sex, John vowed not to become the overprotective father figure with the metaphorical shotgun. As scary as it was to consider, he knew human beings were sexual creatures. He hoped she'd be safe, but he also wanted her to explore the world as he or Bethany did.

The rest of the flight continued smoothly. It wasn't a long flight to begin with, but John was glad to be freed of the confines of the plane. They landed at the John Wayne Airport, south of Anaheim. With dusk approaching, and the children worn out from their first flight, the families opted to stay in that night at their hotels. The hotels were close to Disneyland, so there was no need to get up earlier than they had to. They spent most of the night playing in the pool, enjoying the warmer weather of southern California. John and Bethany played in the pool with the four children, while Nick and Ashley watched from the chairs on the deck. Ashley was heavier than the women John and Nick had dated in the past, and even Nick had put on a few pounds himself over the past several years. John had always eaten healthier than his friend. This didn't matter much in their twenties. Yet they were now past forty, and the physical differences were far clearer.

John and Bethany were also in great shape, thanks to several years of rock climbing. To prove her hard work, Bethany wore a bikini in the pool, and John didn't mind at all. They could keep up with the playing and splashing children with ease. Both their children started taking swimming lessons when they were in preschool, so they knew their strokes and how to stay afloat. Nick followed suit with Chloe, but Alex had to learn later in his life, and his technique was poor as a result.

That next day was their first at Disneyland. The children, Alex included, were ecstatic. The adults had been there at least once each, but enough time had elapsed that the experience was fresh. There were also new places that weren't there when they last visited the park, notably the Star Wars–themed area. They spent lots of time there but also enjoyed the classics as well.

When they were walking back to their hotel that evening, Ashley asked the children, "So what were your favorite rides?"

"Splash Mountain!" said Olivia.

"I liked the frog one!" yelled Chloe.

"I thought Space Mountain was pretty cool," said Alex.

"Pirates of the Caribbean was the funniest," said Emma after much thought.

"Well, tomorrow we're going to California Adventure!" said Bethany excitedly.

"Never been there myself," Nick said, shaking his head. "I was a little one when I was here last, before that place existed."

Once they were back at the hotel, Bethany and Ashley were with the children in Nick's room. John was with Nick in his own family's room, recalling the events of the day in a more juvenile fashion.

"Man, I never saw Chloe so excited before," Nick mused. "She was fucking going crazy when Jasmine showed up."

"Yeah, that was intense." John took a sip of some bottled water he had purchased at the park. "And she was pretty hot too."

Nick grinned. "She's probably half your age, dude."

John shrugged. "Yeah, so?"

"Well, whatever happened to half your age plus seven or whatever?"

John looked away while pondering. "I mean, yeah, but..." He stopped, completely at a loss for words. "It's not like it's illegal."

After recovering from a deep belly laugh, Nick continued. "No, you're right. Whoever was playing her was quite the looker."

Nodding, John said, "Well, yeah, just because we're approaching middle age don't mean we're dead."

"Yeah, it's hard convincing myself of that," said Nick. "You got nothing to complain about. Beth looks great. After two kids too!"

"Oh, believe me, I'm not complaining one bit. I'm sure she'll appreciate that compliment." John felt guilty by not paying Nick's wife a similar respect. He liked Ashley; she was a fun and kind individual. But he didn't personally think of her as attractive. It didn't matter, as she was attractive to Nick, and that point counted above all others.

"Speaking of which, do you mind if during, like, the afternoon tomorrow you guys can take control and look after the kids for an hour?" Nick sat down on the bed with a mischievous look. "Like, it would be cool for Ashley and me to come to the hotel room."

"An hour? You only need ten minutes."

"Hah hah hah," said Nick sarcastically.

John smiled at his own joke, then pulled up the calendar on his phone out of pure habit. There was no itinerary for the trip saved on there. On instinct, he always conferred to his calendar for planning anything. Before he put the phone away, he made a note of the date: April 13. He turned the screen off and set the phone down on the counter behind him. At that moment, he froze.

April 13.

"Oh my God," uttered John. He meant to say it quietly, but it escaped his lips.

"What?" asked Nick.

John looked at his friend with fearful eyes. "Yesterday was April 12."

Nick nodded with concern in his own eyes. "Yeah, we flew in on April 12."

John's spirit sank, and his body sank with it as he found the nearest chair and sat down. He gazed openly at the space in front of him.

"April 12 was the day of the accident."

At first, Nick nodded confusingly, but soon he understood. "Oh. Oh, yeah."

John frowned. "And I completely forgot."

Nick said nothing. With no change in John's expression, Nick broke his silence. "We were busy. A lot was going on."

"I have never forgotten." Being in the presence of his friend, he tried to keep a stiff upper lip. He battled the precursors of tears. "I've always expected it. It just... completely passed my mind this time."

"I'm sorry, man."

"Yeah," said John, choking on his words. "Fifteen years too."

Nick whistled. "That's a long time." After a long, thoughtful pause, he continued. "I have to admit, John, I'm kind of surprised you still care as much as you do."

Chapter Twenty-Three

John's hypnotism broke. He turned to face Nick. "What do you mean?"

Shrugging, Nick answered him. "I know it was a huge deal for you. Believe me, I was there. It hit you like a ton of bricks. To this day I still can't imagine how hurt you were. I'm pretty sure that it's probably the worst day of your life. It's just… I don't know. Like, if she was your final love, and you never met anyone again, I could get it. But you have Bethany, dude. She's your wife. And I know you love her. She's everything to you. Well, her and your kids. You've lived and done so much more with her. I mean, what, you've been married eleven, twelve years now? You'd been together longer than that even. You were with Isabel, what, three years?"

John understood that Nick was trying to help ease his shock, but it was driving him down the road of anger. "And so she shouldn't matter anymore because the math doesn't balance out?"

Nick sighed. "No. I don't know what I'm saying. Most of your adult life has been spent with Beth. I hate seeing you hurting, and if you keep remembering that shit that went down, you'll always be hurting."

"I can't forget her. I promised her I'd remember her to the end." At that point, John was seething under his skin, but he kept his anguish in check.

"You know," Nick said, followed by an underhanded laugh, "I think it's because when I put myself in your shoes, I think of Michelle. God, that… Goddammit. Just, nothing good comes from me thinking of her, you know? Any sort of good times we had I just buried and never revisit. And trust me, there were some good times, as hard as it is to believe."

"Yeah," said John, calmer.

"I wouldn't wish your pain on anyone, but if I had memories of a lost love, I sure as hell wish I had yours."

John returned his eyes to Nick. After a moment of studying each other's faces, John smiled. "Thanks. That kinda helped."

"Of course. Look, John, I didn't mean to demean you or Isabel or anything having to do with that. I know you care, and that's cool. You may disagree, but I think the phrase 'it's better to love and lost' is true for us. She was taken away from you, but she never betrayed you. I would take that any day of the week." Nick looked down. "While we're reminiscing about this, I kinda miss her too. It's been a long-ass time, and I definitely don't think about her anywhere near as much as you do. But she was one cool chick. I'm glad she was my friend too."

Nick stood up to stand next to John, who remained seated. "Just think about your own wife, okay? This week is for you guys, your family. Just think about her a little more. I think she may appreciate it."

John pondered his words. A lot of what Nick was saying made sense. John was old enough that if he analyzed his life on a spreadsheet, Isabel was a minor blip. Yet despite its small size on his timeline, it was a powerful blip. Bethany hadn't brought up Isabel in years; John taking down the shrine when Olivia came along probably helped in that regard. He fought that step, but as with most things he had done in the past ten years, he did it for the sake of the family. In the end, it was easier than he imagined it would be.

24

CHAPTER TWENTY-FOUR

Emma was sitting on the floor in the living room, reading a book that had been assigned to her at school. It was a dreary day outside, and the glow from the overcast clouds permeated the room. John's thirst for the rain had never been quenched after so many years, and the lack of rain ruined his mood.

"Dad, what's the point in studying books you don't want to read?"

John was in the kitchen, wiping down the counters and cleaning off a pot by hand. Emma was at the age where she'd question the point of her education. He remembered his classmates in middle school asking about the point of pre-algebra or biology or anything else being studied. Unbeknownst to Emma, he thought her inquiry about literature studies was a good one.

"Well, Emma, it helps with critical thinking," said John loudly so she could hear him in the other room. "You can look at a fictional situation and study it, ask yourself questions about it. That way, when something in the real world happens, you're smart and can figure it out yourself."

"But can't you do that with anything? Why does it have to be from boring books?"

"Probably a specific issue your English teacher wants to talk about." John put the pot away and studied the kitchen. It definitely looked better than it did a half-hour earlier. "It used to be worse. Used to be a bunch of books written by dead white dudes. I had to read a bunch of them myself."

"Aren't you a white dude?" she asked flippantly.

"Yes, but I'm not dead." John grinned, even though she couldn't see him.

"Jamie's older sister says the books she reads in high school are even more boring," said Emma.

The doorbell rang, breaking their discussion on literary critique. Sighing, John took one last look at the kitchen before heading to the front door. It was a drab Saturday afternoon. Bethany and Olivia were away at a weekend workshop class for visual arts. His younger daughter was becoming invested in her craft, improving every day. Olivia was a quiet yet talented child.

John wasn't expecting anybody that day, so he cautiously opened the front door. Standing on his front porch was a bespeckled man with a smaller stature than John. His face was round, despite his thin frame. He was wearing a sports jacket with jeans. No tie. Despite his thin hair, the man appeared a little younger than John.

"Hello?" John asked. He wasn't paranoid about the situation, but he was wary due to his teenage daughter being in the next room.

"Hey!" said the man with an odd look on his face. He tried to smile, but his face kept shifting to an uneasy expression. "Are you John Poland?"

Nothing unusual so far, aside from the fact this wasn't a salesperson. Or at least a bad one. "Speaking. Can I help you?"

The man's smile looked more natural, but it still seemed to hide nervousness. "So my name is Andrew Nimz. You probably have no clue who I am. I, uh... This is kinda awkward. Sorry."

"Okay?" John angled his head, perplexed by the man's behavior.

"So, um, there's a reason I'm here, believe me. Kind of a long story. When I was a kid, I had an older sister that disappeared. Cut off contact with the family, completely gone. Lot of things happened. I've spent the past couple of years trying to find her. Private eyes, looking through records. You know, the works."

John nodded. "Okay." He still had no clue what the visit was about.

Andrew nervously laughed. "Sorry, um, there's just no good way to segue into what I need to ask you. So I found out my sister changed her last name, and, um, your name came up in the investigations. You don't happen to know Isabel Breton, do you?"

Any pretense John had about the stranger evaporated. His body froze, his eyes locked on Andrew. He skipped a breath, feeling the shock seeping through his body, numbing his diaphragm. At first, he was unable to acknowledge

Andrew's question. His mind was racing. What did Andrew know? Did he know what happened to her?

Instinctively, John turned around and raised his voice. "Emma, can you go upstairs to your room?"

He could see her head rise out of her book. "Yeah, sure, I guess."

Once John saw her putting the bookmark in her book and preparing to get up, John turned his head back toward Andrew. "Yes. Yes, I did know her at one time. Did you want to come in?"

Andrew relaxed. He sighed, and his subtle smile seemed genuine. "Don't mind if I do, thank you."

John backed up to let him into the house. John could hear Emma's feet at the top of the stairs behind him. She knew nothing of that subject. For the first time, John felt like he knew nothing either.

Leading Andrew into the dining room to take a seat, John asked, "Want a beer?"

Andrew nodded. "Yeah, don't mind if I do. Long past couple of days, that's for sure."

He sat at the dining room table while John turned on an overhead light. John ducked back into the kitchen to grab two bottles from the refrigerator before returning to entertain the stranger. Despite the mystery, John never paid heed to Isabel's smoky past, while they were together or even after her death. He still maintained that if she didn't talk about it, it wasn't his business to know. But now his curiosity had been piqued; he had a chance to learn something new about his lost partner.

"Well, Andrew, yes, I know Isabel." John took a seat and used his bottle opener to open the two bottles on the table. "I, uh, don't know what you know about her either. This is kind of a bit awkward too…"

But Andrew interrupted John. "If you're referring to the fact my sister is dead, yes, I know that." His face wasn't pained, but there was a soft sense of loss in his eyes.

His admission relieved John. At least Andrew was aware of the elephant in the room. Still, John was hesitant to answer questions that Andrew had. It was personal for John, and he didn't talk about Isabel to just anybody. "Well, it's good that you know. I'm not even sure where we should begin here."

Andrew took a swig of his bottle. "This whole process wasn't easy. Spent the past two years doing all this work. I was hoping to find her somewhere. I just found out a few weeks ago that she had passed. Uncovered her death certificate. Found she was in a coma and that her plug was pulled. Took some doing but found your signature authorizing it." His eyes darkened, and he gave John a pointed look.

John took a deep breath. "I did… I did."

Andrew took a moment to study John, collecting his own words. "You weren't just a friend, were you?"

John bit his lip, wondering if it was time to start answering. "Isabel, yes, she was my friend. She was…" He closed his eyes and took a deep breath. "She was my partner."

Silence befell the room. Andrew's face wasn't quite sad, but it was almost as if he missed her. "You loved her, didn't you? My sister?"

"Yes, I did." John's breathing returned to normal.

Andrew scratched the top of his head. "Was that her

child? The one who ran up the stairs?"

John shook his head. "No, no. Isabel and I never had children. I got married again after she died." He didn't intend to indirectly refer to Isabel as a wife, but it felt natural to say. As he took a deep breath, his gaze floated away from Andrew. "Even so, it still hurts."

"It's funny, you know," said Andrew. "I didn't cry or anything when I first found out she died. To me, she died when I was twelve when she left home. Things were quite a bit different back then. How I felt about her then. I guess finding out about her actual death is a bit of closure for me."

John finished a sip of his beer, leaning forward in his chair. "Isabel didn't really talk about her family at all. She mentioned her mother once. Never mentioned anything about siblings or anything specific. I remember her talking about stuff that happened when she was in school or shenanigans with her friends, but nothing about her home life. Look, I'm sure you have a lot of questions about what her last years were like, but, dude, I have to know. Something had to have happened."

Andrew took a deep breath and looked down at the table, adjusting his glasses. "Yeah, I suppose I should tell you about all that first. So there were three of us. The oldest was Mary. I was the youngest. Isabel was the middle kid. We were, on the surface, a pretty typical suburban middle-class family in the Midwest. Mom was a school librarian. Dad worked at a newspaper. Dad was..." And then Andrew stopped. He took a swift drink from his beer. "Dad was my hero." He made sure to emphasize the "was."

"Mary and Isabel were two years apart in age, so they

were very close. Me being a boy and seven years younger than Isabel, I didn't really relate to them all that much. So I was closest to Dad. Well…" Andrew took another sip. "What we didn't know is that my dad was abusing Mary. Starting from when she hit puberty, he would molest her, sometimes beat her. He hid this pretty damn well. Nobody really knew anything, family or friends."

"Jesus," said John, taking in all the terrible history.

"Isabel, however, found out about all that crap when she was in high school. After all, she was pretty close to her sister. I don't really know exactly how she found out, but she did. And she confronted my dad. Isabel was really freaking smart, would always help out with my homework. I remember Mary did not do well in school at all, barely graduated. And you know what my dad did? He blamed her accusations on some sort of feminist brainwashing that she was reading or something. It was really easy to get Mom to side with him. Mary was too freaking scared to say anything herself. I kinda remember her being mad at Isabel for saying something.

"Needless to say, it drove a pretty bad wedge through our family. I was pretty young, but I remember I was so mad at Isabel for saying those cruel things about my own father. I remember she was gone a lot, keeping busy away from home. Dad accused her of partying hard and drinking and doing drugs. Well, when I first began my search for her, I first talked with some of her old school friends, and according to them she just spent time reading books and studying subjects and just being, I don't know, smart. She just couldn't stand being at home with my dad.

"But the abuse didn't stop. Isabel did stay around to

help Mary as much as she could. Mary obviously didn't go to college, couldn't even hold down a job. She just stayed at home because she had nowhere else to go. Once Isabel graduated high school, my dad pretty much told her he'd pay for her school, full ride, if she would move away and not come back home. I mean, heck, that sounded great! My mean sister gets to be away from us, and we'd be a happy family again. Win-win for everyone.

"Well, her first year away at school, my mom came home one day and found Mary's body with her wrists slit open."

John put his hands on his face. This was the past Isabel tried to run from. This was the baggage that only she carried, the event that made her who she was.

"Bel never told me any of that," John softly said, still taking in the terrible history. He shook his head one more time.

"I find it interesting as to how she just put that all to rest, because as soon as she found out, she got the police involved, but they couldn't find enough evidence to bring Dad to court. Mom sided with my dad again, and I, of course, stood by him too. I wouldn't let anything happen to my hero. Isabel told us to just fork off and we never heard from her again."

"So what did your dad blame the suicide on?" asked John.

"That Mary was 'emotionally disabled,'" Andrew said, creating air quotes with his hands. "Mental illness. You know, the works. But Mary was dead and Isabel was gone and I was an only child. It sucks to say in hindsight, but, man, the rest of my childhood was awesome. No sisters to divide my parents' attention. Dad would buy me video games and we'd play all the time. My teenage years were awesome. And no one was the wiser to what really happened."

"Amazing," said John. "And no one bothered to look her up?"

"None of us wanted to. Even if we did, she did a very good job at covering her tracks." Andrew looked out the window. "According to my research, she changed her last name, changed her address like ten times while she was at university. I think the only reason I was able to get this far at all is that she had died long enough ago that her records were just easier to access."

"It went the other way too," said John, reminiscing about his former partner. "We couldn't find her parents to act as next of kin. They tried but they couldn't really backtrace anything, which I thought was very odd. You'd think the state would be good at that. Come to think of it, wouldn't surprise me if she did some illegal things like fake a social security number, that sort of thing."

"Yeah, she got one of those right away, actually."

John rubbed his chin. "So I guess this begs the question: how do you know all of this now? That is, everything about your dad?"

Andrew finished the last of his beer before he continued. "So life went on normally. I became an electrician. My parents retired. Well, three years ago, Dad had a stroke. Didn't live the healthiest lifestyle. He died a few months later. At the time, I was devastated. He was my hero. But once we went through his affairs, that's when the evidence came up."

He chuckled as if what he was about to say was a joke. "He wrote down everything that he did. Almost like a confession. We found videos and pictures of some of the, shall we say, encounters that he had with Mary. He even kept some of her underwear in a safe."

John's eyes widened. "Wow. I guess the news didn't just subtly show up, huh?"

"No, it didn't," said Andrew, shaking his head. "We finally realized the monster that my dad was. And to top it off? Mom suspected the whole time. She didn't want to say anything because she didn't want to upset anybody in the family. She also didn't have proof. And she was in love with him, somehow. For the first time in my life, I was mad at my whole family for letting this happen. And for the first time in my life, I forgave Isabel. That's when I decided that I had to find her, if for no other reason than to just apologize to her. I didn't care so much about forgiveness or reconnecting with her or anything like that. My biggest regret is that I won't be able to do even that. She died thinking her family was sick and evil. And the worst stick in the mud about it is that she wasn't wrong either."

John nodded. "She said she always valued friendship above family. I can see why the concept of family meant nothing to her."

"And now I kind of agree with her too," said Andrew, regret painted on his face. "I talk to Mom a few times a year, but I still haven't forgiven her either. She was an adult. She should have known better. Isabel was a teenager, and she was the responsible one."

"She was definitely the responsible one in our relationship," said John, chuckling to himself. Andrew even smiled. John scratched his head. "She gave up on society. She loathed it. She hated the rules, hated things being the way they were just because they were the way they were. She loved the city. She loved the country. She hated the suburbs. Now I think I know why."

"She wrote a lot of poetry and short stories in high school about that," said Andrew. "I discovered them during my search. At first glance, it looked like typical teenage angst, but there was real emotion behind every word she wrote."

"You know, I was thinking about what you said a moment ago." John took a quick look at the stairs to make sure there was no eavesdropping. "About you regretting that you won't be able to apologize to her in person."

"What do you mean?" asked Andrew, skeptical.

Here was a stranger who'd be privy to something not even John's own family knew about. "When she got in her accident, and she was in a coma, as weird as it is to say, talking to her really helped. I got to say things and confess things to her, and I felt better doing it. When she died and I'd visit the place where her ashes were laid to rest, I would do the same thing and feel the same way. I can tell you where she rests. Only a few of our close friends know where that is. Not even my wife knows where that is. But you are her brother, and you are here to make amends, so I think you deserve to know too."

Andrew smiled. "Thanks, John. That really means a lot." He looked around the house, studying the pictures and photos that lined the walls. "You live a good life, it seems. I'm glad that my sister chose to spend her time with you."

Isabel chose John. She didn't choose her relatives; she rejected any association with them. She abandoned her past. The one person she cared about the most in her old life was killed, and she tried to seek vengeance. After that failed, getting up and leaving was the best option. In the months and years after, she healed herself from the ordeal. When her orbit finally joined John's, she was the strongest person he had ever met. Knowing how she reached that point made John appreciate her more.

Learning more about his first love filled him with joy. He smiled and felt warm. It was almost as if he was falling in love with her again. But it wasn't new love; it was always there. It had stretched across time, over almost twenty years, but was renewed. The feeling likely wouldn't last, but it was worth experiencing again.

The two men continued their conversation late into the afternoon. John told Andrew about his experiences with Isabel, what she was like as a young adult, and more about her worldview and perspectives. Two beers later, and the hour was getting late. Bethany and Olivia were almost due home.

"Where are you staying?" asked John. Andrew had flown in from across the country.

"Staying at the Marriott downtown," he said. "Never been here, so figured I'd hang around for a few days."

"If you want, I'll take you to her resting place. I have to admit, I've neglected seeing her as often as I should, so it'll mean a lot to me to go with you."

Andrew smiled. "Yeah. That sounds great, actually. I'll check my schedule and we'll make it work!"

The two exchanged contact information. John also

promised to send photos of Isabel, as the newest photo Andrew had of his sister was her senior portrait. Andrew then drove away.

"Who was that?" asked Emma, walking down the stairs as soon as Andrew left.

"An old friend," said John. It wasn't quite accurate, but deep down, there was a shred of truth in his words.

25

CHAPTER TWENTY-FIVE

Mirrors were always honest. There were those designed to flatter or entertain, but mostly, they were the bearers of the visual truth. John knew this as he stared into the face of one, alone in the bathroom. His hair was starting to show strands of gray. Some wrinkles had shown on his face; they weren't noticeable to the average onlooker, but he could see them. John was getting older, and although he took it in stride before, that was the first moment he discovered the destruction of time.

He leaned against the sink, one hand firmly planted on the edge of the counter, the other around a glass of wine. It was a hard day. It had been quite a long time since he had experienced pain of that magnitude. John couldn't keep his eyes off himself, but they were no eyes of admiration. He could only focus on the negativity of his world and the people no longer in it.

Outside the door, he could hear the chatter of pleasantries. Guests socializing with new acquaintances, and guests socializing with friends from the distant past. Some of those discussions were sure to be authentic; others were more shallow, family and friends struggling to reconnect after decades of not seeing each other. John was unwilling to take part in any of that; he wanted to be alone.

He heard a knock on the bathroom door, shattering his moment of self-reflection. A door to the bathroom of his childhood home. He spent many hours in that bathroom as a teenager for many reasons. That old familiarity returned to him. Following the knock, a muffled but familiar voice spoke. "John, are you in there?"

While he was hiding in the bathroom to avoid other people, this was the one exception. Waiting first, he eventually responded with, "Yeah, I'm here."

"Can I come in?" the scratchy voice said with calmness, not trying to attract attention.

"Yeah," said John, defeated.

Bethany opened the door and squeezed herself into the small room. She wore a long-sleeved ribbed black shirt, with a lengthy gray skirt. Her curly hair was the same length it always had been, yet it was paler than in the past. Despite the circumstances of the day, she was still beautiful.

"Hey," she said in a comforting tone.

"Hey," he said in response. He was wearing nicer clothes than usual; he was even wearing a tie for the occasion.

Keeping her head down, Bethany walked over to him and gave him a hug. John continued to lean against the sink, yet he appreciated the gesture.

"That was a nice service," she whispered in his ear. "How are you doing?"

John shut his eyes, hoping that all the pain outside that room would go away. "I should go back out there," he said softly.

"How are you doing?" repeated Bethany, her soft voice unchanging.

He sighed, hoping the answer was obvious. She had been analyzing him since they first met, and she knew more about him than even he did. There was a lot of experience there, and John trusted her expertise and knowledge. Her insistence that John verbalize his anguish wasn't a pleasant request, but John knew from all his years by her side that it was another step in the healing process.

"I'm better than I thought I would be," he said. "I know I said this before, but I just wonder if sudden death is easier to cope with than a long, drawn-out one."

Bethany looked intently at him. "I think you can make that judgment now."

John nodded, not quite understanding Bethany's words. A heart attack out of nowhere. Enough to not only debilitate someone but to outright kill them. That was all it took this time. Quick and unforgiving. He stirred, turning his head to lock eyes with Bethany. "How's Mom doing?"

"She's alright. Your uncle is with her, last I checked. I can't even imagine being married to someone for over fifty years and then just lose that person suddenly."

John looked forward at the mirror, again facing his own cynicism. "It's gonna happen to one of us."

Bethany offered a half-smile; John resorted to black

humor as a way of coping with the loss of his father. "I know. And I hope it's you that has to go first."

Before John could offer a retort, there was another knock on the bathroom door. Bethany turned her head toward the door and shouted, "We'll be out in a second!" She leaned in and softened her voice. "I just don't want you to have to go through that a second time."

After kissing him on the nose, she turned around and opened the door. Waiting outside was one of John's cousins, someone whom John had met a handful of times over the years. He wasn't even sure of his cousin's name, but that was a common oversight for him. He stiffened his back, awkwardly exuding a stance of strength, and followed Bethany out of the bathroom with his wine glass.

About two dozen guests drove from the service at the funeral parlor to John's childhood home, a home he lived in for twenty years, back when he still had two parents. It was a suburban home, newer during his childhood, but now it had been reduced to a vintage, if well-kept, state. Gray rugs from the 1990s permeated the floors in nearly every room, leaving little for variety. White textured walls with wood trimmings on the floor provided further proof of the moment when time had stopped in that house. All was frozen in there for years, until one of those two parents perished.

With his mother widowed, he wasn't sure what would happen to that home. Would she stay as its sole resident, or would she flee the memories she helped shape and retreat to greener pastures in a retirement home? Those questions stayed in John's mind, yet everyone probably asked themselves those same questions.

Moving their way through the claustrophobic hallways, John and Bethany came to the dining room, where some desserts were arranged on the table. Aside from random guests entering and leaving to gather food, there were two young women in the corner, talking softly with tears covering their faces. Their eyes showed the strain of pain that could only be known by someone who had never experienced it before.

"Hey, girls," said John in an attempt to be sympathetic while ignoring his own anguish.

Both Emma and Olivia turned and immediately hugged him. They said nothing as soon as they saw him. There was no longer any active crying, but from the intensity of their embrace, John knew they needed help. This was the first family death they had experienced, and they weren't yet sturdy enough to handle this kind of emotional anguish, especially when the person who passed was as close to them as their paternal grandfather.

Emma was taller than Bethany. She had grown so much in the past several years, both physically and mentally. She had been the captain of her varsity volleyball team as a junior. Olivia was thirteen; she still had time to close the gap and had grown so much on her own. Part of him wished that Bethany would handle their pain, but their daughters wanted his guidance at that moment.

"I miss Grandad," said Olivia, her mouth muffled against John's shirt.

"We all do, sweetie," whispered John. Olivia was the more emotional of the two, undoubtedly because she was an introvert. Even then, both Olivia and her older sister were equally in pain, equally in need of care.

Bethany kept guard so as to not allow anyone to disturb their group hug. John wasn't close to his extended family. Aside from the pain associated with reflecting on his father's life, John didn't look forward to the reception after the service because he didn't want to show his vulnerable face to strangers. Those strangers would want to talk to John to "catch up on old times" and to "reconnect." John desired none of that. He wanted none of them to be present to share in that moment; they were not his life. Yet his mother insisted that as many family members as possible show up to offer their personal eulogies and to offer support in her time of need.

Thinking now of his mother, John let his focus of concern drift to her. He didn't talk to her much since they left the service, but she needed his support the most; she was the most affected by the loss. Loss John was already familiar with. After another minute of silence, he kissed the top of both his daughters' heads and said, "I'm going to find Grandma. Are you two going to be okay?"

The embrace cracked apart as his two children backed away from him. They both hesitantly nodded as they wiped away drying tears from their eyes. John vaguely remembered when the first of his grandparents had passed, but they had lived in a different state. He wasn't as close to them, and his reaction was subdued. There was a certain level of envy John had toward his children; they were so close to all four of their grandparents.

With a quick smile, John backed away to hunt through the house and find his mother. Bethany remained behind with the children to continue comforting them. Bethany's parents were much younger than John's; they were still in their mid-sixties. They would be around for years to come, pending any sort of random illness. John wondered how much longer his elderly mother would wish to remain living. For so long, there was someone who needed her every day. Now that person was gone. He'd have to talk to his children about dedicating more of their time to visit her.

Ejecting those dire thoughts out of his head, John made his way into the living room to find his mother sitting with his uncle Mike, her younger brother. His own wife had died a couple of years earlier from complications related to diabetes. John passed by a few people standing by the door and sat down on the couch next to his mother.

"How you doing, John?" asked his uncle.

"Not too bad, Uncle Mike," said John. "When you're married to a counselor, things do tend to be easier."

"I bet." He nodded. Mike was the one he knew the best of his aunts and uncles. Mike slapped his hands into his lap. "Well, Carol, I see there's some treats that people are eating. I'll go see what there is. You want any?"

John's mother shook her head. "No thank you. I'm fine for now."

Mike offered a courteous smile and slowly stood up, groaning as he did so. He wasn't the smallest man himself, and although he spoke with a youthful zest, John had doubts about Mike's health. John turned toward his mom and smiled.

"Hey, Mom. How you doin'?"

His mother gave an expansive smile that wrinkled the area around her eyes. "I'm fine, John. We're supposed to celebrate your dad's life right now. It's okay to be happy."

John nodded. "Yeah, I know. It's easier said than done though. It didn't help seeing Emma and Olivia crying at the service. I haven't seen them cry that hard since they were little kids."

"I know. Poor girls. They really loved him." His mother sighed. "I can understand why you're so sad too."

Cocking his head, John asked, "Oh? What do you mean?"

"Well, John, this must be hard for you as well. This is the first really close death you've had. You've never had anything like this happen before. You've never hurt this much before."

John was initially surprised and hurt; how could she be so ignorant and callous as to make such a bold claim, especially about a subject John cared so strongly about? Then he wondered if his mother was sincerely ignorant, if her age was collecting too many numbers. After gathering his emotions, John decided to test which was the truth.

"Mother," John said strongly, "what do you mean this is my first time having someone close to me die?"

"Well, John, you've never had another family member like this die. I mean, you lost your grandparents a long time ago, but they all lived far away. This is the worst for all of us."

John remained confused. "But, Mom, don't you remember Isabel?"

"Isabel?" she muttered under her breath as if a verbal reminder would help her remember. "Isabel. Oh, yeah, Isabel! Wasn't that your girlfriend you had right after college?"

John nodded intently, offended by how his mother remembered Isabel. "Yes, Mom. Remember, she died?"

"Yes, of course I remember! But, honey"—she set her hand on his hand—"she was just a girlfriend. That was years ago. I'm surprised that anyone would remember that. Oh dear, I knew it was tough for you, but you weren't married and weren't with her that long. I'm kind of shocked that you're comparing the death of your own father to a girlfriend you had when you were twenty-five!"

He wanted to blame her words on her advanced age, where she no longer cared about social etiquette, but it wasn't the first time she had spoken that way about Isabel. John wasn't sure what to think; he wasn't emotionally stable at that moment and lacked the fortitude to stand up for his long-dead partner. His mother's words seeped into his soul and there wasn't much of a defense mechanism to ward them off. It was just a short-term relationship over twenty years ago. Why was John letting her get to him like that? She was contradicting what John always thought was the truth.

John never experienced an assault on Isabel's memory like that before, yet he lacked the conviction to defend any aspect of her. He could only yield the argument before it started; this wasn't the time or place for a debate. Nodding subtly, he grabbed his mother's outreached hand with his other hand and smiled. "Sorry, I just miss Dad."

His mother smiled sympathetically and scooted over in her seat to get closer to her only child. The two went into a hug on the couch. Twenty years earlier, John vowed to remember Isabel for as long as he lived. But he relinquished that vow for a moment to avoid an argument at a perilous time. He was fine with that. His gut was fine with that. His apathy hurt, but he was compelled to consider his mother's words—words he often ignored or passively considered his entire life. There was so much pain going around. John was numb to everything at that moment. There was no rain to save him this time. He had to respect his father's memory and then go home to his wonderful family. A family he spent a large part of his life with. A family he supported and loved. A family that supported him and loved him. That was his life. That was always his life.

26

CHAPTER TWENTY-SIX

Most of the vehicles waiting in the pick-up zone for the high school were running, likely to power their radios; blasting music or audiobooks or political opinions through their speakers. Or, unable to cope with the light rain spring was known for, they had their heaters on. When he was younger, John would be angry at drivers who wasted fuel in such a manner. Exhaust and pollution were deposited into the air for future generations to worry about, and for what? Hearing some blowhard's opinion on abortion?

Fortunately, most modern cars were electric-powered, although the occasional gas-powered automobile pitter-pattered across the roads. Years of creature comforts had made John more tolerant of that behavior. He even noticed that one or two cars had no drivers; driverless cars had finally taken off after years of promises and setbacks.

He could hear no sound or bell where he was parked. Yet the sudden swarm of teenagers blasting through the doors would tell anybody that classes were done for the day. Their spread was like that of an amoeba viewed through a microscope. Students in their groups were breaking apart in every direction, trying to make their way to their destinations.

After the initial storm of young adults subsided, John eyed a specific teenager who was heading in his general direction. Other students had already gotten into their respective cars. Olivia, with her straight dark hair and intense yet curious eyes, walked up to John's car. She opened the back door, threw her backpack into the back seat with little consideration for its contents, and settled into the front.

"Well, how was school?" asked John before Olivia buckled in.

"Fine," she said calmly. Unlike her older sister, Olivia was more reserved and detached. This was more noticeable the older she became. While this concerned Bethany, John took little worry in her behavior; it reminded him a lot of himself at that age. Olivia's grades didn't meet her mother's standards, but she was a renowned artist; some of her charcoal works were featured in small local galleries around town. She had a few good friends but had been drifting further from both her sister and mother over the past couple of years. Bethany felt it was due to Olivia taking herself too seriously and tried to get her to engage more with the world.

Normally Olivia rode the bus home from school. However, she had to go to the dentist to get some cavities filled.

Her dentist was deeper in the city, so John took half a day off work to take her to the appointment. It thrilled neither father nor daughter, as it was probably preventable. She shook her head. "I always thought cavities were some sort of boogeyman to get us to brush our teeth when we were kids. I never thought it was an actual thing."

John paid attention to the road as he pulled away from the curb. He had to watch out for the other parents and students leaving the school. She was always a skeptical child. John admired that in her. Even though her skepticism in science was silly, she began showing doubts about the social order, about the playbook. That aspect of her worldview pleased him, even if that same doubt had left him.

"No, it's real," he said. "Now, when I was a kid, you know that stuff that would stain your teeth if it was dirty? I thought it was fake. I thought it was just a way to shame me. Lo and behold, turns out that it was actually a thing."

Olivia said nothing. Even though she was usually quiet, today seemed unusual. No music played over the car speakers, but John was tempted to end the silence by turning something on. He did not, keeping his focus on the road as he turned onto a major avenue that led its way toward the central downtown area. It was the beginning of rush hour, so their trip would be longer.

John would glance over at Olivia and notice a look of worry and concern on her face; he initially assumed it was about the dental procedure she was about to have. But John knew Olivia well; she was brave in the face of adversity. Her lips parted as if she meant to speak, but she didn't. She continued looking forward, focusing in on herself as if nothing else mattered.

This went on for several minutes. John had stopped at a red light when his daughter turned to face him. "Dad, can I ask you something?"

"Sure!" He tried to play off the seriousness of her question, but he knew it was hard for Olivia to ask what she was thinking about.

"Well, I don't want to get in trouble." She turned back to look at the road.

John made a subdued laugh. "Olivia, what do you mean? I told you when you were a little girl that you can't get in trouble for asking questions."

"I know," she said. "It's just… I'm afraid I'll get in trouble because of how I found out what question to ask you."

"I see," said John, who was now curious. "It's okay. Go ahead and ask."

Olivia stayed quiet for another minute before she collected the courage to speak. "So, Dad, I was trying to find some of the drawings I made as a kid, like back when I was in kindergarten."

"Aren't they in your room? I thought they were in a box in your closet."

"Well, no, they aren't. I knew you and Mom boxed them up, so I went to the garage to see if I could find them there. I tried to keep it on the down-low, which was stupid. I just didn't want to ask."

"It's okay, honey," said John, smiling. "I get it. So go on. What's your question?"

"Well, I just went through a bunch of boxes. I know some of them were Emma's stuff. Some of it was probably you and Mom's stuff. I didn't want to stumble on any private things, but, Dad…" Her teeth clenched. He could tell she was nervous. "In this one box, I came across a bunch of pictures of you when you were younger and this lady. You were both naked or something, in some sort of swimming pool. I never seen that lady before. I just know she's not Mom." She was going to say something else, but she stopped herself, saying, "I'm sorry, Dad."

"I see," John said. The fatherly instinct in him wanted to be angry with his daughter for going through things she had no right to be in, but his heart sank into sadness. He knew exactly what those pictures were. It had been years since they saw air outside of their boxes. When had John last looked at them? Five years ago? Ten years ago? Despite ignoring them all those years, he started longing for them again. Any anger built inside of him was swept away.

"Dad, I just… I always thought you and Mom were, like, always together. Which is silly. Emma's had, like, four boyfriends, and she's only nineteen. I just never thought there was anybody else." She finally looked at her father. "Who was she?"

Now it was John's turn to be hesitant. He licked his lips, trying to think about how he would answer. She was young, but she was intelligent and observant. John never talked to Emma about this subject, and it rarely ever came up with Bethany. But Olivia always thirsted for knowledge, and she deserved the truth. John looked back at Olivia. He looked at her long dark hair, thought about her middle name, then started thinking about the drawings she was trying to find. Her crafts.

He returned his focus to his driving. "So I was thirty

when I married your mother. We had first started dating two or three years before that. You're right, there's a lot of unaccounted years there that I never told you or your sister about. I had dated in college here and there, but there was another woman. A woman who was a very big deal to me."

Olivia could see the sadness in her father's eyes, and she nodded. "I see." She took a deep breath. "I didn't spend a long time looking at the pictures. It felt kinda gross, but the two of you seemed so happy. What happened?"

"She was my partner," said John. He didn't think about Isabel as often as he used to. The accident was almost half his life earlier, and after losing his father and the subsequent conversation with his mother, that brief period of time slowly lost its relevance. He hadn't even visited those hot springs since Olivia was in grade school. Her peek into his past brought back the sense of longing, the sense of sadness John had stopped feeling.

"Partner," whispered Olivia, chewing on the word as if to interpret its meaning. "Like, married but not officially, or something?"

"Pretty much," said John. "We met a year after I graduated college. We fell in love very fast. She was very unorthodox, broke all the rules. Hated norms, hated the idea of getting married. You would have liked her."

"Huh," she said, curious. "She could have been Mom then."

"Well, probably not. I mean, half your genes would have been different, but you and your sister probably wouldn't even be alive. She was against having children, period."

Olivia cocked her head, her brow furrowed. "That's strange. I never heard of someone not wanting children before." She stopped to think more. "But it also makes me wonder why people feel like they have to have children. It's almost like they're not aware of the alternative."

John cracked a smile but tried to hide it from her. He could see the dots connecting in her mind.

"Dad?" she asked, becoming nervous again. "This lady, she didn't want children. How about you? You wanted children, right?"

John's heart sank, but not due to sadness or longing. That was a question he had hoped he'd never have to answer. He couldn't lie. "At the time, I agreed with her. We both felt the same way. We saw this idyllic future, if you will, where we grew old and died on our own terms, living the life we wanted to live. Not subscribing to anybody else's fantasy. Children were not part of our goals."

"I see," Olivia said, concerned. "Dad? Were Emma and I wanted?"

He had to think quick to avoid damaging his relationship with her. "I love your mother. She wanted to have children, and I was willing to be convinced, to soften my mind on some things because your mom is very important to me. And honestly, once your sister was born, I understood that I could pass a little of myself onto you guys. If I died childless, everything that I am, that I was, would die with me. The two of you would remember me, just like you remember Granddad."

Olivia nodded. "That makes sense. So we were wanted?"

"Yes," said John with great affirmation.

She smiled. After processing the discussion more, she continued. "But I dunno, I think this lady-friend of yours was on the right track. I'm just trying to imagine pursuing my art career with babies hanging off my arm. I think all children should be wanted, but if you don't want one, you don't want one."

"You have no idea how bad it gets," said John, thinking about all the people he had known and had children because the playbook dictated that they should. Michelle, Nick's ex, was at the top of the list, but there were many others.

"So tell me more, please?" asked Olivia. "She sounds smart."

"This conversation stays between us, okay? You promise?"

Olivia looked toward John, her eyes more alive than they had been in quite some time. "Yes. I promise. I won't tell Mom or my friends or anybody."

"Okay, good," said John. "She was the smartest person I ever knew. I looked up to her. Your mother's smart—don't get me wrong. She's got a good head on her shoulders and is very intelligent. But there was something different about Isabel."

Olivia perked up with surprise. "Isabel? That's her name?"

John nodded solemnly. "Yeah. Isabel. I called her Bel, but yeah, that was her name."

"Isabel, not Isabella?" asked Olivia, referring to her middle name.

John nodded. "There's a small difference so it wouldn't be so on the nose. But, Olivia, I named you after her. Well, your middle name anyway."

Her lips parted as if she meant to speak, but no words came out. She always assumed her parents had randomly picked her name. Emma's middle name came from Bethany's great-grandmother, but Olivia's name lacked any meaning. For the first time in her life, she knew the truth.

"Why haven't you told me about her before?" asked Olivia.

"I don't know, really," said John. "Your mom and I thought that we were our own family, and Isabel wasn't a part of that. We wanted to affirm that we were always a loving family. And also, your mom kind of wanted me to slowly phase her out of my thoughts, partly out of jealousy maybe. I dunno. I just kind of had to bury her and just never intended on telling you or Emma about her."

"Where is she?" asked Olivia.

"She's dead." John couldn't have been flatter in his delivery.

"Oh," said Olivia, and for a moment her face grew sad at the news as if she had lost a friend. "What happened?"

"So we were together for a few years. Had our own place, madly in love, had dreams of owning a country cottage. Typical dreams for twenty-somethings. Well, she got in a car accident and was put on life support. We couldn't find her family, which is another story altogether. But they determined me a common-law husband, and I kept her going for a lot longer than I should have. I had hoped she would wake up someday. She never did."

Olivia was silent.

"That's how I met your mother, actually. I was the saddest, most depressed I had ever been in my entire life. That accident hurt me in ways I would never wish on my greatest enemy. I hate saying it, but it really was much worse than Dad dying. Then I went on one of those old Internet dating things, found Beth. She was fresh out of college, knew what had just happened to me, and, well, I know this is gonna sound gross, but she was my first hookup since the accident."

"Oh God, Dad. That's gross," said Olivia, shutting her eyes. "I don't want to hear it."

"Sorry," said John, upset at himself for becoming too frank with his daughter. "But yeah, we always told you and your sister that we met at a coffee shop. Well, kinda true but not exactly. So there was a year or two there where your mom and I dated but Isabel was still technically alive. It got to the point where she did not want to play second fiddle to a living corpse, so I had to pull the plug." He paused, feeling a tear forming. "It was, to this day, the hardest decision of my life."

Olivia looked over at him. "I'm sorry, Dad."

John smiled. "It's okay. This happened long before you were born. So those pictures you saw, we took them at these hot springs out of town a few miles. They were kind of our engagement pictures, but not an actual engagement."

"Oh, I think I heard about those hot springs!" said Olivia excitedly. "My friend Ella said she went to some hot springs a little ways east."

"That's probably it." Word of the springs' location had traveled. It was probably good that John had stopped his visits, as it was becoming a tourist hotspot. John sighed. "Very few people knew about them back then. That was like our special spot. When Isabel finally passed, we cremated her, and I put her ashes in those pools. I used to visit her there quite a bit."

"That's sweet that you did that." Olivia scratched the

top of her head. "I wish I knew her. She sounds really cool."

"I'm very sure the two of you would have got along great," said John with certainty. "She was very crafty, you know. Didn't draw like you, but loved making things. Remember that afghan blanket that you loved as a kid? That red and brown one?"

"Yeah, don't we still have that?" she asked.

"Oh yeah, of course," he said. "It's in a closet somewhere. But she made that. We didn't buy it from a store or anything. In fact, that box you found should have a lot of her stuff in there, assuming it hasn't been damaged or anything."

"Cool," said Olivia. They were getting close to the dental office, but there was still more time for them to continue their conversation. "I wish Mom didn't freak out about me so much. You know what she said the other day?"

After John shook his head, Olivia answered her own question. "She said she can't wait until I'm in college so I'm out of the house, but she also thinks that I'm so lazy I'll drop out. Why would she say that?"

"Believe me, Olivia, I try to talk to her," John said. "I know you'll turn out okay. You'll turn out to be a better person than I'll ever be."

The smile on his daughter's face told John everything he needed to know. She was still young and had a few hurdles to face on her way to maturity, but she was in the right place. They pulled into the parking lot. The rain intensified, but neither John nor Olivia, in contrast to the other half of the family, minded the falling drops as they left the comforts of the car.

"If you ever wanted to know anything about Isabel or

have any questions about anything, don't feel embarrassed to ask," said John.

Olivia smiled. "Okay, Dad. Thank you."

That day's conversation informed John of a fact he knew but had never admitted. Ever since Olivia was a toddler, John secretly noted similarities to Isabel. John didn't believe in the ancient superstition of the Buddhists, but it was the closest evidence he had of reincarnation. Olivia carried more of Isabel than her middle name.

27

CHAPTER TWENTY-SEVEN

John's father passed away less than two weeks before his forty-ninth birthday. No longer was his birthday associated with positive memories of parties and presents and friends. He thought about his lost father, about the service, about the celebration of life at his childhood home. The concoction of events and emotions was too much for him to separate from his birthday.

As he learned with other drastic life experiences, time never healed, but it did stretch. The pain was the same, but it was spread out across longer years. After a long while, he could afford a celebration. For a milestone like his sixtieth birthday, people expected him to celebrate.

One by one, the guests arrived at his home. Bethany organized the entire event. Even though John had retired several years earlier, Bethany still had at least one more year left as a school counselor before she'd be eligible to retire. Yet she loved her work so much that she planned on continuing for a few more years. She had less free time for organizing social events than he did, but she still managed without a hitch.

The first guest to arrive was the most important: Nick. He brought along Ashley, and the two were still happily married. They had moved across town when their children left home, and because of distance and schedule conflicts, John only saw him once a year. Even though there was no need for the gesture, Nick instinctively brought some beer to the occasion, like he was coming to a party of young bachelors.

"Thanks. Maybe I'll have some after I finish my glass of wine," said John, grabbing a bottle opener and handing it to Nick. Nick laughed as he opened his bottle, and Ashley rolled her eyes. She split off from her husband and migrated to the living room.

"How you doing, man?" asked Nick. They were the same age, but life hadn't been as gentle on Nick. Thanks to years of hard living, due to losing his job during the recession, splitting from Michelle twice, and episodes of alcohol abuse, he had aged more acutely. Even though he never got outright obese, he spent most of his thirties and forties overweight. Thanks to a heart scare seven years earlier, Nick had put some effort into slimming down and lost some of his excess weight.

John remained active throughout middle age. He and Bethany continued rock climbing, and thanks to having more free time due to the children graduating college and moving out, they could devote more time to other physical activities. John's hair was almost all gray, but he still had a complete mane.

"Not bad for sixty!" said John, sipping on his glass as Nick drank from his bottle.

"Five more years until I can retire. Can you believe that?" Nick's statement held a lot of pride. John nodded; he was eligible to retire in his fifties because he started with the company when he was young. Someone like Nick had several jobs before he got his life back on track. The job market had changed in the years since they were younger. When they were first starting out, tenure was disregarded in performance reviews, so there was no incentive to ever stay with one company. Now, with increasing automation and the realization that disloyalty was hurting companies, the pendulum had swung the other way.

"Hopefully Beth's done by then," noted John. "I swear she'll die working."

Nick shrugged. "Unlike us, she does good work. She still do middle school?"

"Yeah," said John, nodding. "She moved to an elementary school for a few years but switched back to middle school. Says it's more rewarding, and the kids don't hug as much."

A second knock on the front door revealed one of John's old coworkers, Madison. She brought her wife, Hannah, whom John had never met before. He was introduced and brought them into the fold of the growing party.

"They just promoted me to your old job," Madison said while sipping on a glass of wine Bethany had provided.

"No way!" said John, legitimately shocked. "What happened with Emmerson?"

"He quit a few weeks ago. Didn't really give a reason. Honestly, I didn't really care either way. Always seemed a bit odd."

"Well," said John, taking a sip of his wine, "wasn't I pretty odd?"

"Yeah, but you're a good odd." Madison playfully punched his arm. "Besides, I worked with you for twelve years. I think I got to know you pretty well."

She was in her early forties. While John was usually youthful for his age, he definitely felt older when he talked with her. During one of their conversations at work, he found out that she was starting kindergarten around the time he started working for that company. So much time had elapsed in his life, and he would never adjust to the reality that time never reversed and never forgave.

The next to arrive were Emma and Olivia, accompanied by Emma's husband, Liam. John hadn't seen them for almost a month, thanks to their busy schedules. He gave his daughters tight, long hugs; even Liam got a hug from John. Bethany came over from the living room, an apprehensive smile on her face. She hugged Emma and Liam but only offered Olivia a half-smile of recognition.

It would be nearly impossible for John to be prouder of his daughters. Emma got her bachelor's in political science and became entrenched in community outreach programs. There she met Liam, and they quickly fell for each other's spells. They married two years ago in a flowery garden. Emma began a master's program, hoping to complete it within a few years.

Olivia went to the same college as her older sister and emerged with a degree in fine arts. Her experiences were more tumultuous, as she and Bethany had a falling out after she graduated high school. John maintained a strong bond with his younger daughter and gave her the support she needed to succeed. Once she graduated, she worked part-time to supplement her minimal income from selling art and found herself living with Emma and Liam. She reconnected with her sister, and now they were closer than ever. The division between mother and daughter had yet to heal.

"Happy birthday, Dad!" said Emma, all smiles.

"Thank you so much!" He turned toward Liam. "How are you doing?"

"Fine, John, thank you," his son-in-law said. "Working as a campaign manager for a state senator is definitely time-consuming though."

"Well, just you wait until Emma runs for office," John said, watching her blush in response. He always knew she would be a politician, ever since his father had made the suggestion on the day she started kindergarten. His father didn't live to see his prediction come true.

Feeling that he was needed elsewhere, John broke away from that crowd and scouted the house. He noticed Olivia seated in the living room, isolated from the other conversations. John walked over to his younger daughter, and she smiled.

"Hey, Olive," he said, referring to her childhood nickname.

"Hi, Dad," she said.

"How're you putting up with Emma and Liam? Everything still okay?"

She nodded. "Yeah, everything is still good, although

I hear them having sex all the time."

John had a blank look on his face. "Well, they are married."

Olivia shrugged. "Yeah, just makes me feel lonely at times."

"Olivia!" shouted someone from the other end of the room. John knew the source of the voice without seeing its face but still turned around as a courtesy. After getting Olivia's attention, Emma continued. "Tell Mom and Dad what you did!"

John turned a curious look toward Olivia. She blushed and tried to playfully hide her face. Bethany gracefully bowed out of talking with Madison and Hannah to join the commotion. When Olivia volunteered no information, John asked, "Well, what did you do?"

"Nothing really," said Olivia, shy from all the attention. "I just sold a drawing at an auction."

Even though John was silently overjoyed, it was Nick who verbally responded as he was leaving the bathroom. "Oh, nice! How much did you make?"

Olivia's face grew redder, and her smile grew more sheepish. Softly, she answered, "Sixty thousand dollars."

A collective gasp filled the room. Nick nodded approvingly. Emma and Liam were all smiles. John and even Bethany's mouths were agape.

"Wow!" said John. "I'm so proud of you." He walked over and leaned down to hug his daughter in her chair.

"If you could do one of those a year, you could afford an apartment just on that," said Bethany, still fixated on her younger daughter's financial stability.

"Well, to be fair," said Olivia as her father pulled away,

"I can't guarantee I can do that every year. I'm not gonna quit my job at the ice cream shop, but I think I'm gonna put it away and save up for my studio."

"You do that," said John. "Wow. Wow."

"You should start selling prints," said Nick. "You're a name now. You can easily make one to two hundred dollars a pop on a good print."

"I thought about that," Olivia said. "Think I might do that on my next drawing."

With the excitement calming down, they heard another knock at the door. The next guests to arrive were Amanda and Jacob, John's old friends from the Isabel era. They kept in communication throughout the years, and even though they came in and out of his life, they always kept in touch. The couple had divorced some years earlier, but they recently got back together and tried things again.

"Glad you guys are here," said John with a slight but firm smile.

"We're always here for you," Amanda said. "Even when things were dicey between Jacob and I. We made a promise then, and we like to keep our promises."

Had John always kept his promises?

"Well, my promise to you is that I got beer and wine in the kitchen!" The couple grinned and disappeared into that part of the house.

Nick took advantage of John's solitude and approached him. "Hey, how's your mother doing?"

John blew the air out of his lungs through a narrow circle in his lips. "Not great. She's still recovering from surgery. Otherwise, she would have been here. She's probably gonna be ready to go home next week, but long term, things aren't looking good. She's nearing ninety, after all."

Nick nodded. "Yeah, still amazing that you have at least one parent alive. Been two years for mine now, and I definitely think about them a lot." He looked toward Bethany in the other room. "It kinda helps to have parents who had you young."

John shared Nick's stare. "Yeah, Beth's folks are in their mid-seventies. It's fucking crazy. They're still younger than my dad was when he died." He paused, remembering that horrible time. "That was over ten years ago now. I'll bet good money that Beth's parents will see great-grandchildren and be healthy enough to play with them."

"I wouldn't doubt that," said Nick. "I mean, in our lifetime, medical science has come such a long ways. More people are living into their nineties, very healthy. I have no doubt you and Beth will live to see a hundred and enjoy it."

"You think?" asked John, skepticism in his voice. That was another forty years away, which was a lifetime's worth of experiences. Forty years earlier he was in college. Most of his life was forged in the interim. Would his final forty years see him slow down and grow feeble, or would he maintain the same exciting intensity of his past forty?

Nick pointed down at John's body. "Look at you. Do you want me to admire your body? Don't you have a wife for that?"

John winked. "I like hearing it from you the most though."

The two of them laughed. Bethany and Emma walked past them on their way to the kitchen. Bethany asked, "John, want me to get the cake ready?"

Chapter Twenty-Seven

"Sure," he said.

Nick's eyes followed them longer than John's. He hesitated for a moment, sighing before speaking. "You know what Alex told me a few weeks back?"

"How is Alex doing, anyway?" asked John immediately after, curious about Nick's oldest child.

"He's doing okay. Struggling with relationships, but that's not surprising, considering who his mother is. I'm just glad he moved out before he turned thirty. But anyway." Nick cleared his throat. "You know what he told me? He said that he and Emma took each other's virginity. Can you believe that?"

"What the hell?" said John, spacing the words enough to make each sound like its own sentence. "Wait, what?"

"I know. I asked him if they were drunk or something. He said they were sober. I then asked him how old they were, and he didn't really answer that question. Kinda makes me wonder."

"I see," said John. He wasn't sure if Nick's son was telling the truth; he had a history of lying. Regardless, John had to take the revelation seriously, noting the four-year age difference between the two. John was certain she was sexually active during high school, which didn't bode well concerning certain laws. To celebrate this news, he took a long sip from his wine glass.

"I figured I'd tell you. Apparently, they did it to get it over with because they trusted each other enough or something. Like, they didn't want anything weird to happen in an actual relationship."

"Well," said John, "I've always trusted Emma to do the right thing. If Alex ain't lying, then despite how much legal shit he could end up with, I know that Emma was, and is, a smart girl."

"Are you gonna ask her?" asked Nick. "You know, to corroborate this story?"

John shrugged. "I dunno. It's her past, not mine. I never played the sex cop that many dads fantasize about." He finished his glass as he saw Emma and Bethany light the cake on the dining table. "Besides, remember we predicted that something like that would happen?"

"Oh, yeah!" said Nick, recalling the memory. "When we took the kids to Disneyland! Man, I was hoping that we were wrong, to be honest."

"I kinda was too," said John. When he thought more on it, it could have been possible that this hypothetical event happened when Emma was an adult and she lied to Alex to make him feel better about himself. There was no way of knowing without asking Emma directly.

"Okay, candles ready. Everyone here?" called out Bethany. Almost everybody at the party had already congregated in the dining room, but Ashley and Liam arrived a few seconds later. Once everyone was assembled, they launched into the typical cacophony that vaguely resembled the "Happy Birthday" song. No one tried any fancy harmonies, but the actual result was little better. John looked down at his vanilla-based cake with minimal frosting. The candles were arranged to resemble the number "60." John forewent making any wishes and blew out the candles. He was far too old to hope that the impossible would ever come true.

After the applause ceased, Emma handed John a knife, and he sliced the cake into pieces to pass around. There was enough for everyone to have one piece each, but this was a conscious decision by John. He didn't want to be an enabler of unhealthy eating habits. While there were chairs, almost everybody remained standing as they ate from their plates. He noticed that Emma had retreated into the kitchen to put the knife in the sink to let it soak. John followed her.

"You still doing good?" asked John.

"Yes, Dad, I'm good. Why?" She wiped her hands on the towel.

"Is it okay if I ask you an offensive and personal question?"

Emma laughed. "Oh, Dad, you're always offensive. No, go ahead."

John looked behind him to make sure they were out of earshot of the other guests. "So I was talking with Nick and he was saying something about you and Alex being a thing or something."

She smiled. "Oh my gosh, that kid's something else, isn't he? I haven't talked to him since high school. Real awkward guy. I mean, he's not bad, but just a little strange. Yeah, he asked me out, took me on a few dates. Tried kissing me once. I really wasn't into it."

"Oh, okay," said John, satisfied that his daughter was telling the truth. At least Alex didn't completely make up the story, despite massive embellishment. "And you were in high school? How did I not find out?"

Emma giggled. "Well, you know, I was dating an older man. Felt kinda rebellious, you know? I didn't want you to freak out on Alex's dad anyway. You two were best friends. Did Alex just tell Nick about this now?"

John nodded. "Yeah, his story was a little different."

"Oh God, I can only imagine," she said, leaning against the counter and folding her arms. "I heard that he bragged to his friends about how I slept with him. He put me on some pedestal since we were kids, so I dunno. I always felt guys who put women on pedestals are just weird. It's sad that he's still bragging about a lie years later."

"Look, Emma, I honestly don't care if you did sleep with him. It was just so out of left field that my curiosity got the best of me."

"Oh, Dad, it's fine," she said, brushing his arm. "Just be thankful that I didn't tell you about the guys I did sleep with!" She winked and walked past him to leave the kitchen.

"I did not want to hear about that!" said John. He heard her laugh loudly as she walked out of the room.

After the cake, the party died down. Madison and Hannah were the first to leave; John congratulated Madison on her new position one final time. Nick and Ashley were ready to go, but they were waiting to sober up. Amanda and Jacob were the next to leave.

Olivia was inebriated, resting in a chair in the living room. Emma and Liam were standing in the front of the room, and both of them looked nervous. They kept looking at each other, then back at the room. Finally, Emma broke the silence. "Mom? Dad? We have something to tell you guys."

John turned his head as Bethany walked in from the bedroom. Nick and Ashley were in the kitchen, sobering up with snack foods.

"Yeah, we're here. What's going on?"

"Well," said Emma, whose look of nervous apprehension had morphed into a shy grin. "We wanted to wait until after your birthday so we wouldn't steal your thunder. But I want to let you two know: we're pregnant."

Bethany screamed and immediately ran up to hug her daughter. John grinned, taking the news more slowly. He hadn't noticed she didn't drink any alcohol that day. Unlike both of Bethany's announcements, John had zero doubts and concerns. He was going to be a grandfather.

"Oh, honey, that's wonderful," said John. "Did you just find out?"

"Earlier this week," said Liam. "We told Olivia first thing, but we wanted to wait until we were all together before telling you two."

Bethany kissed her daughter's cheek. "Oh, you two will be wonderful parents. I just know it!"

"Still going to finish up your master's?" asked John, feeling pragmatic to the point of lacking emotion.

"Oh yeah, Liam's going to help support me through this. Shouldn't be many speed bumps." Emma rubbed her flat belly, giggling. "I wanted to wait to pursue any bigger goals until after I had a kid, so I felt this as kinda a good time to get started."

John grinned again, nodding in approval. He looked over at Olivia, who was still seated in the chair. She had a thin smile on her face, but part of her eyes echoed sadness. John wasn't sure if she was sad because she would spend less time with her sister or if she was sad that the pregnancy announcement trumped her artistic achievement. He acknowledged Olivia, and his smile grew bigger from looking at her. She saw her father's look, and her thin smile turned into a grin. Anybody could produce a child; few could produce art.

28

CHAPTER TWENTY-EIGHT

"Come on in!" called out John. He backed up into the entry-way to let Emma come in with her two children, Matthew and Will. They ran past his knees with clever agility, found Bethany sitting on the couch, and jumped on her.

Emma laughed as she entered her childhood home. John looked behind him to see his grandchildren hugging their grandmother with unconditional love. "They seem to be more excited to see Grandma than me!"

"Oh, Dad," Emma said, shutting the door behind her. "They love you too. Don't worry."

"How are you doing, honey?" asked John, returning his attention to his eldest daughter.

"I'm good, Dad," she said, smiling. "You sound better, that's for sure."

"Yeah, finally got over that damn cold. Do you want

anything?"

"Water's fine. Too early in the day to start boozing up." Being familiar with the home, she walked past John to hang up her coat. "How are you, Mom?"

"Oh, I'm fine, dear," said Bethany, holding one grandchild on each side of her. They buried their heads into her sides, calming down from their initial burst of energy. Her hair no longer had any hints of blonde and was fully white by now, but it still retained its classic curliness. Her freckles had also faded with age but were still visible.

"Matthew! Will! Can you take your coats off for me so we can hang them up?" Emma walked over to her two children as they took off their coats, which looked abnormally large on them. Matthew, being the older one, didn't have too many issues getting his own coat off. His younger brother, Will, had some difficulty getting his arms out of the sleeves. Bethany helped him out, and once both coats were off, Emma took them to the coat rack.

Bethany rubbed her hands through their shaggy hair. "Not much different from when you and Olivia were that age."

"Yeah, but we were girls!" said Emma with pride. "Boys are tougher. There's no way we were this difficult."

"Well, wait until you have teenagers. Then you'll be glad you had boys," said Bethany, noting the difficulties in raising her own children.

Emma had a stable nuclear family; she was still married to Liam and had won a race for city council. Olivia had been ignoring the rules and expectations set for her. She had moved out of her sister's apartment before her first nephew was born and found scattered success with her work. After a few years, she got a steady job as a graphic artist for a local agency. Her relationship with Bethany had warmed, but there was still a long way to go; years of judgment was a lot for Olivia to get over. She still didn't feel comfortable with Bethany without John around.

John returned to the living room with a glass of water. While giving it to Emma, he turned to his grandchildren. "Matthew? Will? Do either of you want some juice?"

"Yes, please!" they said, not quite in sync with each other.

Smiling, John left the room to return to the kitchen. He grabbed two small plastic cups. They were the same cups they bought for Emma and Olivia all those years earlier, and he kept them around for sentimental reasons. John prepared two cups of orange juice and brought them to their dining room table.

"Okay, boys, your juice is at the table!"

John heard the running of tiny feet, and it didn't take long for the two boys to run into the dining room and into their chairs. John smiled. Matthew had darker hair that could have been influenced by John's side of the family. Will's sandy hair probably came from Bethany. Aside from hair color, their faces were very similar.

"Yummy," said Will. He was four, still a little young to have developed a distinct personality.

"Matthew, can you take your cups to the sink when you two are done?" asked John with a gentle, grandfatherly voice.

"Yes, Grandad," he said between sips.

John returned to the living room to enjoy the company of his wife and daughter. He sat on the couch alongside

Bethany, listening in on their conversation.

"We've been trying a lot," said Emma, a hint of defeat in her voice. "The spark is not really there. I'm more willing than he is. I just don't think he's attracted to me anymore."

"Emma, you are a beautiful person," said Bethany reassuringly. "Liam's a great guy, and John and I really like him. But for him not to like someone like you?"

"Well, how did you and Dad handle it?" asked Emma. "After you had me and Olivia. Did the spark leave you guys too?"

John and Bethany both gave each other a mischievous look, prompting Emma to roll her eyes. "Ugh, forget I asked."

"No, but seriously," said John. "For those first few years, it was an every-so-often thing. By the time we got Olivia enrolled in pre-school, there was less stress. We always made sure we took some time off for ourselves. My mom and dad were retired by that point, so they loved having you guys over."

"Yeah," said Emma, nodding in remembrance. "I do remember being over at Grandma and Grandad's a lot at that age."

John knew where Emma's mind had drifted. His mother had finally passed two years earlier, at age ninety-four. She had a good quality of life toward the end, even if she had to spend the last couple of years in assisted living. Emma had said in confidence that it was John's parents she preferred; she had more fun at their house as a child.

"You do know I wish I didn't have to sell their house." When John's mother died, she still owned the same house. John was three when they moved into that house; it was the only home he remembered. He had hoped he could pass along the house to Emma or even Olivia, but medical expenses from treating his mother put Bethany and him in debt. Selling that home paid off those expenses and allowed them to upgrade the appliances and some furniture in their own aging home.

Emma nodded. "I know. It's okay, really."

Sighing, John said, "Anyway, the older you got, the better our spark was, I guess you can say. We kept healthy and ate well. Hell, we only quit rock climbing last year because Bethany's shoulders finally had it."

Bethany looked at John with a knowing grin. Even though they had to stop that rigorous activity, they took up weightlifting at a gym to continue maintaining their physical health. She looked back at Emma. "You know, you should get involved with something with Liam. That might help your marriage."

"I don't know," said Emma, looking down on the ground. "We'll have to try something."

Matthew and Will skipped into the living room. John asked them, "Did you put your cups in the sink?"

Matthew nodded. "Uh-huh, I did!"

"Good job, boys!" said Emma. "You make Mommy so proud!"

The two of them grinned widely.

"Well!" said John, clapping his hands. "I got that board game that you liked!"

"Which one?" asked Matthew, his voice rising with excitement.

"The one with the mountain that you try to climb, with the monster that comes down?"

Matthew gasped, his grin growing wider. "Can we play, Grandad?"

"Of course we can! Let me go get it." John stood up out of his seat.

"Can I play too?" asked Will.

"Sure, and if you need help, Mommy and Grandma are here for you!" John hurried up the stairs to Olivia's old room, where they stored their games. It was more difficult to climb the stairs than it used to be, but his knees didn't mind. He had friends his age who had problems with stairs in their forties. Many of them he had lost contact with. Nick was one of the few exceptions, but no one else from high school or college kept in touch.

John found the game, still unopened in plastic shrink wrap. Once upon a time, he'd make a comment about the wasteful use of a petroleum byproduct. These days, John hardly cared anymore. Despite worsening conditions around the world, with oft-ignored reports of flooding and starvation, at least his immediate surroundings were safe and secure. Best not to worry about unseen suffering; seeing his smiling grandchildren was paramount.

Downstairs, John set the game on the floor, slowly lowering himself to sit. Matthew clapped his hands, maintaining his wide grin of excitement. Will was more subdued, his mouth agape in wonder. John looked at his grandchildren. "Okay, boys, brand new, still wrapped. You want to help me set up the pieces?"

"Yes!" exclaimed the two.

John easily tore through the wrapping and removed it. As he removed all the pieces and parts from the game that had to be assembled, Emma said from the couch,

"Matthew, why don't you tell Grandma and Grandad what you've been learning in school?"

"Oh, yeah!" said Matthew, trying to recall his most recent lessons. "Ms. Hazel is teaching us about, um, time and calendars and things."

"No way?" said John, trying to recall how old he was when he first learned about that subject. "Like what?"

"Like, we have to, um... We have to add and subtract time." As Matthew was explaining this, he stopped helping John set up the game. "Like, if it's 4:55, and we add thirty minutes, that would be, um... That would be 5:25. And thirty minutes is half an hour!"

"No kidding!" said John with the right balance of snarkiness that could be picked up by the adults but completely ignored by the children. Bethany glared at him.

"And you also learned about how to read the calendar and the months?" Emma was trying to encourage Matthew to divulge further what he had learned.

"Oh yeah," said Matthew. "Like, we learned the months last year in kindergarten. But this year we are... We are learning about, like, more about the months and years."

"That's great!" said John. Will was still trying to help set up the game, but he wasn't that useful at it.

"Do you know what today is?" asked Bethany.

"Oh yeah, um..." Matthew looked up at the ceiling. "It's April 12!"

"Oh, wow!" said John, smiling. "Very good!"

"We should hire you to schedule our doctor appointments," teased Bethany. Matthew grinned.

"Are you gonna finish helping me?" said John.

"Oh, yeah!" said Matthew, suddenly remembering he

had a task to complete.

After another few minutes of work, the setup was complete, and the game could begin. Emma slid down to the floor to help Will, but John and Matthew were in a competitive mode. Bethany sat on the couch and watched.

"Aunt Olivia is really good at this game!" said Matthew as he made a move.

"Oh, she is?" asked John, this time with genuine curiosity.

Emma jumped in to explain. "Last time she came over she played them, and you know her: show no mercy."

"Well, glad to know that I raised one of my daughters right!"

Emma squinted at John. She refocused her efforts on the game itself, casually using Will as a means to beat her father.

John commented on that toward the end of the game. "You know, millions of people died because countries have been fighting puppet wars since forever. I thought I raised you better, Emma!"

"We'll see after I—I mean after Will wins." Emma's determination to defeat her father had never been stronger.

After a few more turns, Emma's rhetoric matched reality as she won the game. John was a few squares behind her, and Matthew had been lagging further behind due to a few poorly drawn cards.

"Good job, Will! You did it!" Emma made her younger son feel as good as possible about the victory, but the real winner subliminally looked at her father and smiled.

"Yeah, you did it, Will!" said John, singing false praises.

"I'll beat you next time, Grandad!" said Matthew, who

was surprisingly a good sport about the whole competition.

"Oh, I know you will!" John smiled and rubbed his hand through his shaggy hair. Matthew giggled and flopped to the floor in an attempt to escape John's hand.

"Okay, boys, it's getting late!" announced Emma. "We have to get home and make some dinner. I bet you guys are hungry."

"A little," said Matthew. His voice rapidly shifted from energetic to lethargic and sad.

"Well, go ahead and get your coats and your shoes on!" she said, standing up from the floor. Her lead prompted the two children to get up and run over to the coat rack. Bethany stood up from the couch, and John followed suit, although he was the slowest of the five.

Emma turned to face her parents. "Thank you so much for having us. They wanted to come over for like the past week."

"We are always so happy to have them," said John. "You are always welcome to come over."

"Call first," said Bethany. "You wouldn't want to catch us—"

Emma held her hand up. "Okay, Mom. Yes, I think I get it." She then laughed. "I'll talk to Liam, see if we can do something else."

"Is Dad gonna eat with us?" asked Will, looking straight up at his mother with a wishful look in his eyes.

"I hope so!" Emma grabbed her jacket. "I'll call him before we leave to see if he'll be home tonight."

Both boys ran to the front door, quickly putting on their shoes. The three adults followed them to the door, led by Emma. She grabbed the door handle and looked down at the two. "Okay, boys, we're leaving now. Say goodbye to Grandma and Grandad!"

"Bye, Grandma! Bye, Grandad!" The two of them took turns hugging the legs of John and Bethany.

While they did that, Emma looked at her parents. "Thank you again. Love you guys."

"Love you too, Emma!"

After one final smile, Emma opened the front door, and her two children ran out into the world. She followed and shut the door behind her. John and Bethany migrated to the window so they had a better view as they walked to their car.

"Do you think everything with Emma and Liam will be okay?" asked Bethany nervously.

"At this point, who knows?" said the ever-skeptical John. Any separation would not only hurt the grandchildren but also interfere with Emma's future. It was a wonderful visit, and there was some hope, but in the short term, things weren't the most optimistic.

29

CHAPTER TWENTY-NINE

Wiping sweat from his forehead, John stood up and took a deep breath. John never loved June. To add insult to injury, the heat accentuated the grueling work he tasked himself to complete. He paused, studying the mostly empty room surrounding him, his present company a collection of boxes by his feet.

This was Emma's room. In John's mind, it was always Emma's room and always would be. Even with the walls empty, the furniture removed, the things boxed up, his imagination filled in what was missing. He could see her bed, her desk and chair, her dresser, her posters of cute male celebrities. Even though most of those things were long gone, every time he walked into the room, he could see them all.

Liam poked his head into the room. "Hey, John, everything good still?"

John nodded, taking deep breaths. "Yeah. It was a lot easier the last time I moved."

Liam grinned. "But you weren't seventy-three either."

John shook his head. "No, that's the damn truth, isn't it?" He gestured toward each corner of the room. "This was Emma's room. Did you know that?"

"No, I forgot about that." He looked around the room. "I think Emma showed me once. Well, back when we were married, anyway."

"Right," said John, nodding. "Still appreciate you helping us out."

"Not a problem." Liam took a step into the room so he could lean on the doorframe. "Hell, I'm forty-two and I can feel the difference." Liam was always tall and lean and maintained that physique into the beginning of middle age.

"Emma also appreciates it too," said John.

Liam shrugged. "Don't think she cares that it's me specifically. It's just that someone is helping out her parents. Just happens to be me."

"Well, between you, Olivia, Mateo, and then Beth and me, we'll get this done."

"Right on, boss!" Liam grinned. "These boxes ready to go?"

"Yeah, I just boxed up the last one."

There were five boxes left in that room, and John and Liam took several trips up and down the stairs to the front door. Mateo took them from the staging zone and loaded them into the moving truck outside. Climbing the stairs reminded John why he and Bethany decided to move. While they were still able-bodied and could do most everything they had always done, the soreness would only get worse. There would come a point when they would be in their eighties or even nineties, and something would happen that could affect what was left in their life. Wanting to prevent any such mishap, they opted to move into a different house.

They picked that house because they planned to have a family. Olivia moved out nearly twenty years earlier, so children were no longer a consideration. They decided to not only downsize to a single-story home but to move out of the metropolitan area they both spent their lives in. A few hours away was a lovely town with many amenities that attracted both John and Bethany. They no longer craved proximity to the city.

Mateo had finished packing a few boxes into the truck and walked over to where John and Liam stood. He smiled, wiping sweat off his shirt. "Aw, man. John, you're gonna kill me. I knew being with Olivia was too good to be true."

John laughed. Mateo was a good man, a couple of years younger than Olivia. When he was younger, he was an EMT, but when he turned thirty, he quit the medical field completely and became a welding artist, crafting large metal sculptures for businesses and universities across the country. Through their mutual friends, the two met and had been partnered happily for the past five years. Mateo came from a Catholic background, but he rejected his faith, including the need to have a large family. That attracted Olivia, and they remained childfree, despite pressure from both friends and family as well as society as a whole.

"I hope he's not slave-driving you to death either," Mateo said to Liam.

Liam shrugged. "Trust me, I've been dealing with John for years. This is nothing new."

John grinned at the suggestion of having a reputation. There was an outdoor chair he sat on to take a quick break. He looked up and down the street he had spent over half his life on. There had been some changes, primarily new roofs and paint jobs on some of the houses. Some homes, significantly older than his, had been bulldozed and replaced with newer structures.

The demographics had changed as well. He and Bethany were on the younger side when they first moved in. Most, if not all, of the original residents had moved out or died, and changing popular tastes meant many young, hip people lived on that street. There were more young children playing in the road and the front yards than ever before. Emma and Olivia would have loved that when they were small children. That was a different time.

"Should have brought Matthew and Will out," said John.

Liam studied the children playing everywhere. "Think Matt and Will are a little old for them. Will's going into the fifth grade, you know. Matt's starting eighth."

John shook his head. "It's so true. The older you get, the faster time travels."

"Believe me, I've been noticing it too." Liam squatted next to John. "It feels like yesterday that I held Matt for the first time. I'm sure you could probably say the same thing for Emma."

With a half-smile, John reminisced. "Yeah, kinda. Beth's parents were there, not too much older than you are now.

I thought Emma looked like an alien."

They both giggled. Mateo had finished with the remaining boxes, and he took that opportunity for a short break as well, setting himself down on the grass not too far from them.

"How is Beth's dad, anyway?"

"Not terribly well," said John, recalling that his mother-in-law had passed earlier that year. "Kind of wasting away. He always seemed so young to me. They were a lot younger than my parents. But now he's just… old." John wondered if the two younger men thought the same thing about him.

"Well, I'm glad that they got to spend time with great-grandchildren," said Liam. "I never had that."

"My last great-grandparent didn't die until I was in high school," said Mateo, looking up at the clear blue sky. "But everybody popped out babies when they were young."

"Come to think of it," said John, trying to concentrate on filtering the plethora of memories in his mind, "I think I'm the oldest person I know before I had my first kid."

"Well, John, that just means you're the smartest," said Liam. "Unless Mateo and Olivia decide to have one, then they'll have you beat."

"Not a chance," said Mateo, his voice no longer being entirely playful.

"What are you boys arguing about now?" said a scratchy voice from the front door.

John looked over. "I was just bragging how I was the oldest person I know to have their first kid."

Bethany shook her head, smiling. "Well, you're probably right. Where is Emma? Wasn't she supposed to come and help?"

Liam stood up to stretch his legs. "She's down at the capitol today. Some important tax law is being debated right now. Besides, I don't think she'd be happy to be at the same place as me."

"Well, tough!" said Bethany, stepping down onto the walkway.

"Well, at least you got Olivia," said Mateo. "She still inside with you?"

"Yeah, she's finishing up what she was working on. She's really taking her time. I think she just wants to see the house before we give up the keys."

"She is a sentimentalist, that's for sure," said Mateo, standing up to stretch as well.

As John stood up out of the chair, he considered Bethany's words. The rift between her and Olivia lasted years. She was a counselor, yet she failed to save their relationship when Olivia was a teenager. Bethany would have easily known Olivia was the sentimental type. He never tried to understand how or why things collapsed when she left for college; he was just happy everything was okay now.

"How are you two doing in there?" he asked.

Bethany sat down in the empty chair. "Well, our bedroom is almost packed. All our clothes and bedding are in boxes. Just a few more trinkets need to be thrown in. The bed is ready to go."

Mateo and Liam looked at each other with unenthusiastic glares. "That'll be us."

"It's not too bad to take apart," said John. "It was pretty easy to put together. Better than most of my old beds, that's for sure."

Liam and Mateo sighed as they picked up their pride

and walked back into the house. John and Bethany continued to look at the door after they shut it behind them.

"Can't believe it's really happening," said John. He walked behind Bethany and gave her a shoulder massage.

"I know it's surprising to you, but I'll miss this place," said Bethany. "Everything that we are happened here."

"Well, aside from those first several years when we were dating," John said.

Bethany grinned. "Well, aside from that. And speaking of that, we'll be moved in by the time of our anniversary."

John looked up at the sky. "I never had to be reminded. The blistering sun did that for me."

"Oh, John, this isn't that bad. You just like complaining about any heat above sixty-five degrees. And you do know where we're moving it'll get even hotter?"

"Yeah, but I'll be inside most of the time." John continued to rub Bethany's shoulders. "And whenever our daughters visit, I'll ask them to bottle up the cool air from home and bring it with them."

"Yes, because that will work." She reached her hand to touch John's. "Any plans for our anniversary, my love?"

Before John could answer, the front door opened and out walked Olivia. She had a forlorn face as she approached her parents. "Hey, Mom and Dad."

"Are all the boxes in our bedroom done?" asked Bethany.

"Yeah," she said. "I didn't know how sad I'd actually be until I saw all the rooms empty. I had to spend some time in my old room. It's just so surreal."

"It is for us too," said John. "We were here a lot longer than you were."

"Yeah," she said, looking down. "Did you guys feel the

same way when you sold Grandma and Grandad's house? When Grandpa sold his house?"

"It didn't bother me," said Bethany. "Probably because I kind of resented being poor when I was younger. I just did not want to live in such a small home. And Mom and Dad never moved out, even though they could afford to after I grew up. And when Mom died, we just had to sell. Dad's care just cost too much."

John said nothing. He stood silently, watching his daughter's reactions. She looked away, processing her emotions. "Yeah, that makes sense. Getting old sucks."

John and Bethany had been aging gracefully, but even then, their real ages would poke at them. John's hair had thinned, but he was lucky to still maintain a full head of gray hair. At the weightlifting gym, many younger members mistook him for a man in his fifties. Bethany's skin was rougher and had lost some of its youthful tightness. Yet at her gym she could outpace any middle-aged person.

"It's not bad," said Bethany with a smile.

Soon, a mattress came through the door, carried by Liam and Mateo. The two passed them on their way to the truck. "Is there enough room for the box springs and everything?" asked John.

They set down one side of the mattress on the edge of the truck. "Yep, room for the box spring and also the folded-up bed part," said Mateo, "and then the last of the boxes in that room."

"We should probably help out with the boxes at least," said John. Bethany got out of her chair. The three of them walked back into the empty house, through the barren living room, and into the back where the remnants of the master bedroom remained. There were still several boxes, so they moved those by the truck while Liam and Mateo loaded the rest of the bed. Once the bed was fully packed, they added the boxes of the bedroom to the puzzle of the packed truck. There was even room to spare.

"Is that the last of it?" asked Olivia, admiring the contents of the moving truck.

"Think so," said Bethany.

"Well in my experience, it's good to do a once-over throughout the house, just in case," said Mateo. "It's really easy to forget something. Happened to my family a couple of times."

Olivia went over to peck Mateo on the lips. "You're so helpful. Thanks for helping my parents out!"

"It's not a problem, Olivia," he said with a big smile.

"Am I going to get a kiss of thanks?" asked Liam.

The other four laughed. John and Bethany rubbed each other's backs as they embarked into their former home to follow Mateo's suggestion. Mateo and Olivia went upstairs to check those rooms, while John, Bethany, and Liam remained downstairs. In each room, everything was gone. Only the paint of the walls and the carpet on the floors reminded him that this was once his home. A home he abandoned to a young, eager couple.

"Hey, John!" called Liam from another room. "There's a few boxes left in the garage. Totally forgot about them, since we packed most of that shit up last week. Wanna check it out?"

"Probably a good idea," said John, following the younger man. "It's probably just junk anyway. Mostly my stuff. Beth didn't keep much out there."

"Got it. Well, worth a look anyway."

They walked into the garage through the house door. A single light bulb illuminated the concrete chamber, but the back door was open to let some air flow. True to Liam's word, there were about a dozen ancient boxes, many of them dusty beyond compare. John walked over to take a quick look at them when he noticed a particular detail on a couple of them. They were the oldest boxes there, yet they seemed to be in the best condition. They were practically unused. Those boxes were marked with green ink. Green ink that John had used to distinguish them decades earlier. Green ink that never faded.

"Did you need to look inside of them at all?" asked Liam.

John took a deep breath and considered Liam's words. He hadn't looked into those boxes for a long time. For years he didn't even think about those boxes—boxes kept as a promise to someone from another life. A life before Emma and Olivia. A life before Bethany. If John forgot about the promise, was that promise even worth keeping? The display was whittled down and put away when Olivia was born. After she left for college, John didn't even consider putting the shrine back up. He did not care to.

So much time had passed. The pain had stretched beyond what he thought possible. All that was left was an empty promise to somebody who stopped caring when they passed on. Any guilt John had was swept away at that moment. There was room for those boxes, of course. But the reason for the move was because John was preparing for an easier life involving less physical stress. It would just be another box that would be in the way, just another box he'd have to strain to move. He'd eventually become so elderly he could no longer move anything. Was it worth keeping under those circumstances? In his new house, it would still not see the light of day. It was no longer appropriate for it to see the light of day.

"No, it's fine," said John. "You can leave these. Someone else will get them. May be useful to someone else."

Liam nodded. "Okay, cool. Well, that's it in here. I'll check the backyard."

He left John alone by going through the back door. John followed him but stopped at the doorway. He saw the three cedars he planted when he first moved in. They were now tall trees that dominated their surroundings. They were originally a symbol of his youthful confidence, reminders that he could do something about the world, but now they were merely representations of memories. The empty garden beds reminded John that it was the first summer he didn't grow a vegetable garden. He hoped he could grow something in his new place. The climate was drier, but he'd be able to work with it as long as he was well enough. Accepting the reality of what he was doing, John turned toward the house door and stepped through it. No tears, no cries, no verbal recognition. No goodbyes.

30

CHAPTER THIRTY

John wasn't sure why he was nervous. It wasn't his health that was under scrutiny, yet his stomach churned as if it was. Shaking off the anxious chills, he continued toward the open door. Inside the doorframe was a woman in a white frock. She was smiling, yet there were more complex emotions behind that smile.

"This way, please," the woman said. John gestured for Bethany to go into the room first. Once she was through, John followed.

"Have a seat over there!" she continued, gesturing to two chairs on one side of the desk while she shut the heavy door. A copper name tag adorned the clean desk, reading "Ava Santana, MD." That woman had been their doctor since they moved to town six years earlier. When they moved, Dr. Santana had recently started her own practice;

not only was she half their age, but she was even younger than their two daughters.

"Thank you," said John. He and Bethany sat on their side of the desk. Dr. Santana sat across from them. She set down her tablet and several pieces of loose paper on the desk. It was a relief on John's legs; they had mostly recovered from being broken earlier that year, but minor symptoms still reared their head.

"Leg still doing okay?" asked Dr. Santana.

John nodded. "Yeah, still a bit sore but I can walk around and annoy the children better than ever."

Dr. Santana smiled. "That's great. For anybody else at your age, it would have been debilitating. Staying active is probably the smartest thing the two of you ever did."

"I knew those annoying deadlifts would pay off," said John, coughing. He was older. He knew it; he felt it. He also knew it could have been much worse.

Their doctor smiled, but her face changed to address the business at hand. "Thank you for coming. I know this must be agonizing for you, to know what's going on."

Bethany nodded. "I'm not gonna lie, it is a bit scary."

Dr. Santana silently studied them. She looked down at her tablet and pulled up the documents she needed for their visit. "So the test results have all come in."

"I figured," said Bethany, the scratchiness of her voice more prominent. Under the desk, her hand reached over to John's. He gripped back equally hard.

Dr. Santana stared at Bethany, continuing to gauge her emotional response. "It's what I feared it would be. Pancreatic cancer."

Bethany took a long, deep breath in, her face unchanged.

John gulped and looked over at his wife. The trapdoor opened beneath his body, and his stomach and heart entered a free fall. His lips quivered. Yet Bethany remained stoic, keeping full attention on their doctor as if breaking eye contact would concede the battle to the invasive cancer.

"I understand," said Bethany. The inflection in her voice remained the same.

John wanted nothing more than to accept that the tests were wrong. That the years of training from many doctors and specialists and laboratory assistants were all for naught and that they all erred in their assessment of the situation. John wanted to call out the false positive, to insist that Dr. Santana do all the tests again and do them correctly. The logical side of him would do no such thing. The logical side of him knew the doctor was right, that the diagnosis was final.

"And that's the bad one, isn't it?" asked John, his own voice unsteady.

Dr. Santana nodded. "Treatment has improved drastically over the past couple decades, but the five-year survivability rate is still lower than we'd like. Bethany, your cancer is a stage two. It hasn't spread yet to other parts of your body, but it has advanced more than we'd prefer."

Bethany remained devoid of emotion, and she remained silent. John spoke for her. "So what's the prognosis. What can we expect?"

"Well, I think regardless of the outcome, you can expect to maintain a fairly good quality of life. It's not like the old days where you're bombarded with radiation that would kill you almost as bad as it would kill the cancer cells. Treatment is much, much better than what you grew up with."

Bethany nodded.

"But you also probably want to know if we can cure it." Dr. Santana passed them loose pieces of paper filled with graphs and diagrams. "We measure life expectancy based on five-year survival rates. With stage-two pancreatic, as you can see on your papers, about thirty percent survive five years."

John pointed at the graph. "It also has survival rates for each year. Like one year is eighty percent, two years is fifty-five percent, and so on."

Dr. Santana nodded. "Yes, exactly. Bethany, all things considered, you are very healthy for your age, so I can almost guarantee that you'll go through these first two years just fine." She then sighed, looking down at her desk. "I'm not so sure after that though. Three, four, five years, or longer, I just can't say."

John put his elbows on the desk, resting his face in his hands. Bad news was never welcome and could never be processed rationally. "Man, growing up as a kid, it was like the cure for cancer was going to be the next big thing. It was just around the corner. I thought that maybe by the time I was forty or fifty we'd find a cure."

"I know, I hear that a lot from your generation," said Dr. Santana. "Each cancer is different though. Each cancer requires a different treatment, a different cure. I mean, to be fair, we've practically cured many forms of cancer. Catching them at stage one or even two, we can eliminate them pretty quick. But not all cancers are equal. And when it comes to pancreatic, I can slow it down, I can make it not painful, but I can't stop it or revert it."

The doctor sighed again, this time looking Bethany in the eye. "I'm glad we caught it as quickly as we did. You telling me that your mother died from it probably gave you a few years of life you wouldn't have gotten otherwise. I guess we can be grateful for something."

Silence befell the room. John stopped asking questions. He stared at Bethany. They had mentally prepared for several weeks now. Her symptoms came out of nowhere. She had lost some weight and had a pain in her back that wasn't muscle-related. Dr. Santana even warned them during testing that it was likely to be cancer. Now they knew it to be the truth, making it harder to process.

"We can start treatment pretty much right away," said Dr. Santana. "The second page has a brief overview of the process. We'll get an appointment set up so you can begin next week. Do you have any other questions?"

"Yes," said Bethany, breaking her silence. "Will there come a point that it will become unbearable?"

Dr. Santana tilted her head. "Probably not. Like I said, the treatments are damn good these days. Even the symptoms can be managed well until the end. If it becomes too much, we can discuss end-of-life options, but I don't suspect it will get to that point."

Bethany nodded but didn't speak.

"Well," said their doctor, standing up and grabbing her tablet, "I'll leave you two alone. Take your time. I'll have my assistant give you a call to schedule the start of the treatment. And if you ever have any questions, please give me a call." With one final, weary smile, she walked out of the office, shutting the door on her way out.

Both remained silent for a moment, collecting their

thoughts and deciding what to say. If there was even a point in saying anything. But John loved Bethany and cared for her more than anyone, so something had to be said, even if it was inane or dense.

"Beth," said John, turning to face her.

She continued looking down into her lap, a slight smile on her face. "At least I know what it is."

"Yeah, I know, but..." And John's mouth froze. He scooted his chair closer to hers. He feared that tears would follow, but none came.

"It's okay, hon," said Bethany. "If what she says is true, I'll still have a great life to share with you."

"I know, but you're so young still. You're younger than my dad was when he died, and he was younger than both your parents when they died. This wasn't supposed to happen so soon. So young."

"Climbing rocks can't cure cancer," she said.

"I know," said John, defeat in his voice. "It's just... It's not fair that I'm about to be older than Dad ever was, and all these years later, all these medical advancements, and I'm still gonna lose you."

"We have a few years ahead still," said Bethany. "And who knows? I may be that thirty percent. You may keep me around for longer than you think. Or want."

"Hey!" said John, which prompted a brief coughing fit.

Bethany's eyes met John's. "No matter what happens, it'll be okay. I'll be alive and happy until the end. That's better than I could have ever wanted." Her free hand felt his face. "I love you."

"I love you too." Both of them cried.

Wanting to escape the room of bad news, they left their

seats and made their way out of the building. Despite the numbed soreness of his recovering leg, he still had full mobility, not requiring any canes or walkers. But he tired more quickly, and much of his youthful vigor had evaporated. He was older, but he wore that age better than most.

John drove them home, a five-minute trip. It was the fifth car John had ever owned. He bought it when they first moved into town. With both of them retired, they only needed the single car. It had a driverless option, a feature John consistently ignored; as long as he was able, as long as he resisted age-related ailments, he still insisted on driving.

"It was two years for your mother, right?" he asked. "From when she found out?"

Bethany was looking out her window at the now-familiar buildings passing by. "Yeah, I think so. She had stage three, I think, at the time. But that was ten years ago. Medicine is better now."

"I hope so," said John.

She turned to face John. "I trust Dr. Santana on this. She's young, but I trust her. That's part of the reason why we went for a younger doctor, because they'd be up to date on the new and fresh things coming out."

"May want to do research ourselves," said John. "See if there's anything experimental or anything like that."

"John, I understand you want to help me," said Bethany, "but it's my body. It's my decision. You of all people should know that."

"I know."

Bethany eyed John as he was driving. He was paying

attention to the road, making sure he was driving safely. He lacked the reflexes and finesse of his younger days, so he prioritized concentration over conversation.

"Be glad that you don't have to make any decisions this time." She faced forward again. John remained silent.

They pulled into their new home. It was a single-story abode on a larger lot. John still grew a beautiful garden. The house itself was relatively new, about twenty years old. The entryway was larger and more formal than that of their old house, but the other rooms were roughly the same size. There were two bedrooms, and the smaller room was a study. While their old home was mostly carpeted, this had mostly hardwood floors. Society's tastes changed over the years, and this newer house reflected those changes, even if no one knew who authorized them.

John and Bethany walked up the steps of their front porch. Even though they had a ramp on the side for accessibility, should they require it, they both used the steps while they were able. It was likely the steps would be all Bethany would ever need. She wouldn't fade into a decrepit old age like John likely would. She would be Bethany to the end.

They spent most of the early afternoon letting their close friends and family know. They called Emma and Olivia first; Emma burst into tears, while Olivia maintained her composure. John let Nick know; those days, he spent most of his time taking care of his ailing wife. Liam and other family friends were informed next, but the two of them didn't want to spend any more hours of their day fulfilling their obligations to their loved ones; they wanted to spend it together.

After pouring glasses of wine, they walked back out onto the porch to sit on their swing. It was wide enough to fit three people, so there was always more than enough room for both of them to sit comfortably. This time, they wanted to sit as close to each other as possible. Bethany leaned her head onto his shoulder while they watched their neighborhood. School had gotten out for the day, and children populated the quiet streets as they walked to their families. Even though the sun wasn't shining down on them, there were a few blue breaks in the otherwise dreary sky.

"I almost feel fall is more bland here than at home," said John, looking up.

Bethany took a sip from her glass. "We've been here six years, and you still think of where we used to live as home."

"It's not the house specifically," said John, defending his words. "You live in the same area for over seventy years, it really seems like home to you, no matter where you end up."

"I guess so," said Bethany, skepticism in her voice. "I would just hope that after all these years, you'd consider me home."

John smiled as he kissed the top of her head. "Beth, my love, you are always home to me."

She sighed. "Still find it funny that we've become the old 'get off my lawn' couple that we always used to make fun of."

John noted their advanced age and how they were sitting on their front porch, watching children coming home from school. "I'm glad we were never as bored as I thought we might be once we retired."

"You're talking like it's my last day on Earth. I do have a while longer, you know."

"I know," said John, his voice cracking. "Still getting used to it. Maybe I have this fear that you'll slowly decay like our parents did."

Bethany lifted her head up and kissed John on the cheek. "Nonsense. As long as it's fine with Dr. Santana, I plan on still going to the gym with you. May have to cut back to one day a week, but I want to be alive when I die."

"You seem ready to go," said John, a frown on his face.

"Babe, I'm seventy-four years old. I was a school counselor for thirty-four years. I made hundreds of children's lives better. Children who otherwise wouldn't have had a chance. We raised two of our own, and they both came out at least half-okay. And for most of those years, I had you. I could not wish for a better life. Would I like to live that better life longer? Of course. But I did what I wanted to, and that makes me the happiest, luckiest woman. No cancer can ever take that from me. From us."

John leaned his head onto hers, and they both closed their eyes. He smiled with the thin realization she was right. She was always right, and she was the most successful person he had ever known. He was lucky to have had her in his life.

"I regret nothing, then," said John, his words still heavy.

Bethany opened her eyes and pulled back to look at him. "What do you mean?"

John stiffened his back. "Everything that ever happened in life. Everything that I did, everything that you did, everything that happened to me that I had no choice in—I regret none of it. I would live my life again. All of it. Through all the pain and tears and sadness, and all the joy. Everything that happened that led me to you. I'm glad of it all. I was always a hopeless romantic, and, honeybun, you made my whole life worth it."

Her eyes reddened, welling with tears. "You... You mean that?"

He nodded slowly. "It took me long enough to realize it, but yes. Yes, Beth, I really mean that. I just wish I realized it when I was much younger. I could have given you a better wedding night."

She punched his shoulder playfully. John laughed softly. "But no, really. I regret nothing. Thank you for being you."

Bethany sniffed and rubbed a tear from her eye. "That's the most beautiful thing you ever said to me, John. I... I guess even after all these years, I still had that sliver of doubt."

"You shouldn't have," said John before coughing. "You should have known more than me."

"I guess so," said Bethany, tears streaming down her face. She went in for a long kiss, and they spent the rest of the afternoon holding each other on the porch swing.

31

CHAPTER THIRTY-ONE

Emma walked up to the podium, her face neutral, but John could see through the façade to the emotion behind it. She was usually larger than life in front of an audience, commanding her crowd. Now, she was small, conflicted, cautious. Weak.

"I want to thank everyone for coming today," she said in her best politician tone. John knew his daughter too well to understand that it wasn't her heart speaking, but her face. "I think it's comforting to know that my mother would have loved the fact that every one of you was here."

Despite her prominent position in politics, there was no entourage with her, no media to report her speech. Just her in a small speaking hall, with four dozen guests in attendance: some passing acquaintances, many close friends. Also in attendance was a black coffin, displayed at the front of the room, closed as per the request of its inhabitant. John couldn't bear to look at the coffin, spending most of his time leaning forward and looking at the ground. Occasionally he glanced up to see Emma speak. Olivia squeezed his hand as she sat next to him.

"I have given many speeches on the floor of our state senate, I have faced down many lobbyists, yet talking about my mom is about the hardest thing I've ever done." She nervously laughed as she wiped her hand at her eyes. "I remember when I was sixteen. Grandad had just passed away, and I remember how hard it was for me. But Mom comforted me and my sister, Olivia. She's seated right over there, at the front. And I remember one thing Mom said to us that I'll never forget. She said, 'The more you cry, the more good that person did for the world.' And I truly believe that to be true.

"Mom was a counselor. It was not just her profession. She was a school counselor for thirty-four years. But more importantly, she was a counselor at home. Whenever Olivia and I had a fight, or somebody at school said some less than savory things about me, and I came home crying, or I had a bad day at a town hall meeting, or during my divorce, she was there for me. I didn't trust anyone else like I trusted Mom. She knew exactly what to say and how to say it. I'm not sure if that's just a mom thing—God forbid if I was even half that good to my own two kids—but even if it was, she was the best at it. She could love like no one else could. Whether it was Dad or Olivia or myself, or even her two grandchildren, she could love."

John didn't stir. He could not speak; he dared not speak at Bethany's funeral. The result of a two-and-a-half-year battle with cancer that couldn't be beaten by the geniuses of humanity. She remained strong and happy until the end. After training to run a half-marathon, after making a trip to Costa Rica, she was ready when the cancer metasta-sized. She knew no pain that last week, spending it in the hospital, but she was never alone. John spent most of it with her, having wonderful conversations. Conversations that weren't one-sided. Once the time came and their two daughters were summoned, she went to sleep with a smile on her face. The three of them wept, but they weren't tears of heartbreak. Those new tears were tears of celebration.

"Mom was definitely not a religious person. She didn't want this to be a somber, drawn-out experience with prayer and rituals. She left us happy, and she wanted everybody else to be happy. I don't think she realized how hard that is for us."

A few laughs rumbled throughout the small chamber. Emma took a few beats to collect her thoughts. "Everybody always said I took after her. My hair, my looks. Even my personality. Not sure about that last one. She came from a working-class background, and she clawed her way to success. I didn't know her at the time—that was before I was born—but I did see that in her ever since I was a small child. She was the biggest inspiration I ever had. I don't mean to bring politics into this or make this about me, but my drive to do the right thing came from her. I know a couple of former students of hers are here today. I've talked with all of them, and they all say the same thing. They were floundering in school, and she inspired them to try. And they did, and now they're successful in all aspects of life. They have careers, they have passions, they have dreams.

They didn't compromise. Mom didn't compromise."

She wiped a tear from her eye. "I'm going to be turning fifty this year. I remember when Mom turned fifty. I was in my last year of undergrad. I teased her so much for growing old. God do I regret saying that." Another round of subtle laughter rumbled throughout the room. "Another thing she told me. She told me she didn't feel old at all. She told me to stay feeling young, and you'll never grow old. I always took that to heart. My blood pressure medication may disagree, but I digress."

Emma looked at John in the front row. He was still looking down, not making eye contact. "But even saying all of that, I'll miss her. We'll all miss her. And seeing Dad and my sister right now, right here, devastates me." She shut her eyes, took a deep breath, then turned to the left to face the ominous coffin. "I love you, Mom. I love you so much." That was the moment the politician broke, the face cracked, and the heart commandeered the body. Emma collapsed into uncontrollable tears. She could barely stand and used the podium to support her weight. Olivia jumped out of the bench and ran up to her older sister. They exchanged some words, and Olivia helped Emma walk away from the stand and seated her on the front bench with her and their father.

John remained silent.

There was another speaker, an old college friend of Bethany's, but she kept her eulogy short. John ignored everything she said. He had two concerns: maintaining self-control and caring for his daughters. His focus consumed him, and he hoped Emma and Olivia were fine with his emotional distance.

After the final speaker, the service concluded. The funeral home had a room with snacks and desserts for the guests, and some attendees rose to visit that room. Many others stayed in the main hall. John looked up to see his two grandsons, Matthew and Will, walk up to the blank, black coffin. They seemed to stare into it like it was an eternal abyss. They had grown so much. Matthew was graduating from college in the spring, and Will was finishing up trade school for welding work.

Mateo stood up from the other side of the row and walked over to what was left of the original family. "That was nice."

Olivia looked up at her partner. "Yes, it was."

Emma was still crying in great torrents, and Olivia was holding her in her arms. Mateo looked over at the statue that was John. They briefly made eye contact before John returned his stare to the floor. Mateo patted him on the shoulder and walked away.

Once Emma calmed down, she and Olivia whispered a conversation. Olivia looked over at John. "Dad, I'm going to take Emma to the other room. Do you want me to come back and stay with you?"

John shook his head. "No, Olive. I'll join you in a moment."

Olivia nodded. Before standing up, she hugged John tightly and whispered in his ear, "I love you, Dad." Sniffling, she stood up, and she led Emma out of the room. Mateo followed them. John remained motionless before being joined by Liam. Relations between him and Emma had warmed over the years, but he kept his distance at the service.

Liam sat down alongside John. "Hey, John. That was a lovely service."

"Yes it was," he said, echoing Olivia.

Liam's age was catching up to him. He was still tall and thin, but his hair was now all gray. He looked noticeably older than his ex-wife, although there was no specific reason for that. Liam looked behind John, toward the back of the room where the door was.

"I'm proud of Emma. I mean, it sucks that things ended up the way they did between the two of us, but you and Bethany raised a really fine daughter." He paused. "You know, I think the reason why I loved the two of you so much was because I was a thousand miles from my family. I moved far away after college, rarely saw my real parents. But you and Bethany, man, you gave me family. Thank you for that."

John nodded to subtly acknowledge Liam's compliment. He continued. "I know you've probably been told this a thousand times already, but if you need anything, I'm here. And you can count on that. I'm not gonna move to be closer to you, but if you need help with something some weekend or have a large project, I'm your guy. You can always count on me."

Swallowing first, John said, "Thank you, Liam." His voice was old and gravelly; it was the oldest John had ever sounded.

Liam nodded before walking toward the back of the room. A long minute passed by with John internalizing his thoughts before two other attendees came by to give their condolences. These two sat down next to him. John looked to his right to see Nick, Ashley sitting on his right. Nick looked twenty years older than John and walked around with a slight hunch. His wife had lost a lot of weight to combat her heart issues, but she still needed a cane to move around and couldn't stand for extended periods of time.

"Hey, man," said Nick, his voice old and tired.

"Hey," said John.

Nick leaned back on the bench, looking up at the ceiling. "Here we are again. Although I'm glad we're inside, I don't think I can make a hike into the woods at my age."

"Yeah, this one is a bit easier."

"How are you doing?" asked Nick, injecting added concern into his voice.

John shook his head. "I don't know."

"Alex and Chloe send their condolences. They weren't able to make it."

"I got their cards," said John.

"Beth was a wonderful woman. I'll never forget when the two of you helped me get back on my feet that one Christmas. Before I met Ashley." She looked over and smiled. "But you were concerned that she'd be upset. And she wasn't. She fully supported me, helped me out with applications. I never told you this before, but she even gave me some free therapy sessions to help sort my shit out."

"I didn't know that," said John.

"I know, because I just told you for the first time." Nick grinned. Once the smile faded, he looked at the ground. "I've been with you off and on since high school, John. We've seen each other's worst—and best. And I'm glad that this isn't your worst."

John nodded.

"Really, though. I'm no sentimental type, I'm no good

at speeches, but I know she made a lot of people happy, and I'm sure that happiness will linger on for many years. Embrace her memories. You had a wonderful woman in your life, and everybody should be jealous of that."

"I guess so," John said, fiddling with his hands.

Nick put his hand on John's shoulder. "When are you leaving to go back home?"

Where was home anymore? Bethany had said that she wished she was his home. But she was gone now. Her warm smile, her curly hair, her scratchy voice were erased from the world. The only thing left was the memories. The memories of that nervous first date at that coffee house when they were two twenty-somethings. One searching for healing and salvation, the other searching for knowledge. Their feelings morphed into genuine affection and then love. Finding their way through life, blind, and achieving success in their own careers. They owned a place they could call their own and gave birth to one child, then another.

Before the service, John tried to remember when they went out with Nick and his ex-wife at that fancy restaurant. It was the night he and Bethany first became an exclusive couple, when he could finally call her his girlfriend. She was his, and he was hers. For fifty-four years, they were each other's.

John had prepared for this day. It hurt that her death hadn't gone according to his preordained plan: he was five years older than her; he should have been the first to pass. She hadn't even met the average life expectancy. Her smile was still young. Her wrinkles tried to betray that reality, but no one who knew her believed those wrinkles.

It wasn't fair that she went out when she did, and how she did, and why she did. But John was accustomed to things not unfolding according to his plan. He hardened himself to that at a young age, and that experience made Bethany's death easier to bear. That burden was still astronomically challenging. No matter how numb he was, it was never enough to preemptively cure sorrow.

John addressed his friend's question: "In a couple of days. I'm staying with Emma for the time being."

"Well," said Nick, "the youngins might think we're too old to be hitting the pubs, but if you want to hang out before you leave, I'll appreciate that. I think you may too."

John focused on Nick's eyes as he said that. There was a hint of finality in Nick's tone, the suggestion that it would be the last time the two would hang out as friends, alone and on their own terms. John would go back to his newly adopted town, Nick to his. With Bethany gone, there was no longer a large desire to travel. It could be several years before John visited his hometown again. By then, it could be too late.

John smiled. "I'd like that."

"Good," said Nick.

Ashley spoke up for the first time. "I'm going to go into the other room. I'll meet you over there." She stood up with great effort, leaning heavily on her cane. "John, it was nice to see you again. I'm so sorry."

"Thanks, Ashley."

Nick stared at Ashley as she slowly walked away. He shook his head. "That's gonna be me in a few years. Hard enough to walk as it is."

"Let's hope that we all die before then," said John.

32

CHAPTER THIRTY-TWO

"Please have a seat, John," said Dr. Santana as she pulled out the chair on her side of the consulting desk.

Reluctantly, John sat down. His bones reacted strongly to the movement, reinforcing the certainty that his future was coming quickly. A future he was experiencing alone.

Dr. Santana sighed. "It's been a while, hasn't it?"

John wasn't sure what she meant. He had visited her many times over the past several weeks to address some bouts of nausea he had been feeling. Before that, his check-ups were seldom. After Bethany died, he stopped lifting weights, stopped paying attention to his body. Stopped caring. Dr. Santana could have also meant that it had been a while since he met her in that particular room. It had been several years since Bethany received her final con-sultation on how to handle the end of her life, a fact that cursed the room in John's mind.

"You could say that," said John coldly.

"Well, the information that I'll be telling you could have been much different if you had come to me when you first felt the symptoms."

John nodded. "It didn't bother me enough to care."

Dr. Santana gave him a sympathetic smile. John's disposition toward life had changed upon the death of his life-long partner. His cynicism was kept in check by decades of love but had now returned to wreck him. John was better prepared this time. Whether that was due to experience or the acceptance of his advanced age, he wouldn't know.

"So we had noticed that mass that was pressing up against your rib cage, which was concerning to me." She looked at her tablet, dissecting the information on its screen. "That's why we ran all those biopsies and tests. Well, we got the results back. Are you ready to talk about this?"

"Better to get this over with now." John already had suspicions and hypotheses from his own research, so confirmation wasn't a big deal for him.

"So the mass in your rib is from a cancerous growth in your liver."

John wasn't surprised by the result. "I figured."

Dr. Santana gave him a pointed look. "Which surprised me, because you were not an alcohol abuser, and you never had Hep B or C when you were younger. So we studied your other test results, and we discovered that it's likely that your cancer didn't originate in your liver. We also found it in your stomach."

That took John out of the moment. "Oh."

"It's rare, but we've seen it happen where the cancer

doesn't show obvious symptoms in one spot, yet it can spread to another organ where it flourishes. That's what I think happened here. Based on the rate of growth, it wouldn't shock me if your cancer developed at the same time as your wife's." She passed a paper over to John. "I'm sure you're familiar with these charts now. Best-case scenario, if we can guarantee a liver transplant and we can remove the original tumor, assuming it hasn't spread elsewhere, I can get you going another ten years, maybe more."

John asked, "Aren't I a little old for a transplant?"

"Well, the oldest recipient of a liver transplant was in their nineties." Dr. Santana sighed. "But you are right. It used to be, decades ago, doctors rarely did transplants for anybody over seventy. Now we're seeing more and more patients in their seventies and eighties. But due to the severity of your cancer, and the fact it's no longer localized, the likelihood of being approved for a transplant anytime soon is slim."

"That makes sense," said John, returning to his cold, apathetic attitude.

"If we ignore the transplant option, it could be possible to remove both masses, but it would take a pretty big toll on your body. You're definitely healthy for an eighty-six-year-old, but your health has been slipping for the past several years, so your recovery time isn't close to where it was even five years ago."

John nodded, reflecting on his life since Bethany left. He stopped going to the gym, stopped going on hikes, and was reduced to a sedentary lifestyle. The only real physical activity he did was his gardening, but even that was becoming increasingly difficult. With no one to share an energetic life with, the effort was no longer worth it. The result of that decision was never made plainer to him. By him mentally giving up, his body physically gave up too.

"It doesn't look good then," said John, lamenting his life choices.

"There's a lot more variables here than there were with Bethany." Dr. Santana pulled up some information on her tablet. "Best-case scenario you recover okay from the surgery, cancer goes into remission, but then we're looking at maybe five years, but those five years would be hard on you. And this is all assuming the cancer doesn't return right away. What's probably more likely is that we do that, the cancer returns, and you got a year or two, and I can't guarantee a quality of life that you'd be okay with."

"What about the treatment that we did with Beth?" asked John.

"The cancer is more advanced than what she had. You're also much older than she was. So that's the main difference. At this point, using similar treatment methods, you're looking at one year, tops."

"But it would be pleasant?"

Dr. Santana nodded hesitantly. "Your experience would be similar to Bethany's, just accelerated. The main difference between you and her is that we couldn't do surgery on her. That's why it's an option for you."

John leaned forward and looked at the desk. He realized he wouldn't see his ninetieth birthday. Back on his sixtieth birthday, he predicted he would live to one hundred, due to advancements in medical science and improvements in his general health. All those years of effort, on both his and Bethany's part, were for naught; cancer was still the silent killer. At the same time, Bethany went on her own terms, feeling well and happy about herself. John would likely not have that same experience.

"How about anything experimental?" John put his hands on the desk, propping himself up so he could look at Dr. Santana. "Like, something the FDA is testing? Anything new that's not approved yet? Surely you would know something."

A faint smile grew on her face. "I just knew you'd ask something like that." She went back to her tablet and accessed another screen. "There is actually something that's brand new. They literally just approved this on conditional terms maybe a month ago."

John perked up. "Wha-what is it?"

Dr. Santana's optimism faded. "Well, before I really get your hopes up, it's not something that will make you live longer."

John sat back in his chair. "Oh. Then what's the point? What is it?"

She studied her tablet more. "It's an experimental drug, a very, very powerful type of hallucinogen. It triggers very powerful, very real images in your mind. Without going into the sciencey specifics, it allows your brain to generate a false reality that is indistinguishable from our own. This reality comes from your subcortex, which is deep in your brain. You'd probably refer to that as your subconscious."

John's curiosity was piqued. "Wait, so like virtual reality? But instead of video games, it's all in your mind and more real?"

Dr. Santana nodded. "Yes. Yes, if you like to think of it

like that, then yes."

"But why isn't this bigger news?" asked John, his confusion growing. "This would have been all over the news. Surely even I would have heard about it by now. And what the hell does this have to do with my cancer? I mean, you said it won't make me live longer!"

She smiled. "I haven't got to that part yet. There is a massive side effect. Once the effect wears off, which is about twelve hours, it causes irreversible brain damage, massive hemorrhaging. Your brain turns to mush and you'll be permanently disabled at best, coma if you're lucky, or you'll just die from brain death."

"Interesting." John's eyes narrowed in anticipation of what was coming next.

"This drug has been in development for many years now, and it's only just been approved for a single application, to be administered to those who undergo voluntary assisted suicide. Basically, the drug is injected into the patient right as they're made unconscious. The doctor lets the drug take its course, and at about the tenth or eleventh hour, the lethal dose is provided. It's been nicknamed the 'heaven drug' because the idea behind it is that it gives someone the experience of heaven before they expire."

Silence enveloped the office. John looked away from his doctor, processing the information she had provided him. "So if I opt to 'die with dignity,' as the politicians used to call it, I can have this drug?"

Dr. Santana set down the tablet. "Yes. I will warn you right now that you are still healthy enough that I will not authorize this procedure at this time. But depending on which course of action you want to take, if it comes down to it, we can revisit this later."

"When you say the effects last for twelve hours," John said, "does it appear to last for twelve hours in dreamland?"

"Interesting question," she said in response. She picked up the tablet and researched his question for a minute. "Inconclusive at this time. Brain scans have determined that brain activity increases dramatically during the entirety of the duration. One of the reasons for the hemorrhaging, actually. Researchers weren't sure if that was from the extra power needed to simulate a world or if the internal clock ran faster, meaning there was more time available during the dream."

"So if no one wakes up from this, how do we know what it does?" asked John. "I mean, I know you can scan the brain, but how do we know it creates this imaginary reality?"

"Well, people have woken up during trials," said Dr. Santana, scrolling up on the tablet, "but odds are low. Special testing was done for inmates on death row who volunteered. They were given lethal injections if the normal side effects occurred, but their sentences were downgraded to life in prison if they survived. Wow, that seems really unethical. No idea how that passed through committee. Anyway, out of the ten that tried it, three managed to live through it unscathed, and they explained what they saw. Testing only lasted a couple of years, but apparently they still authorized it for its current use."

John ran his hand through his hair. If there was a mirror, he could see how white it was, but he was fortunate to still have a natural head of hair. Hair-replacement technology was of a high enough quality and affordable enough that there were few bald men anymore. Nick had work done when they were in their fifties. John wasn't sure about Liam. Mateo had been shaving his head for as long as John knew him.

"So getting back to business," he said begrudgingly, "how long would I wait on the transplant?"

Dr. Santana set the tablet aside, once again speaking about something she knew well. "Six months tops. We'd want to remove the stomach mass at the same time, to prevent it from growing back. Any longer than that and we'd have to make a decision quickly to mitigate future growth. Regardless of which choice you make, we're getting you on treatment right away."

"Good plan," John said. He sighed. His lack of fear could have been a side effect of losing Bethany and the apathy that came from that. Or he approached the bad news much as she did. He never understood how she was so accepting of her fate, so at peace with herself. Maybe it took until that moment for John to finally understand where she was coming from. Maybe his fear was locked away, buried beneath his denials, and that fear had yet to metastasize.

Yet he was alone in dealing with this. Emma and Olivia could comfort him and visit him, but they were more than a four-hour drive away. While Bethany appreciated their presence, John was more apathetic about their support. What his daughters could provide him wasn't enough. Despite feeling guilty about his true feelings, he still wanted more. That more had died the same way he was going to. It was beyond tragic. It was pathetic.

33

CHAPTER THIRTY-THREE

The room was smaller than John expected, a small hospital bed in the middle of the far wall, with many machines and IVs surrounding it. The walls were a green pastel color, but there were no windows. The artificial light had a calming yellow hue. The design was intended to comfort those who spent their last precious moments there.

"So this is it," said John, walking farther into the room and standing in its center. He tried to mentally photograph the colors, the paintings, the smells.

"Yes it is," said Dr. Datta, closing the door behind him. He went to the side of the room to give John space to digest his surroundings.

"This is the last thing I will see that is actually real."

"Well, it depends," said Dr. Datta. "When the drug takes effect, what you see will be real. Your brain will make

no distinction between what your ocular receptors interpret and what your own genius will create. It won't be real
to me, or the nurses, or anybody else, but it's real to you."

John nodded. The time had come. It didn't take long
for his cancer to become a social animal and invite itself
to every party in his body. Part of him regretted waiting
for a transplant; he should have done the double surgery
immediately after the diagnosis. Part of him was glad the
process was quick, quicker than Dr. Santana had originally
estimated. He could still walk, breathe, talk, eat, and feel
emotion. If it wasn't for the cancer, he still would have
many years left; reaching one hundred would have been a
possibility. But they would be empty years. Even with his
loving children, going on with his life became a chore. His
aggressive cancer agreed with him.

He found himself by the hospital bed. There were blankets folded on a shelf nearby. At least he'd be warm in the
real world. He turned around to the end-of-life specialist
most familiar with the drug at that hospital. "What will I
see?"

"In heaven?" asked Dr. Datta, referring to the potent
effects of the drug he was about to administer. "What you
want to see. People you want to see. The people who survived the ordeal recalled seeing things they had no chance
of seeing in our world. People long gone. Places long gone.
Memories long gone."

"I see." John wasn't sure if that was comforting or not.

"Are you sure you don't want your daughters here with
you?" asked the doctor.

John thought about whom he was leaving behind. Emma
and Olivia would become parentless. They would have no

one to look to for help, for guidance, for support. Their last parent would be gone. But they would be okay. They were strong women, powerful women, powerful people. Emma was one of the top politicians in the state and had plans to either run for governor or even U.S. representative. Olivia was an independent artist whose works had become famous worldwide. They trained their whole lives for their positions, and John was there from the beginning to encourage them. His daughters were more successful than he ever was. He was no longer in a place to help them. John couldn't rise above his station, not in his condition. His blip on history would be a footnote, and that fact was fixed.

Emma and Olivia would carry on his name and memories for as long as they lived. They easily had another forty to fifty years in their future. A future full of rich opportunity. Once they passed, his two grandchildren, Matt and Will, would remember him. Beyond that, John would be forgotten. Everything he was, everyone he knew, would phase out of existence, and no one would care.

John didn't want his children with him at the end. Their pained faces would convince him that ending his life was a mistake. He couldn't afford to take that chance; he didn't want to go on anymore. Yet their well-being was secured. They would be alright.

"No, I'm good," he said. "I'm at peace with myself. They're at peace. I just want to be alone."

Dr. Datta gave a knowing nod. "Do you wish to proceed?"

Shutting his eyes, John tried to imagine what his brief afterlife would look like. It proved a difficult endeavor, at least while sober. Hopefully, he would spend a long time in that new reality. Nick would be there. His parents. Bethany.

"I am ready."

"Go ahead and lie down on the bed." As John complied, Dr. Datta left the room for a moment. John was nervous and could feel his old heart pounding, but his breathing was calm. It was a new, irreversible experience, yet John surrendered his survival instincts.

A nurse came in next and prepared the procedure. She hooked up the sensors and IVs to John. He shivered; he was only wearing a hospital gown. Smiling, the nurse grabbed the blanket from the shelf and put it over him. It gave him the warmth he needed, even if it wasn't for long.

"How are you doing?" the nurse asked.

"I'm ready to go," said John. Part of him wanted them to hurry up before he changed his mind.

Dr. Datta and another nurse came in with the drug. "So we mixed the 'heaven drug' with a general anesthesia. The 'heaven drug' does take a few minutes to start taking effect, so you'll be unconscious before it happens." He glanced at his watch. "We'll be monitoring you the whole time you are under its effects. At the eight-hour mark, we'll ready the drugs for the final death. You will have no idea this will happen. Once the effects of the 'heaven drug' start wearing down, I will personally administer the lethal dose. You will not know you die, and you will pass with no pain. Do you understand?"

John's mouth was dry. He tried to swallow. "Yes."

"Are you ready to go?"

John smiled for the first time in a long while. "Yes."

Dr. Datta nodded at the nurse. She injected John with some fluid through the IVs she had hooked up before. It was quick, and John's brain had no time to figure out what was going on before the only reality he had ever known faded away.

*****

Reality slowly reassembled itself, darkness morphing into blurred light. That light transformed into a gray haze, and as John's senses attuned themselves, he noticed the haze had resolved into a horizon. He blinked several times before realizing he had been holding his breath. A deep rush of air soon entered his lungs, shocking the rest of his body into consciousness.

John took a minute to analyze his motor movements. He could feel his heart beating deep within his chest. He raised both of his arms and moved each individual finger. While looking at his hands, he noticed that his skin looked more youthful than it had a moment ago. There were no protruding veins, and his skin lacked many of the blemishes that marked his elderly body. Looking down, he noticed that he was wearing a black T-shirt and some slacks. The surrounding air had the gentle hint of a breeze. Yet the temperature was lukewarm, almost moist. It was comfortable.

There were a distinct ground and a distinct sky, but it was all muddled shades of gray. A fog-like haze blended the two together in the distant horizon, which was perfectly flat in every direction. The ground was smooth yet mirrored the sky, resembling a calm overcast. Every direction John looked had the same mystical appearance.

When John took a step, he heard splashing water. Looking down, he saw a big ripple emanate from his foot, spreading farther out, before weakening in the distance. Strewn across the ground was a thin layer of water he hadn't noticed before. As the initial ripple calmed itself, the reflection of his face materialized. Brown hair topped his head in a style he hadn't worn since he was a young man.

He resumed walking, each step creating a new ripple. His body, his muscles, his bones had a youthful vigor to them. John was no longer fatigued by the slightest physical exertion. His body was young again, yet his many years of life lingered in his thoughts, weighing down his mind.

After walking for several minutes, John saw the first break in the monotonous scenery. A black object faded into view on the horizon, emerging from the foggy haze. John squinted, but it was still too far away for his younger eyes to resolve. Undeterred, he continued his slow stroll toward the mystery. It reminded him of scenes from video games he played years earlier.

Soon, the black form became a figure. This person was wearing a large dark gray robe, masking details of their body. They were turned away from John, their hood shielding their head from his eyes. John approached cautiously, yet this figure didn't move. He stopped when he was several paces away. When the last ripple subsided, there was only the noise of his breathing and that of the faint ambient surroundings.

"Uh, hello?" asked John. He could speak, and his voice carried across the flat void.

The figure stirred. It turned around with slow dramatics. When it faced him, most of the face was obscured by the oversized hood, with only the chin exposed. John didn't know if they were an ominous guide to this world or something else. He gulped. "Where am I?"

The figure remained silent. Yet after a moment, it lifted its arms to take the hood off in a slow deliberate fashion. When the shadow passed over the mysterious face, John gasped. His eyes bulged, and he stumbled backward, barely able to keep him standing.

Isabel stared back in silence.

John continued to stare, his mouth agape, looking at Isabel as she appeared right when she left their duplex for the last time many, many, many years earlier. Many decades earlier. Her dark hair was tied back, fully exposing her emotionless face. But her eyes clawed into John's. She showed no reaction, no hint of what she thought. She just stared.

"Be-Be-Bel?" John corrected his posture but kept his distance. She was unmoving, save for the subtle motion of her breathing. Breaths she made with her own strength. Her eyes kept their intensity, but the emotion behind that had become clear. She had no reason to be happy, to be glad of seeing John again. He soon realized why, and his entire world, his entire life, his entire soul crumpled upon that stare. In an instant, he was broken.

"Oh my God, Bel!" John shook and fell to his knees, splashing the shallow water upon impact. Tears enveloped his eyes, his emotion freezing his body. "Oh my God, Bel. What have I done? Oh my God." He leaned forward, hands on the ground. "I forgot you. I betrayed you. Everything I was, everything I wanted to be, I betrayed myself. Oh my God! Why the fuck did I do this? Why did I put your memories away? Why did I kill you? Oh Jesus!"

His hands no longer had the strength to hold himself up, and his head lowered to the ground. "Oh, Bel! I fucking ruined everything! We were going to help save the world! We cared more about life. About each other. About ourselves! And I fucked it all up! I became the very thing that you despised."

John's crying continued unabated, uncontrolled by the undammed emotion in his heart. "Oh God, I cheated on you with Beth! You were here this whole time! You listened to me ramble about her. I thought I loved her. Oh God, why did I think that? She needed to follow the Goddamned playbook. She needed her white picket fence, and... Oh God. I'm sorry. I'm so sorry. I wasted my whole life. I wasted my whole..." And he couldn't finish his sentence, the last word transforming into an inaudible cry of despair.

"All I have to show for it are two kids. Everybody has two fucking kids. I'm no different from anybody. I'm a fucking failure." He got enough strength to sit upright, still on his knees. Through the distortion of the thick tears, he made out the ominous figure before him, who cast judgment on his entire life. "And I die knowing that I fucked it all up. Oh God, Bel. Isabel. You were right. You were always fucking right!" He collapsed onto the ground again, drowning in his self-pity.

"And the worst crime I committed was forgetting you. Your words, your memories were more important, more unique, more... you. And I threw them all away. I broke my promise to you, Bel. Everything that was left of you I just threw away. I should have taken those boxes with me. Remembered you at the end. But I didn't. I never got that stone cottage like I promised. I know you'll never forgive me. Bel… Bel, I'm sorry." A cry erupted from John, and the last of his energy was spent, leaving him on his knees, completely wrecked, completely alone.

John lay there crying. His breathing slowly calmed, but the pain kept flowing. If it was going to end like this, if it was going to end with John in the deepest gutter of his soul, it was a meager price to pay to see Isabel one final time. Yet his selfish grief was interrupted by a voice—a voice he barely recalled from the ancient annals of his youth. That voice said one word with complete and absolute calm: "John."

His cries stopped. He lay still for a moment, registering what he heard. Sniffling, he sat up, looking at Isabel. He rubbed his eyes, allowing him to see her looking down at him. She retained that intense stare, but there was something different behind her eyes. One more time, she said, "John," then walked a few steps toward him, holding out her hand, palm upright.

John stared at her hand. It was welcoming him. It spoke comfort to him in ways no words ever could. He grasped it, and she helped him to his feet. Neither his knees nor his hands appeared wet, or if they were, he didn't notice. Isabel let go, allowing John to stand on his own again. Her eyes softened, and the look became familiar.

"John, it's okay," she said. She tilted her head. "John, no matter what you did, what choices you made, what mistakes you made, you had something that I always wanted but never had a chance to have. You had a life."

When he jolted his head back, Isabel finally broke into a smile. "You did so much with that life. You clung onto what you thought was really precious to you, what you thought was really important to you, and you took that happiness with you to the end. Yes, you may have compromised on our beliefs, but in the end, you were happy. I wanted you to be happy, more than anything else."

"Really?" said a tepid John. He sniffed, and another tear came down, yet it wasn't from sadness.

"All my beliefs, all my philosophies, all my answers, none of that mattered in the end. I died. I had no chance to live any life. And I am so happy you got that, even if I never shared it with you."

John smiled. "But, Bel, you did share it with me."

Her smile grew wider. "I did, didn't I?"

"You were always with me," whispered John.

"Well, I guess I was finally wrong about something."

They both giggled. Isabel offered both of her hands. John looked down and held them in his own. Her smile retracted, yet her disposition didn't change. "I would not have expected you to remember me at all. But you did, and I can't tell you enough how grateful I am for that." She offered a half-smile. "You know, what's funny and kind of poetic is that even though I will soon die forever, at least my final memories are spent with you."

John's eyes welled up again. "Bel..."

She wiped some of the messy tears off his face. "It's okay. I'll be fine. You'll be fine. You carried my soul when I passed. Your daughters will carry your soul when you pass. Even when you die and I disappear forever, I still have to thank you. You did save me. You didn't kill me. Don't ever blame yourself for that."

"I'll try not to," he said, nodding with his eyes closed.

Chapter Thirty-Three

"I... I feel terrible that Beth's not here right now."

"That's good. You spent so many wonderful years with her. She was so lucky to have you. It would have killed me—" She stopped herself and giggled. "I mean, it would have metaphorically killed me to see you lonely and miserable for the rest of your life. You never deserved that. But you did deserve her."

John took his hand and touched Isabel's face. Her cheek was warm and soft. She wasn't an apparition of his mind but living flesh and blood. "You have no idea how long I wished for a day like this. To see you one more time. To talk to you one more time."

"It's okay, John," she said, her own eyes starting to water. "I'm not leaving you. I'll never leave you again."

With that, the two embraced. John buried himself in her robe, and she clutched him in return. There was no need for anything more; all they wanted was the touch of the other. It was all that was needed to put both souls at peace. Their eyes closed. For the first time in his life, John stopped worrying about the future. Worrying about how much time he had left until the end. The end no longer mattered anymore. In the midst of their embrace, the two could feel light sprinklings of water on their clothes and their heads. The weather was not cold or bitter, but welcoming and loving.

It was raining.

About the Author

A lifelong native of the Portland, OR area, Justin Radford is a writer, musician, composer, and artist. After writing his first novel at age ten, he has gone on to compose rock musicals, perform in Lady Gaga tribute bands, and travel the country with his Las Vegas showbear, Julie. Life in the Rain is his first published book, an amalgamation of his life experiences and thought experiments in exploring his emotions. You can check out his current projects on his website www.vainastudios.com.